THE
CLAW AND THE
CROWNED

THE BOOK OF ALL THINGS

USA TODAY BESTSELLING AUTHOR
SARAH M. CRADIT

ISBN: 978-1-958744-17-8

Cover and Interior Design by The Illustrated Author Design Services
Map by The Illustrated Author Design Services
Hardcover Art (Freedom Comes in Many Forms) by Leah Fry of The Sketching Hour
Imryll and Drazhan Portraits by Nora Adamszki
Mine by Stephanie Brown of Offbeat Worlds
Editing by Novel Nurse Editing

Publisher Contact:
sarah@sarahmcradit.com
www.sarahmcradit.com

SARAH M CRADIT

WEAVER of WORLDS

For all the good girls

PRAISE FOR
THE CLAW AND THE CROWNED

"Dark and sexy, The Claw and the Crowned is skimming the line between what love demands and what hate allows. Freedom comes in many ways!"
~Angelina J. Steffort, award-winning author of The Quarter Mage

"The Claw and the Crowned took my breath away. It has Sarah M. Cradit's signature epic worldbuilding and addictive plotline, but it also has a fan-your-face-steamy romance that kept me flipping pages well into the middle of the night. The Book of All Things is a must read fantasy series- it truly has all the things I love in my favorite books."
~Michelle, @BookBriefs

"Cradit is one author I will always read! I absolutely love this highly-addictive and swoony world that rips all the emotions out of me!"
~Candace Robinson, Author of Vampires in Wonderland Series

INTRODUCTION

There exists a realm set upon an isle, surrounded by a sea no one has ever traveled beyond.

Let's begin again, shall we?

There exists a realm set upon an isle, surrounded by a sea few have ever traveled beyond.

As with all histories, truth begins where the victor decides. It was the Rhiagains—and their handpicked favorites from the Noble Houses of their realm—who washed up on the shores of a rocky, bereft crop of land twenty years past, fleeing inevitable destruction of their homeland, the Sceptre of Ilynglass. The Rhiagains claimed to not know how they got there, citing an inhospitable sea.

More than a thousand started the journey from Ilynglass.

Barely a hundred made it to the end.

In Ilynglass, the Rhiagains were kings. In the White Kingdom, only three of the survivors have Rhiagain blood at all. They are outnumbered by their own people, collectively distrusted by a kingdom that has never traveled to the mythical land of "Beyond," and whose inhabitants have their share of doubts surrounding the origin of these manlike intruders.

The lords and ladies of the Reaches, who ruled unto themselves for centuries, have no love for foreigners claiming to be gods. The uprising that followed brought bloodshed and uncertainty to a once-stable land, dividing both hearts and beliefs.

Distrust turns to awe when the surviving Meduwyn sorcerers, the true gods of the Sceptre of Ilynglass, are sent into the kingdom to perform seemingly impossible feats of magic, which leave the realmfolk of the kingdom bowing in submission.

Once again, the Rhiagains find themselves wearing a crown.

Carrow Rhiagain established the small isle as the seat of his kingship, naming it Duncarrow, which translates to: Fortress of Carrow. He built a keep on the inhospitable land and forbade the customs and traditions of Ilynglass from infiltrating their new life, committing to the kingdom that he will rule with their best interests at heart. That he will become one of them.

But most of Carrow's plans perished in the Passage. Carrow lost two of his sons, his First Chosen, and numerous grandchildren. His age and infirmity prevent him from siring more desperately needed heirs.

His last hope is a son who was a babe when they came to the White Kingdom—who was raised in the strange shadows that had formed on a land foreign to everyone. Torian has grown up to become a quiet, sensitive young man, who isn't prepared for the burden he's expected to one day carry.

But Carrow can no longer wait for his son to be ready. The Rhiagains teeter on the brink of extinction.

Tradition determines Rhiagain kings take two concubines, but Carrow has chosen five for his son—a tall order for any man, but an impossible one for Torian, whose heart has always belonged to just one young woman.

Imryll of Glaisgain.

Spirited Imryll wants nothing more than to leave Duncarrow and forge a life of her own in the kingdom. Her heart belongs to a future that is being ripped away. The spark within her transforms into a bid for survival as her family's future is secured at the cost of her happiness.

Torian has no choice but to put aside childish ideals and embrace his fate or be forever known as the last Rhiagain. The one who could not rise.

But there are still those who remember the Uprising, who watched fathers and brothers and sons perish for daring to question the intention of the outsiders who refused to explain where they'd come from.

Drazhan Wynter is one such man.

The Uprising took everything from him.

The Rhiagains took everything from him.

He's spent a decade training. Preparing. Transforming into a warrior.

A deadly one.

Drazhan has come to Duncarrow to take everything from the Rhiagains.

The father.

The son.

And Imryll of Glaisgain? The one whom all of Duncarrow looks to with hope for their future?

He has plans for her too.

RHIAGAINS

King & Queen
King Carrow
Queen Godivah, First Chosen

Surviving Children
Lady Clarisan, 28
Prince Torian, 20

Rhiagains Who Died in the Passage
Queen Yvaine
Prince Dacian & family
Prince Calder & family

Sorcerers/Meduwyn
Mortain
Oldwin
Lysanor
Isdemus

Head of Torian's Guard
Janus

NOBLE HOUSES

Glaisgains
Duke Drushan
Duchess Melantha
Marquess Octavyen, 22
Lady Imryll, 19

Dhovaeys
Duke Drummond
Duchess Alyse
Marquess Luthyas, 22
Lady Aloysha, 20

Privaines
Duke Fenring
Lady Adamina, 20

Farrestells
Duchess Teleria
Lady Tasmin, 18

Tindahls
Duke Rahn, 28

KNIGHTS OF DUNCARROW

Queens' Guard
Drazhan "Stormclaw" Wynter of Witchwood Cross, Northerlands
Farradyn Blackfen, Rush Rider of the Westerlands
Owen Strong of Sandycove, Southerlands
Kav Garrick of Iron Hill, Southerlands
Tarsten Waters of Bythesea, Easterlands

WHITECHURCH

Lord of the Easterlands
Lord Marius Quintus

Others
Lady Marcelina Quintus (sister of Marius)
Steward Francis Oakenwell

KINGDOM
OF THE
WHITE SEA

JOYLESS,
ROCKY ISLE

ONE

CAGED. TETHERED. YOKED. DEFEATED.

Imryll hastily stuffed the contraband vellum into her leather satchel when Torian came striding her way down the rocky path from the courtyard. When his bright eyes stopped drinking in her face, they went straight to the bag.

Not quick enough then.

Torian wouldn't punish her for writing. But she couldn't afford to be careless, even with him. He was terrible with a secret, because he wore his thoughts in the very last place a future king should: on the outside.

But then, he hadn't spent his life mastering the subtleties of the precarious world around him like Imryll of Glaisgain had.

"Writing your memoirs?" he asked, with the lopsided smile he reserved just for her.

"They're not memoirs," Imryll said, biting back annoyance he didn't deserve. Even the question recalled the way others turned their nose up at her desire to be educated. *Women should be lucky they're even taught their letters at all, with how much work we have ahead of us if we're going to rebuild our bloodlines.*

Woman or not, unsanctioned writing of *any* kind was forbidden on Duncarrow. If anyone found out Duke Rahn had slipped her the vellum and ink in secret, his punishment would be more than she could live with.

"You're really not going to tell me, Ryl?" he asked as he chose the rock next to hers, his knee about an inch too close to be mistaken as innocuous. She almost slid onto another rock, but she didn't care about impropriety. Quite the opposite. She *welcomed* the reputation that accompanied such a discovery if it kept her name out of the mouths of those desperately planning and plotting the unions within Duncarrow. *A dozen marriages by wintertide* was the rumor, a rush to ensure future generations were not as decimated as the present ones.

"No," Imryll said without elaborating. She closed her eyes and tilted her face back to invite a fine mist of sea spray from the crashing tide. It ran into her eyes and down the sides of her face, the brine scorching the inside of her nose. Her dress was already half-soaked, but she liked it that way, clinging to her warm flesh, reminding her of the cage she still lived in...would always live in if she couldn't find the courage to leave. All she had to do was slip onto one of the weekly provision ships that traveled to and from the mainland, but even thinking about it was a dauntless prospect.

She wondered if the White Sea was anything like the sea of her parents' world—the one everyone refused to talk about because Torian's father had forbidden mention of Ilynglass.

Imryll felt his gaze traveling her exposed neck.

"Are you embarrassed to show me?" he asked. A wounded lilt touched the end of his words. "You think I'd tease you?"

The insinuation forced Imryll to pitch forward. She rolled her elbows back to her knees and aimed an irritated look at him. *You sit like a common-born,* she heard in her mother's voice. "Really? All these years we've been friends and you think I'm *embarrassed* about my passions?" She pulled back. "Others might think less of me for them, but I don't think less of myself."

2

Caged. Tethered. Yoked. Defeated.

Torian sputtered an answer that made him shake his head before finishing. He breathed in with a quick flutter of his eyes, as he often did when preparing to weather her capricious moods. "There must be a reason then."

There wasn't. Not one he wouldn't harp on anyway, with his enduring need for reasoning in all things. It wasn't as if he'd glean the underlying truth. There was no risk of Torian leaning on magic to explain facts, despite that he'd been raised in the shadows of four formidable sorcerers.

Imryll didn't need a reason not to show him her writing though. The words were her own, and she could say that about very little in her life. The "memories" prompting the words were not, but since she didn't know *why* the visions of the Sceptre of Ilynglass—of the world they were forbidden from speaking of—were given to her, or where they'd come from, she hesitated to name them anything but dreams. Waking dreams that began and ended on their own schedule.

Whatever they were, no one could ever know.

Not even him.

"You used to tell me everything." Torian lifted his chin and turned his eyes toward the sea.

"When we were children, you mean."

"We're closer to those days than the ones where we have children of our own."

Imryll judged him from her peripheral. It took so little to shift his fair mood into a full-on sulk. He was a man now, not a boy. Nothing underscored that more than the responsibility awaiting him.

"I shouldn't even be out here with you," Imryll muttered. She picked at the fabric of her gown, soaked from sitting upon the wet rocks of Duncarrow in the cold season. *Midwinter,* the people of the kingdom called it. She didn't know if her own people had another word for it. Maybe it would come to her in one of her visions. "You'll be bound soon. Your chosen will have no tolerance for your female friendships, of that you can be certain. I'd like to

3

not add angering our future queen to my grievously long list of sins."

"*Chosens.*" Torian corrected her with a twitch of his nose. "And I don't care what they think, Ryl. Everything else in my life has been decided for me. I won't let others pick my friends. I'll already be giving up enough. I won't give that away too."

They understood one another on the topic of unwelcome duty, but she resented that he could never grasp how different it was for her as a woman. "The king will select only the finest young women for his son." *And the man has made it clear it will not be me.*

He sighed. "I'm already dreaming up ways to escape them."

"When you're bound, you'll have too many eyes on you for that, Tor." Imryll couldn't help but snicker. "Though I suspect you'll be too exhausted to care."

Torian flushed at the insinuation. She wondered, not for the first time, how he was going to satisfy five concubines when he couldn't even speak of sex without looking scandalized.

Imryll though…Imryll couldn't wait to take lovers. Not on Duncarrow, of course. She'd always be a veritable hostage on the joyless, rocky isle, but when she left…Ahh, when she finally found a way to *flee* the damp, cursed place, she'd be a woman of her own means. With independence and confidence and power. They would whisper across the kingdom about the one who had chosen her own fate.

Soon.

"My father is announcing my chosen five to his minor council right now. He wanted me to be there, but I couldn't bear to hear my future discussed in that way. To hear the future of five young women spoken of as if they were property to be sold. Young women who were once my friends and playmates." Torian pulled his knees to his chest. He seemed so young compared to how Imryll felt, though he was a year older than her and being groomed to be king. "And do you know, sometimes…" He shook his head, with a heavy glance pointed at the sea. "Never mind."

It was evident Torian wanted her to push, but she asked the question from her own curiosity. "Do I know what?"

Torian lowered his face to his knees and turned it toward her. His dark-red hair had grown a touch too long, and it fell over his eyes, dipping against the freckles on his golden-brown skin that became a dense forest on his cheeks.

Imryll's heart lurched in her chest unexpectedly.

She loved him too.

But not enough to stay.

And soon, it wouldn't matter.

"Sometimes," he said through a weighty exhale, "I wish I was already king, so I could make my own choices."

Imryll forced a laugh to quell her uneasiness. "You think the choices the king makes are always easy?"

"No, Ryl, I don't. But I could be content with it if I could make the one choice that matters to me."

"And what's that?"

Torian unwound one of his hands and trailed it across the rocks to her. She eyed it with suspicious reluctance but a glance up, into his solemn gaze, had her sliding her fingers to meet his.

"So I could choose you."

Imryll withdrew her hand with a wounded gasp. Why his words had stung her was as much a mystery as why he'd said them at all. Lamenting was the business of fools. There could be no gain, no joy in speaking life into impossible potential.

She loaded a sound scolding but didn't get the chance to unleash it on him.

Torian twisted his other hand behind her head, into her hair, and pulled her in for a kiss that stole her breath. He tightened his grip in her thick curls and kissed her the way she'd seen her brother kiss his wife, with fire and tongue and a moan that stirred something familiar and forbidden under her dress.

He lifted his other hand away from hers, and his fingers brushed across the curve of her bare ankle. A chill shuddered through her and settled between her shoulders.

She'd never kissed a man before, but a real kiss was less fluid, more messy and inelegant than the ones she'd received in her dreams. She was too distracted by the uneven strokes of a tongue that didn't seem to know what it was doing to decide whether she were enjoying herself.

When Imryll didn't object, he slid his hand higher, and she allowed that as well, curious how far he would go…wondering if he had the courage to see through what he'd started.

If *she* did.

His kisses lessened when his palm cupped the inside of her thigh, dangerously close to her undergarment. Imryll could feel the debate raging within him.

"Light of Enivera, you are going to get us all expelled from Duncarrow!"

Imryll snapped her eyes and mouth closed, dragging her teeth over her bottom lip. Her forehead lingered against Torian's for a final moment before she gathered the grit to face her mother.

"Duchess Melantha." Torian cleared his throat. He dropped his hands to his groin, folding them there as though what he attempted to hide wasn't already apparent.

"Mother…Duchess." Imryll pushed to her feet and brushed the sea spray from her dress. She pursed her mouth into a tight line. "I—"

"Your Grace," her mother said with a heavy bow, cutting Imryll off. "You'll forgive my daughter for her lack of good sense. She's always been a most exasperating girl, as you are well aware. Her indelicacy stems from her lack of fear of punishment and an unattractive candor she did not inherit from *me*, of that I am certain."

Torian shot a helpless glance at Imryll, who shrugged. She'd heard her mother's speech a thousand times. It no longer affected her.

"Duchess, it was I who acted untoward and should apologize," Torian said, sounding like a proper prince and not the dreamy-eyed boy who'd almost convinced Imryll that giving away her

6

maidenhood on the wet, jagged rocks wasn't a half-bad idea. "I forgot myself for a moment, and it will not happen again."

"To the contrary, Your Grace," Melantha said with a roguish grin. Imryll caught the twinkle in her mother's eye and held her breath. It never led anywhere good. "You should kiss my daughter, and often. Just not today."

"Pardon?" Torian's head cocked like he hadn't heard her, though the rattled look on his face made it clear he had.

Melantha turned her gaze back on Imryll with a heavy, satisfied sigh. "Darling. Your dreams are about to come to life, in spite of your ill manners."

"You're sending me to the mainland to help build the reliquary?" Imryll quipped, knowing very well it wasn't what her mother meant, and that whatever she *was* about to say would be the opposite of anything Imryll wanted.

"The king has just concluded with his minor council. He's made his formal decree on the matter of the prince's future queens," Melantha replied, clutching her hands to her chest in anticipation of delight. "And my darling Imryll has been selected for the astonishing honor of being First Chosen to Prince Torian!"

Imryll took a heavy step back and lost her footing on the rocks. Torian reacted quickly, diving forward to catch her before she fell.

"But I'm not…no. No." Imryll shook Torian off with a flurry of swats. It wasn't right. She was supposed to leave Duncarrow. She wasn't fit to be queen. Her mother had said so, the queen had said so, *everyone* had said so, enough times that Imryll had turned it into a deep-rooted personal belief.

Torian's searching gaze burned her from the side.

"Darling?" Melantha asked.

Imryll flexed her hands, which had gone numb in the intervening moments between her mother's terrible declaration and Imryll finding her voice. "No, that cannot…That *cannot* be, Mother, because the king himself already said I was unsuitable, that I was precocious and stubborn and willful and—"

"You are all those things, yes," Melantha said with a disappointed breath out. "But in addition, you will also be Prince Torian's First Chosen. His First Chosen, darling! Which means that one day, you will also be—"

Caged. Tethered. Yoked. Defeated.

"Queen," Imryll whispered right before she passed out.

Drazhan massaged his ancestral blade over the whetstone, indulging his desire for mindless utility. It wasn't, strictly speaking, necessary. Stormbringer had not dulled since the last sharpening. Stormbringer hadn't dulled at all in the ten years it had belonged to him.

But there was naught else to do on the wretched ship, and it was preferable to needless conversation.

The other four knights watched him in the dim light of the cargo hold, each wearing looks that gave away more about themselves than they should ever allow another man to see. *Judgment. Envy. Curiosity. Pity.* If Drazhan had worn his own emotions so clearly and brazenly, he'd never have been selected for the "privilege" of competing for the Queens' Guard.

No, he'd be rotting in a cell somewhere.

"Aye," the one who called himself Kav said. He'd been narrowing his eyes for hours, even through the hard rise and fall of the choppy swells, watching Drazhan work. *Judgment.* "I ken it's sharp enough."

"Sharp as his mother's slit," came the slithery one, Waters. *Envy.* Tarsten Waters's awkward, desolate laugh died when no one joined in—not even Kav, who pretended to be enthralled by the water coursing through the boarded slats above as the storm knocked the ship about. "One would think you were going to Duncarrow to take a bloody life, not protect one."

Waters being right didn't make him perceptive. Most guesses paid off with time and luck.

"Thing'll break, he keeps havin' a go at it like that," Kav said.

Waters didn't resist the setup for another tasteless jest. "What do you know, just like his mother."

That pulled a laugh from Kav, and the two passed more barbs, each less clever than the last. They eyed Drazhan in dark distrust, the man who would let others speak of his mother like that without drawing steel or raising fists.

Drazhan put no stock in the opinions of men who couldn't hold their tongue long enough to listen, to *read* a situation.

The other two knights wisely kept their counsel, quietly observing from the shadows. Farradyn Blackfen was a Rush Rider from the Westerlands, a longbowman. *Curiosity*, his eyes indicated when they met Drazhan's.

The other was a Southerland lad like Kav, but more solemn, focused. *Pity* rolled across Owen Strong's stern face when he eyed Drazhan's isolation. He had a broadsword, a left-hander, but also a mace for his right. Drazhan had watched him wield both in training, roaring like a mythical beast as he slammed the hilt of both weapons against his chest. Strong was one of the few he'd noted to keep an eye on.

Waters and Kav eventually grew tired of hearing themselves speak and returned to their silence.

Drazhan hardly noticed because the alternating high and low keen of the metallic ringing pacified him. He'd trained himself out of a requirement for sleep, but in its place, Drazhan meditated. That he could do while sharpening his sword. While practicing with it. While running a man through with it.

But it was with his fist weapons—his claws—when Drazhan was most in his element.

None of the other knights had seen the skill in action.

They would.

"Heard they all have red hair. All of 'em, not just the Rhiagains," Waters was saying. "I don't know where they washed up from, but sounds like a dream to me. Ever fuck a redhead, Kav?"

I haven't, thought Drazhan. *But I will. I don't care about the others, but the prince's First Chosen, his queen, is mine.*

9

"Aye, aye," Kav said, a little too insistent. It was unclear whether he was answering the question or acknowledging the potential. "Imagine there'll be some for us?"

"If you think King Carrow will allow his knights anywhere near those pert little highborn maidens, you're deluded. The only lass you'll be spending time with is the one you're guarding, and you touch her? You're as dead as all those Rhiagains at the bottom of the White Sea."

"We're highborns too."

Waters snorted. "Not like *they* are. My father says they're looking for husbands from all over the kingdom. *Husbands*, not hardheads who swing their cocks like they swing their swords."

"Aye, speak for yourself. I know my letters."

"All two of them?"

Drazhan blinked to clear the men from his thoughts. They talked too much. Men who talked too much were a danger to themselves.

He reached down for a sip from his wineskin, his first in hours. When his eyes swept back up, they caught the gaze of Blackfen. The longbowman nodded once. Drazhan almost returned it but decided not to.

These men were not his friends.

They might be his enemies.

But only time would tell if any of them had the courage to stand against Drazhan when he went to collect the heads of King Carrow and his last surviving heir.

TWO

A CANVAS OF SHAME AND FRECKLES

Torian stormed through the halls of the Keep of Duncarrow, wearing an eye-narrowing glare that silenced those conferring their respects as he passed. If he heard another *Your Grace*, he'd throw himself into the sea just to drown the words.

The keep gleamed with newness, the stones not yet stained by the time and grunge his sister had described when she spoke about the castle of their homeland, a place where the tapestries no longer held fast to their vibrance and life, the dyes long wept of their original color. Torian had been only a few months old during the Passage. He was too young to have known that life and would not live to see the Keep of Duncarrow fall to the same trappings of age.

Twenty years his people had been in the White Kingdom, on Duncarrow, and it had taken ten of those to build a stronghold worthy of kings. Was it like the one from their homeland? What traditions had they kept when so many had been abandoned? His father and mother offered no answers about a past they were determined to pretend never existed.

11

They were powerless in their old world, Clarisan liked to say. *They might have been kings, but the sorcerers were gods. The Rhiagains were just their pretty pawns.*

His sister Clarisan was nearly a decade older and the progeny of his father's other concubine, whose name was lost along with everything else from the Before. Clarisan had been eight years old when she made the Passage, and she was the only one who would tell Torian *anything* about their old sceptre—their word for kingdom. But even she was evasive. King Carrow tolerated his only daughter because there were so few Rhiagains left. Her continued favor was not assured.

The sound of Torian's boots slapping the always-damp stones only flamed his angst higher. It had the ring of petulance, of a boy clinging to childhood because he wasn't ready to be a man. Wary eyes followed his movements, inciting his paranoia, and he wondered, Were they thinking the same? That *this* was the future of the crown? The one upon which all their hopes rested?

His father was likely still preening before the Noble Houses after his proclamation, which meant his mother would be courting the remaining duchesses, whose daughters were about to become chosens. Still, Torian raced up the narrow servant staircase instead of taking the regular way to the royal apartments. He had no desire to run into anyone who might want something from him.

When he reached the top, he checked the long hall to confirm he was alone and then darted into his apartments, bolting the door behind him.

"Ahh, there you are," Clarisan said, startling him into an unseemly groan. "I expected you *minutes* ago."

Torian turned toward his older sister. Her amber eyes flickered open, closed, then open again from the other side of the room. She wore her red-gold hair long and flowing, a defiance making her seem younger than she was. She grinned, a mischievous mien rife with affection. *A dose of reality with your comfort,* she said when delivering unsolicited advice, which was often.

"Isa." He shrugged away the shock of finding his chambers occupied and stepped farther in. "I'd ask what you're doing here, but..."

"You already know," she answered, widening her generous grin. "What's a mystery to me, however, is why you look as if you've just had all your favorite toys taken away."

"This isn't funny, and it's not a game." Torian brushed past her and made for the drink cart. Atop it were five different wines from the Westerlands, gifts from Lord Blackrook. The choice flustered him. He didn't know them apart. He couldn't discern how they were any different from the ones sent by Lord Quintus in the Easterlands. He didn't know anything he should know.

"The one in the center will be to your liking," Clarisan said in a light, teasing way that clashed with his sour mood.

Torian clenched. She knew him well. Sometimes he welcomed that, but others...

He ripped the glass bead from the decanter and launched it to the corner, where it shattered. Clarisan gasped as if he'd just committed murder. Torian inhaled a deep breath and poured himself a glass of the wine he probably *would* like but wished he wouldn't, because she was so damned exasperating when she was right.

He downed it in one gulp and poured another.

"Better?" she asked in a simpering tone. It almost had him lying to her.

Torian steeled himself and turned around. "You enjoy my suffering far more than you should."

"That's not true." Clarisan moved to stand behind a chair. "I'm having trouble contemplating why you're suffering at all, Tor."

"I'm not in the mood for your riddles." He rolled the glass over his forehead to cool it.

"You never are," she said with a tight laugh. "But I thought you'd be *happy* Father chose Imryll as your First Chosen. It was certainly a surprise, after he'd made such a point about you never bonding to a Glaisgain, but now that it's been announced, he

13

won't go back on his word. To do so would humiliate himself in front of the men he desperately needs to keep respecting him."

"It wasn't that she's a Glaisgain," Torian muttered. He drew another sip and winced, following it with a sharp gulp of breath. "It was Imryll specifically he had a problem with."

"Because she can't stay her tongue."

"Because she has a mind of her own." Torian slid his glass onto a table and paced away from his sister. He threaded his hands through his hair. "Because she's intellectual and clever and beautiful and…" *And he knows how I love her.*

"Yes, and now she'll be yours to play with," Clarisan said. "So I ask you again, why do you choose to suffer?"

They both whipped their attention toward the wailing hymn echoing down the hall, carried by dozens of voices. The tinkle of bells rang out of harmony between the wordless notes of the mourning song. Torian passed a glance to his sister, who shrugged.

"Another one?" he asked with a pointed look. "How many of us does that make?"

"You come to a world that doesn't belong to you, perhaps you deserve to die of foreign illnesses," she said lightly. "And since last week? Two? Since we arrived two decades ago? About thirty. We'll have to go down later and see who's name they've added to the wall."

"Thirty," Torian whispered, musing over another thing no one would speak about. Over a thousand of his people had left their old world for this one. Only one hundred and twenty-seven made it. But it hadn't taken long for the illnesses of the White Kingdom, to which his people had no immunity, to sweep through Duncarrow. It got so bad, they made outsiders isolate for a year before coming to work on the isle. Though there'd been a couple dozen births in the past twenty years, new life had yet to keep pace with the passing of the old. There were three times as many realmfolk working in Duncarrow as there were nobles.

"Not to worry. I'm sure you and Imryll will have a passel of little ones running around these halls soon." Clarisan was back to her favorite sport, prodding him.

And when she does, she'll have no reason to come to my bed anymore, because she won't be my wife. She'll be one of my chosens, the one from whom my heir will come. Because Rhiagain men don't have wives.

Torian collapsed onto the hearth. He pressed his hands to his sides and let his head tilt in surrender. His back was swallowed in delicious warmth. "You know I love her."

"But?" Clarisan tilted her head.

"But what is love if you must share it with others?" Torian slumped to a crouch when the weight of the words left him. "How can I look into her eyes, knowing I'll be expected to lie with *four* other women? How can I make the one I love most happy when duty bids me to spread that attention equally?" He buried his head in his hands and shook them together. "She deserves so much better."

"*How* will you do it? Well, the answer is simple. You just will. Same as she'll be able to take as many lovers as her heart desires when there's no risk of their seed taking root. Rhiagains have incubators, not wives." Clarisan left the chair and approached. She knelt before him. "But you speak of the happiness of others as if it is your sole burden."

"That's not—"

"But what of yours, Torian?"

"What of my what?"

"*Your* happiness."

"You aren't listening," Torian replied. "Whatever love she has for me will die. In having to share me, she'll resent me." He didn't have the heart to address the claim that Imryll might take other men to bed.

"I *am* listening," Clarisan gently said. "All I hear is how you will satisfy *her*. Your *chosens*. Oh and, though I know you loathe him, our father too. But how will you satisfy yourself?"

15

Torian lowered his hands from his face and gaped at her. "And where in all of this am I supposed to find room for *that*?"

Clarisan patted his head and stood again. "I suggest you take the opportunity to learn."

He wanted to roll his eyes, but he was too distracted, thinking of Imryll. Her high-spirited smile, the freckles spraying her light-copper cheeks…How many times had he wished he could run his hands through her strawberry-colored hair? Today he'd finally worked up the courage. But then everything had changed.

"I can see your thoughts whipping you into submission," she said, gliding toward the door. "Don't take too long with your self-imposed sulk. Mortain will return soon with the rest of your chosens, and Father doesn't intend to wait a moment longer than he has to. We all keep dying like this, we won't have anyone to raise all those children you're going to sire."

The mention of one of the Meduwyn sorcerers made Torian look up. He didn't trust any of them, but he trusted Mortain the least. "Mortain? What has he to do with this?"

Clarisan clucked her tongue and glanced back at him as she reached for the door. "Hadn't you heard? Three of your chosens will be coming from the kingdom proper."

"What?" Torian pushed to his feet. "But what of the disease? Has he kept them in isolation?"

"The sorcerers could heal it if they wanted to. They can heal anything."

"That's not what I asked."

"No, but it's what you *should* be asking. Why do they do nothing as the old ones die off? Could it be that the younger generations are more pliant, easier to mold and shape?"

Torian groaned. "Say what you mean. Please."

"I already have, but you never listen. Mortain is bringing three of your incubators from within the kingdom. Daughters of stewards. Daughters who will be missed." Metal screeched when Clarisan unbolted the door. She grinned at the dawning horror

16

on his face as her meaning came into clarity. "Oh, and in case any of that was unclear, *none* of them are coming willingly."

Imryll had to speak with Tasmin. Tasmin would understand. She was the *only* one who would understand.

Her face tingled with raw, dangerous energy, spots swirling before her eyes as she entered the split in the hall, each side leading to the apartments of the Noble Houses. She made a left, headed toward the Farrestells' end of the corridor, and ran straight into Adamina of Privaine.

"Lady Imryll." Adamina's violet eyes narrowed with malice disguised as impishness. A grin as dark as her eyes spread over her pinched but pleasing face as she seemingly noted the flush in Imryll's cheeks. "Where are you off to in such a rush?"

"Adamina." Imryll squared her shoulders and buried her disgust for her once childhood friend. They'd been close for years, until Adamina decided she had an affinity for scheming.

Adamina lifted her chin in another sweeping appraisal. "Congratulations are in order. First Chosen. What an honor they've bestowed upon you. You'll be the mother of our future king, if you can rise to the occasion. A confusing honor, rife with questions, but an honor nonetheless."

"Thank you," Imryll muttered. Any reaction would be shared among Adamina's circle. It would be dissected, then used to judge and diminish her in the eyes of the intimate Rhiagain court.

She darted her eyes down the hall toward the Farrestell quarter.

Adamina turned to follow her gaze with a curious twitch of her eyes. "Are you not going to congratulate me then?"

"What?"

"Have you not heard?"

Imryll's neck flexed in pained impatience. Sweat beaded around her temple and brow and between her breasts. She needed Tasmin, her real friend, her *only* friend other than Torian. She needed to speak openly before the truth burst out of her like a sea monster clawing its way to the surface.

"Heard what?" she asked through a tight jaw.

"Oh," Adamina said, feigning a crestfallen look that did nothing to hide the joy in her eyes. "Well, I suppose they would have told you eventually." She flashed a quick smile. "I'm to be the prince's Second Chosen."

Imryll recoiled. She forced herself to internalize her reactions, shoving the terrible thoughts of sharing Torian with her rival to the back of her mind until it was safe to entertain them.

Adamina feasted upon weakness. Imryll refused to feed it.

"Does this upset you?"

"No," Imryll whispered. She tried again, finding her voice. "Torian must have five chosens, so why would the king not choose from amongst his inner circle?"

Adamina's jaw dropped. "Using the prince's first name so casually? Even now, when you've been given a second chance to prove your value to our blessed and benevolent King Carrow?"

"Perhaps he'll allow you such familiarity one day too, Adamina," Imryll said with a satisfied grin, which hollowed her even as she enjoyed the anger flashing across Adamina's smug face. She shouldn't lower herself. It was no victory to best someone if it required using the monster's own tactics to do it.

Adamina's upper lip curled toward her nose. "If you were sensible, Imryll, you'd see the wisdom in us allying through this."

"Why would there be wisdom in that?" Imryll couldn't help asking.

Adamina lowered her voice as if her words were dangerous. "The other three will be outsiders. *Realmfolk.*"

Realmfolk. Adamina had perfected the art of elevating her status by demeaning others.

But the implication stuck in Imryll's chest. There was a general distrust of outsiders, even beyond the illnesses they brought. The Rhiagains and their nobles were feared and thus were tolerated, but there were so few of the old families left from the Before. Had the king really selected three of his only surviving son's chosens from outside their inner circle?

"I see that is as much of a surprise to you as it was to me," Adamina said.

The last thing Imryll wanted was to show herself at a disadvantage, but there was no point in trying to cover her disbelief. *Outsiders selected as Torian's chosens. When every Noble House in the court has been preparing their daughters for this.* "Yes," she confessed, evening out her expression. "It does surprise me."

Adamina enjoyed Imryll's revelation, but a dark look quickly replaced her gratified expression. "It's a surprise to us all. And while we are not…We do not question our king, who is right and just in all matters, does it not give us pause?"

Imryll slowly nodded. "He must have his reasons."

"Indeed. And if these realmfolk chosens are a success…rumor is, they won't be the last to come. It will be important for us, Imryll, to be the most pleasing. To show everyone why the Noble Houses are now, and always, the best choice for a Rhiagain."

Imryll acknowledged her with a nod, unwilling to throw her weight behind any scheme of Adamina's, however sensible it sounded.

Adamina lifted her skirt with a curt nod in return. "We'll speak more on this later."

When Adamina had disappeared around the corner in a whirl of layered skirts, Imryll forgot about Tasmin and slumped against the wall. She took in her first satisfying breath since turning the corner.

Everything in her life had changed in an afternoon.

But nothing had changed in her heart.

She had to find a way off Duncarrow.

Not tomorrow, but *tonight*.

The midwinter air swept a crisp wind over and into the open-air lyceum, bouncing between the vacant stands as it turned into a whistling song. Drazhan held the back of the line as they marched into the arena on the south side of the keep.

It wasn't much of a march or even a line—only the five knights who had advanced to the end of the yearlong trials in Riverchapel. Five hundred they'd been when they began, most of them fresh-faced youth looking to prove themselves in the wrong way. A waste of a year it had been for Drazhan, to get to the same place he knew he'd end up. On the first day, he'd accurately picked out three of the four men who'd made it to the end with him. Only Waters was a surprise, but Easterlanders were known for their underhandedness, and the boy's father was a favorite of Lord Quintus.

They'd docked mere minutes before, taking a short path from the port that passed so quickly, Drazhan had to remind himself how small Duncarrow was.

Some said the isle was cursed.

"This coliseum is grossly out of proportion," Blackfen, the longbowman, muttered, and Drazhan had to silently agree. There were hardly a hundred residents of Duncarrow, but the lyceum had been built to house thousands—thousands who would never be invited, from the Rhiagain fear of the sickness. That had been another reason for the trials lasting a year…to keep the knights isolated from the rest of the kingdom long enough to be sure they wouldn't bring death.

Drazhan had brought death, just not the kind they expected.

He inhaled the briny air whipping across the modest isle. Duncarrow had been an abandoned stronghold from before written record. The island was inhospitable, a pile of jagged rocks and fickle tides that made even the sturdiest sea travelers brace for the worst. Before the Rhiagains had claimed it, no one in the kingdom wanted anything to do with the wretched place. Nothing grew. Nothing thrived. Little survived.

The Rhiagains said it was where they'd washed up from their perilous crossing, a sign they were meant to settle there, but anyone not fooled by their charm knew they'd chosen isolation from a place of pragmatism. To maintain the illusion of gods without the inconvenience of scrutiny. No surprise visits they would not see coming for miles. A perfect siege defense.

The commander leading the five, Ofal, didn't seem to know how to address the knights. He was a first commander of the Rhiagain Guard, a high-ranking officer who bowed to few men, but the freshly formed Knights of Duncarrow had already become a matter of legend. No one yet knew where the elite warriors fit into the hierarchy. Drazhan and the four men in front of him were the first of their kind.

"Ah, right." Ofal stopped in the center of the arena and cast his gaze around the empty seats. He seemed at odds with himself on whether he should explain that, but he pulled his shoulders back with a stern face and apparently decided not to. "This is the Lyceum of Duncarrow."

"Original feckin' name, never could've guessed that," Kav muttered, pulling a snicker from Waters.

"It is here where you will train, and it is here where you will fight." Ofal seemed out of place giving his speech. He, like all of the Rhiagain Guard, was a man of the kingdom. And like all men of the Guard, he spent most of his life sequestered on the nearby Isle of Belcarrow—an even more foul place than Duncarrow, or so Drazhan had heard.

"Fight what?" Owen Strong, the other Southerland lad, asked. He nursed his broadsword and mace in his palms as though the battle might begin at any moment. "Our trainer said there might be beasts?"

"You'll only fight each other. No beasts," Ofal answered. "And there will be no death in this arena, boys. You have all come to serve one of our chosen five. What you are competing for is the honor of the order."

"Of the order?" Kav asked.

"The order of queens, of course."

Kav shrugged, still confused.

Blackfen shot Drazhan a look he read well enough from his peripheral. *This idiot really didn't listen to a thing this past year, did he?*

Drazhan kept his eyes on Ofal.

"The queens are ranked in a hierarchy," Waters said, looking both put out and elated to be the one explaining things. "The First Chosen is always queen. Second, third, fourth, and fifth wives are minor queens, ranking in order of importance. If the first queen dies, ah, well, there's four more, in carefully chosen order, to step into the honor."

"Thank you, Waters. But I feel compelled to add you are here to ensure our queens do *not* come to harm," Ofal answered, a stern frown creasing the flesh between his brows. "And that's why you are competing. So the most capable among you will be chosen to protect the one who is most important to the future of this crown. The one whose son will one day be king."

"Oy, well that's gon' be me," Kav said, throwing an elbow at Waters, who didn't smile this time.

"You have one week to practice for the Tournament of Choosing," Ofal said.

"One week!" Waters cried.

"You had a whole year, Syr Waters," Ofal replied, unmoved. "If you're not equipped to win today, you won't be a week from now." He gestured behind him. "Your living quarters are just beyond the gates. That's a generous description, mind you. It's five cots stuck in a hall for rest. No use complaining, you'll all be sleeping in the keep soon enough."

"And we'll be doing this in front of all of Duncarrow," Blackfen said, not quite a question. "How many live here?"

"Roughly four hundred, if you include the servants. A third of that if you don't. Not much of an audience," Ofal said, agreeing with what went unsaid. "The ones who matter will all be present; nothing else should concern you. His Grace King Carrow. His Grace Prince Torian. The Noble Houses of Duncarrow, of course. And...your queens."

"That won't even fill—" Blackfen was silenced by Ofal dropping to one knee. The knights exchanged perplexed looks and then did the same in disjointed order.

Drazhan was the last to kneel, and as he did, he saw the object of Ofal's flustered call to respect: a young woman, with wavy red hair catching the hard wind like loose ribbons. She wrapped her arms over her chest, but the gusts snapped her dress as if it might carry her away and out to sea. She squeezed her eyes hard twice and then swallowed a deep breath, attempting to not appear startled by the scene she'd walked into.

"Lady Imryll," Ofal said without looking up.

Drazhan had never looked down to begin with. He caught the young woman's furtive eyes, which were splotched with more red, as were her cheeks, a canvas of shame and freckles.

"This isn't necessary." Lady Imryll wiped at her face and held her head high. "*Please,* Commander. Ask your men to stand."

Ofal reluctantly climbed to his feet, nodding behind him for the others to do the same.

"I didn't know anyone would be here. The lyceum is usually…"

"We're preparing for the Tournament of Choosing, my lady," Ofal said with a bow that made her more visibly flustered. "Knights, you asked about our future queens. You have the most important one standing before you now: Lady Imryll of Glaisgain, only daughter of the Duke of Glaisgain, soon to be First Chosen of Prince Torian."

Imryll. Drazhan mouthed the word without sound. He watched her sweep her uncertain gaze over the knights, who each looked down in reverence. But when she met his, a look of hard surprise darkened her expression. What could she be thinking about his refusal to bow, to even nod? Could she glean his thoughts from his eyes?

Behind her troubled expression was something dark and tortured, but that was not Drazhan's first thought when he took her in.

23

No, his first had been to imagine what she'd look like bent over one of the rocks, the rough waves crashing over her bare flesh as he cupped the swell of her ass.

Imryll. Imryll. Imryll.

Her name would sound just right in his mouth.

On his tongue.

As she let him claim her.

As she let him *ruin* her.

As he brought Duncarrow to ash and rubble.

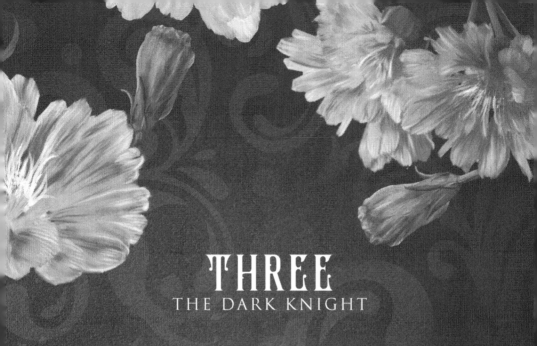

THREE
THE DARK KNIGHT

Imryll had never been so unsettled by something as innocuous as a look.

She'd come to the lyceum to be alone after Adamina's numbing revelations, no longer having the heart or energy for conversation with Tasmin. She did her best thinking alone, and she had only a few hours to discover a way to sneak onto the ship leaving that night.

Instead, she'd stumbled into five soldiers and Commander Ofal. Four of the men were silenced by a call to reverence, lowering their gazes as tradition demanded, but the fifth...The fifth, with his bold, jutting chin and narrowed eyes, challenged her. Incomprehensible loathing singed his mossy irises that had not averted, not for a moment, when the commander announced he was in the presence of a future queen.

Imryll's mouth watered in confusion. She didn't know whether to run or to stay and confront the warrior.

Knights the commander had called them, conjuring vague memories of her father speaking of the elite warriors chosen for the Queens' Guard.

One of them will be mine if I can't find my way off this isle. Please, gods, not that one.

"Lady Imryll?" The commander tilted his head in concern once the men had risen to their feet. "Are you all right?"

"I…" Imryll tried to answer, but the fifth knight's glare demanded her attention.

"Shall I have someone escort you back to the keep?"

"No, that will be…" She swallowed, her eyes drawn back to the intensity of the knight and the darkness rolling off him like plumes of smoke. *Do none of them see this?* "I came for some fresh air, but I see the lyceum is in use, so I'll…" She squeezed her eyes once to keep herself from looking again to the impudent man still boring holes in her. "I'll find my own way back."

"Forgive my boldness," the commander said nervously, "but now that His Grace the King has made his announcement, my lady would be better served with an escort at all times."

Imryll burst out laughing, despite the unease flowing over her. "Here? On Duncarrow? What exactly is a danger to me here on this pile of rocks?"

Him, she thought, refusing to look at the fifth knight. The dark knight. He's *a danger to me.*

"Just the same, my lady. Will you indulge my concerns and allow me to send one of our knights with you?"

Imryll's face burned, even through the wind chilling her bones. Her pulse was a fluttery mess of everything before the moment and everything during. How strange it all seemed in light of the future others had planned for her.

The commander didn't wait for her confirmation. He nodded at one of the men—mercifully, not *that* one—who stepped forward to her side. She noted his longbow and checked it against what little she knew of the kingdom. *A Rush Rider. Father says their bows are carved to match their heights.*

"Syr Farradyn Blackfen, my lady," he said, introducing himself with a respectful bow. He had hair the color of night, his chin and nose perfectly linear.

Imryll inadvertently looked past him and saw the dark knight smirking with his eyes.

"Or simply Blackfen, if it serves you."

"Blackfen," she said back to him. She felt light and disconnected. Weightless. With a shuddering inward breath, she quickly nodded. "Thank you." She didn't—couldn't—meet the eyes of the commander when she repeated her gratitude. To look anywhere but where they were headed would be to risk another dangerous silent exchange with the foul one.

Blackfen held out his arm. Once she took it, fully turning away from the unnerving situation she'd regretfully stepped into, her pulse started to return to its normal cadence. She indulged a deep breath when they were free of the lyceum altogether.

"You're a Rush Rider?" she asked. Words soothed her, replaced the image of the dark knight still haunting her thoughts.

"Yes, my lady."

"Just Imryll is fine."

She felt him tighten at her side. "Perhaps to you, my lady, but I do not expect that others will share your desire for familiarity."

Imryll nodded to herself. The towering keep spiraled into the thick haze of clouds at the end of the rocky path. Her belly clenched at even the thought of going back inside, but there were few escapes on Duncarrow, and the knights had co-opted the path she needed to get to her favorite one safely.

Once Blackfen left her, she'd take another path to the cave.

"I hear the Westerlands is beautiful. Green and lush," she said.

"It is, my lady."

Imryll laughed. "And you would give that up for this?"

Blackfen's jaw moved before he spoke. "My people, the Blackfens, are servants of land and lord. It's in our blood to go where honor demands."

"Honor demanded you come to this cheerless pile of rocks?"

A smile played at his mouth but didn't form. "Honor brought me to Duncarrow to protect our future queen."

Imryll pondered his words. The fifth knight's hostile expression played in the space of her thoughts, unwelcome. "And…the other men? They feel as you do?"

"I cannot speak for the other men."

"But you do know them? They're your friends?"

"I wouldn't go that far," Blackfen answered. His breath furled in a soft white cloud immediately stolen by the wind. "We spent a year training together, but that doesn't make us friends."

"Enemies then?"

"You would provoke me to say something untoward, my lady?"

Imryll's brows rose. "Untoward? Now you've piqued my interest."

Blackfen chuckled. "I meant only that we come from different parts of the kingdom. We have different pasts, different impetuses."

"And the one who defied your commander and didn't lower his eyes, what of him?" Imryll snapped her mouth closed, stunned at her own brashness.

"Oh. Him." Blackfen nodded with a long inhale. "No one knows Syr Wynter. I think he prefers it that way."

"Wynter? Name's a fine match for his chilly demeanor."

"I suppose I've gotten used to him." Blackfen angled his face toward her. "Don't take it to heart, my lady. Some men just desire not to be known."

No.

He wanted me to know him.

"Tell me, Syr Blackfen. Who is your favorite to win the tournament?"

His mouth screwed into an attempted grin. "You're looking at him."

"If you win, then you'll be my guard?"

"Yes, my lady."

"And as my guard…you would have to do whatever I ask?"

Blackfen cocked his chin. "As your guard, I would have to act always in the interest of your safety."

She laughed under her breath. "What a politic answer."

"For a politic question. My lady."

Imryll froze when she saw who approached them on the path. Her blood cooled, stiffening her hands and feet. Sickness spread across her chest. "Thank you, Syr Blackfen. I can take it from here."

Drazhan glowered in the direction Blackfen had left with Imryll.

Her presence lingered like a phantom.

The others were talking. About *her*. About the tournament. About things so inconsequential, his mind filtered all of it out, allowing his thoughts to come to complete suspension.

"Syr Wynter?"

His body obeyed the call to return to the conversation, but his mind no longer existed in the present, with the commander and the other knights.

He was no longer in the lyceum at all.

The acrid brine of the sea air disappeared.

Snow speckled his face, becoming ash.

Drazhan hovered in the space between his past and his future, mingling grief and hope and rage and vengeance until they were all the same, swirling through his mind like a tempest of promise.

Imryll.

Imryll. Imryll. Imryll.

"Mortain." Imryll steeled her jaw to subdue her unease for the creature standing before her on the path.

And that was what he was. A creature. For though the others called the Meduwyn sorcerers, it wasn't just their magic that separated them from her people.

The differences lived in their disturbingly vivid eyes and the movements of their waxy faces, which seemed more like they were mimicking complex emotions than experiencing them.

Their slow, measured movements left her with the unsettling sense they weren't even aware of their own hands, their own feet. Immortality wrapped them in a blanket of imperishability, a disturbing, persistent reminder of how fleeting life was for everyone *but* them.

And yet they were also beautiful, in the way dolls were when crafted to perfection. Their hair was lustrous…their lips full, cheeks high. They held their secrets close, and their intentions closer.

Even Mortain, who scared Imryll the most, had a way of wrapping her attention through his fingers and making it his own.

Only four Meduwyn had survived the voyage from Ilynglass. Four too many, in Imryll's estimation. King Carrow had mercifully sent the other three into the realm on a secret assignment years ago, leaving Mortain the sole Meduwyn on Duncarrow until they returned. Somehow, he was everywhere, always. In the corners and shadows…uninvited, judging, listening, guiding.

"Lady Imryll." The words rolled over his tongue like a trill. A shiver raced down her back. "Shall I even ask what has you so flustered, or would it be easier for me to pull the truth from your mind?"

"Not flustered. Only cold." Imryll folded her arms over her chest. She couldn't meet his eyes. Her mind flooded with thoughts of the sea and the wind to cover what she hoped wasn't too late to hide from him.

"Cold. I see." Mortain's tone was light, almost teasing, but it made her skin tingle. He'd always had this effect on her. There was nothing inappropriate about his words or actions, but his bewildering intentions left her in a state of constant distress when he was around. "Little need of that when there are a hundred fires burning in the keep."

"I was on my way back." She wanted to gather her skirts and push past him, but the fear of him snapping his bony arm out to keep her in place—of him touching her at all—held her fast.

"Your mother is in a state."

"What?" Imryll snapped her gaze to his and instantly regretted it. Dread sizzled through her collarbone. She lowered her eyes back to the side.

"Duchess Melantha has been looking for you." His even tone rode the line between soothing and frightening. "So has the duke."

"My mother just saw me."

"Ah, yes, and you're in no condition to be running off on your own, no? As upset as you were when you ran from her and the prince?" Mortain's smooth words floated across the wind like a warning.

"If I was surprised by the news she brought me, I had good reason." Imryll couldn't help defending herself, even if it was wasted on him. "For years, King Carrow has declared me unfit to even be the prince's friend, let alone his concubine."

"Unfit." Mortain drew the word out with a thoughtful tap of his bony fingers against the arm crossed over his torso. "That can mean many things, Imryll."

"It meant just one thing…Mortain."

"The way my name flounders upon your tongue wounds me," Mortain said, sounding as he must have thought a wounded man should. "Are we not friends?"

"Friends?" Imryll's laugh forced her head back up. Mortain's deeply solemn expression stilled her again.

"I've looked after you since your birth." He moved closer.

She willed herself not to step back, to restrain her fear of him, which was perhaps more irrational than earned. He'd never harmed her. Never threatened her. Never done anything to frighten her beyond being himself.

"I've always had your best interest at heart."

Imryll blanched and turned her face to the side when he stopped right in front of her. Her heart shuddered despite that she *knew* he would never hurt her. He'd be thrown in the Sky Dungeon for even touching one of Carrow's people, powerful sorcerer or no.

31

"What do you want?" she asked, straining her words through her teeth. *Breathe. He will not hurt you. He will not hurt you. He will not—*

"I've come to take you back, Imryll."

"Why?"

"You know why."

Had Mortain seen through her intentions? Did he know she would leave that very night if her plans aligned?

Imryll swallowed hard.

"You're going to be First Chosen," Mortain said. "And you're going to be First Chosen not because Carrow has changed his mind or because you've miraculously changed your ways." He uncoiled her hands from her chest and gently lowered them to her sides. He waited for her to meet his eyes, an unspoken command she had no choice but to obey.

Imryll blinked hard and gathered her courage. She looked up and into the abyss behind his violet eyes. "You want me to ask why. Is that it?"

"I want you to be curious. To question everything, as you always have," Mortain replied. "The incuriosity plaguing this isle is illicit. It's unfathomable. But you have somehow been exempt from this plague." The way he said *somehow* left her with the sense he already had an explanation. "And yes, Imryll. I want you to ask *why* you've been selected not only as *a* chosen of Prince Torian, but *the* chosen."

Imryll dug her toes into her boots and forced herself to ask the question. "Why then? Why am I, the unfit one, the intemperate one, the *curious* one, suddenly the right choice for our future king?"

Mortain's grin started small, but then it stretched across his face as though carved by a blade. His eyes remained the same: dark, lifeless. "Because I told the king that Imryll of Glaisgain is going to be our First Chosen, and the king always answers to Mortain of Ilynglass."

Imryll's breath choked in her throat. She tried to speak but couldn't.

"Does that surprise you?"

Imryll started to nod but found herself shaking her head instead, her tongue shoved to the roof of her mouth to keep her teeth from clacking.

"And when you're ready for the truth, for the answers to questions no one else will answer for you, you come to me. For, unlike the others, you have earned this gift of truth." Mortain reached forward and smoothed rogue hairs off her face. "But for now, Imryll? We both know what must happen. And you'll come with me, knowing what must happen, because despite the fight in you, the insubordination brewing in your heart, you understand duty as well as anyone. As well as I."

Imryll's legs turned to jelly but Mortain steadied her, extending an arm just as Blackfen had. But where the bowman had promised safety, the sorcerer could only offer darkness.

But he wasn't wrong.

Her life had never been about choice.

Imryll took his arm and left her hope wilting on the jagged path.

34

FOUR
RUNNING BACK INTO THE STORM

Imryll winced through tight blinks as she fielded the barrage of questions from the duke and duchess of Glaisgain. Melantha allowed her daughter to call her "Mother" in private, but the dressing down wasn't private. Imryll's brother, Octavyen, was in their parents' apartments, and so was Mortain, who hadn't left after delivering her.

"You sit there…You sit there and you *glare* at us as if you were not just handed the greatest gift anyone has ever given you." Duke Drushan's eyes flared with confusion. Imryll's reticence to become a glorified mistress of the prince truly confounded him, but that was because he'd never listened to a word she said.

"She's not glaring. Ladies don't *glare*," Duchess Melantha said in a clipped, hushed tone, as if glaring were an insult too great to be borne. She smoothed her crimson gown with an affronted look at the wall.

"You believe you've raised a lady, do you?" Drushan asked, followed by the expected eye fluttering Imryll had come to know as part of his favorite pastime: belittling anyone whose opinion varied from his in any way.

"You would hold your own daughter to the standards of a woman when she is only just?"

"I married you when you were fifteen. You fell in line easily enough." The sneer on the end of his words made Melantha blanch.

"You're assuming she will not fall in line, Drushan. She has only today learned she will be queen, after years of everyone telling her she will not be. I assure you, there is *no one* who wants this more than our daughter."

Because all women dream of being trifles of men, right?

Imryll used the last of her patience to resist rolling her eyes. "I'm right here," she muttered. Then she did roll them, but off to the side, and as she returned her gaze to her parents and their row, she caught Mortain watching her. He lifted the corner of his mouth in a grin his eyes never caught up with.

"No? The same daughter who still sees our future king as a playmate?" Drushan snapped back, ignoring Imryll.

It was then she knew her mother had not said a word about what she'd witnessed on the rocks.

"She will learn to see him otherwise," Melantha said in the same patronizing tone she employed on Imryll when she was being disobedient. "Just as I learned to see you as otherwise."

Imryll's eyes rolled again, for an entirely different reason, when a vision unexpectedly grabbed hold of her.

I'm in the Sceptre of Ilynglass.
Again.

I know this not from the sea with the tides climbing as high as the blue stone cliffs, nor because I see the trees with rope-like branches that are used to make everything from clothing to homes.

I know because I know, in the same way I "know" things every time I'm pulled away.

36

We've traveled away from what I recognize though, because there is no sea breeze, no brine with each intake of breath. Still, there's an unmistakable familiarity to the air. A foul, cloying humidity gets into my skin, through my shirt, and melts my energy.

There are others here, sensed more by the perception of movement around me than anything I've seen. All sound is garbled, but it's better than the silence that greeted me when the confusing visions first began.

There's a mountain. I think…I think I need to be there. There's something in the mountain—an oracle of sorts, though it isn't me who knows that but the vessel I occupy. My thoughts are not my own. They're a mix of mine and the owner of these eyes I look through, but I know what this creature desires. To be atop this mountain. To collect an important truth.

I glance to my side and see…ah, well. At last, after almost a year of being rudely ripped from one reality to another without warning, I see someone I know. Oldwin, one of the four Meduwyn who made it to the White Kingdom. He's grinning—no, smirking—one tooth sharpened to a point. He knows what we'll find up this mountain. He licks his lip with a vigor that matches an animal who has just taken down a meal.

Imryll swallowed a gasp as she returned to herself, her chest rising and falling in her effort to breathe normally before someone realized she'd disappeared for a spell. Her eyes darted around in a panic, but no one had seen. No one paid her any mind at all.

What's at the top of that mountain?

"And gods help us all if she's still hoarding vellum and *writing*," Drushan spat with a pained groan. "Melantha, you indulged her way too much as a girl. I blame you for this."

"She's not, Drushan. Not anymore. She wouldn't," Melantha said uneasily. "She knows better, don't you, Imryll?"

"Imryll will be fine," Octavyen said, speaking for the first time. He sat in a broad chair, his legs spread as he picked at his cuffs with a bored look. "As long as His Grace has taught his son how to be a man in the bedchamber."

37

"Octavyen!" Melantha declared. Her head trembled in tight shakes. "Your sister is still a maiden, and you will not speak of such things in her presence."

Octavyen grinned at Imryll. "You'd let her go to the prince's bed ignorant?"

"If you're implying she should behave as you did with your wife, fooling around before it was proper, you can leave," Drushan said with a hand thrust toward the door.

Octavyen had been married two years to Duke Drummond's daughter. Negotiations had begun, to sell Imryll to Drummond's heir, before the king's surprising declaration.

But Imryll wasn't even going to be a wife. She was merely the one who would bear Torian heirs, useful only for her parts.

She tapped her feet together under the chair. *I need to get to the cave, so I can write this vision down before it leaves me.*

So I can gather the courage to get on the ship later tonight.

"Of course not," Octavyen replied. His smile dissolved. "But it doesn't mean someone shouldn't tell her what to expect. What her *prince* will expect, and what *she* should expect from *him*."

"As if the prince will know any better." Drushan snorted and fingered the top button on his tightened collar.

"For her sake, I hope you're wrong," Octavyen muttered. "The Rhiagains may not take wives, but that doesn't preclude them from pleasing the women they take to their bed."

Imryll knew her brother liked to satisfy his wife, because he bragged about it to everyone who would listen. Aloysha walked around with a skip in her step and a grin permanently carved into her face.

"Since when has coupling ever been about pleasure for women?" Drushan retorted. He quaffed the last of his liquor and huffed a bitter laugh into the glass. "*This* is the sort of talk that leads to dissatisfied wives, and husbands who are left to deal with them."

Imryll again felt Mortain watching her. She shivered and rolled her palms over her dress, quietly plotting her escape. They hardly knew she was there anyway. The conversation would happen with or without her.

"Well, does it matter then? How she feels?" Melantha flipped her hands up and turned away from all of them. "Why are we even speaking of this when the matter is decided and her feelings are irrelevant?"

Imryll swallowed a groan. *Why indeed.*

Octavyen winked at her and pushed out of his chair with a huff. "I really hate to interrupt this deeply important discourse, but Imryll promised to help Aloysha pick out patterns for her springtide gowns. The seamstress is due in our apartments now."

"We're not done here," Drushan said. He paused as he refilled his glass. A dark look passed behind his eyes. He rapped his knuckles against the wall. "When your sister is queen, we will have climbed higher than any of our peers. She needs to understand that what she *wants* has no place in this room. This keep. This kingdom."

"By now she's more than well aware," Octavyen replied. "There's little point to her sitting here while you exchange words over her head. In the end, she'll do whatever you ask, just as we all do. Won't you, Ryl?"

Imryll nodded, impatient to be free of the mawkish apartment and her grasping parents. Glaisgains being crown favorites meant her growing up hearing her father plotting at all hours. There was always intrigue, always a new way to rise to the top.

This time, *she* was the way.

If she failed, the honor would go to the Privaines, and there couldn't be a worse outcome in her father's eyes than losing favor to Fenring Privaine.

Drushan and Melantha's eyes locked in a silent, heated debate they didn't vocalize.

Octavyen snagged Imryll's hand in his and dragged her out before they could argue.

She caught Mortain's piercing gaze once more on the way out. His restrained, knowing nod stuck in her chest like a dagger she never saw coming.

"Thank you," she whispered to her brother when they were free of the room. Imryll ran her hands along her neck with a grimace. Her gaze traveled instinctively toward the north of the island, where her cave awaited her. "I owe you."

"You owe me nothing," her brother said with a scoff. "But you know they're right, don't you?"

Imryll crossed her arms and turned toward the row of windows lining the hall. Clouds dulled the light, dimming the stones. She'd have no time to pack anything of use. She'd have to leave with only what she wore. No gold. Nothing to trade for food. If she was clever enough, she might steal a few things on the voyage, but that was only if there *was* anything to steal. Provision ships brought food and supplies. They didn't leave with them.

"Ryl?"

She was still mulling the holes in her plan, only half-present. "You rescued me just to subject me to the same speech?"

"No." Octavyen sighed. He stepped behind her. "Unlike them, I actually care that this is making you so unhappy."

"Do you?" Imryll's face tingled; tears tickled her eyes at his open display of affection. The urge to cry came from all sides, from past and future. Whether she stayed or left, her immediate future held only the darkness of fear and uncertainty.

"You know I do." Octavyen laid a hand on her shoulder. "But it's *Torian*, Imryll." His voice lowered to a whisper. "You already care for him."

Imryll shook her head. She trained her eyes out the window, to the vast, endless sea. To what lay between her and what she wanted most in the world: to be free of the lies and oppression that had built everything on Duncarrow. "Not like that."

"You're looking at this all wrong, you know." He didn't want to argue; she heard it in his voice, agitation creeping in. Octavyen loved her but was used to not having to fight very hard to win. "Friendship in a marriage is a gift most never receive."

And freedom an even rarer gift. "Are we done?"

"Imryll…"

"It's as you said, Tav." Imryll spun back at him with a scowl that she hoped hid the grief humming just under the surface. Her voice cracked, the familiar preamble for tears. "I have no choice in the matter. I'll fall in line. You can report to Duke Drushan that his daughter is *agreeable* and *pliant.*" What she said was unfair and she knew it, but when had equity ever entered her life?

Octavyen's face fell. "You know I would never do that."

"Doesn't matter to me either way." She held her chin high and her shoulders back. "In the end, is it not the same?"

"It won't be as bad as you're making it out in your head. Unlike a marriage, there are no expectations of fidelity. You can take all the lovers you desire once you're with child." His mouth quirked into a frown. "That was not an invitation to tell me about them."

Imryll wiped at her tears, which had betrayed her and fallen anyway. "Does Aloysha really need my help?"

He shook his head with an exhale, clearly relieved for the subject change. "I just said it to get you out of there."

Imryll nodded. She should thank him. He'd always been good to her. Always looked out for her. Other than Torian and Tasmin, and perhaps Duke Rahn, he was the only one she'd miss.

But finding gratitude for anyone on Duncarrow—anyone who played a part, no matter how minor, in keeping her world small and boxed—seemed a feat currently beyond her ability.

"Good, because I doubt she'd like my choices today. Black, black, and more black," she said instead and brushed past him, her emotions torn between hoping it was the last time she ever saw her brother and mourning the same.

Drazhan flipped the thick pages of his tiny leather journal and ticked a single mark with his charcoal at the end of a long line of them, as he'd done every day since his father and brother had died—since his sister had been irrevocably traumatized watching her entire world burn. He was nearly out of pages, but before the paper ran out, Carrow and Torian Rhiagain would be dead, and any heir of Imryll's would be called into question.

It wouldn't bring his father or brother back. It wouldn't bring the light back into his sister's eyes. It wouldn't revive the lost souls of the Cross or restore the futures denied them.

But the stolen crown would crumble, and the kingdom would return to the Reaches once more.

He thumbed the pages, full with marks, for a second longer than usual, indulging himself in a rare moment of reflection. He'd come a long way since becoming orphaned in the Uprising. Everything that had mattered in the years between was reflected on the pages.

The other four knights were drunk. Even Blackfen, who seemed to possess the modicum of restraint the others lacked. They'd been throwing rocks at the fire they'd made in the center of the arena, roaring with laughter as if there were anything humorous about acting like beasts. As if they were not sitting upon land seized by men who had stolen from their people.

Drazhan's head whipped upward in rapid fury when a rock hit his shoulder.

Kav and Waters curled toward each other in a snicker. Owen glanced at them both with stunned disgust, while Blackfen followed Drazhan with his eyes, waiting for him to react.

Drazhan tucked his book back into his boot. He didn't drop his gaze from the two churls still cackling to each other with anxious glances. He tightened the buckle and sat back up, folding his hands over his lap.

Their laughter dissolved to titters. One of them coughed.

Drazhan continued to watch.

"I ken you two have a death wish." Owen raised his brows at Blackfen as he swept a hand down to lift his ale from the dirt.

"Nah," Kav said. He swiped at his nose and then his eyes, full of tears from his puerile attempt at cleverness. "Just tryin' to get a rise out of him. A full year we've known each other, lads. But this one? Doesnae grin. Doesnae speak. Doesnae show *any* emotion, while the rest of us are practically kin now."

"Perhaps he just has better sense than to run his mouth out," Blackfen muttered. "That's enough for tonight." He started to kick sand into the fire, but Waters snaked a hand out and stopped him.

"I fight for my wife and son." Waters slurred his words. "Kav here fights for the same thing. Strong here thinks his family has something to prove, and maybe they do, so I know why he's come this far. And you, Rush Rider, you're just oozing with honor, aren't you? It probably comes out with every shit, swims in your piss." He spat into the dirt. "But Stormclaw?" He ground his mouth. "Don't know a thing about him, do we? Couldn't even tell you why they call him that."

Drazhan ran through the start of one of his meditations, waiting for Waters to wear himself out. Drazhan's gaze hadn't wavered. The longer he stared at the two men, the more they worked themselves up.

"None of your feckin' business, aye?" Owen said, rising suddenly to his feet. He drunkenly swayed into Blackfen, who'd stood right after him. "Man has his reasons. You donnae need to know 'em."

Drazhan saw Imryll bent over her bed with her ass peaked in the air, fresh off his most recent command as he told her exactly what he was going to do with it. His sword-formed callouses scratched her velvety soft cheeks as he palmed them—branded them. He watched her glance back over her shoulder, her eyes flaring with anticipation and her undefined red curls half blocking her flushed face. Timid but ready.

Kav shot off the log and went for Owen, but Waters had him by the collar before he could take a step. Blackfen stepped to Owen's side, weary resolve streaming through his hard sigh. His longbow was propped against the stands, but Rush Riders didn't pass their trials on their archery skills alone.

43

"He's not worth it," Waters said, though his eyes, flashing with anger, said the opposite.

Drazhan wouldn't enjoy fucking her. That wasn't the point.

But he wouldn't hate it either.

"And Stormclaw? He doesn't give a rat's cock," Waters spat. He released Kav, who snarled at Owen before dusting himself off and sidestepping away. "Look at him, staring as though he's not even here but somewhere else."

Drazhan plunged into Imryll in one sharp thrust, impaling her on what other women had called a very generous cock. She cried out with a high whimper, but she didn't inch forward for reprieve. She didn't need to after the hour he'd spent with his face between her legs. He didn't care about her pleasure, but readying her, tonguing her from end to end until she had nothing left to give, was part of turning her against the Rhiagains. Ensuring she took only shame to the prince's bed would allow Torian to know, *Carrow* to know, that the heir to the crown didn't have a drop of Rhiagain blood.

It would be the final humiliation to Carrow and the few left of his treacherous brood.

"See?" Waters wagged his arm. "He's not natural. He's more beast than man."

Blackfen crossed his arms. "Why does that bother you, Waters?"

"He should be fighting me right now! I struck him and he's just...sitting there." Waters flapped his arms around in disbelief.

Blackfen nodded at Drazhan. "Seems to me he's already won this fight."

"Ah, and how's that?" Waters charged forward a step. His face burned bright red.

Drazhan took a fistful of Imryll's hair, coiling it like a rope as he continued his campaign of claiming. He liked the way she arced up off the bed with a guttural moan, the sensual curve her back made. The princeling would never command a sound like that from her.

"He's got you all worked into a proper tantrum," Blackfen answered. "And all he had to do was look at you."

"Doesnae bode well for ye, in the tournament," Owen said. "Ye ken he's getting under your skin now? Wait 'til it counts."

Drazhan finished fast. There was no need to draw it out anymore. She looked back at him with her doe-like amber eyes and nodded once, giving him permission to spill his revenge inside of her with far more gratification than he'd ever take from the sex itself.

He left her like that, panting and confused, caught in an unexpected squall she'd never learn to navigate.

The kind of storm she'd run right back into, over and over again, unable to resist the rain.

Perhaps he'd enjoyed it after all.

Drazhan lifted himself off the rock, filling his lungs with the repressive air. It burned his lungs on the way in, but he was grateful for the dearth of comforts…for the tiny cot shoved into the circular hall of the lyceum and the leftovers from the kitchens after the staff had eaten. He'd forced himself to leave luxury behind when he'd departed his ancestral keep in Witchwood Cross, because comfort was a shackle that excused cowardice when the moment called for so much more.

He nodded at the other four knights, still squabbling, and decided to go for a walk.

Imryll took the less-sure path she'd hoped to avoid, traversing the cluster of treacherous rocks that lined the northern shore of Duncarrow. The precarious tides were calm one moment, deadly the next. Residents were cautioned against going there in any tidal phase, but Imryll couldn't cut through the lyceum with the knights training there.

One in particular had used his brusque first acquaintance with her to take her apart and put her back together, the pieces out of order.

The Rush Rider would win. Everyone knew Rush Riders were fierce and formidable.

No matter the outcome, she wouldn't be there to see it.

Imryll slipped and slid on the slick black rocks. Sea spray knocked her sideways, and a crashing wave left her dress soaked, but she gasped and pressed on until she reached the only stretch of beach land on Duncarrow.

The strip was narrow, the sand gritty enough to cut the soles of feet open of anyone foolish enough to go bare. It wasn't as ugly as the rest of the isle, but it was a trap when the tide was in, and a rugged wasteland when it wasn't.

Imryll turned her back on the sea and marched, her boots sliding through the fine rocks, straight to the stone wall that stretched to the tallest natural point on Duncarrow.

She confirmed she hadn't been followed before approaching the wall. She ran her hand down the smooth columns carved into basalt, down, down until she found the overhang that blended with the rest of the wall.

Imryll dropped to a crouch and angled her head upward to find the opening to the hidden cave. *Her* cave. She'd always come alone.

She tossed her satchel up first, then slid her arms along the smooth, damp stone overhead, feeling around for the dug-in rocks that would give her the purchase needed to hoist herself into the dim passage. When she found them, she pulled herself up and in with a gratified grunt.

The cave was as spacious as a small keep. It stretched so far, she thought it might reach the other side of the isle, though she'd never wandered farther in. She never outran the small band of natural light from the outside. Bringing a lantern was something she'd only chanced a few times, but poking around dark corners at night, alone, exceeded her courage.

She settled into her usual spot, close to the entrance to make use of the dwindling illumination outside. A puddle spread more cold wetness up through her hips, but her dress was already soaked, and she didn't intend to stay any longer than it took to write down her vision. At the break of dusk, while the provision ship was readying for departure, she'd sneak to the port and take control of her future.

If she couldn't summon the courage to take the chance, she'd be a bride in a week's time.

No.

Not a bride.

A chosen.

The next queen.

Imryll could hardly still the dizzying energy whirling through her long enough to focus. But she *needed* to focus, to play out the next few hours with careful precision. Sneaking onto the ship wouldn't be easy, but if she could manage to evade the men at port, no one would ever think to look for her onboard. Not until it was too late.

She nibbled on her mouth with a grin, trying to keep her thoughts from slipping too far ahead of her. It would be easier to forget the visions, leave them behind with everything else, but she couldn't shake the sense they mattered.

Imryll pulled out her notebook and balanced it on a dry spot of the rock's table. Before her troubles returned, her charcoal came to life in her hands. When she was done transcribing the vision, she added her thoughts to the end.

*They speak of a voyage. I don't know who "they" are, but I know **what** they are. I can see it in their eyes, in their unnatural smiles. They're sorcerers. Meduwyn. The ones who never made it to the White Kingdom. They're plotting, and while I now hear **something** more than the silence of the early visions, the sound is distorted, almost worse than hearing nothing at all.*

The others defer to me. They respect me. When I speak, they listen.

I know now I'm not merely a detached narrator, observing something from afar, invisible. I am someone they respect. Someone they need. Someone they will follow.

The question is are these remnants of a life spent or memories of a heart still beating?

Now that I know Oldwin was there too, I can no longer rule out that I am seeing through the eyes of a Meduwyn still very much alive.

"Shoulders straight!" King Carrow barked. Torian snapped his posture so erect, it choked his breath. "Are you a prince or a hedge-born?"

"A prince, Your Grace," Torian answered. He modulated his voice to keep emotion from creeping in, how his father had taught him. Even. Regular. No excitement nor disinterest. A careful middle.

Nothing like the red-faced storm of annoyance swirling the king at present.

"Do you want your wives to whisper about the imbecile who was so easy to wrap around their jeweled fingers?"

"Of course not," Torian answered, screwing his mouth in lieu of the fire the response demanded. Kindness and respect had no intersection for his father. Respect was fear. Fear was obedience. Obedience was the mortar holding their entire reign together after all but a handful of Rhiagains had died during the Passage.

Carrow bowed over in a phlegmy, productive cough that spanned almost a full minute before he straightened and stopped. He dragged his hand across his chin in a pensive study of Torian. Those never ended well, not for Torian. He didn't need to be reminded of all the ways he was unlike his long-dead older brothers.

Torian's mother, Queen Godivah, added nothing to the conversation. She was occupied with examining the rouge on her cheeks in the tall mirror across the room. Her part yet awaited her, when she'd guide and mentor the five chosens after the ceremony. Godivah wouldn't even *be* First Chosen if Carrow's hadn't died in the Passage with both of her sons, but she played the part like she'd been born for it.

Torian's stomach dropped toward the stones and coalesced into a puddle at the thought of the ceremony facing him. He'd known for a while the number was a daunting five, but now that Imryll was among them, the task ahead seemed not just overwhelming but impossible.

There are two kinds of love. The love we afford possessions, which we are obliged to protect, to keep safe from harm or tarnish. And then there is the love that makes us weak and unable to rise to the difficult charges that await all kings. You may love your wives, Torian, as long as this love extends only as far as preservation.

All his father's wisdom over the years was burned into him like lashings of shame. There was too much to know and even more to understand, and none of it aligned with the man Torian wanted to be.

Not that his own desires mattered at all.

"You'll have your work ahead of you with Lady Imryll. She's willful, full of dangerous ideas, and cannot hold her tongue to save her life." Deep lines grooved into Carrow's forehead, in the space between his eyes. The whites of them were dotted with muddled yellow, causing him to look even more sickly than usual. He paced away from Torian, giving his son a few moments of peace. "She's ill-suited to be a queen at all, let alone First Chosen, and this has no doubt already created division in the Noble Houses."

All that and more, Torian thought, but he feared asking the obvious question, lest the answer be clear to everyone but him.

"But…" The buckles on Carrow's boots jangled as he made purposeful strides. Every landing was intentional, as if he'd mapped the chambers out in his mind so as to land only in the center of every stone. "Perhaps Mortain was right. The Glaisgains make a more powerful ally than the other houses. And Lady Imryll will produce comely children for you, which cannot be overlooked as a benefit. Handsome kings command greater respect."

Mortain *chose Imryll?*

49

"The sorcerers always have their reasons," Godivah remarked with a flip of her hand in the air, a move to indicate she had no idea what she was speaking on, but she assumed she was the only one aware of it.

But only a fool would dismiss or underestimate her.

"If Mortain is wrong, and she fails, your second will be a Privaine, which will suit us equally well. Lady Adamina would have been a better choice for queen, but…"

Torian snapped his eyes toward his father, who wasn't inclined to trail off for anything. But whatever the king was thinking, he kept it from his expression. His rage of earlier had been replaced by a more careful countenance.

"But what?" Torian asked. He winced before the last word was out. He'd regret asking this, as he came to regret asking any questions the king had not intentionally coaxed from him.

But his father's anger didn't come.

"Mortain insists. Imryll is the one," Carrow answered. There was only a hint of annoyance in his response. "She's the mother of our future." The second statement seemed more for himself.

It wasn't the first time the sorcerers had swept in and arranged a situation to their liking. He remembered what Clarisan often said about them…how they'd not been servants in their old sceptre, but the ones wielding the power.

"If she's not the one now, I'll be there to make sure she becomes the one." Godivah turned with a feral grin, but it settled. "Dear gods, we have so much to do. So much to do in so little time."

"No one is more up to the task of making queens out of girls than you, my dear."

"And what about…" She threw a not-subtle nod at Torian.

"No man knows how to fuck until he does it."

Godivah cackled before she could stop herself. With a cough, she cleared her throat. "Ada has that pretty little face, but she looks like you could break her with a single snap. Imryll has the kind of hips that could bring a dozen children to our legacy. Polish can be taught."

50

"Or broken in," Carrow said, and they laughed together.

Torian steeled himself as his mother and father bantered the qualities of Imryll of Glaisgain like she were property at auction. He'd never share what lived in his heart, the love for Imryll that threatened to swallow him whole, to drown him in unrequited wanting. It would be easier to watch her marry someone else than to watch her approach his bed with remorse.

Duty would crush the love between them and grind it into dust.

Drazhan checked his sword belt as he approached the rocks. The tide was still out but fast returning, and when it did, most of the area would be submerged in water.

He'd spotted the narrow strip of coastline when they'd made landing. It made him think of home…of the choppy white peaks of the Howling Sea and her mournful call through the land of endless winter.

Kav and Waters were both already half passed out when they'd stumbled into the hall. Blackfen and Owen weren't far behind.

But it was yet early. And Drazhan wanted to touch the sand.

He jogged down the rocks. His boots hit them in perfect time, sliding but not falling, almost bouncing from stone to stone until he hopped onto the sand in an effortless landing.

Drazhan's boots didn't sink; they crunched. He frowned before he'd even knelt to scoop some into his palms. It wasn't sand at all but jagged rock, ground into the consistency of broken glass. Thousands of years left before it would smooth and turn to proper sand.

He watched it fall from his palm, in inelegant plops, and dusted his palms against his pants.

His hands twitched, missing his claws. He had even less privacy than he'd had in training, and he *needed* a release. Like air, like food, when Drazhan went too long without indulging his claws, without turning them into a hurricane of strength and fury, he diminished.

Drazhan squinted into the last of the day's light. The sun was setting, and the tide had come in quicker than he'd anticipated. Now that he knew about the place—and how to keep the others from following him—he'd come back.

He'd turned to leave when a sound piqued his attention. He waited to hear it again.

A voice. He didn't hear a second.

Drazhan's hand twitched to Stormbringer as he continued to listen. He expected Kav and Waters to corner him at some point, but they'd be fools to accost him when they were drunk. Drazhan could take down both of them handily, inebriated or not.

But the voice was distinctly feminine. Smoky and deep, but with a softness that ruled out the ungainly boars he'd been training with.

Drazhan stepped quietly across the shifting-rock sand. The strip of coast was too narrow and exposed for there to be anywhere to hide, but the sound hadn't come from his imagination.

He moved toward the basalt columns that stretched up into the cliff. They were carved by the sea into uneven fingers, like pipes from an organ, and as he approached, he saw the illusion this created, and what it covered.

They were not all flush. Several jutted out a couple of feet. When he dipped low and looked up, he saw what the trickery was hiding.

An entrance, to what seemed to be a cave. If he stretched back to his feet, the floor would hit him at chest level, but he didn't know what—who—was inside.

The feminine voice came to life again, and it became evident she was talking to herself.

Drazhan considered his next move. He should leave. He hadn't come for company, and the woman in the cave was none of his business.

Then he remembered the shifting tide. Whoever was in there would be stuck, or worse, if they didn't leave soon.

With an eyeroll and a disgusted grunt, Drazhan rose and hoisted himself up into the cave by his forearms in one fluid move.

He heard a gasp, then what sounded like something falling to the rock with a series of clinks.

It took a moment to adjust to the dim light. All around him were more of the same basalt columns, stretching on into the darkness. He forced his eyes to quickly dilate—a skill he'd taught himself—and saw her.

Her.

Gaping at him, her mouth hung wide. Her breath hitched as she crossed an arm over her chest in alarm, the other slapping the damp stones behind her as she tried to crawl backward and away from him.

Her features were blurred by the twilight, but he knew those red curls. He'd already smelled them, held them, pulled them... even if she didn't yet know it.

"You," Imryll whispered, an accusation with a question somewhere in the middle. One she seemed afraid to ask or even form.

Drazhan denied her a response. He didn't want her to see how she'd unnerved him.

"If you've come here to..." She didn't complete the thought. To assault her? To rape her? The very suggestion was offensive. He'd never forced a woman's hand, and he'd never force hers.

He resisted the urge to clarify things for her. *I have come to Duncarrow to fuck you, Princess, but by the time it happens, you'll be begging me for it.*

But that began to feel unlikely with the way her eyes blazed with fear in the escalating darkness. Daring him to confirm or refute the unspoken charge.

"Are you going to say anything or just stare at me like a churlish beast?" she asked, her voice shaking. He discovered it wasn't only her arm pressed to her chest. She was holding something against it. Vellum.

"Tide is coming in." Drazhan swallowed the rock in his throat and took another step, enjoying the way his shadow fell around her—not a threat, but definitely an insinuation. *When you invite me to your bed, I'll teach you things your prince will know you didn't learn from your own imagination.* "You'll be trapped."

"*What?*" She almost squeaked the word.

"Tide's here. Leave. Or drown."

Her response was throttled into a whisper, too low to hear, but Drazhan turned away before she could repeat herself. He knelt to stabilize his hands and dropped back down through the hole, then landed on the rocky beach with a crunch.

He didn't turn back and offer her a hand. She knew her way out. But as he started back up the shore toward the rocks, he spotted others coming toward the beach.

Drazhan squinted. There were a half dozen or more guards on the way.

A soft thud sounded behind him when Imryll dropped back onto the beach.

Drazhan's mouth tightened as she stepped closer, but she held her distance. A small, strangled sound escaped her throat at the sight of the guards, and it seemed as if she might clamber back up into the cave to hide.

Perhaps the only thing restraining her was him, thinking he'd rat her out.

Would he? He wasn't sure.

"Lady Imryll!" one of the guards cried.

Imryll moved forward, cutting a wide berth around Drazhan when she passed him. She made haste toward the rocks, lifting her skirt in her near sprint.

Imryll came to a stop, and her shoulders lifted and fell with a shudder bloated with defeat. Her gaze wasn't on the guards though, but the sea.

Drazhan snorted under his breath. She might not be happy to see the guards, but she'd be less happy for them to find her little clandestine hideout.

Now there's at least one other person who knows your secret, Princess.

He watched her take a step back as the guards neared. Then another. She turned and nearly ran straight into his arms—would have if he hadn't maneuvered to the side.

"Go on!" one of the guards cried, jackknifing his arms. Drazhan got out of their way and watched the strange scene unfold: six of them handling Imryll like she were a man four times her size, while she hurled insults about their mothers. Her eyes caught Drazhan's, pleading with him to do something.

He had no intention of doing anything but watch and laugh at the soldiers getting flustered by a wily girl.

Imryll's eyes widened at him in disbelief, which made him laugh harder.

"Lady Imryll, your father has deemed you at risk of flight or harm, so you will be contained to your apartments until the ceremony."

"I will *not*," Imryll cried, wrenching her arm free, then another, only to lose the first again. "Touch me like that again, and I'll drag you to the Sky Dungeon myself!"

It was impressive to watch her maneuver in and out of their grasp, like a dance they all knew the steps to. Less inspiring was how useless the guards were. Six of them and one of her? Should have been over before it even started.

Drazhan hoped all the guards were this stupid. If so, his tenure on Duncarrow would be quicker than he thought.

"Thank you for cornering her, Syr," a guard said to Drazhan with an exasperated head shake. He nodded at the others to cart her off, still screaming threats. Sweat slid down his temples. "She's been eluding us for hours. Isle is only so big but…"

"Mm." Drazhan grunted. He held his gaze on the sea but could see them dragging a screaming Imryll back up the rocks. She hated him already, which was exactly what he'd wanted. There was no risk of a vain highborn falling in love with someone who would so easily hand her over, but he was *precisely* the sort of man a girl like her conjured in her fantasies.

"She runs off a lot," the guard said, scratching his head, lingering as though Drazhan had intimated an interest in conversation. "Always has."

Drazhan arched his brow.

"Duke and Duchess think she was planning to make a go for the mainland tonight. As if she'd get far on her own."

That so?

"This is why women need a firm hand. Won't be making a go now, will she?" He laughed to himself, glancing out at the sea before clapping Drazhan on the back. "Thanks again."

Drazhan grunted.

He waited until Imryll's screams faded into the roar of the incoming tide before making his own way back.

FIVE

FOR THE TOP PRIZE

Imryll passed most of her week of imprisonment alone. She wasn't allowed farther than the Glaisgain apartments, but she hardly left her own room, unable to summon enough deference to overcome the devastating anger gnawing at her heart.

The only thing the duke and duchess had agreed on in years was that their only daughter must be protected from herself at any cost, until she was the problem of another man.

Hours separated Imryll from that fate. She'd never warmed to the idea of marrying someone. Love intrigued her, but it had nothing to do with marriage.

But what lay ahead for her was less than marriage. In a marriage, one could expect a sense of cohesion and trust…a veneer of equality and respect for the wife a man had chosen to build a life with. They could ply her with pretty titles and more sumptuous gowns, but all she'd ever be was a vessel to a prince who had more need of a womb than a wife.

From her window, Imryll could see the lyceum gleaming in the distance. Construction had only finished a couple of years ago, and it had been used precisely once, for the unveiling. Since then, the arena—fit for a much more prolific populous than Duncarrow—had sat unused. *Planning for the future,* her father had said, though they both knew there was no future where King Carrow would fill the stands with anything more than idealism.

The outer walls obscured any view of inside the arena. Were the knights eking out a final few hours of preparation? Was the honorable bowman, Syr Blackfen, practicing to win his place at the top, saving her from that ill-born, Syr Wynter?

She prayed to the gods that was so. Why she prayed at all was a mystery. They'd done nothing to intervene in Imryll's fate. They could not possibly be on her side.

You can't blame them for your hesitation. Fear kept you from going straight to the ship. You have no one but yourself to fault for failing.

At any moment, the knock would come. The seamstress would sew her into a dress, perfectly to Imryll's proportions. Imryll would spend these excruciating minutes trying not to cry, the only outlet she had left for her anger. The seams would be left loose so Torian could rip the gown off her later.

No one on Duncarrow would risk their lives to help the First Chosen of a Rhiagain prince escape, but they'd risk their lives to see that she didn't.

"You're overthinking right now." Tasmin rocked in the corner of the bedchamber, working on her latest needlepoint. Tasmin hated needlepoint, same as she hated any of their "ladies' instructions," but she'd brought it to calm herself on behalf of Imryll. "It's all very simple. You'll allow him to choose you before all of Duncarrow. Bed him—well, perhaps, if he's up to the task, and I wonder about that…"

Imryll turned her head back to the window with a hidden snicker.

"And then…" Tasmin went on, set to the whistle of her fast threading. "When the king sends his son on a diplomatic mission—and he will, so the prince can prove his worth…You use that. You do whatever you need to do to convince some powerful man to whisk you away. Pray this happens before the prince impregnates you." She set her work aside. "I see you smirking in the reflection, Imryll. You have more power than you'll ever know. But it does you no good if you won't use it."

Imryll chewed the inside of her mouth, enjoying the tinge of copper. She rolled the back of her head on the cool windowpane and looked sideways at her friend. "If the implication is that I become a plaything of some realm highborn, I wouldn't consider that an improvement to my circumstances."

"True," Tasmin agreed. She tucked her legs underneath her and rocked in the chair. "And by staying, you're spending your evenings in the bed of a man you love."

Imryll snorted. "I love Torian the way I love you."

"Marry me then." Dark mischief twinkled in Tasmin's eyes.

Imryll rolled her gaze toward the ceiling. "You miss my point."

"No, I've just heard you saying the same things for five days, and I'm not sure what the repetition offers toward solving the problem. I can't tell if you're trying to be useless or if your pragmatism has simply failed you."

Imryll was grateful to her mother for allowing Tasmin to visit, but over the passing days, her friend's wry humor had made the room seem smaller, even more cramped. "What would be your suggestion then, Tas?" The cold from the window nipped at her cheeks, sending a shiver through her. "One that doesn't send me from one powerful man's bed to another's."

"I'm only suggesting that while escaping a powerful man's bed on an island is nearly impossible, it is, in a practical sense, simpler on the mainland."

"So you *are* suggesting I become another man's whore to steal my freedom."

"Careful. That's their word for us, Imryll. Let's not give them more power over us than they've already taken."

Imryll had several retorts ready, but Tasmin was right. It was a terrible thing to say, and she'd only said it because they were alone.

She turned her eyes back toward the lyceum, wondering again what the knights were doing. Perhaps fighting...over which of them would take the top spot, winning her as the prize. She didn't care who won, as long as it wasn't the one who had laughed when she was dragged away from the beach. "Tas, do you...You don't suppose there's any way to alter the outcome of the tournament?"

Tasmin's rocking stopped. Her boots landed square on the floor. "What's churning through your devious little mind now, Imryll?"

"Nothing." She regretted saying anything.

"No, it's *not* nothing." Tasmin pushed to her feet. The creak of the rocker mixed with her footfalls as she approached. "I forgot you met the knights the other day. Have a fancy for one in particular?"

"*No.*" Imryll practically hissed. Tasmin's eyes widened in skepticism. "No," she said, lower this time. "There's one who seems to take pleasure in my unhappiness, and I worry about what happens if he wins."

Tasmin settled in on the opposite side of the window with a knowing grin. Her dark hair framed her face in luscious waves. She was easily the most beautiful of the eligible ladies at court. She'd be married already if the dukes weren't so threatened by her clever mother, Duchess Teleria, the only woman on King Carrow's minor council. "Why would a man who doesn't even know you, who has competed for a *full year* to guard you, take pleasure in your unhappiness?"

"Don't do that."

"What?"

"Sound reasonable when there's no reason to be found in this." Imryll scoffed and turned toward the window. Her breath fogged the pane. "I sensed a darkness in him, Tas. Don't laugh at me, please. I mean it. I read it so clearly; he would revel in my pain. Grind me under his boots."

"I won't laugh," Tasmin said, "because you asked so nicely. But I desperately want to. Listen to yourself."

"Forget I—"

They both turned toward the bedroom door swinging wide. The duchess and the seamstress stood side by side with matching harrowed expressions.

Like we're going to a funeral, not a Choosing.

"Darling," Melantha said, her features tightening as she held a smile that didn't make it into her eyes. "It's time."

"For the third and final time, Syr Garrick, we will not be attending the Choosing. We were not invited. We will remain here and wait for our part." Commander Ofal looked ready to send Kav back to the mainland and request a replacement. So did the others, even Waters, who seemed to be realizing he'd aligned himself to the wrong man.

Drazhan would rather see competent soldiers like Blackfen or Owen stay than men he could best in his sleep.

Blackfen was a fighter, but he'd spent his entire life becoming one with his longbow. There'd be no archery in the tournament—swords, maces, and daggers only. It made Owen and his beast-like combat the favorite to win.

Waters and Kav knew it too. Their eyes followed him, clearly dreaming up ways to sabotage the warrior.

Drazhan would win on his own merit. He'd come this far on skill alone.

If he couldn't win fairly, he didn't deserve his vengeance.

He checked the sky. In an hour, the arena would be scattered with Rhiagains—not remotely full, but filled with everyone who mattered to the king.

"Are you truly so curious? Fine," Ofal was saying, though his eyes betrayed his excitement in sharing something he knew but others didn't. "I was there when the commanders were given the order of events. First thing you need to know is the Cycle of the Chosens is not like any 'wedding' we'd recognize."

Ofal's use of the word *we* had Drazhan casually wondering where the man was from. With a careful ear, Drazhan heard a Westerland accent. South, perhaps Greystone Abbey or Greencastle.

"It's not actually a wedding at all, for Rhiagains don't take spouses like others do. They acquire women suitable to carry on their line. It's more like…"

"An auction?" Waters quipped.

"You'll keep that opinion to yourself if you're wise," Ofal countered with a stern frown.

"Never been to a wedding." Kav spat. "Never will."

"Not even his own," Blackfen muttered.

"Aye, and weren't you the one just asking a hundred questions about this one, Kav?" Owen retorted. His mouth hung open with a head shake at Blackfen that said, *This guy.*

"Know thy enemy," Kav said, tapping a meaty finger against his temple.

"Who, exactly, is your enemy here?" Blackfen asked, moving his head back and forth in incredulous strokes. "If your enemies are on this isle, son, I reckon you've come to the wrong place."

Drazhan wouldn't have figured Blackfen for a crown sycophant. The Westerlands had lost as many men as the Northerlands in the Uprising.

"Not what I meant," Kav muttered with a look at Waters, who seemed all too eager to distance himself from Kav's nonsense. "'Tis an expression."

"Feel free to enlighten us," Blackfen said, folding his hands over his chest. "I'm listening."

"Men," Ofal barked. His earlier excitement had dulled during Kav's outburst of stupidity. "As I was saying, it's not a wedding at all. It's a *Choosing*. The prince will stand on the dais and his chosens will be paraded by him, prizes to be picked. Of course, that's all been decided and his selection is purely symbolic. When it's done, he'll escort his First Chosen, Lady…ahem, Princess Imryll and lead the rest of the court to the lyceum to begin the entertainment portion of the festivities."

"Entertainment." Waters snorted. He squinted, looking around the empty seats as though imagining them full of men, cheering him on. "Won't be so entertaining for the rest of you when you lose. Badly."

Only Kav rose to the bait, huffing like a bull about to charge. The others knew better.

"You'd do well to remember none of you will be going home today. *This* is your home now," Ofal said. "No matter who wins, you have all bested four hundred and ninety-five of your peers to be here. You've already won."

"Some prize, eh? Guarding a bunch of lasses on an isle no one leaves or arrives to," Kav quipped with a meaty hand wave around. "Unless they ken it's the other lasses we're protecting them from? I'd not turn away a good catfight, aye?"

"You're not just guarding their lives, Syr Garrick," Ofal said darkly, no longer wearing his good humor. "You're guarding their *chastity*."

"Aye?" Kav cackled, oblivious to the scowl growing on Ofal's face. "Aren't they getting chosen today so they can spit out bairns for the crown?"

"Guarding their chastity from men like *you*, ye dullard," Owen gruffed with a stern, impatient glare he shared with Blackfen.

"Syr Strong speaks true. Mostly," Ofal said with a long-suffering sigh they'd already become familiar with. "The prince can only offer his attention to one princess at a time. There can be no question…no *whisper* of a question that all heirs born to the five princesses are Rhiagains and thereby worthy of their inheritance. The princesses are welcome to have their amusements on the side. But they must reserve those activities for when they are with child or are beyond their childbearing years."

"Aye, they can fuck whoever they want when there's a loaf of bread in the oven," Kav said back, scratching his head. "Does that mean…*We* can…"

"Do you prefer your head attached to your shoulders?" Waters shook his head with a heavy eyeroll.

Blackfen shifted to Drazhan's side. "Should we take them both out early? Make a true competition out of the rest of it?"

Drazhan grunted. His lips twitched in a grin that Blackfen took as confirmation.

Blackfen clapped him on the back with a wink. "Right then. The three of us, fighting for the top prize. I can live with that."

I'm glad you can live with it.
It will make it easier to beat you.

SIX
SYMBOL OF HOPE, SYMBOL OF BONDAGE

Raised flesh dotted Imryll's arms. She was surrounded by those sworn to keep her in line. Her mother and father. Duke Fenring. Duke Drummond and his wife, Duchess Alyse. Duke Rahn and Duchess Teleria were there too, but their presence was a solemn comfort. They were the only two adults in her life who had given any thought to her as an individual and not a token for bargaining.

Mortain was conspicuously absent. Imryll overheard Drushan telling Melantha the sorcerer was attending to the three chosens he'd brought from the realm proper.

Imryll had forgotten all about the strange conversation with Adamina until then. *Realmfolk.* Her chest burned with a fear that had no name. It spread outward, across the soft flesh of her exposed arms, and settled into her hands, which she'd been commanded to clasp in front of herself, lest she turn them on one of the highborn sentries to make a run for it.

Had Mortain really stolen young women from their homes, to give them to Torian?

And did it make her angry, for them, or jealous, for herself?

She tried adjusting her hands to lift the long train on the violet gown she kept tripping over. Violet was the color of the Rhiagains, one of the few traditions they'd carried from the Sceptre of Ilynglass. Her bodice plunged into a V between her breasts, and it reached nearly to the center of her belly. Only a thin sheen of lace covered the exposed flesh, an effect her mother said was supposed to *show all others what a prize the prince has won.*

A prize.

Less than a wife.

The showpiece of the Rhiagains. The broodmare who would save the line and secure the monarchy.

She didn't know where the other chosens were. Whether they'd all be at the Choosing ceremony with her or if they'd be bound to Torian separately. Imryll had no idea what to expect at all. No one had bothered to explain anything to her.

The halls were decorated with pink and purple blossoms strung along the trim. She wondered where they'd come from. Everything with color and vibrance had to be imported. There were no flowers on Duncarrow. No signs of life.

The walk—*death march* were the words playing in Imryll's head—seemed to stretch on forever, her steps echoing like a chorus singing her sentence, until Imryll and her escorts finally entered the banquet hall.

Like the lyceum, it was a room built for many and rarely used. Great hulking candelabras made of stone and wood eclipsed the senses, lighting up the room like the midday sun. The tables had been removed, replaced by benches, upon which the meager, noble population of Duncarrow sat waiting.

To the left, upon the raised dais, she spotted the king and queen with Torian, all three bedecked in purple-and-silver raiments. Farther down stood Mortain wearing his usual black cloak, and next to him stood Adamina and several young women Imryll knew had to be the ones stolen from the kingdom.

Everyone on the benches rose to their feet in a commotion of clicking heels and rustling fabrics when Imryll entered with her gaolers. She picked up some groans and grimaces and guessed they'd been through the dance of sitting and standing and sitting and standing a dozen times already.

It was Torian's eyes Imryll searched for in the madness of light and whispers. He looked her way, waiting for her. A generous smile spread across his soft face, big enough to catch the attention of Queen Godivah, who gave him a subtle swat from behind. His smile dimmed but didn't vanish. His deep-blue eyes promised safety he had no power to deliver.

You love him. Perhaps not the way you should, but he will not be careless with you. He's your friend, and you know his heart.

She did know his heart, but what of her own, which was breaking, *bursting* with every step that brought her nearer to a future she'd been too weak to avoid?

Melantha whispered something Imryll couldn't hear, but the meaning was clear enough: smile or pay for it later.

Her father had nods for everyone else as they entered, but no warmth or kind words for the daughter he'd sold to the crown in return for favor he'd already begun to enjoy.

Drawing closer, Imryll could see the unbridled excitement brimming on Adamina's face. The purple she wore was a more understated shade, same as the other young women, whose faces were still hidden. The duke of Privaine sat in the very front, beaming with pride, his eyes glossy. What must *that* be like, Imryll thought, to have a father who loved his daughter enough to be reduced to tears in front of the other noble-borns?

Duke Rahn gave her a solemn, supportive nod, filled with more words than he'd ever be allowed to say. He wasn't even a decade older than Imryll, but he'd been her teacher and, at times, a trusted confidant. His dangerous encouragement of her writing was a secret she'd take to her grave.

At his side, Duchess Teleria lifted her shoulders in a heavy sigh. Tasmin forced a smile.

King Carrow stepped forward and approached the narrow steps leading up to the dais. He held out his hand, which Imryll kissed as expected, and then offered it to her. She took it, feeling the heated, demanding eyes of her mother and father on her back, silent threats to represent them well *or else,* as she ascended the steps at the king's side.

Imryll kept her eyes on Torian as she walked across the dais. She refused to look into the small crowd, at Ada, or especially at the girls standing off to the right. Nothing was real anymore except the friendship she shared with the boy who had become a man overnight, as quickly as she'd become a woman.

I do love him, she thought again with a skip in her pulse, pressing the words in a line across her thoughts with the insistence they deserved.

And just as immediately came *but it's not enough.*

"You look divine, Lady Imryll," the king said, despite having not looked directly at her once. His bloated hand still held fast to hers, one of his garish rings pinching her flesh. He wheezed with every step. There was a reason Carrow wasn't taking more chosens for himself. He'd left his best days in the sea, with the rest of his brood.

"Thank you, Your Grace." Imryll swallowed the words she wanted to say.

"Duke Drushan has explained you will stand at Torian's left?"

"Yes," Imryll lied with a pained swallow, though she wasn't sure who she was protecting.

"And that you are not to interact with the other chosens?"

"What?" Imryll asked before she could stop herself. *Not interact with the others?* "Of course, Your Grace."

"Ever," he said with emphasis. "Queen Godivah will mentor you in the ways of a Rhiagain princess. She will explain why the First Chosen must never intermingle with the others beyond what is expected in front of the court. They are servants. Vessels. *You* will be queen."

Vessels? And what does that make me?

Breathless, all Imryll could do was nod. She held her gaze on Torian, whose light frown mirrored the change in her expression.

"There will be much for you to learn. None of it inconsequential."

"Of course, Your Grace."

"The queen will guide you from here. Your mother's instruction has ended."

Imryll didn't know how to feel about that. Melantha wasn't the warmest mother, but underneath all the layers of service and spectacle was genuine concern for Imryll's security. Godivah was the ice queen, the Second Chosen who had become first only after her predecessor had died in the Passage. She'd clawed her way to favor, ensuring Carrow never took another chosen, despite the need for more sons.

Imryll was so caught in her thoughts, she hardly noticed the king releasing her. Her hand dropped from the change in weight and she looked to the side, in a stupor of light and dizzying heat, to see Torian watching her. His smile was quick, tight, but his eyes said what his expression could not.

Until that moment, Imryll hadn't realized what a difficult day this would be for him as well. The stoic strength he wore was for her, but he'd need some for himself.

Love you, he mouthed. Her nod in return was less than he deserved.

Another failure.

Another ache across her chest she couldn't soothe.

Breathe in.

Breathe out.

Mortain was speaking. She tried to make herself listen, but the sound of his sonorous voice droned into the other sounds, mixing with the throb of her out-of-step heartbeat.

Breathe in.

"A representation of all that is great about this realm." He was saying something about the young women he'd brought back to Duncarrow. She needed to focus and listen. The king might not want her interacting with them, but the First Chosen had a responsibility to make the others feel welcome, to see to their needs, and…

No. No, you are not giving in. You are not pretending this is anything but the worst possible outcome.

Torian's peripheral stare filled Imryll with shame. It coursed up from behind her ribs, saturating her cheeks. It wasn't his fault she felt this way. He knew she had a restless heart but he had a stalwart one, and he always, *always* put others first.

Breathe out.

For him. For Torian.

Breathe in.

Shaking, she turned her eyes on the gathered. Duke Rahn. Duchess Teleria. Tasmin. Octavyen, Aloysha, and their daughters. Her focus faded to a fog until everyone blurred with the harsh light of the sea of candles.

"Miss Senna Rosewood of Greenfen."

A young woman stepped forward, but Imryll couldn't look at her without stepping forward herself. Low murmurs followed the name, but Mortain didn't wait for them to subside.

"Miss Theodora Bristol of Valleybrooke."

Another quick slide forward by the girl and the shortest of pauses from Mortain, as though he was in a great rush to finish.

"Louissa Rutland of Whitecliffe."

This one came closer to the edge, and Imryll caught a flash of ebony hair before she whipped back into place.

"And our very own Lady Adamina of Privaine. Your reserve chosens. The assurance of our glorious future here in Duncarrow and the White Kingdom. The Rhiagains will rise once again, even better than before."

Polite applause rippled through the celebrants. There were only three Rhiagains by blood left, and one of them was a bastard, recognized but not elevated. They were outnumbered, and if enough of the Noble Houses banded together, they could overtake the Rhiagains with little effort.

No, that should *be true but it's not. The sorcerers have chosen the Rhiagains, and so it must be them.*

Mortain's icy hand lifted hers, and she jumped. She hadn't seen him approach. He flashed a glacial grin at her before turning it back on the gathered. "And the greatest hope for our future, the most exquisite of them all, Lady Imryll of Glaisgain. May her days be long and her womb light aplenty."

Imryll's stomach clenched at the dread his words produced. She was no less a concubine than the other girls, just the one with the most pressure to perform.

Torian whispered something, some soft comfort when she returned to his side, but it was lost in the confusion of thoughts swarming her mind.

"Our Grace, Prince Torian of Rhiagain, will select each of his chosens in the order they will serve him. He will make his selections in silence, offering them each a circlet of silver that they will henceforth wear around their arm as a sign of their sacred place in the Rhiagain dynasty. Their crown."

Torian stepped away with a deep sigh and followed Mortain down the row. Imryll felt the air leave with him. Suddenly, she wanted him back—to take his hand in hers and pull him close so they could be strong together.

You're being so unfair. Confusing him. You always have.

Dots circled her vision. Another waking dream threatened to take hold of her, but she fought it. *No, no you don't, not now!* She blinked to clear it, inhaling a handful of failed breaths, none giving her the relief she was after. She felt Torian again grow near, heard the rustling of activity to her right. Then he was with her once more, holding out a silver band, each end formed into tight coils that reminded her of what Duke Rahn had told her about snakes hiding in the grass.

A crown had never looked or felt more dangerous.

Imryll looked up and into Torian's glossy eyes. He bit his bottom lip with a groan swollen with emotion. She nodded as the first of her tears fell…as his eyes followed them as though he would catch them if he could. His gaze fell on her arm, and she gasped in understanding.

A symbol of hope.

A symbol of bondage.

She held an unsteady arm toward him. With his free hand, he cupped her under the elbow to still her, offering a tight smile as he worked the cold circlet up her bare arm. It brushed her flesh like a cruel whisper, passing higher until it stopped on the natural curve of her bicep.

She was now his.

Now *theirs.*

Imryll inhaled her sob and trapped it in her throat and chest as Mortain announced that all should proceed to the lyceum for the next event in the Cycle of the Chosens: The Tournament of the Queens' Guard. None of the words made sense. She was learning alongside everyone watching her life change.

Torian broke tradition and slipped his hand through hers. She looked up, catching his eyes, and a sense of peace came over her.

No matter what else happened, he would never intentionally hurt her.

"How lovely," Godivah muttered as she linked arms with the king to lead the way.

Torian was helpless.

He'd never been so damn helpless.

He'd just been bound to the only girl he'd ever loved, but in place of joy was hollow regret. Her grief echoed onto him, which he wore like a mantle of shame, just as he'd absorbed her rolling fear and angst throughout the brief but intense ceremony.

And just like that, he had five chosens?

Three of them had been *stolen* from the kingdom, if Clarisan was to be believed, and he had no reason to doubt her, especially after the terrified looks on all three of their faces. She enjoyed turning her words into games, but she never lied to him.

He couldn't recall the poor girls' names. There was a Louissa. He remembered hers. The others...

Imryll fidgeted to his left, watching the citizens of Duncarrow slowly stream into the lyceum.

Clarisan leaned in from his right. "Her disquiet is far from subtle. Calm her, or Father will."

Torian grimaced and clasped a hand over Imryll's. He felt her abrupt shift of energy as he stilled her nervous trembles. Her head twitched as though she might say something, but all she offered was a clipped smile in recognition of his effort. He felt a change pass over her as she moved her torment inward.

The queen whispered to the king in the row in front of them. Carrow remained as still as stone, forcing Godivah to do all the leaning. His neckless head bobbed into a nod occasionally through the one-sided conversation.

In the row behind Torian, his other four chosens sat in quiet patience. Was he supposed to address them? No one had bothered to explain the protocol for a prince with five mistresses.

Though he'd fantasized about making love to Imryll of Glaisgain many times, now that mere hours separated him from that experience, he could no longer conjure the same excitement for the task.

Torian spread his gaze over the thin crowd. They could have all fit into one octant, but instead they scattered like bugs, making the lyceum look even bigger than it had before they'd all arrived.

Imryll craned to see down into the arena. Her foot tapped in quick beats. She flashed Torian an apologetic look and stopped.

I don't want your apology, Imryll. I just want you. I want us back.

Gasps echoed across the lyceum, and a hush followed. All around the octant, citizens were rising to their feet. Torian had started to do the same when Imryll clapped a hand atop his thigh with a small head shake.

Ah. They were rising for the Rhiagains.

Imryll's arms were crossed, one hand fingering the silver circlet cutting into her upper arm. She chewed her bottom lip so

73

hard, a band of blood appeared, but she seemed unaware as she strained to see what everyone was gasping and aahing about.

Then he saw them. Five knights, all donning different colors and sigils, marched into the center of the arena. They wore leather and cloth, with a shirt of mail protecting their center, but there was no plate to be seen. No shields.

"How…" Torian whispered to Clarisan. "They're all meant to survive this tournament?"

"These are the five who rose to the very top of their training. They'll survive."

Duke Fenring of Privaine started to announce the events, but he was on the other side of the lyceum, and his voice was lost in the distance.

"I can't hear what's being said."

"Duke Rahn explained it to me earlier. There will be four events," Clarisan said, her eyes pointed toward the arena. "As the knights are eliminated, they will be paired with one of your chosens. The winner gets Imryll."

Torian scrunched his face. "Gets her? That sounds crude."

"No one else in Duncarrow will spend more time with her than the knight who wins this tournament. He will be at her side at all hours and will even sleep in her bedchamber. Her safety will be secondary to his primary charge, which will be to ensure she opens her legs for no one but you until your seed has done its job. So what word would you like me to use?"

Torian's heart sank toward the bench. *Will even sleep in her bedchamber.* He hadn't considered that the guards would be with his chosens at all times, because Janus lived in the background of his life, enough that Torian sometimes forgot he even had a guard.

"Is that really necessary?" he asked, though he knew the decision had been made long before today.

"It's to ensure," Clarisan said, "there's no question of the legitimacy of the children the women bear you."

Torian swallowed.

"I should think, despite everything, this would give you some comfort. To know the children bearing your name also bear your blood. That is the point of all this, no? To fortify the Rhiagain bloodline?"

"Imryll wouldn't…" Torian's words disappeared when the knights came into view. Their faces were obscured by the gleam of the sun, but they carried strength in their shoulders, and a confidence that was entirely foreign to him.

"Of course she wouldn't, Your Grace," Adamina chirped from behind, reminding him she was there—and listening. "Duke Drushan will have made certain of her obedience."

Torian turned to admonish Adamina for the dig, but Imryll was too agitated to notice, and he couldn't find the right words anyway.

"They all think they'll win," Clarisan mused aloud with a laugh.

"Do we…That is, is there one favored to win?" Torian asked.

"As long as it isn't *that* one," Imryll muttered, and both Torian and Clarisan snapped their gazes her way.

"What? Which one?" Torian replied.

"The one standing off on his own."

"The dangerously handsome one?" Clarisan quipped with a quirk of her mouth.

Imryll glared at the lone knight. "I've met him. He's a rude creature, and I won't let him anywhere near me."

"How?" Torian turned toward her. "How have you met him?"

"By chance, and hopefully never again," she answered and then set her jaw in a stubborn line that meant she would say no more.

Clarisan started to question Imryll, wariness crunched between her knitted brows, but the first melee was already underway.

Torian volleyed his attention between Imryll's strange confession and the fight that held everyone else's rapt gazes. He squinted against the midday sun but could see very little. The clang of swords meeting in battle set his heart on edge, but all he could think about was that something had happened to Imryll that she hadn't shared with him.

Clarisan cheered and whistled in time with the other celebrants. Torian followed the excitement and saw the first knight had been eliminated. He strained to hear the name and barely caught it. *Syr Tarsten Waters of the Bythesea, Easterlands, is declared the guard of our Fifth Chosen, Princess Louissa.* He angled back and forth to see the face behind the moniker and was disappointed to see it was not the warrior who had upset Imryll.

That knight was glaring their direction.

Imryll's nervous tapping started again. She raked her teeth across her bottom lip in hard, grating passes, scraping the rouge off. A low moan escaped her mouth.

Torian didn't stop her this time. No one would hear her anyway above the screams of the chosens behind them, and the clashing of steel.

Minutes passed in suspension. Another knight was eliminated. *Syr Kav Garrick of Iron Hill, Southerlands, is declared the guard of our Fourth Chosen, Princess Theodora.*

Imryll's tension mounted in time with the rabid cheering.

"One more elimination and then it will be time for—" Clarisan winced. Her eyes flared wide with some new horror, and this time he followed her to see…No, he could *not* be seeing that.

"He's not a man at all," Clarisan said, breathless, as together they watched Imryll's knight slash sheathed fists—*claws,* they were *claws*—in a flurry of rapid blows against the air, a hurricane of man and beast and darkness. His opponent was bigger and brawnier, wielding both a mace and a sword, but his rhythm was thrown by the incredibleness of the feral assault.

Clarisan's mouth hung wide, her decorum forgotten. Torian realized he was doing the same. His mother and father leaned together to whisper.

When the clawed knight coiled to strike, slicing his tines of metal through the air, the warrior stumbled. He wiped his brow and squared up once more, but he was visibly shaken. He said something to the other knight, but he hadn't even finished speaking before the clawed one was *climbing the air,* loading his muscled, sinewy arms like they were weapons and hurtling toward the warrior.

The warrior jumped and waved the violet flag, declaring his surrender.

Imryll whimpered. Torian was too dazed to wonder about it.

The duke of Glaisgain announced the defeat. *Syr Owen Strong of Sandycove, Southerlands, is declared the guard of our Third Chosen, Princess Senna.*

"Ooh. There goes my favorite to win. But who could stand against such a strange assault? Did you s*ee* that, Tor? Are those his actual hands? Every day I wonder just how much we *don't* know about this curious realm." Clarisan waved her own violet scarf in the air as the one named Owen Strong was escorted away.

Torian couldn't respond in words.

"The last two will vie for first and second place."

"One last fight," he muttered, relieved to be nearing the end and unnerved at how events had led them closer to that soulless beast winning the right to be Imryll's forever shadow.

"The fighting is done, if one could even call it that. Hardly half an hour of men dancing around one another, pretending there was any danger at all. What kind of fight prohibits men from landing blows?" Clarisan shook her head with a scoff like she'd been denied something. "No, it will be a demonstration of honor that decides matters."

Torian tensed. "A demonstration of honor?"

Before Clarisan could answer, Torian's mother stood and held her hand out toward Imryll. Imryll's open-mouthed stare lasted long enough for Godivah's expression to darken.

"What's this?" Imryll asked.

"You are required for this next part," Godivah explained with a sour smile.

"Why?" Imryll looked too frazzled for etiquette.

Godivah pinched her face in disgust at Imryll's artless unraveling. "The two knights remaining must contend for the right to be your personal guard. Come." She waved a hand. "Others are watching, Princess."

"What do I…" Imryll glanced at Torian for help, but he could only shake his head in helplessness.

Godivah groaned with a furtive glance to her left and right, to those watching and waiting for Imryll to stand. "Each knight will make his attempt to woo you. A display of chivalry," Godivah said, her jaw tight. "When they have completed their display, they will each be honored with a moment alone with you, where they will use their charm and wits to try to sway you to choose them."

Imryll sagged as she exhaled against a pillar. "I get to choose the one I want?"

"The *crowd* picks your knight. Your guard," Godivah said, her smile icy and tight. "Their selection will be based on his show of chivalry and your reaction to whatever is said in your private moment alone."

"I don't understand." Imryll looked to Torian, to Clarisan. "Why am I needed at all if the choice isn't even mine?"

Adamina made a snide comment to one of the other chosens, too low for Torian to hear.

Godivah snapped her fingers and waved her hand at Imryll, a warning. "Everyone is waiting on *you*."

"It's just for show," Clarisan said to assure her.

Imryll took Godivah's hand and tentatively stepped around the bench and down the steps that led into the arena.

When she was gone, Clarisan leaned in. "So. Are you going to tell me what the story is with the sexy one and Imryll?"

Torian shrugged and shook his head all at once. He watched Imryll descend into the arena like a lamb entering a den of tigers.

"Have you been watching him, Tor?"

"I can hardly see over…" Torian nodded at his father's swollen form.

"So you have *not* seen him eye-fucking your crush?"

"*What?*" Torian paled, torn between his sister's crude suggestion and Imryll. "I don't even know what that means."

"Yes, you do." Clarisan settled back against the wall and folded her arms. "And if I noticed it, you can be sure Father has."

SEVEN

IT WILL BE MY FACE YOU SEE

Imryll had never wanted to disappear so badly. Standing face-to-face with the dark knight left her feeling like she'd climb out of her own skin to be away from Syr Wynter.

Worse, he *knew* it. Victory flickered in his hazel eyes and on the corners of his mouth, curved into a smirk. She could neither look at him nor away. All of her discomfort and fear played out across his expression in reverse.

Blackfen can still win. The crowd can't possibly want this terrible man guarding their queen.

Godivah's expectations hung over the huddled group awaiting order. Wind whipped across the valley of the barren arena. The expectant eyes and ears of Duncarrow left Imryll even lighter on her feet. She hadn't realized she'd swayed until Blackfen righted her with a polite nod.

Her father emerged from a glare of sunlight to join them. She realized he was there to guide the men, just as the queen was there to guide her.

Mortain was conspicuously absent. She hadn't seen him at all since the Choosing.

Duke Drushan waved his arms to bring everyone closer. Imryll stayed beside the queen, which said something about her dislike for the knight—even now, staring at her with coarse knowing, as if he knew what she looked like without her dress—as she was terrified of Torian's mother.

"Syr Wynter. Syr Blackfen," Duke Drushan said. His voice was loud enough only for their group. "You have both trained well. Fought well. But you will set aside your skill in the arena to prove your worth to Princess Imryll, First Chosen of Prince Torian of Rhiagain, your future queen and mother of our one-day king."

Imryll lightly snickered at the mild discomfort this produced in Wynter. *Can't wield your strange claws here, can you?*

Blackfen, mercifully, had a more prepared air about him.

Wynter's gaze whipped up to hers in a violent, demanding pass that had her hand flying to her throat. She tried to lower her eyes, but he held them in an unsaid command she didn't know how to disobey.

Did neither the queen nor the duke see how this vile man treated her? In front of all of Duncarrow no less?

There's no way he can win.

"First," Duke Drushan said, "you will each be granted the opportunity to make your declaration, to all of Duncarrow, why *you* are the most worthy to serve as Princess Imryll's Queens' Guard. You will be succinct, selecting your words carefully and with the understanding they cannot be changed. There are no second chances." He looked at each of the knights to obtain their understanding. "When that is done, you will each have a moment alone with the princess to privately sway her to your cause. You will go to the center of the arena for this, so that all watching can gauge her reaction. The citizens of Duncarrow will vote with their applause for the knight whose chivalry is best suited to guard our queen and protect the future of crown and kingdom."

Imryll gripped the wooden railing like it were the only thing holding her upright. Her toes curled in her boots; sweat dripped between her breasts and under the plunging lace, something she was certain everyone watching could see. Wynter's eyes fell precisely to that spot, and a short, forceful huff escaped his mouth.

"The princess and I will wait here while you make your declarations to Duncarrow," the queen said when the knights didn't move. She ticked her head into a dismissive nod and off they went, the duke knitting his brows before following them.

"In the end, it won't matter what you think," Godivah said. She tapped her bony fingers on the railing with a soft chuckle. "The people will pick the one they like best. Simple as that."

"Is that how your guard was chosen, Your Grace?" Imryll asked. She didn't care about the answer. It kept her talking, and talking kept her breathing, and breathing kept her from making a scene she'd never recover from.

"You mean Queen Yvaine's guard?" Godivah answered, her voice thick with reprimand. Imryll winced at her foolish error. Of course Godivah had never done this. She'd been Second Chosen at her own ceremony.

"My apologies, Your Grace. I wasn't thinking."

"No, Imryll, your problem is that you think too much." Her chin chucked upward as the duke and knights fell into place. "My original guard died in the Passage. I'm less fond of his replacement." She tapped her hand. "Now hush. Listen."

Syr Blackfen stepped ahead of the other two men. He wore his longbow, which he'd not had on him earlier. He held it aloft, and it stretched to the left and right over the top of him like wings of a hawk, his fists wrapped over the perfect curves. "The Blackfens have served this realm for hundreds of years. Service runs in our blood. It powers our souls and ignites our hearts. The coming of the Rhiagains was a gift to our lands, turning a realm into a kingdom and giving my family an even more important cause to rise for. I was born to serve our queen, and I bring the

83

spirit of my ancestors with me into this charge. I lay all of this before our future queen, alongside my life."

"Ooh. He's *good*," Godivah cooed with a seductive purr. Applause and cheers echoed around them, though they didn't count, not yet.

It was a good speech, though she wondered how many had actually heard it with how scattered the crowd was.

Imryll hoped it was enough.

She swallowed the lump in her throat and waited for Syr Wynter to take his turn.

He strolled into place as though he'd already won. His sword hung secure in its belt, his hands spread out to the sides like he was ready to call for applause. "Syr Blackfen speaks of honor. That he has, and with more to spare."

Blackfen nodded in respect.

A shiver tore through Imryll at the sound of the dark knight's voice, husky, throaty...like a velvety smooth blanket that, if flipped to the other side, would leave a thicket of scratches on her flesh.

"Do I have his honor?" Wynter shook his head and tightened the edges of his jaw as if to say *oops*. "No."

The crowd tittered, laughter spreading in scattershot beats.

Imryll tilted her head with bemused relief. Her tension eased. He was sabotaging himself, but why?

"Do I *require* his honor to be the best choice to guard our future queen and her heirs?" Wynter asked, spinning to collect the gazes of everyone in the octant. "If our queen's life were in peril, would you want a man with honor at her side, ready to stand for what was right, or a mercenary who has no place for goodness or rightness and would cut down any man, woman, or child who dared breathe even a *word* of threat in her presence?" Metal rang as he brandished his sword.

She didn't see the clawed weapons he'd shocked the crowd with earlier. She began to wonder if she'd imagined them.

"Who would not stop to consider whether he should run a man through before doing it? Who would collect heads and hearts to present in veneration at the feet of his beloved queen? A queen who would never have cause to question whether her guard had the mettle to stand for her, for she knows that a man without honor will never need to stand in defense of choices he made to keep safe the only one who matters."

Roaring applause followed his bloody confession. A name sounded from somewhere in the distance, and then rippled through the crowd.

Stormclaw.

Blackfen lowered his head to the ground and shook it, laughing.

Imryll passed her agitated glare around at everyone, not knowing where to land it. Her step faltered when her pulse skyrocketed so high, it made her audibly gasp, drawing Godivah's penetrating disapproval.

"Duncarrow, it seems we have a proper competition!" Duke Drushan yelled, receiving more joyous applause. He, too, laughed, as though what that godless heathen had said had any place on Duncarrow...any place with *her.*

"Well," Godivah said with a tight exhale. "He's even better." She looked up, catching the duke's gaze before nudging Imryll forward. "Go on then. It's your turn."

"Uh..." Imryll pitched into step, almost tumbling over the bottom step before planting her feet in the dirt. She'd walked the arena many times on her way to the cave, but all pleasing familiarity was gone. Her hand traveled to her arm, fingering the tight silver coil that felt like a collar before remembering that everyone was watching, scrutinizing everything from the way she held her head to the depth and shape of her smile.

She moved with her eyes closed, pretending to be fussed by the harsh wind so she could claim her few last moments of peace. But she was there before she knew it, and with no warning, no explanation or transition, her father nodded at Blackfen.

"Stand with Syr Blackfen, Princess. Syr Wynter and I will be just over here until it's Wynter's turn."

Imryll's cheeks had gone numb. The sensation traveled downward. She turned her back on her father and Wynter and tried to smile at Blackfen.

He fell to his knees. She shook her head, waving him up.

"You know I must, Your Grace," he whispered when he was again standing.

"I don't know what this is," Imryll said quickly, the pricks from dozens of eyes stabbing her from all sides. "But I need you to win. I *need* it to be you. It cannot be him."

"Your reaction will tell the people how you feel about both of us," Blackfen said. "I can say all the right words, Princess Imryll, but you already know I would die for the honor of serving you. I would die *for* you, and I came to Duncarrow expecting that day would eventually come to pass. I would serve you well, for the remainder of my days. There is nothing more for me to say."

Imryll clenched and unclenched a hand before shakily raising it toward his face. He winced at her bold choice to touch him, but he recovered with an easy smile that reached her cupped palm. "You're a kind man and a stalwart knight. Let them all see that I see it."

Blackfen reached for her hand on his face and turned to kiss it before giving it back to her. This caused a stir in the crowd—a good one, she prayed. "The arena has never been about honor. It's about blood and lust and vice. I am not these things, yet I hope they still choose me, because I would never look at you the way Syr Wynter has."

Tears welled in Imryll's eyes like liquid fire. "I know."

"If he does win this day—"

"No, don't say it. Don't even think it."

Blackfen tightened his mouth into a hard line of resolve. "No matter the outcome, I will always look out for my queen."

"Thank you, Syr Blackfen," Duke Drushan called. The bowman was already walking away from her, taking most of her courage with him.

"Nice speech, Wynter. More words today than I've heard from you in a year," she heard Blackfen mutter when the men passed each other in the dirt.

She was still watching Blackfen walk away when Wynter approached. The suddenness of his presence made her stutter back a step. He was far taller than she'd initially realized, and as he dishonored her precious space, he cast a shadow that stole the light from the sky. The unyielding warmth of his nearness radiated into her like a heatwave. When he stepped closer, closing the gap she'd created in her discomposure and leaving no room for decency, she believed she might actually burst into flames.

If she did, the ice in his eyes would put out the fire.

"Look at me," he commanded. No honorific. Not even her name.

Wynter pressed the underside of his hand to her chin and jerked it up. He didn't let go. Her jaw trembled under his hard touch, the pinch at her jawline reminding her who was in control of the moment.

"You cannot…You cannot speak to me this way." Her teeth clacked, and he fixed it by closing her mouth for her. His thumb traced the edge of her jaw as though tucking her words in for the night.

His leather armor creaked when he bent down toward her. His stunning eyes narrowed on his approach, following a grin she caught only the corner of before he coated her ear with his breath. "Here's how this will go, Imryll of Glaisgain. In a few moments, your people are going to declare me the winner of this tournament. And when that happens? Forget everything the queen or your mother told you about this day and all the ones that will follow."

Imryll choked on the push and pull of her breathing.

"Your life will be in my hands. I *will* keep you safe. But that is not the only thing I'll keep." His voice lowered even further, his lips brushing her earlobe. "I didn't come all this way just to guard you, Princess."

Imryll couldn't speak with how he held her. Couldn't turn her head to catch the eye of anyone who might save her from what must look to others like an unorthodox attempt at flattery. She shook her head tightly instead and squeezed her eyes closed.

"Their laws determine you now belong to them," he said. "But I make my own rules, *Imryll,* and in all other ways that matter, you now belong to *me.*"

Why is no one doing anything?

Why is no one helping?

Why can no one see what this ill-born is doing to me, in front of all of Duncarrow?

Imryll's knees went soft, but Wynter held tight to her face, nearly crushing her teeth together as she lost her footing. He lifted her with one hand, with what sounded like a *tsk.*

"The first time you come for any man, it will be for me. I'll have you on *my* face, writhing with need." Drazhan paused to let her catch up, smiling when he saw she'd returned her full, scandalized attention to him. "I'm going to mold your cunt to my cock so that it will know but one path to pleasure, and it's through me." In demonstration, he pressed his swollen length against her torso, driving a shiver through her that didn't stop when it reached her tailbone. It turned to an unwelcome ache she had no time to make sense of. "Tonight, when you go to your husband's bed for the first time and he doesn't know what to do, how to please you, you'll think of me. It will be my face you see when you fuck the prince."

Never. The word didn't make it out. She couldn't even mouth it with the way he held her face between his fingers.

"Though how will you explain to him that you've come to your marriage bed already soaking wet?"

Imryll's throat constricted. Could he see the burning flush in her cheeks? She couldn't blame the wind, not with the way he'd blocked out the rest of the world. He could spill filth from his mouth, but he'd never get the pleasure of knowing how his vile words had landed. Never know of the throb between her legs, her own body betraying her.

"And the best part, Imryll?" He flicked his tongue out against her earlobe, and she liquefied with a moan. "You look at me now with disgust. With confusion. But when I finally bury myself inside of you, freeing you? It will be because you begged for the release you know in your marrow, in your *blood*, only I can deliver you."

Wynter broke the spell and stepped back, leaving her boneless and shaking from astonishment. Her chin was branded with the impression of his fingers. She was exposed for all to see the effect of his work. She loathed him, so why, *how* had he left her wet and aching? Had he spelled her, or was she depraved in the mind, determined to punish herself?

"I'll tell them what you said," she croaked. She cleared her throat and tried again. "You'll never get away with what just happened."

Wynter's eyes glinted in amusement. "You'll tell them? Who?"

"My father, my—"

"And which word will trip you up the most, Imryll? Cock or cunt?"

Imryll panted so hard, the desperate sound echoed in her ears. She caught her father regarding her with an odd look and straightened herself with a lift of her chin and a smile that took every bit of courage still left to her.

What happened next seemed the inevitable conclusion of a day that had been designed to break her.

The crowd chose Wynter.

Unequivocally.

The foul knight who had whispered disgusting, forbidden things in her ear was going to be her shadow.

Following her every move.

Sleeping in her room.

As though reading her thoughts, Wynter again joined her at her side, placing his hand to her lower back like he were claiming his prize. Her disgusted look only made him laugh.

"Don't touch me," she hissed. The others were heading back to the keep. They milled around her as though part of another reality, another timeline.

"Remember those words when you're on your knees begging me to let you come." His tongue passed along his bottom lip, quick enough to miss if she hadn't been reading him like a book. "Shall we?"

"I'm not going *anywhere* with you."

"Duncarrow has decided I'm going everywhere with you."

Imryll shook herself loose of his touch. "You think I won't tell them what you said? That I'm ashamed to repeat words you wield as weapons? My father will be far more horrified to hear them than I am to say them."

"Hmm. Will you also tell him that his little girl is soaking wet for her guard?"

"You're a disgrace to the Queens' Guard," she spat, fumbling to gain the control he'd stolen from her, bit by bit, with every word. "A disgrace to your realm, your family."

"Yes," he agreed with a curved smile. "And yet, I'll be taking you to the prince's apartments now, just the same."

Imryll recoiled again. "We have the banquet first, you hedge-born."

"Highborn actually. House Wynter of Witchwood Cross, not that I'd expect you to know something as prosaic as the geography of the realm your son will rule."

Imryll flapped her mouth, unable to find words for the abominable creature. How in the gods had he made it past four hundred and ninety-five others, all the way to the end? To her?

"And the banquet, Princess? There's not one, but five, starting tomorrow. Five full nights of stuffing your jeweled faces with imported food. Tonight, you'll be expected to perform a more *sacred ritual.*" His last words dripped with dry amusement. "You're welcome for readying you for your prince."

Imryll scrunched her nose. "You're disgusting."

Wynter nodded with a light bow.

"I'll have you sent back. I'll find a way," Imryll said. Her cheeks darkened when he laughed at her again. He didn't fear her. He didn't respect her. He probably didn't even *want* her but rather desired control over her in order to humiliate her. She might never know why he'd loathed her from first sight, and she could live with that if she could sway the court to banish him. "Your behavior is beyond the pale, and I will not stand for it. Nor will the king when he finds out what you are."

"Until then, you have no choice but to play the part assigned to you." His hand grazed the middle of her back as he leaned in to whisper, "Princess."

EIGHT
LAVENDER AND RASPBERRY

Torian's quaking intensified with each step as they neared his new apartments. He'd only seen the freshly accoutred rooms for the first time the day before, when his father had given him the *you're no longer a boy, but a man* speech, which had only shoved his fears into the light to reveal their parts. Like rubbing salt in an infected wound.

Imryll walked at his side, her face pointed forward and unreadable in the dark of the windowless inner hall. He thought he'd seen a tear cutting down her stone face, but trying to steal a better look had drawn unwanted attention.

Her guard, Syr Wynter, matched her pace. Imryll's shoulders rolled up in stiff defiance anytime the knight drew too close. Something awful had transpired between them, and her hesitance to explain it at the tournament deepened his worry. He'd never seen Imryll react that way to anyone. Like the need to be away from the man was visceral, clawing out of her.

Torian added it to his list of concerns making him sick and rounded the last corner, where he and his new chosens would spend their private hours.

Duke Drushan pulled to a sharp stop and turned to face the small retinue made up of the duchess, the queen, and a handful of guards. "Your Grace, your new apartments have been prepared according to Rhiagain custom. Your comfort tonight is the top priority of everyone in Duncarrow." Drushan curved a wry smile at his daughter. "This is where I leave you, Your Grace, but your mother and the duchess will remain until Princess Imryll is adequately prepared for your bed."

Torian winced. Imryll intensified her effort to look at nothing but the wall in front of her, but her jaw twisted in subtle response to her father's words.

"Syr Wynter and Janus will be stationed just outside the bed-chamber, but there are five other guards at the end of your hall should you encounter any trouble this evening."

"Trouble?" Torian asked. From what, falling rocks?

"One can never be too careful with the future of the royal family," Drushan muttered, eyes on his daughter as though she alone could discern his meaning.

Torian felt the blood rush from his face. Was he implying that if Imryll didn't come to his bed willingly, they would come *restrain* her?

Did any of the men and women standing in the hall believe Torian would *ever* participate in anything so vile?

"Your Grace?" Drushan asked, eyeing him.

"Sorry?"

"I asked if there was anything else you needed before we leave you."

Torian shook his head, stuffed and heavy, as he tried to turn toward Imryll, to step inside, or to do anything that would signal the others to leave.

Drushan left, taking several of the guards with him—the ones who would linger at the end of the hall in case Torian needed their help taming Imryll.

Bile crept into the back of his throat.

"Duchess Melantha, I can take it from here," Godivah said. She flashed a smile, her eyes dark and full of menace.

"Your Grace? Am I not to stay and help my d—"

"She is a princess now. The only woman suitable to groom a princess is a queen. You are dismissed."

Duchess Melantha sent a helpless, almost sad look at Imryll, who returned nothing. Torian almost felt bad for her, if he didn't know how much she'd failed Imryll as a mother.

"Duchess Melantha, was I not clear?"

"Yes…Yes, of course, Your Grace. Imryll, will you need—"

"Whatever she will or will not need is my concern now. The longer you stand here, Duchess, flapping your mouth in surprise, the longer you prevent a Rhiagain heir from taking hold in your daughter's hopefully ample womb."

Imryll's upper lip swallowed her lower one. She turned away.

"Thank you, Your Grace. May the gods be with you tonight, daughter. Prince Torian."

The duchess lifted her skirts and fled down the hall.

Godivah turned back toward the couple. Her eyes crinkled, hollow, matching her smile. "Let us waste no more time, Princess. Come with me."

Godivah led Imryll into a room just off the bedchamber, full of mirrors and powders and racks of dresses.

No, not dresses…nightwear.

A full bath sat in the center of the room, flocked by two attendants.

"Won't be very hot after all these delays, will it?" Godivah muttered and marched toward the young women. Like many of the Duncarrow staff, they'd been brought from the mainland years ago, quarantined for so long, some of them went mad. "Strip her, bathe her, rub her clean flesh down with oil…the lavender, I should think. Reserve the raspberry oil for her nethers. You know the one, I mean? Not the very pungent one, but the one he can taste."

They bobbed in uneven curtsies. "Yes, Your Grace."

Imryll's knees threatened to give. There was nothing to brace herself with other than sheer will.

At least they left the vile one outside.

"Shall we leave her dress on her, Your Grace, or shall we select some nightwear for her?" one of the attendants meekly asked.

"Neither," Godivah barked. "Seduction is for the ugly. My son has been dreaming of dipping his wick in the princess since he was old enough to hold it."

"You wish her naked when we send her into the prince's bed-chamber, Your Grace?"

"Is there another way to interpret 'neither'?"

Lowered eyes. More curtsies. "No, Your Grace."

So much for ripping me out of my dress.

Godivah rolled a finger through the air, one final assessment. She spun back toward Imryll. "Can I provide you with any clarity, Imryll?"

"Your Grace?"

"Drop the scandalized look. I'm not offering an instruction. You will become skilled at the art of lovemaking over time, but tonight you need only to spread your legs and allow my son to do what the gods made him to do."

Imryll's jaw slackened.

"What I'm asking is if there's any confusion about what's expected of you tonight."

Is there any confusion about me being no more or less than an incubator to the Rhiagains?

No, none at all.

"No, Your Grace. I understand the…the expectation."

"Good." Godivah leaned in. "Don't think me too heartless, Imryll. The raspberry isn't for him…It's for you."

Imryll's throat locked up. She didn't know how to respond to that, or if she should.

"A woman pleasing a man? Takes so little. They'll rise to any occasion offered. Fill any hole put in front of them. But when a woman knows pleasure, her whole world opens up. And when your world opens, your womb lights. So *let him taste you*, and discover how you can serve this crown and yourself in the same breath."

Godivah clicked her tongue and retreated to the door. "Your first time will hurt. The second will not. The sooner you quicken with child, the sooner you can rest."

The door opened and closed, and she was gone.

Imryll closed her eyes and rolled her head back as the young women bathed her, dried her, and plied her body with oils. When they slipped their fingers between her legs to spread the raspberry, one of the girls whispered to the other that Imryll was *already prepared.*

Shame flooded her from head to toe. She braced herself against the bedpost while they worked, trying desperately not to think of Drazhan Wynter and his licentious words in the arena.

How will you explain to him you've come to your marriage bed already soaking wet?

Imryll bit her lip and forced her mind to clear as the young women finished.

Torian gasped when the small door in the corner of the bedchamber creaked open. He never got the chance to resume normal breathing. The sight emerging from the back room left his blood stilled in his veins, his thoughts shapeless.

Imryll walked toward him entirely nude. The arm wearing the circlet was crossed over her chest, her breasts spilling above and beneath. Her other hand dipped between her legs, just the right size to conceal her sex. She had no defense against the sheen of oil coating her soft skin, traveling up her neck to the prettiest face he'd ever laid eyes on—or would be, if her eyes were not swimming with grief.

She's yours. Bought and paid for, for you. You can do whatever you want to her. Whenever you want.

Torian swallowed and fought the desire burning in his loins. It surprised and pained him how much more turned on he was, knowing he had the power now. That if he were to spin her around and bend her over the desk, she'd have no choice but to comply with his demand.

"Ryl." Torian's voice cracked. If she could read his mind, she'd never speak to him again.

"Can I…" She nodded toward a quilt folded over a nearby settee.

Torian followed her gaze and realized she was asking to cover herself. He almost said, *You don't have to ask, none of this is mine,* but everything was his now.

Including her.

The lump in his throat swelled in tandem with the one in his pants.

"Tor?"

"Ah, yes. Yeah, of course, Ryl. I…What did they do to you in there?"

Imryll dove for the quilt, dropping her arms away from her privates long enough for Torian to catch a glimpse. He reconciled the image with the one from his fantasies.

She wrapped the blanket around herself with a hard shiver and sank onto the settee.

"Prepared me," she muttered, hunched over her lap, rocking. "They rubbed me with oil, said…" Her head dropped lower, softly curled red hair spilling over her knees in buoyant waves. "It's like I've forgotten how to breathe, Tor."

Torian imagined wrapping her hair in his fist with a claiming tug, driving into her from behind as she cried for a second to catch her breath.

What is wrong *with you? You* love *her. Are you going to comfort her or treat her like everyone else has since the announcement?*

Those thoughts belonged to his fantasies, and his fantasies belonged to a past that was over.

Imryll was there in his bedchamber, vulnerable and distraught and sharing both sides of herself with him because he'd earned her trust over many years of tears and confessions. She couldn't be *my Imryll* and also a conquest. Her faith in him was predicated on his differences from the other men in Duncarrow.

"Can they see in here? Is there…" Imryll shook her head and wrapped herself tighter. With a shuddering breath, she looked his way, her eyes ringed with red. "I don't know what to do. None of this feels real to me."

Her words—an echo of his feelings—broke Torian from his confusing trance and spurred him into action. He tentatively sat beside her on the settee, crowding the far end. "It doesn't feel real to me either. I've tried not to think about this day…this night…" His cock stirred at the lie. "Are you all right?"

"No," Imryll said so quickly he almost asked her to repeat it, to confirm it was what she'd meant. Imryll never betrayed weakness. Never admitted defeat.

Her confession had the same effect as throwing him into a vat of cold water.

Torian's heart melted toward the plush divan.

Strangely, though, her admission also relaxed him. Imryll said she wasn't all right, which was all he needed to know to decide his own conduct. It was that simple.

"They'll expect us to be in here for a few hours before we retire," he said. He didn't recognize his own voice, aged and hard. It was as foreign as the room, as seeing Imryll so out of sorts. "Let me find you something to wear and then we can talk."

"Talk?" She asked the question without lifting her head. She was still bowled over her knees. Her oiled, bare upper back shone from a gap in the quilt's cover.

99

"Or we can sit in silence,"Torian said as he went to find something for her. He exited the bedchamber into two others before he found the wardrobe room. Moments later, he emerged with a thick hooded robe and passed it to her.

Imryll accepted it without moving anything but her hand. She nodded her thanks and waited.

She's waiting for you to leave.

Torian cleared his throat and stepped back into the wardrobe room. His flesh buzzed, worries bouncing between what to do about the next few hours and what to do about the rest of his life.

"You can come back," she called.

He returned and found her still sitting on the settee, but she was cloaked and using the quilt only for her lap. He noted her shivers and went to stoke the fire someone else had made.

"I'm not cold. I don't know what I am," she said, shaking her head. "I'm sorry, Tor."

"For?" Torian fingered the mantle, eyeing the fire as if it required his scrutiny anyway.

"You must be feeling…Well, I don't know how you're feeling. You said if you could make your own choices, you would choose… but…Here I am, and I can't even…"

Torian fisted the hot stone and steeled himself before turning. "I love you, Imryll. I have always loved you. But this is not how I saw our future either." The porous rock burned his hand but also gave him another avenue for the pain without borders. "When I said I wanted to choose…*This* wasn't what I meant."

"I know," she said softly. "But if I don't give you a child soon, none of that will matter."

Torian felt her beneath him, receiving him with wide, wanting eyes, hot and warm and welcome, and…He shook his head. *That* wasn't the way he wanted to finally be with her. "That's a problem for tomorrow, Ryl. Tonight…Tonight we just have to make it a few hours, until we've satisfied others our duty is fulfilled and we can both put this strange day behind us."

Imryll nodded, looking away from him.

Torian turned and leaned against the edge of the hearth. "Your guard. Syr Wynter."

Her spine straightened, but she left her eyes on the shadows. "Awful, isn't he?"

"I don't know," Torian answered. His pulse quickened as he neared a question that might stir her famous defensiveness. "You said you met him before today?"

Imryll slid her legs under the quilt. "I accidentally stumbled across the knights with Commander Ofal a week ago. They were in the lyceum. Practicing, Ofal said."

"Why were you in the lyceum?"

"I just needed some air." Tension crept into her tone. "I didn't know they'd be there."

That wasn't my question. "And he was rude to you?"

Imryll's head shook. The exposed hollow of her gleaming neck rippled with a swallow. "He was...yes, rude. Impertinent. He treated me coldly and with a shocking lack of respect for a man who trained a whole year to be here. He wouldn't even lower his eyes when Ofal announced me."

Torian snickered. "You hate when people defer to you."

"Yes, but to so defiantly refuse?" Fire jumped into her face as she spun on the settee, turning toward him. "He just *stood* there, staring at me. Smirking at me. And Ofal did nothing."

"He smirked at you?"

"That's what I said."

Torian screwed his mouth. "That's why he has you so unsettled?"

Imryll balked. "If you were there, you'd understand. I don't want to talk about it."

Torian looked at her flushed cheeks and wild eyes and could see that was true. But there was more she wasn't saying. "I could ask my father to have Wynter and Blackfen swap duties."

Imryll snorted and thrust her hand to the side. When she did, her small arm slipped past the swimming cuff of the robe. The sheen of oil still clinging to her flesh caught the candlelight, creating the impression she was glowing gold. The entire bed-chamber smelled like lavender. "After that garish display? He'd punish you even for asking."

"Do you have another idea?"

"Not talking about it at all was my suggestion."

Torian sensed the hard shift in her, that whatever ground he'd gained in freeing her of her marital obligation for the evening had been lost in his insistence to talk about her guard. The itch to do it anyway was palpable.

You've never seen her show such strong emotion about anything except leaving this isle.

Torian returned to her side. In a rush of confusing, clumsy emotion, he reached under the blanket to gather her hands in his and, fumbling, brought both to his mouth.

Imryll neither pulled back nor encouraged the gesture. She only watched, waiting.

"Why don't you go lie in my bed and rest?" He kissed both her hands, slick with oil. But the scent—lavender mixed with raspberry, mixed with *her*—left his bones weak with wanting. *They readied her for you. She's yours. The power belongs to you.* Torian inhaled sharply. "I'll keep watch in case anyone decides to surprise us, and when a few hours have slipped away, I'll escort you to your new apartments. All right?"

Imryll nodded, blinking tears away. "I'm sorry," she said, so softly he leaned in.

"There's nothing to be sorry for," Torian told the woman holding his heart in her palms. "We'll figure this out, Ryl. Just not tonight, yeah?"

Her expression shifted, and she leaned in to kiss him. Torian braced, breathing in, but the peck was chaste, over before the warmth had even risen to his face.

And then she was gone, peeling away.

Torian watched her long legs as she approached the bed. The gleam of her muscled calves as she climbed up—*as she climbed over me, cradling me between her thighs, and*—and nestled herself under the covers. He started to ask if she needed anything, but the question was answered with soft snoring before he could.

Light of Enivera, give me the strength to navigate this.

Torian pressed a palm against his cock to relieve some pressure and turned his eyes and thoughts toward the door.

Imryll stepped out ahead of Torian with both hands holding the robe closed. The exhaustion on her face was far from feigned. Anyone watching would think exactly what she wanted them to think, and she didn't know how to feel about everyone she knew assuming she'd spent the past few hours in Torian's bed.

He's not just Torian anymore.

He'd handled her with kindness and patience. She wondered if she deserved either of those things. It was the fate of all women to become a man's possession and the mother of his children. Few were as fortunate as she was, to be sold to a man she already cared for. A *prince.* Someone gentle and thoughtful, who loved her and put her needs before his own.

But not even for all that could she lie back and play the part.

Imryll swayed gently as her limbs returned to life after the fitful nap she'd taken in his bed, alone. He'd never say she'd wounded him, but she knew she had. Nothing would be the same between them after she'd come to his bed too shaken to let him touch her.

It would be worse if she confessed it wasn't just the ceremony, nor the attendants slicking her down with oil, that had turned her into a shaking mess.

I didn't come all this way just to guard you, Princess.

"I'll escort the princess, Your Grace." Syr Wynter stepped away from the wall with a bland expression. His eyes were hidden by the midnight shadows of the dim hall. The edge of his mouth twitched.

Imryll flushed with shame, as though he'd heard her thoughts.

"Syr Wynter. I didn't see you there," Torian said with a breathy exhale, hand to his chest with a short laugh. "Janus, you can go in now. I won't be long."

Torian's guard offered a short bow before brushing past and into the bedchamber.

Imryll's toes curled at the stinging reminder of what awaited her when she returned to her own bedchamber. The lingering sleepiness weighting her fell away, and the urge to bolt—to *run* fast and far—was so strong, she almost laughed. Run *where?* She was a known flight risk, so stealing away on a provision ship was out of the question. She was as likely to sprout wings and fly away as she was to escape unnoticed.

"Your Grace," Wynter said again, with the same inflection he might address a tomcat.

Torian either didn't notice or was too caught up in more pressing thoughts. He smiled and chuckled again, stifling a yawn. "I don't mind escorting the princess, Syr Wynter. It's no trouble."

"After the night you've had, you'll need your rest, sir," Wynter answered, with something nearing a grin of his own. His eyes flicked toward Imryll just long enough for her to note it. "The king brought me here for a reason."

"Ahh...Yes, this is true." Torian rubbed a hand against his face, suppressing another yawn, and looked at Imryll. "But why don't we ask the princess what she wants. Would you prefer I take you, Ryl?"

He might have downplayed her reaction to the knight, but he'd heard her just the same.

But if she accepted Torian's offer, it would only prove she was the weak, submissive plaything of men Wynter had presumed her to be when he'd said such abhorrent things to her in the arena.

Abhorrent, and yet the ache between your legs has found no relief. It's multiplied and taken on a life of its own.

Imryll was so sensitive and swollen, she feared a rogue breeze might send her straight over the edge.

She wanted to bury her face in the robe, but that would give Wynter another victory to stoke his arrogance.

"That won't be necessary," she said. She had to loosen her hold on the garment to stretch to her toes and plant a kiss on Torian's mouth. The short sound he made after she broke away told her he'd noted the disparity in her treatment when others were there to observe. If he wasn't already wondering what Wynter had to do with her shifty behavior, he would soon.

Imryll forced a smile and turned down the hall before the look on either man's face could melt her burst of resolve.

She made it several paces before Wynter's heavy steps fell in behind her. When she heard Torian's door close, she shuddered, grateful there was no one in front of her to see whatever was painted on her face.

Wynter's presence at her back was like a painful shadow of judgment. She thought she heard him mutter something under his breath, but to acknowledge *anything* he said or did would encourage discussion.

When they reached her private entrance, Wynter stepped in front of her, brushing his tall, thick frame against hers when he reached beyond her to open the door.

His warm breath tickled her face on his retreat, stirring what should have come alive for Torian but hadn't.

Imryll clenched her legs and marched inside, her arms wrapped so tight and high, she didn't see the pelted rug until her foot caught, causing her to release her robe and stumble forward without it. She shrieked at the sudden loss of balance, flailing her arms toward the bedpost as both of her feet came up off the stone, but she was too far away. She closed her eyes and braced for impact but came to a sudden, jarring halt before she could land.

Imryll opened her eyes and saw the floor inches beneath her face, only her toes brushing the stones. The rest of her senses returned in a discordant rush, and the awareness that it was Wynter's arm hinged across her still-slick lower belly, keeping her from calamity, sent stars to the back of her tired eyes. He held tight despite the slickness, his forearm straining and his fingers splayed, one of them low enough to graze the soft mound of flesh the attendants had shaven only hours ago…low enough to feel what she'd been desperate to hide all night.

His middle finger twitched. Imryll swallowed a gasp as another hard throb nearly rent her in two.

With an effortless tug, he had her back on her feet. She reached for the bedpost, surging forward to grab it instead of going for her robe, which she should have done, because her whole backside had become exposed to the same man who just that day had claimed she would be *begging him for it.*

Imryll adjusted her legs, sending another tingle of pleasure straight into her head from the breeze of friction. She feared moving at all. Her breathing was shallow, her knees weak as she tried in vain to consider her next move—*any* move that would keep her from coming undone in front of him.

His lips made a soft smacking sound, as though tasting something. He chuckled. "Raspberry. And is this lavender?"

Imryll froze. Had he just…He could not have…

Wynter stepped closer. She wrapped herself tight to the bedpost, hiding a moan as her legs squeezed tighter together. *Say something. Say something. Say something!*

"Imryll," he whispered, his breath like a warm draft against her scalp. "You've had a long day. A rather…uneventful night."

Imryll squeezed her eyes closed at the insinuation. Of course he'd heard.

"You've been so patient, haven't you?"

Imryll dug her nails into the bedpost. The throb was coming so hard, it was deafening, vibrating in her belly and behind her ears. *Nothing* about it made sense. There was no man in the world she wanted less, but if he reached around her and dipped his hand between her legs, to deliver her of the divine torture, she knew she'd do nothing to stop him.

Take this from me, you loathsome creature.

Wynter's rough hand hovered just above her arm, raising her flesh with bumps that had her toes curling. He landed the touch and trailed his fingers down her bicep, across the cold metal of her circlet, and up the curve of her forearm until he had a hand wrapped around one of hers.

He peeled each of her fingers from the bedpost and pressed her palm to her oiled belly. Then with a nudge, he slid her hand downward.

Imryll ground her forehead against the bedpost. She needed... no. No, she didn't want it. She didn't *need* it. She was stronger than that. She had to be.

But nothing, *nothing* about the day had been about her, and when Wynter guided her hand between her legs, encouraging her to end the day by taking something for herself, she didn't stop him.

He released her and backed away a step. "Go on. You've more than earned this."

She shook her head against the soft wood, wondering where her objections were when they'd come. One of her fingers stirred to life, brushing the swollen knot that she'd tried so hard, so desperately hard, to ignore all those hours.

The resulting surge sent her to the tips of her toes.

"That's a good girl, Imryll. You're almost there."

You can stop. You can wait until he's asleep. You don't have to give him this. He's a disgusting, vile man, who—

Imryll's back arched as she crested the final hill. Her mouth gaped open, suspended between breaths, the bedpost wedged in the space between her breasts as she greeted the blissful oblivion she'd been fighting all day. She clamped her teeth onto the wood and moaned into it, a futile, final attempt at modesty that had Wynter growling behind her.

She rode out the waves, one after another, no longer caring about the man watching her nor the one she'd failed. The moment was hers, and when it was over, she'd be someone else again, but for now...for now...

Imryll sank to her knees in the throes of a straining gasp as the last of her energy melted to the floor. One arm was still stretched above her head, clinging to the bedpost, slick with sweat and oil.

As her breathing slowed and the world returned, Imryll heard Wynter's heavy steps retreating to the other side of the bedchamber.

Imryll dropped her arm from the post and fell asleep on the floor in a naked heap.

Once he heard the soft sound of her snores, Drazhan returned to her. The candlelight caught the sheen of her oiled, naked form, crumpled where she'd collapsed. He knelt to sweep her into his arms, so he could transfer her to the bed, but the thought of touching her again had him instead reaching for her cloak.

He draped it over her and returned to his corner with a slow smile.

Lavender and Raspberry

FREEDOM COMES
IN MANY FORMS

NINE

FEAST FOR THE MOTHER OF KINGS

Imryll's eyes glazed, morphing the flickering heads of the candles into the actual heads of the men and women twirling around the opulent banquet hall. It took a conscious, willful act to return the sparkle to her expression. That had been Mortain's word, *sparkle*, when he'd insisted that to do so was her highest duty during the Week of Feasts. To smile with sparkle. To speak with it. Dance with it. *Swoon* with it. *They must look at you and feel validation in their choice. Validation that exceeds their doubts.*

Sparkle.

She didn't even know the meaning of the word. She supposed what he was really trying to say was for her to try not to look like the rotting corpse she felt like inside. But after a week of feasts celebrating Torian's newly anointed role as harem master, the lines had blurred. Each of the past four nights had been for the other chosens, but *tonight* was hers, the Feast for the Mother of Kings. The last of the events was reserved for the most valuable among the vessels.

Imryll wondered why any of it was necessary. The food, the dance, the singing, and the speeches might wear the illusion of honoring her, but beneath all of it were the silent, pleading prayers that Imryll was as fertile as they hoped. The other chosens would have their sons, but the Meduwyn were clear on their shared prophecy: only from the queen would the next king rise.

Imryll laughed at whatever Torian had just said, though she couldn't hear anything over the din of song. Minstrels from the Southerlands sang in a clash of cymbals and falsetto cries about love and redemption, yet as talented as they were, all Imryll could think of was how the musicians had been isolated from their families for a full year. They had sacrificed their precious time for festivities that most on Duncarrow would forget by next week.

"Imryll?" Torian leaned closer. His hand dropped onto her plate, accidentally nudging the untouched boar off the edge. He groaned in apology but didn't right it. They both knew she wasn't going to eat it. "Did you hear what I said?"

"Charming," she replied, agreeing to the question he was most likely to have asked, her gaze weaving through the sea of violet. Boots clickety-clacked on stone while women laughed, swaying in the arms of men they could hardly tolerate. Those not dancing clapped in time to the music, escalating into a more lively beat with each climbing verse.

"Of course you didn't. Can hardly hear ourselves think in here," he said, easing some. With one hand on her shoulder, he pointed toward the middle of the dance floor. "I asked if you wanted to try a little dancing ourselves?"

"Us? Dance?" Imryll's eyes widened into saucers, watching the strange choreography the women must have learned somewhere. Was she supposed to possess this skill? And had they been danc- ing this way the entire week?

"I danced with the others on their nights," he said. "Don't you remember?"

The others. Had he even learned their names? She was ashamed to realize she could only remember two. Any time she'd tried to speak with them, she'd been thwarted by the queen or her attendants, whisked back into the dense surrealism of the celebrations.

The past days had been a fever dream of too-loud sounds and too-bright lights.

Imryll tried to keep the edge from her voice. It teetered there anyway, on the verge of every word she spoke. "They'll expect us to do the same?"

"Yes, though it's not as if we've made a point of fulfilling expectations this week, have we?"

It didn't sound like a jab, but it was. Almost a full week they'd been bound. Every day was the same droll, contradictory instruction from the queen. *Smile, but offer no warmth. Ensure your sister chosens are represented, their needs met, but do not speak to them, and Light of Enivera, don't you dare befriend them.* And her favorite: *they may call you my son's chosen, but you are nothing until you give him heirs.*

Her nights weren't much better, running down time to erase suspicion. Torian had made no further attempt to kiss or touch her. Disappointment pooled in his eyes, widening the distance growing between them, but none of it made it into his words.

She didn't need to read his mind to know what he was wondering. Was he really so terrible? So hard to love? But these were the wrong questions. They assumed her discontent had anything to do with him at all.

"I don't want to make things harder than they are," Imryll murmured. On the other side of her, Adamina hopped in her seat, clapping in time to the strange music. If she wasn't actually enjoying herself, she was making a damn good show of it. Imryll wished she were as skilled at playing pretend.

But was she really the only one who looked around at the garish display of violet everywhere—every gown, every flower, even the vegetables had been dyed—and thought, *This place is bruised?*

"Imryll, we simply *must* request these musicians come more frequently!" Ada cried in precisely toned delight. Her slippered

115

feet tapped a little too far to the side. Imryll nudged hers away to avoid impact.

"They had to isolate themselves for a year to come here, Ada." Imryll cringed. If Godivah saw them speaking, it would be Imryll admonished, not Adamina. "A year away from their families. Perhaps once in a lifetime is enough."

Ada's cheeks remained swollen with her plastered smile. "Ah, but you cannot know the honor that must have been. For them *and* their families."

"Honor warms some hearts, I suppose," Imryll murmured. And what did honor mean to the mothers and fathers who had their daughters stolen from their beds, without warning? Or to the daughters themselves, who were supposed to feel a part of a world they had no choice in belonging to?

The three young women who'd become linked to her sat only a few feet away, likely terrified and homesick. Imryll's heart ached for them, but even if she had counsel to offer, she couldn't get close enough.

In spite of her sour mood and absent appetite, she caught her fingers dancing along the cloth tabletop. Some small part of her wanted her to enjoy herself, to not dwell on every last thing haunting her.

Imryll reached for her wine goblet and drained the last of it. She lowered it again with a deep sigh, revealing Octavyen's smiling face as he dropped into a half bow on the other side of the table. His plum collar was popped, accenting his ridiculously coiffed hair.

"A dance, Princess?" he asked with a teasing wink. His cheeks pinched with a grin.

Imryll looked from her brother to Torian. Torian's mouth twitched, but he offered no verbal response.

He waved her on.

The moment she fell into the familiar swath of Octavyen's arms, some of Imryll's tension melted. He could do nothing about her melancholy, her sense of failure, but his good humor was a relic from simpler times.

"You know it's a feast, don't you, Imryll?" He nodded at her untouched plate before sweeping her out and back in with a chuckle.

She smirked over his shoulder. "I'm not hungry."

"All week?"

"Maybe I just don't like eating in front of an audience."

"Get used to it. Queen Godivah might pick at her plate like an obese pigeon who daren't fathom another scandalous bite, but she still *eats*."

Imryll gasped and laughed in one shocked breath. "Don't you ever let anyone but me hear you say such a thing."

"Should probably hold my tongue with you too, now that you share a bed with her son," Octavyen said as he drummed the song's beat along her midback. She kept her focus trained on the stone walls, blurring out the sight and sense of dozens of eyes following her movements. Eyes that had paid her no mind a fortnight ago.

"You think all the Glaisgain secrets belong to the Rhiagains now? That I've forgotten who I am?" she answered.

"Mother and Father certainly hope not." He peeled back and waggled his brows, drawing another giggle from her. It felt good to laugh, even if there was no longer any depth to her joy.

It wasn't for lack of trying. She'd spent hours on her knees, beseeching the gods to steel her toward her new life, to open her heart to what she knew *should* make her happy, if only she could disassemble the stone encasing her wounded heart.

But all they'd sent her were more confusing visions she no longer wanted, of a land that would never be hers.

In her anger, she'd blocked them out.

They couldn't forsake her and then expect her to be their scribe forevermore.

"Mother and—" Imryll snapped her tongue to the roof of her mouth at the sight of Syr Wynter and his latest attempt to level her with his cutting gaze. He didn't even have the good manners to look away when caught. He only shifted in place, recrossing his arms over his torso as though settling in for a longer glare.

"Mother and what?" Octavyen asked, pivoting so he could follow her attention. "Ah. I meant to ask you. Is he always like this?"

"Yes," Imryll said. Dry air swarmed her mouth, and she urged her brother on, to change her view before Wynter's knowing eyes layered another problem onto the troublesome evening.

That's a good girl, Imryll.

He'd said more than his share of words on the night of her choosing, but not one since. Thank the gods all he'd done was train that fervent scowl on her for the past week. She'd almost grown used to it, like the other changes in her life. New apartments. New gowns. New prince. New *shadow*. Only sometimes did it catch her off guard, and in those moments, she was one failure of willpower away from becoming a puddle.

"He looks at me the way I'd look at a man who came within an inch of my wife without my permission," Octavyen said. "Takes his charge that seriously, does he?"

Raspberry. And is that lavender?

"Couldn't say," she muttered, opting for the inelegant choice of closing her eyes to avoid passing Wynter's when she and her brother swung around again.

"I thought I'd landed on a rather benign subject, Imryll, but if there's another that will lift your spirit, by all means, let us switch to it."

"How's Aloysha? I haven't seen her tonight."

"She's splendid. I left her with her brother when I came to find you. Are you asking because you care, or to shut me up?"

Imryll sucked in a short breath. "Forgive me, Tav. I *am* trying to be more merry. I'd like to be. I...I will be."

"Have you a plan for that?" Octavyen slowed their dance and pulled back to watch her from the side. "Or is idealistic hope your strategy?"

"Don't forget prayer," she said with a half smile. "I want to be happy about this. I know I should be. With time, I will."

"Not still devising an escape from Duncarrow?"

"Would you keep your voice down?" Imryll shook her head. It seemed years ago that she'd snuck down to the shore, plotting the life of her dreams. "Even if I wanted to, there's no chance of it now. I can't even visit the privy without…that one…" She couldn't make herself say his name.

"Your guard joins you in the *privy*?"

Imryll shut her eyes in annoyance. "I meant it to be hyperbolic, Tav. But he shadows me at all hours. Watches me sleep. I don't think…That is, I'm not *certain*, but I've seen no evidence that he himself sleeps at all."

"Disturbing."

"Quite," she said with a hearty exhale. It was a relief to speak of her dark knight with someone, without having to share the darkest parts.

"And you and Tor? You're doing well?"

Imryll caught Queen Godivah giving her a thorough examination from her throne behind the table where Torian and the chosens sat. "Of course. Always."

Octavyen angled back to look at her. "Are you?"

Imryll snapped him back into position. "We'll find our way."

"That doesn't sound like a couple in the throes of newly chosen bliss, Ryl."

"Not everyone can have your relationship, Octavyen."

Octavyen's hand stiffened at her back. "I think I'll go have a chat with your guard."

"What?" Imryll's dancing came to a halt. She followed her brother's stern look, but she already knew what she'd see. She groaned. "Leave it. He's just like that."

That's a good girl, Imryll.

An unwelcome feeling twisted low in her gut, tickling a familiar path farther south.

"He should have better breeding than that and, in lieu of it, better training." Octavyen released her, but she reached for him again, snaring his hand. He looked down at it in confusion. "You don't want me to talk to him," he said slowly. "Why?"

Because he'll make my life miserable for it. Taunting *me, eliciting unwanted sensations I don't yet have a defense for.*

"I'm the one who has to live with him." Her tone was less insistent. If Octavyen suspected there was something even slightly more to her distress, he'd confront Wynter no matter what she said. "He just takes his charge seriously. Like you said."

Octavyen's eyes were still fixed on Wynter. "Imryll, unless he wants to find himself on the wrong end of the king's ire, your *shadow* needs to learn to control himself, at least when he's standing before the court."

He ripped out of her grasp before she could reel him back a second time.

Shame.

If Drazhan had ever felt it before, it had not made itself quite so known. It had not overtaken his thoughts, slipping into his meditations like a thief. Had not stolen his very words, which were already so few.

To not have seen it coming was a failing.

Seducing the prince's favorite should have been the easiest of the three feats Drazhan had planned for his short tenure on Duncarrow.

All the years of training…the seasons he'd passed competing with other men, knowing he'd win but proceeding with the fear of a man who might not.

And yet *none* of it had prepared him for how gutted he'd felt after speaking such filth to Imryll.

How dizzyingly hard guiding her to come undone had left him.

He'd retreated to the corner and fisted himself into oblivion. It hadn't taken him long, deepening his sense that he'd already lost himself in the one place with the key to making him whole.

For the first time in a long time, he'd slept through the night.

The next morning, she'd come to him with questions she didn't know how to form and was afraid to ask, still wound in the robe he'd thrown over her, her eyes wide with the hope he'd spare her the indecency of saying the words.

All he'd offered her was a glare.

It was familiar—*comfortable*—restoring the balance between them immediately and standing in place of explanation. When she'd retreated, he knew he'd won, and he could see she knew it too.

But the shame remained.

Festered like untended rot, creeping into the foundation of self-control he'd spent more than a decade constructing.

Yet there was one thing even worse than shame.

"Syr Wynter is it?"

Drazhan straightened. He reprimanded himself for losing his sense of presence as he struggled to identify the man standing before him. The answer came not from recollection but from his eyes.

They were *her* eyes.

That's a good girl, Imryll.

"Marquess Glaisgain." He'd almost said *Duke.* But unlike the lords of the realm, the interlopers on Duncarrow didn't share paternal titles until retirement or death. "Good evening."

Octavyen—finally he remembered the name, for it reminded him of the self-aggrandizing men who had long ruled the Easterlands—didn't smile or return the pleasantry. A tight line overtook his mouth, the indignation in his eyes already a beat ahead of him. "Are you enjoying yourself as my sister's personal guard?"

Am I enjoying watching your sister make herself come? Drazhan ground his jaw before realizing he was wearing his emotion.

"Enjoyment does not factor into my charge. I am a servant of His Grace the King."

He'd practiced versions of those words so many times, he could say them without feeling ill.

"Right." Octavyen's cheeks ticked up; he sucked in through his teeth. "See, Wynter, I don't rightly care how you feel about your charge, nor does the king. But I do care about the very untoward way you've been eyeing my sister. It's far from chivalrous. Still, I'll happily give you the benefit of the doubt in assuming it's *not* intentional, if we agree it stops now."

Drazhan considered the best response to the accusation he'd been expecting. He wasn't exactly subtle with the way he watched Imryll, but that was the point. To sow doubt.

He flicked a brief glance past the man awaiting his response and saw, to no surprise, that Imryll's entire focus was on the two of them.

Had she sent her brother to dress him down?

No. That was horror on her face.

"Well?"

"Just weighing how to address an unfounded claim when the claimant has already made his indictment," Drazhan said. The wan expression on Imryll's face almost drew a smile to his.

Octavyen reeled back, his head cocked. He'd not been expecting anything but agreement. "Would you like to try your answer again, knight?"

Imryll's mouth parted. Her bosom, practically smashed into the gown they'd chosen for her, lifted and fell in rapid movement with her tight breaths. She started to shake her head but stopped.

Drazhan held her gaze for a full second before turning his eyes back on her brother. "I will be more mindful of what my face is doing, Lord Glaisgain."

Octavyen shifted, as though deciding whether to turn the conversation physical. All humor left his expression. "Are you being clever?"

"Clever? No, my lord. I'm trained not to make commitments beyond my ability."

Crimson bloomed in the young man's cheeks. "You're insinuating you can't *help* but covet your future queen?"

"Covet is not my word. Sir." *Possess. Claim.*

Drazhan hadn't even released his next word when Imryll rushed in like a hurricane, with urgent eye-widening glares at her brother. When Octavyen didn't react, she stood at his side in suspended animation.

"*Octavyen,*" she hissed, tugging on his arm. "This is hardly..." She cast a look just beyond Drazhan with a steeling breath. "Appropriate. I told you to leave it."

Octavyen burned his gaze through Drazhan as he backed away. "I don't want to have to talk to the king, but I will. I will."

Drazhan crossed his arms and watched.

Imryll jerked her brother forward. She looked back once, careful to avoid eye contact, before pushing him into the melee of dancers.

Drazhan tried not to grin. If her family was already making claims about inappropriateness between himself and the princess, the king's concern would soon follow. Once the future of the crown was in question, he could finish what he'd started in Duncarrow and leave—either in honor or in death, but satisfied in knowing he'd avenged his family.

Then he could put Imryll's flushed face and wide eyes out of his head forever.

The music shifted to a more somber refrain, and the dancers slowed. Torian picked at the last of the boar meat clinging to the massive bone, which was swallowing the entire plate. There were four dishes in front of him, and his own portions would be enough to feed him for days. Everyone expected him to have the hearty constitution of a king, so he'd gorged himself to the point that one wrong move might send it all back up.

He'd done far better than Imryll. The only sign she'd eaten at all was the broken stems on her grape bunch.

But food was the last thing on his mind as he watched Imryll and her brother dress down the guard.

"How does one dance to music such as this, Your Grace?"

Torian felt the intruding warmth of Adamina when she leaned across Imryll's vacant seat to speak with him. His smile was quick, flagging from his lack of intent.

"You adjust," he said with a nod, which she followed. The throng of dancers hadn't thinned with the change of pace. The distance between bodies narrowed, and with it, the once-lively hops and skips took on a level of intimacy that made Torian uncomfortable.

Would Imryll ever let him hold her like that? His arm pinning her waist, her head dropping low to his shoulder...

"Ah," Adamina replied with a soft cluck of her tongue. "There were no dances like this at our feast, or the others. Do you suppose there's a reason for the choice to include it tonight, on the last one?"

For the future king to dance with his queen and show the court they need not worry about their future.

"It was probably just at the end of their list," he mumbled.

Imryll tugged at Octavyen's arm, sending them both skittering back. Wynter poorly suppressed a grin.

"Will you not dance with her then?"

"Imryll?" Torian pretended as though he hadn't been tracking Imryll's movements from the moment she'd left his side. "She's not much of a dancer."

"A queen must learn these things," Adamina said and restored her rigid posture as she returned to her seat. "It's imperative you speak with her before she disgraces herself."

Torian grimaced. They'd all spoken this way before the wedding, familiar and without worry for hierarchy, but his father would expect better of him now. "Adamina, you mustn't...you mustn't speak of her in that way."

"In what way, Your Grace?"

He could nearly feel the bat of her lashes.

"As though…" He pulled in a sharp inhale, in an effort to regain his so-called authority. "You are both Rhiagains now. And, strange as it may be for us all, respecting this early on will help us adjust to the change quicker."

"Forgive me, Your Grace," Adamina said, sounding not the least bit sorry. "Imr—the *princess*—is my friend, and I am only looking out for her."

Torian almost snorted. Did Adamina not know Imryll told him everything?

Used *to tell you everything.*

The only thing worse than having four other chosens for Imryll to imagine him sleeping with was one of those chosens being Adamina of Privaine.

No, the worst part is she isn't bothered by the thought of sharing you.

She's bothered at the idea of being *with you.*

Torian swallowed the truth with a gulp of wine.

He wondered what the king and queen were doing. He couldn't slake his curiosity without turning around, which would invite their displeasure. They'd been at his back all night, raised and on display for all of Duncarrow. One day he'd sit in his father's seat, watching his own son.

His shift in attention caused him to lose track of Imryll. He didn't see her dancing with her brother, who was happily wrapped in his wife's arms.

He then saw Wynter had disappeared too.

"Shall *we* dance then, Your Grace?" Adamina asked with a hopeful lilt.

He became suddenly aware of his other three chosens, who hadn't said a word the entire night.

Their happiness hinged on him, and he'd barely been able to say two words to any of them.

I need to find Imryll.

Torian shoved back from the table and stumbled over his own feet as he brushed past all four women on his way to the dance floor.

"What are you *doing*?" Imryll demanded as Tasmin yanked her onto the balcony. The wind displaced her carefully layered curls in an instant. She didn't care about her hair, or her extravagant dress, but the duchess would. The queen would.

"I could ask you the same." Tasmin's tone held more accusation than her words. "And I will. Right now. What are you doing, Imryll?"

"I don't know what you're implying." Imryll frantically fussed with her hair in the reflection of the glass door, but the wind kept knocking it out of place.

"Are you going to make me say it?" She sighed, shaking her head at her slippered feet. "You know I'm the last of *anyone* in Duncarrow who will tell you to fall in line, be what they ask… but is there a reason you're making it even harder on yourself?" Tasmin's deep-brown eyes narrowed. "No. No, don't you even think of lying to me, or plying me with some trite explanation that might work on others. It'll never work on me, and frankly, it's insulting you'd try."

Imryll gripped the thick stone railing and arched herself higher, breathing the first fresh air she'd had in hours. Tasmin would spot any lie Imryll offered, and it would be an affront to their friendship, which had always been based on raw honesty.

"Torian and I…" She struggled to finish. Saying the words aloud made them real—gave her failure tangibility. "I've gone to his bedchamber every night, as they all expect me to, but…but nothing has happened."

Tasmin didn't look surprised. "I deduced as much with the way you two walk around. You in your tightly coiled angst, as though a poke at the wrong time might snap you. Him in brooding frustration, like *he* might snap but in a much more colorful way." She crossed her arms and leaned back onto the balcony wall. "Is it because you're realizing how you feel about him is not sexual, or is the idea of sex being the sum of your worth in this arrangement too much to bear?"

"Can it be both?" Imryll asked with a sheepish grin. "I don't know *what* I feel for Torian anymore, but there's no spark when we're alone. No fluttering in my belly, no special ache."

Tasmin grinned. "Special ache? You've experienced that somewhere else then?"

"I meant it in a general sense," Imryll answered with a flustered eyeroll. "But whatever I did feel for him, or could feel for him, goes cold against the anticipation of duty. I almost let him have me the day I found out I was going to be his First Chosen." She laughed under her breath. "No wonder he's so confused. One second I was ready to throw my chastity to the wind, the next, I couldn't even remember how to speak to him."

"Your circumstances changed in an instant," Tasmin said. "For both of you. If he loves you, then he accepts that."

"I'm not sure he does accept it, Tas." Imryll wished they could stay outside on the balcony forever, but they'd already be looking for her. Her dark knight would burst through the curtained door at any moment—with an even deeper scowl, no doubt. "I've disappointed him. And though I wish I could make it up to him by taking it all back, it would be a lie. Now Adamina…She'd be *thrilled* to be standing where I am. So would any other young woman of Duncarrow our age."

Tasmin snorted. "Not me."

"I never make the mistake of including you when I speak of the young women of Duncarrow," Imryll said with a cheeky smile.

"Some women were born to be possessions. Others want to be possessed."

Imryll twisted her face in confusion. "Aren't they the same?"

"Not at all. There's being sold to someone, owned by them. Like a trifle they place upon their shelf and only pull down when they're feeling rightly amused by it," Tasmin explained. "And then there's…There's being *claimed* by someone, possessed not because they've paid a price for you or because they have any right to you, but because they eat, sleep, drink, piss, and sigh your name. You're the air in the lungs giving them life, the taste on a tongue providing the only nourishment they'll ever need. The edge of everything they are, blurring cruelty with kindness. Hate with love. Their beginning and their end."

Imryll felt the warmth drain from her face during Tasmin's impassioned speech. "You've never waxed poetic before."

Tasmin laughed.

"But you do know *I* know you just made all that up?"

Tasmin lifted one shoulder with a pert grin. "Only way to know for sure is to experience it for yourself."

"You're implying you have?"

"No." Tasmin shook her head. "But your brother has."

Imryll balked. "Octavyen? He's just a man fortunate enough to marry a woman he's actually attracted to."

"Octavyen isn't just attracted to Aloysha. He's in love with everything about her. And if you were not so cynical about the very idea that love can be a boon and not a burden, you'd have seen it long ago."

Tasmin's words left Imryll unsettled. She shifted against the railing. "How does this help me in my present situation?"

"It doesn't," Tasmin answered with a soft, placating sigh. "But if Torian is *not* that man for you, Imryll, it doesn't matter what the king or queen or duke or duchess say. This is your life. You get but one, and you have never been fond of choices made for you."

Imryll dabbed at her damp eyes. "We're back to your idea of me becoming some highborn's mistress then?"

Tasmin shrugged. "I wouldn't discount the idea."

The balcony doors flung open. First Syr Wynter appeared and then, hot on his heels, Duchess Melantha.

Imryll braced for a lecture, but her mother's wan expression stilled her.

"Mother?" Imryll should have called her duchess, but the shock, the anticipation of waiting for whatever Melantha was about to reveal, slipped her temporarily into a more vulnerable state.

Tasmin closed in beside Imryll.

"You must come with us, Imryll," Melantha said. There were pauses between her words, as though staving tears. "The king has collapsed."

Imryll gasped. She felt Tasmin's hand fall atop hers. "Collapsed? How?"

"I only know as much as I've told you," Melantha said. She sniffled and blinked her eyes upward. "But we must go to him. The prince is already at his father's bedside, as is the queen."

"I…" Imryll glanced back at Tasmin, who nodded at her to go on. As she pushed off the balcony, she caught a predictably dark look from Wynter.

She steeled herself and followed her mother back into the banquet hall.

TEN
A LIFE DEVOID OF CHOICE

Carrow Rhiagain had always worn the jaundiced look of a man perpetually in the throes of illness, but for the first time, Torian looked at his father and saw a man dying. The cluster of candles meant to brighten the room only emphasized the pocks and moles framing his sunken eyes, which were nearly swallowed by saucers dark enough to make it seem like he had no eyes at all.

Torian pressed himself into a corner chair, praying no one asked him to return to his father's bedside.

No one present in the hazy, nauseating bedchamber used the word *dying*. None would dare, despite the dearth of light and warmth. Duke Drushan's animated need to be of aid, buzzing between barking orders and blustering reassurances at the king, was the only liveliness in the room.

"He thinks the king cannot see through him."

Torian cringed his shoulder at the sudden voice warming his ear. He didn't have to look. Mortain.

The sorcerer seemed to move through walls.

"What?" Torian asked.

"Look at him debase himself before a man he thinks won't last the night, praying the king is well enough to declare him your top adviser before the end."

Torian shrugged. Mortain was expecting a more thoughtful response, but what more could be said after such a heavy night? There were too many layers to Torian's thoughts to offer any to others.

"Someone should tell the duke."

Torian rubbed the ache spreading through his arms. "Tell him what?"

The door creaked open and closed. More spectators. *Vultures.*

"It's not the king who decides matters of the crown." Mortain crossed his arms with a corner-of-the-mouth grin. "More entertaining for us to watch though."

How could anyone find anything entertaining about a king on his deathbed?

The moment the word, *deathbed*, flitted across his thoughts, Torian's night crashed around him in shrill strikes. The once-quiet room ripped with high-ringing sounds, and his breath…There was no air for his lungs to catch.

He slumped forward, ready to bury his head between his legs and let his weakness take over when soft arms slid around him from the side. With a gentle tug, he fell into their demand and landed his head on Imryll's breast. She stroked her fingertips down his back and up, squeezing his shoulder. The world righted itself when she planted a kiss at the corner of his moist eye.

"I'm here now, Tor," she whispered, kissing him again. Her hand moved in slow, soothing passes. "Just breathe."

Torian had been asleep in her arms for hours. The sound of his breathing kept Imryll rooted whenever she tried to slip away to the protection of her imagination.

The activity in the room subdued after several consecutive hours of no change in the king's condition. All three of his physicians had been in and out over the course of the night, and all three had said the same thing, in different ways.

We are approaching the end. Whether that be tonight or a year from now, only the gods can say.

The end for Carrow.

The beginning for Torian.

For her.

Imryll mindlessly stroked the back of Torian's head. Losing a parent was different for someone like him. He would have to successfully navigate two paths, one of grief and one of courage, and the people of Duncarrow—of the kingdom—would scrutinize both. The early days of the reign of King Torian Rhiagain would decide whether the crown his family had built would wither or thrive.

She had her own part, and no inkling whether she had within her the skill to play it.

Imryll closed her eyes and—

I'm climbing the mountain, the same one from before. There are two with me, but I can't see them, as they each walk a pace behind me. I am leading, but what? And to where?

Voices behind me warble on a lower frequency, unintelligible but for the word oracle. I know this word. I know an oracle awaits us, but other than the tension seizing between my shoulder blades, I don't know why I should be so eager to hear their proclamation, but I am.

"No," she whispered, forcing an intentional break in the reverie. Curiosity almost compelled her to follow the path to the oracle, but she was weary of being yet another pawn in a life devoid of choice.

Imryll lifted Torian off of her and gently settled him against the other side of the chaise. Once he returned to his dreams, she quietly slipped across the stones, heading for the door. None of the others holding vigil stirred, though she noted that the queen's chair, at Carrow's bedside, was empty.

She returned her gaze to the door and went rigid at the sight of Syr Wynter standing directly to the left of it. He watched her with a more disinterested look than she was used to, which was more unsettling than his scowls.

"Not tonight. Please," she whispered as she opened the door and stepped out.

Her dark knight followed but left a respectable distance, instead of towering at her heels.

Imryll started to round the corner but, from an impulse born of instability, abruptly stopped. She swung around to face him. "Is there a reason you've made it your personal mission to bewilder me?"

Syr Wynter blinked, expressionless. His lack of hostility disarmed her, allowing her a quick appraisal of a man she'd been afraid to look at since they'd met. She'd assumed the scowl was permanently etched onto his face, so she was stunned to find he was actually an exquisite creature without it. His dark wavy hair no longer looked menacing but an accent to his startlingly bright eyes. Amber was their color, but it reminded her of the pale-green jade Queen Godivah liked to wear. There were soft lines around his eyes that made him seem older than she assumed him to be, and when he shifted his expression, dimples dented his rugged cheeks. It was his mouth drawing her eyes the most, made of aquiline curves and unrealized mischief.

Imryll became aware of the seconds as he watched her watching him. "Are you never going to have a proper conversation with me, Syr Wynter? Or am I condemned to either vulgarities or frigid stares?"

"Do you have a preference between the two?"

Imryll was startled by his response. His deep voice bounced off the stones, adding substance to the cramped air in the narrow hall.

"My *preference* would be neither. And tonight, when my focus is on comforting my partner—"

"The partner you left alone in a room with his dying father?"

Imryll's mouth flapped open, then closed. A scoff escaped her throat. "I've been in there for *hours* with him. I needed a moment to myself. That does not make me a monster."

"Monster?" Wynter asked with a cocked head and a look she wished she could slap from his face. He scratched his fingers down the scruff of one cheek. "How your conscience must plague you."

"My conscience is none of your concern."

"Have you told him?"

Imryll sighed. "Told him *what?*"

Wynter didn't respond right away. He let his gaze linger long enough that she almost walked away. "What you did after you left his bedchamber the night of your choosing."

The heat drained from Imryll's face. He'd impaled her with thirteen words. That night still seemed like a dream. A part of her hoped it was, that she'd imagined the way her dark knight had guided her through her depraved desire with a few carefully selected commands.

"Ah," Wynter said with the hint of a grin.

"Why are you like this?" she asked, emboldened by his unexpected willingness to spar. Every word he spoke was a lance, but she preferred it to the cowardice of his silence. "Why train for an entire year only to—"

"Princess Imryll. There you are."

Imryll's mouth suspended midword. Godivah's presence bloated at her back. Her cracked voice had a vulnerable edge, but there was no disguising her anger.

"I'd like to speak with you about something that clearly cannot wait another day." The queen made a disgusted sound. "Alone."

Imryll's eyes climbed back toward Syr Wynter for help. His own fluttered down and to the side in bland amusement. She felt like a fool, and she was. Even if the man could help her, he enjoyed her discomfort.

Imryll briefly closed her eyes, gathered her skirts, and turned with a bow. "Of course, Your Grace."

Godivah spun on her heels and marched away. As Imryll jumped into pace behind her, she was, for the first time, sorry to be leaving the dark knight behind.

Duchess Melantha was already waiting in the Glaisgain apartments, and she rose with a worried frown when Imryll and the queen entered. Her bow came late and imperfect. She straightened her hair with a shaking hand.

Imryll's stomach dropped. She tried to read her mother's eyes for a preview of what awaited her, but the duchess glanced away with a stricken look.

"Melantha, will you be presenting this reprimand, or shall I?" The queen's brusque tone cut the tension and then deepened it.

"I…I will, Your Grace." Melantha fluttered around the hearth, wringing her hands.

"Quickly, please. I would like to return to my husband's bedside."

"Of course." Melantha dropped her hands back to her sides with a wary smile at Imryll. There was no joy in it. No warmth. But there was fear. "Imryll, it has come to our attention—"

"Light of Enivera, Melantha, I said quickly!" Godivah lifted her skirts and stormed in another few feet. Her tired eyes swung upward with a head shake. "Imryll, your behavior with your guard has become a problem."

Imryll's words caught. She braced herself on the back of a chair. "My—"

"Hush and let me finish, girl." Godivah exhaled through clenched teeth. "I have no time or patience for your denials. I can only presume nothing untoward is happening, as you cannot be *that* stupid, but it's clear *something* is going on between the two of you. A man does not look at a woman like that without an intent to possess her."

Possessed not because they've paid a price for you or because they have any right to you, but because they eat, sleep, drink, piss, and sigh your name.

"But that's hardly…" Imryll paused. This could be the chance she'd been waiting for, to convince Godivah that Syr Drazhan Wynter was unfit for service. "Your Grace, I, too, would like him to stop." She lifted her chin. "In fact…I've asked him to. Multiple times. He is impertinent, rude, and—"

"And he won the right to stand in your shadow," Godivah stated, finishing for her. "To remove him would cast doubt on the king and the crown at a time when we have none to offer. Do you understand?"

"But I cannot control this man, Your Grace. He seems determined to break me."

"Are you listening to yourself?"

"Imryll." Melantha spoke up from the other side of the room. Her hands were folded under her chin. "Darling. Men cannot control their base instincts. Not as we can."

"What?" Imryll whipped her attention between the two women. "You're suggesting he cannot be held to account for his own behavior but that *I* should?"

"*Tone,*" Melantha warned with a hiss.

"I lack the patience for this conversation," Godivah said. She swept her thinning hair from her face and closed her eyes with a heavy inhalation. "Imryll, you will keep your guard in line, or it will be your shame to bear. We will not shield you from the fallout."

"But there are other guards! Four hundred and ninety-five of them who would love to take his place."

"The people have chosen. You *will* live with it. You *will* keep him in line. And if you do not, you will wear the shame of the fall of the House of Glaisgain for the rest of whatever years are left to you. Do you understand what I'm saying?"

The room darkened. Of course no one would hear her pleas. They'd established a tradition that could not be cast into question so early in the Rhiagain reign. The queen didn't care how miserable Syr Wynter was, or why. She cared that Imryll had not figured out how to make him be discreet.

"Yes." The word came out breathless. "Yes, Your Grace."

"Good." Godivah shot a sharp look over Imryll's head. "I leave this in your hands, Melantha."

"This will not be a problem going forward, Your Grace," Melantha said. Imryll almost laughed. Her mother was powerless.

"Mm." Godivah narrowed her eyes at Imryll. "Now go retrieve the prince and take him to bed. He deserves a blissful distraction." She started to turn but raised a hand in the air. "Ah, I almost forgot. Carrow's doctors have unfortunately declared him too unwell to travel next week. Torian will make the trip to the Easterlands in his stead."

"To the *Easterlands*?" Imryll asked, stunned. Rhiagains never traveled to the mainland.

"To meet with Lord Quintus," Godivah answered, as though Imryll should already know. She rolled her eyes with a snort when Imryll only had a blank look. "We are requesting use of the Quintus Guard in exchange for our choosing the Easterlands for the future home of the reliquary the king intends to build. I won't waste breath explaining to you how important it is that we not fail."

"I see."

"You'll be accompanying my son. Lord Quintus is known for his…exquisite taste, and no doubt your presence will enhance the deal. I trust you'll play whatever part he writes for you."

Godivah didn't wait for affirmation. She turned and marched out without another word.

Imryll directed a dumbfounded, helpless look back at the duchess.

"You heard the queen," Melantha said, defeat heavy in her tone. "Go find your prince and please him."

ELEVEN
KINGS ARE MORTAL.
CULTURE IS EVERLASTING.

Imryll spent the next few days half-asleep. She stumbled from the king's bedside vigil to Torian's apartments with diluted energy, only to fall into her own bed so spent, she would wake to the breaking dawn before she could even reflect on her day.

Everywhere, always, she felt the eyes of the duke and duchess, of the queen. There was not a second of Imryll's day when she wasn't performing. If they knew it was an act, they didn't care. Only Torian noted wryly, *Lately even* I *could almost believe you loved me.*

To and from the king's apartments she streamed, volunteering to help those fetching water or wine, lending an extra hand to physicians, and even laying out the tools of the soothsayers, eager to be of use. To not be *still*. She caught odd looks for joining the servants on tasks beneath her, but no one said anything, only whispers about what a benevolent queen she'd be. But those gave her chills, not comfort.

There was no comfort to be found in the dark, dank quarters of a dying king. None in the face of his only son, stretched between honor and fear as he weighed the days ahead. None in her own heart, shriveling each day she spent in the void between the Imryll she'd been and the one slowly taking over her thoughts.

And then Godivah had pulled her aside and given her another task.

Mortain escorted her to the Sky Dungeon, the spindly tower where the Rhiagains kept their prisoners. It stretched so lean and high into the sky, it seemed a brisk-enough wind might snap it in half. It was said there were no bars on the windows, for the only way out was down.

Joining Mortain was a part of her training, Godivah had said, but Imryll hadn't missed the cold smile the queen had indulged herself when she'd thought Imryll wasn't looking.

As miserable as she'd been tending to a dying king, Imryll found herself pining for the experience with every step. The somber looks on the faces they passed deepened her desire.

Syr Wynter moved behind them in the shadows of the gradually darkening hall. Since their exchange in the royal hall, he'd said nothing more.

"I can hear the questions rolling through your precocious mind, Princess Imryll. Why not ask one of them?" Mortain said.

Imryll's bones chilled at Mortain's knowing tone. She did have questions. But was it ever safe to ask one in Duncarrow?

"Go on then."

Imryll flicked her eyes toward the side, feeling a shift in the air as Wynter's pace quickened almost imperceptibly. But did she care if he heard? Did she care what he thought at all?

"All right," she said, conceding. "Can this not wait?" She gestured ahead, toward the stairs.

"The Reckoning?"

"With the king…" She gathered her words with more care. "With the current situation in Duncarrow, can this not wait until things are more stable?"

140

Mortain folded his hands over his torso. His lean form glided at her side as though footless. "You think tradition only has value in times of peace?"

Imryll frowned at the way he twisted her words. It was a skill he'd honed over thousands of years, and she was no match for it. "No, I think—"

"If we waited for the calmest days, would we ever *do* anything?" Mortain pursed his lips with a thoughtful look. "When would there ever be time for progress?"

"That's not what I'm suggesting. Only that we have greater priorities right now." Her face flushed. She was fumbling, but in his easy dismantling of her words, he left her wondering what she *had* meant.

"Kings are mortal. Culture is everlasting." Mortain lifted his shoulders in a happy shiver. A strange grin followed. "But that isn't your real question, Imryll, is it?"

Of course it was, she started to say, only to realize he was right. The need to carry on in times of crisis was a very Carrow thing to do.

For this reason, once she and Mortain completed their dark deed in the Sky Dungeon, Imryll would return to her chambers and ready herself for the final event of the Cycle of Chosens: The Courtship of the Restrained.

She'd be forced to stand with her dark knight for hours. On display for all to watch. Compelled to smile. To pretend.

Imryll tucked the thought away. Her discomfort belonged to the future.

Her angst belonged to the present.

It belonged to the task awaiting her, where she'd be forced to choose a man to live and a man to die.

"I suppose I'd like to know why we do this at all," she said. Her gaze blurred at the winding staircase ahead. "Why the Reckoning happens once a year rather than pardoning or executing prisoners on an individual basis."

"You want to know why we pardon and execute but one prisoner each a year?"

Imryll nodded.

"For starters, Imryll, we have so few of them, we rather *have* to save them for special events."

Imryll curved her head toward what sounded like a jest from the humorless sorcerer. "Yes, but the tradition assumes there will always be a prisoner worth pardoning and one worth executing. What if they're all deserving of a pardon?"

"Or what if they're all deserving of a push out the window?" Mortain replied with a quirked brow. "Some years both men are innocent. Others, they're both wretchedly guilty. But the scale of time balances all things. An innocent man must die so that two may live." He slowed as they neared the cramped entrance to the staircase. "Challenge your mind to think beyond the individual. That's what a king must do. Carrow created this tradition with that need central to his thoughts. Though we have forsaken most of the ways of our past, there are yet some customs worth preserving."

"I'm not a king," Imryll said. She eyed the crumbling passage with a surge of disdain. "Nor even a queen."

"Your queen has joined me on this pilgrimage for years. She is confident you're ready to take her place." He held his hand aloft into the passage. "Shall I go first, or you?"

Imryll half turned to look back at Wynter, but his eyes were trained on the ground.

"There's nothing to it. One hand on the wall will keep your senses true."

Sweat beaded on her bodice. Her pulse quickened, thrumming in her ear. The circlet gripping her upper arm felt tighter than ever, pinching her flesh. Even if she made it to the top, would she have the courage to stand with him as they condemned a man to such a grisly end?

If I can't climb some stairs, I never deserved my freedom.

Imryll flashed a tight smile and pushed ahead of him. She ascended the first few steps in a confident sprint, but she'd hardly made it to the next story before the thinning air left her woozy. She took Mortain's suggestion, pressing her hands to the filth-stained walls as she took one step, then another. There was no sense of distance, no landings or pauses to give her a break or to allow her to swallow a lungful of the moldy air.

She listened for the slow scrape of boots behind her. Two sets. Matching her pace. Still with her.

The passage narrowed the higher they rose. Bugs too dark to see skittered at her touch. She blinked sweat from her eyes and kept one hand always on the wall, sliding across the mossy, broken stone without lifting.

Disrepair marked the steps the more they went on, until she had no choice but to watch her feet to keep from tumbling. Then she slipped, and there was no time between when her foot missed the stone and when Wynter's hand landed at the center of her back to steady her.

Imryll again felt the air shift, but for the better. Male voices trickled from above.

"Almost there," Mortain called from the rear. Imryll allowed herself one last brush of her sleeve over her sweaty face and made the final push.

She groaned in relief as she stumbled onto solid, level floor. She first saw two guards huddling over dice on the floor. They leaped to their feet in an almost comical effort that had their chairs toppling and heads bumping.

Syr Wynter nudged her in another few steps and then entered, Mortain close behind.

The guards lowered to their knees, rose, bowed, and fell back to their knees. Imryll eyed them in bewilderment while Mortain laughed without humor.

"They see so few people up here beyond the condemned," he explained and brushed past her.

One of the guards put on a brave face. "Mortain. Sir."

"Men, this is your First Chosen standing beside me. I am the least of your concerns at the moment."

Another show of inelegant bows and bumps played out before Mortain waved them to their feet with an annoyed sigh. "Where's the warden?"

"He…" One guard looked at the other. "He's in the end cell, with the prisoners, sir. Waiting for you."

"Indeed? Is that why you both look surprised to see me?"

"Lost track of time," the other guard muttered at his feet.

"Hmm." Mortain turned to face Imryll. "I will explain things to you now, as you'll be expected to act without direction when we enter the cell. Neither prisoner will address you directly prior to your pronouncement. You will have no occasion to hear them plead their case, nor try to sway you. You must use your own instinct to decide who lives and who dies. Once you've decided, the condemned prisoner will be given a choice how they exit the Sky Dungeon and this life."

Real terror struck Imryll for the first time. Everything she'd been lamenting those past weeks felt pointless and insignificant compared to what was expected of her in mere moments. It was a warning from the queen for Imryll to fall in line, or pay later. The power she'd wield in the cursed prison would be hers year after year, and the weight on her conscience would only grow heavier until it was impossible to carry.

"And…" Imryll cleared the dryness from her throat. "And the one I pardon, he gets to leave?"

"Leave? No. But he returns to the keep as a citizen and not a prisoner."

"And the other, you said he gets to…choose?"

"Whether he leaves on his own terms or ours. If you find you're not ready to perform the execution yourself, I will send him down."

Send him down. As though he would leave the dungeon the same way he'd arrived. "Does the queen…"

144

Mortain dipped his chin. "Does she execute the men by her own hand?"

Imryll nodded. Wynter's sword jingled when he shifted from one foot to another.

"Yes," Mortain said. "Every time. Regardless of their last wish."

"And if I choose neither?" Imryll braced for the answer.

"Then they both die." He turned and started down the narrow corridor.

The guards followed. Imryll passed a quick look to Wynter. His mouth was wrinkled tight, matching his forehead. He nodded at her to go on.

So she did.

Imryll stood before the condemned men, her hands knotted behind her. At her back, Drazhan had the perfect view of her nerves, wringing through her trembling fingers. A twinge of sympathy struck him. He'd taken lives in combat or self-defense, but this was not that. This required a level of thought and consideration foreign to her.

Foreign to most.

As he observed her deliberate, her fingers pulling at fingers only Drazhan could see, he considered the choice he'd make if standing in her place.

The man on the left was haggard enough to have been one of the first prisoners of Duncarrow. His filth disguised his age. He could be thirty or sixty.

The other was far younger, hardly a man at all. No hair scratched his soft cheeks, just grime and shame.

Both, Mortain had said, had come from the realm to serve the Rhiagains.

Both had tried to escape, though not at the same time.

It wasn't lost on Drazhan that Imryll had plotted the same before she'd been discovered and locked away as well, albeit in a much nicer cell.

He could tell it wasn't lost on her either.

Nor, he guessed, to the queen, who had sent her.

"Miss—"

A guard knocked the back of his fist into the young man's mouth. Blood spurted in an arc on the hay-covered stone. Imryll flinched but didn't look away.

"You wanna die before the princess chooses? Say another word."

The older man just shook his head at his feet.

Imryll's wringing stopped. Her fingers twitched against opposite palms. She held her head back and high as though it would boost her courage.

"The same crime," Imryll said. She drew her posture tighter once more with a tiny head shake. "There is no difference between them?"

"Correct," Mortain said, ending the word like a sting.

Drazhan had never believed the Rhiagain sorcerers were immortal.

But evil?

Mortain sweltered with the ripe stench of it.

"And I'm to decide their guilt or innocence?"

"Irrelevant," Mortain said. "You decide who lives and who dies. The longer you draw this out, the more they both suffer needlessly." Disappointment hung on his words. He wanted Imryll to approach the moment with the same ice he had in his own veins.

Imryll's frantic twitching resumed. Drazhan had the unfathomable urge to reach forward and wrap both her hands in his and was immediately shocked at his lapse.

The young man whimpered and shook, whispering prayers. The old man stood in stoic peace.

They were both guilty of what they'd been accused of. Drazhan read it in their eyes.

Neither deserved to die, but one would.

"I can't," she whispered, so low only Drazhan caught it.

He pinned his mouth closed to keep himself from speaking. Feeling sorry for her wasn't part of the plan. She might possess a conscience, but she was still one of *them*. The Rhiagains had selected her as the prince's chief concubine for a reason.

The old man. He's ready to die.

The thought raced across his mind. It took a different path, one he hadn't allowed his thoughts to travel in years. Only his sister, who had also been born with the curse of magic, had traveled it with him, and only until the light in her eyes had died to embers.

The old man prefers death. To be set free to remain in Duncarrow is a worse prison.

Imryll straightened with a light gasp.

Drazhan cocked his head.

Had she heard him?

Not possible.

If she had…no.

It simply was not possible.

But *if* she had, it would be no different than speaking to her, and he had no intention of sparing her words that didn't further his cause.

And yet.

Imryll, the old man woke up today ready to die. He has no life waiting for him down those stairs. But that boy has years yet to reclaim a life.

Her fingers trembled behind her in midair, her breath held. She started to turn.

Don't turn around.

She stopped.

She *had* heard him.

Bile stung the back of his throat. He'd never spoken to *anyone* other than Aesylt this way, and even then…It had been *years*…

Death will be a mercy. A gift you *can give him.*

"That one," Imryll blurted. She waved a shaking finger at the old man.

147

"That one *what*, Princess?" Mortain asked through straining patience.

"He is the one who will die today." She sagged after her words were out, staggering a step to the side. "And I will pardon the other."

The young man whipped his face around at all of them with dubious relief. He laughed and cried in the same breath, only for his face to cave again when he glanced at the old man and realized the price of his freedom.

Mortain stepped toward the condemned man. "Your own terms or mine, prisoner?"

"My own," the man answered bravely. "If you have fairness in your heart, you will honor that wish, unlike the queen."

"I am not the queen," Mortain said. "Princess?"

Imryll nodded furiously. "Yes. Yes, I will honor his wish."

The old man inhaled through his teeth, eyeing the window with almost a smile. "My bones aren't what they were, and I could use a lift up."

"Of course," Mortain answered reasonably. He nodded at the guards, who followed the old man as he made his way to the window, wasting no time.

Imryll stepped back once. Twice. Drazhan pressed his fingertips to her back to keep her from taking another.

The guards hoisted the man up. His knees wobbled as he reached for the stone frame of the window. He dug one foot in, and one of the guards nudged him so he could lift the other beside it.

Without a pause or a final word, the old man leaned out the window and fell.

Imryll's hands flew to her mouth in a scream. She backed straight into Drazhan, but instead of stopping, she rolled around him and fled.

Drazhan swallowed a sigh and followed her.

TWELVE
THE COURTSHIP OF THE RESTRAINED

A knock at the door sent Imryll's heart into her throat. The attendants had arrived to dress her for the bizarre event happening in a few short hours. That *anything* was expected of her after she'd condemned a man to death left her wondering if the act had spun her into another world altogether.

They knocked again. Imryll's mouth hung wide in a desperate exhale.

But Wynter had already answered it. He made a slicing gesture at his neck and shook his head, closing the door on the attendants.

It clicked shut. He looked at her. She looked at him.

Imryll sputtered. There was so much she wanted to say. None of it felt right.

He'd been in her head, but he would deny it.

Wynter dished out words like rationed candy, some of it bitter, some of it tart. But never, ever sweet.

He angled his mossy eyes away.

149

"Shall I call them back?" he asked. His hand moved from his side in a weak gesture toward the door.

"You think I cannot dress myself?" Wild rage coursed through her. It faded to aching grief and then roared back to a flame.

It happened faster than she could track.

Imryll grasped for the bedpost. She recoiled when her hand connected, in memory of *that* night—the lurid act she'd tried to convince herself was wrong but one she didn't regret. It was the first time in her life she'd felt not just living but *alive*. No one had ever…Nothing had ever…

She instead moved to the hearth. The flames needed tending, but all she could do was stand, frozen in reflection. The old man's eyes, resolved and calm, haunted her. She still saw the way he looked at her, as though offering her forgiveness. Forgiveness! For condemning him for a crime she'd been dreaming of committing for years herself. Did the queen know it? Was that why she'd chosen those prisoners for Imryll's first Reckoning?

"Imryll," Wynter said with a calm that had no place in the room.

"Imryll? As though we're friends? As though you have any right to speak to me with such familiarity? Your disrespect will be your undoing." She seethed, flexing her cold, clammy hands. Her whole body was dotted with an icy sheen of sweat. The warmth from the fire offered no reprieve. "Hopefully sooner than later."

"I assumed you didn't like pointless deference."

"Pointless?" She spat the word, pitching forward. "Who are you to determine what has purpose and not?"

"Am I wrong?" Wynter's forehead creased from the lift in his brows. She looked for his smirk, but there were no signs of it. Yet. "Are you not put off by titles and formalities?"

"The preferences of a chosen play no part in her reality." Imryll huffed and pivoted away, switching out her hands on the hearth. Why explain anything to him? Why were they even talking about something so inconsequential when a man had just *died*, at her command?

"That man was ready to die, Imryll."

Imryll snorted. She wiped her sleeve against her damp eyes. *No tears. Not this time.* "Read his mind too, did you?"

Wynter's boots clapped against the stone. She cringed when the sound echoed closer, waiting. Moments passed and then he approached, holding something out to her.

A glass of wine.

Imryll flicked a disdainful gaze between the dark knight and the goblet.

"Drink." The word lay somewhere between request and command.

She ripped the glass from his hand and swallowed a gulp with a glare. "Don't talk to me about what that man wanted. He was imprisoned for desiring freedom, then killed for it."

"Death is a kind of freedom."

Imryll cackled. She slapped the hearth. A wave of delirium swept through her. "How esoteric of you, Syr Wynter. Do you also write poetry?"

He pulled his mouth to the side. "You're the second person to suggest so since I've come to Duncarrow."

"There is no poetry in death. There is only death."

"Such confidence for someone who has never experienced it."

"Neither have you!" Imryll gaped at him. She stepped backward, wondering what she was doing, saying. "Why would you..." She sputtered. She didn't remember what she'd been trying to say.

Wynter leaned a shoulder against the wall. A candelabra above lighted the dark hairs on his unshaven face. The shift in illumination turned his eyes from fresh moss to decaying ferns. But it was his mouth that transfixed her. The perfect arch at the top...the hint of moisture centering an otherwise dry bottom lip.

"You're punishing yourself because you sentenced a man to death for the same crime that's lived in your heart all your life," he said. His head tilted against the stone as he watched her. "The one you could not find the courage to see through."

151

Imryll stuttered through an unfinished gasp. "You…You would offer words of comfort and condemnation in the same breath." She sniffled and blinked her eyes wide, straightening. "Why should it surprise me? It's all you know how to do. Pin me with one hand and…and…" She swallowed the end of her thought.

"Both hands," Wynter said. His voice dropped low, rough. "Because you know there's more than one path to freedom."

"Who are you?" Imryll shot back, shaking her head. "How did you come so far in this competition, and why, when the honor means nothing to you?"

Wynter's eyes flicked to the side in thought. He pursed his mouth with a slow nod. "For such a curious, clever woman, you draw surprisingly linear conclusions. You wanted to leave this isle not because you loathe it but because the mainland has something you will never find here."

Imryll closed her eyes with a draining sigh. She reached for the band on her arm with the urge to claw it away, then dropped her hand. "So, with this circular reasoning, you're trying to tell me that, what, people are complex? *You* are complex?"

Wynter held his hands out at his sides, his palms turned.

"You're here to guard my chastity for the prince." Her words dripped with mordant thickness. They were the words of others, a tidy description of her fate that others could talk about as casually as reviewing supper options. She cleared her throat. "Not ply me with unasked-for wisdom that holds no practical use in my world. Do not…Do not threaten to *take* my chastity—"

"I would never take anything you didn't offer me first."

"The night of the Choosing—"

"I encouraged you to claim the ending you already wanted."

Imryll ground her jaw and shook her head, rolling her eyes. Tears stung but didn't fall. How was she supposed to put on a dress and rouge and pretend for even more hours? How was she to survive an entire lifetime of this?

An odd, unwelcome image of locking herself away in her apartments with Syr Wynter and submitting to his licentious commands for eternity flooded her thoughts.

Had he put that there too?

Heat throbbed between her legs. *I'll remember this betrayal, body.*

"You do not know me, Syr Wynter. My motivations are not so transparent that you can decipher them with your *curious, clever* suppositions. You will not always slide so easily under my flesh with your spiked words designed to unravel me. Now that I know your game, I'll be ready for the next ones."

Wynter nodded at the floor. He dragged his bottom lip through his teeth.

"And if you dare lay a *hand* on me—"

His head shot upward. "So you've taken some of my words to heart and discarded others."

Imryll laughed. "Oh, no, I remember. I'll be the one begging for it. Right?"

Wynter shrugged. "You can beg, if it excites you." He took a single step forward. "But all you need ever do is ask, Imryll, and I'll take every fantasy spinning around in your head, causing you all this unnecessary confusion, and turn them real. Another kind of escape, if not the one you'd hoped for." He sucked air through his nose. "Go on. Get ready."

Different musicians from the ones they'd enjoyed during the Week of Feasts practiced lively melodies in the corner. Thousands of fresh flowers spattered the walls and tables, leaving Imryll to wonder where they'd discarded the wilted ones from the past week. Her twisted imagination saw them floating upon the White Sea for the gulls to ponder.

Scents of gamy, rich meats wafted from the kitchens. Soon the food would be carried in, two needed to bear the weight of each platter, and placed on the long tables that had been placed back where they belonged after the days of dancing.

It was the same banquet hall where they'd host the occasional holiday celebration, but Imryll realized she'd never paid close attention to the architecture. Until recently, she'd been too young to join the duke and duchess for most state occasions, and after her coming of age, they'd had to practically drag her along.

She'd always seen the massive stone pillars supporting the domed ceiling, but until today, she had not noted the bretèches carved into them, matching the ones along the outer balustrades of the keep. Each was open in the front top half, a decorative cutout balcony that could fit no one comfortably.

"I see something new every time we come in here," Adamina whispered at her side as they walked down the long stone floor. "Don't you think, Imryll?"

"I think you're trying to get me in trouble, Ada."

"What?" Ada sounded genuinely caught off guard. "Why would you get in trouble for discussing the banquet hall?"

"With *you*," Imryll said tightly, keeping her words quiet and remaining aware of all the eyes following them.

"You'd get in trouble for talking to me? Your friend? Your fellow chosen?"

"Can't decide if you're still speaking because getting me in trouble excites you or if it just takes you this long to grasp a point."

Ada's response was clipped when Commander Ofal began to speak. The music cut off.

He bowed at the five chosens in order, but his words were aimed at the knights. "You've been summoned early so you'll be in place when the rest of the guests arrive." He glanced upward. "There are six sets of stairs, each leading into one of the bretèches, where you will spend your evening."

Imryll shifted in discomfort, silencing the groan curdling up from her belly. Syr Wynter's oppressive presence lingered at her back.

154

"I will take the sixth," Ofal said. "The king, queen, and their prince will enjoy the evening from their usual places at the head of the room, while the rest of Duncarrow dines at the tables."

"The king?" Imryll couldn't help asking. They weren't really going to parade him out, as sick as he was. Were they?

Ofal cleared his throat without answering. "If you are wondering about your own meals, they will be delivered to your individual apartments after the evening has ended."

"Commander Ofal," Ada said with a deep sigh. "There's hardly room up there for one, let alone two."

"There is *just* enough room, my lady. They were designed with viewing in mind, built for as many as three actually." Ofal looked as though the word three pleased him.

"And what, exactly, are we viewing?" Ada scrunched her nose with a slow blink.

"No, my lady," Ofal said, shaking his head in apology. "The view is for those below to witness the sacred and secure relationship between a chosen and her guard. To see that, in a circumstance that might bend a more malleable man, our knights are capable of great restraint."

"You mean to say everyone will be gathered to watch them *not* bend us over the tiny balconies?"

Imryll didn't know where Ada's impertinence came from, but she liked it.

Ofal's smile was polite, if annoyed. "We refer to this event as the Courtship of the Restrained because it gives His Grace the King the confidence that his son's chosens are well guarded and oblivious to temptation. Your knights are no ordinary men whose resistance would crumble."

Imryll looked down the line of realm chosens to catch a glimpse of them, but her view was blocked by their knights. She'd never heard any of them speak, even on their individual feast nights. Torian had done all the conversating. When the events ended, they were sent to their rooms in isolation.

155

"Why the need to invite all of Duncarrow?" Ada asked. She glanced at Imryll as though they were conspirators, and in a way, they were. Imryll had the same questions. The old Imryll would have been the one asking them, but the afternoon had left her numb.

Ofal glanced at both sides before answering. They were still alone, but others would be arriving soon. "There can never be a question, from anyone, my lady, as to the loyalty of the knight to his chosen, who will spend every hour of every day at her side. His Grace invites all of Duncarrow so they can witness this unmatched fealty for themselves. To understand why he conducted a yearlong search for the right men. So they can see there is no chance at all of anyone defiling our future queens, and therefore our succession. Any lingering doubts are left behind after this sacred night."

"Commander, so we are to be crushed together with our knights in a tiny space for hours while Duncarrow ponders our chastity and their fealty?" Imryll asked, briefly emboldened by Ada's defiance.

Ofal grimaced and then nodded.

Imryll glanced up, squinting her eyes. "The balconies are solid stone. How would you know the knights and chosens are not doing precisely what you want others to believe they're *not* doing?"

Ada tittered, choking. Imryll wasn't sure, but she thought she heard muted chuckles from the other chosens.

She *definitely* heard the sound Wynter made behind her.

"We would…know," Ofal managed to say before a pink flush overtook his face. "This conversation is beyond my charge, my lady, and I would respectfully ask that you all allow me to lead you to your places before the guests arrive."

The curved iron door slammed closed the moment Drazhan's second foot was inside the narrow space. He pitched forward into Imryll, who shrieked as she bowed over the balcony from the impact.

156

On the other side, a key slid in the door, locking them in.

"It's too high for you to fall over," he said, flinching as he turned, smooshed in between Imryll's elaborate gown and the lines of rivets protruding down either side of the door. "I need you to stand still."

"What?" Imryll shoved back, pinning him with an *oof* sound from both of them. She tried to turn but only made it worse. "Hours of this? Really?" Her voice pitched with emotion.

"Imryll."

"What?"

"Face forward and stand still."

"*What?*"

"What part of that is confusing to you?"

"I don't know," Imryll said in a breathy whisper. She eased off and turned back toward the balcony, wrapping her hands around its broad edge.

Drazhan took another two steps in, giving her as much space as he had in the back, which wasn't much. His eyes traveled to her bare neck, tickled by stray red curls that hadn't stayed pinned in their messy entrance.

"I don't understand this tradition. I don't know what we're doing here. I don't know…*anything* anymore, and I hate it. I *hate* feeling this way. I hate that you're here to hear these words, to see me break down. I hate I'm confessing this to you when all it will do is bring you more dark joy. But the words have to go somewhere, don't they?"

Drazhan didn't respond right away. She wanted validation, to hear that the unraveling within her was reversible. To assuage the guilt in her heart over the incident in the Sky Dungeon. He was the last person she wanted to speak openly with, but apparently the only one she could.

He settled on a single word. It betrayed nothing. "Breathe."

Imryll's scoff was buried by the din of voices carrying into the banquet hall below. He chanced a peek over her shoulder to watch the tables filling.

157

From his vantage point at Imryll's back, Drazhan could see Blackfen and Lady Adamina in their bretèche, and also Waters and his chosen. Both were far enough away that Drazhan could just make out their likenesses.

He couldn't see Ofal or the others.

Nor could he gain clear sight on any of the celebrants, including the royal family, who were so far to the right, he caught only the corner of Torian's leg.

Three weeks he'd been on Duncarrow, and he'd made no progress toward matters with the king and prince. And since the Week of Feasts, the king had been wasting away in his sickbed, while the prince carried on in mindless ignorance.

The failure gnawed at him. He'd been patient for ten years, training, plotting, dreaming. Now that he was here, all the repressed angst bubbled up and threatened to undo it all.

It all had to start with Imryll.

To end with her.

Though she plainly felt the opposite, she was the one in control now. She held a power she was only beginning to wield, and under his careful guidance, she'd unleash it all before the end.

"So we stand here. For hours," Imryll said. She wrapped her hands tighter on the stone, rolled them, and stretched them out to her sides. "They *watch* us stand here for hours."

Drazhan grunted his answer.

Imryll thrust one hand out to her side. "They're all just eating and drinking without any thought to...as though..." *As though a man had not just plummeted to his death on my command. As though the king had not been wheeled in like a golem when he should be resting.*

"Would you be eating if you were down there?"

"I wouldn't have a choice," she answered in quick defiance.

"So your appetite has returned?"

158

Imryll's head pulled back in recoil. She began to turn but remembered the trouble with moving at all. "Studying my dining habits now too?"

"I wouldn't be a competent guard if I missed details."

An unwelcome chill rippled down her spine, curving around and down, between her legs. It was an almost reflexive reaction to his deep voice and selected words, which settled in and tore through her disgust for authority. Even when he'd sent those thoughts into her head in the Sky Dungeon, stirring her from inaction…

Especially then.

The ache never dulled. Sometimes she was just better at ignoring it.

"Since we're stuck here," Imryll said, with an inhale she hoped came with some restored control. "You're going to tell me what happened in the Sky Dungeon." She tensed her jaw with a half look back at him. "Putting thoughts in my head. Don't you dare deny it."

Drazhan was still. Not a grunt or a shift.

"Silence is confirmation," Imryll said. She spread her fingers atop the stone. Across the way, she saw Ada and Blackfen laughing in their bretèche, but she could see little else. "If you think… If you think I'd tell others you can do magic, you can put it out of your mind. The only thing I have less time for than tradition is authority."

Drazhan's laugh caught her by surprise. It was over before she'd had time to ruminate on the sound, which had been sort of…lovely.

"Syr Wynter."

"Drazhan." His correction was firm.

Another shiver. Another ache. *Drazhan.* "Call you by the name your mother gave you? I think not."

"My father named me."

"Should it matter?"

159

"You want to know about the thoughts?" He didn't take a step, but she felt him close in from behind, though he didn't touch her. "Then you'll step out of the authority you claim to loathe and ask me as Imryll."

A smile played at her mouth. He was still toying with her, but it was time to accept she didn't hate it. She should, but when had she ever felt or thought as she *should*? His mercurial nature stoked her inherent curiosity, distracting her from everything working against her. It teased a return to who she was and still wanted to be.

"Drazhan," she said. She wanted to say it again. It clung to the insides of her mouth like molasses. "Tell me about the thoughts."

His warm breath dusted across her bare neck as he spoke. "You used the word magic. So you already have your answer."

"I know very little about magic. Only the sorcerers have it on Duncarrow."

"And you."

Imryll laughed. "Me? No." *Then where do the visions come from?* "Back on—" She caught herself. "There's never been magic in any of our houses. It all comes from the sorcerers."

He contemplated what she said and breathed in with a whistling sound. "The only other person who could ever hear the thoughts I sent had magic."

"Had?"

"Has." His voice iced over.

Imryll noted a weakness. She wasn't cruel like he was, storing vulnerabilities to use later, but it did light her inquisitiveness. "That doesn't mean magic is the common thread."

"You know that much about realm magic?"

Imryll didn't have to respond. They both knew she didn't.

"I don't know where you get your magic, Imryll, but it's there," Wynter said. His voice raked low and warm along her spine, melting her against the stones. She could close her eyes and listen to him speak for hours. This urge was as strong as the one to banish him, but even that had waned, revealing itself for a truth she was still coming around to: that she liked him. Liked *this*. And though she hadn't lost the discipline bred into her, it had begun to die, along with the other parts of her losing ground in the battle of deciding who she was.

"Fine," she said. "Then *why* did you send me the thoughts?"

"You know why."

"I know riddles are for children."

"Maybe I expect you to be smarter than a child."

"Tell me why you sent the thoughts."

"You needed them."

"You have no way of knowing what I need."

Wynter's exhale tickled her hair as he leaned in slightly. "Don't I?"

Imryll's eyes closed when a slow rush of heat coursed down from her belly and into her core. "You lead with arrogance. Only weak men employ it in place of confidence."

"Arrogance would have me lifting your skirt and taking what you have not offered." His mouth brushed her ear. "Confidence reminds me all I have to do is wait for you to ask."

"Why..." Imryll's voice cracked. Without meaning to, she angled her ass up and back until it brushed him. "Why do you do this to me?"

"Is that what you want to know?" Wynter asked. One of his hands brushed the pocket of her dress, up and down, like strumming a mandolin. "Or are you afraid to ask yourself why I affect you so?"

Imryll swallowed so hard, she made a choking sound. Her eyes darted toward the other bretèches, to the floor where everyone was distracted by food and conversation. If anyone was watching, they'd see as little as she could. They'd miss the sweat beading down her neck...the part of her mouth, her tongue wetting her lips as she struggled to inhale enough of the thick air to cool the fire laying waste to her insides.

"You don't," she lied. She rolled her lips inward in a wince, waiting for him to call her on it.

"If I were to dip my finger between your legs, what would I find?" There was something indescribably sensual about the way he traced his fingers down the hem of her pocket, but why? *Why?*

"Nothing," she croaked. "For you will not."

"Is that a challenge?"

Imryll couldn't answer, because it was.

"Mm," Wynter said against her ear. "You're frustrated. You have no outlet, except me, but you haven't yet given yourself permission to take what I offer. Because once you do, you'll see the rest of your life for what it is." He tugged at the seam. "There are still parts of you holding tight to your old life. Those same parts kept you from getting on that ship."

"Don't," she whispered.

Wynter's hand pulled back. "Don't what?"

"No, not that…I meant, what you said…" She squeezed her eyes shut. Her eyeballs throbbed with her intense pulse.

"Fair enough," he said. "Then tell me what you do want."

Imryll shook her head with an erratic exhale. She danced her legs farther apart, wondering what—*what*—she was doing, who she was. *You know who you are. You've just given her up because you're weak.* Dark spots blotted her vision, her heart beating higher and higher. There was no escape for this feeling but one, and all she had to do…

No.

Yes.

But a queen should not—

You are not *a queen. You don't intend to* be *a queen. You just haven't found your way out.*

Accept it and remember who you are.

Her eyes opened from the shock of her stunning realization. For weeks she'd been fighting herself, fighting the answer. Becoming bound to Torian had happened against her will, and she'd viewed it as a life sentence without escape.

But what if escape was still a choice?

What if she never had to pretend ever again?

"Imryll," Wynter whispered.

"I want..." *The world. My freedom. To breathe. Him. This.* "Yes."

"Tell me."

"I want..." *You are not like Ada, like others. Who cares why he taunts you, what his motives are? You want it, and all that's left is to ask for it. You used to be unafraid. You saw to your own needs. You were unashamed of them. You are still her.* "I want you to slip your hand inside my dress and feel what you've done to me, but I...I fear it will have to wait until later this evening because there's no room to do it here."

Imryll relaxed. The words had been said, and there was no taking them back, even if she wanted to, and she didn't. Color returned to her fingers, no longer pressed against the stone. She drew a deep breath and released it.

Imryll jumped at the sound of a small blade being brandished. She angled her head downward with a start when Wynter slid it into her pocket and ran it down the inner seam in a single, cloth-ripping stroke. She gasped in delight, in understanding, then gasped for another reason entirely when his hand connected with the flesh of her thigh, his strong fingers spread, and their tips dug in.

"Can you keep a straight face in front of your people, Imryll?"

Imryll exhaled with a hushed whimper, her eyes closing. His fingers brushed dangerously close to the throb piquing with every passing second.

"Can you smile and play the part while I fuck you with my hand?"

Imryll nodded. Her mouth flooded with an acidic tang, and she swallowed it down. She opened her eyes and tried to smile, to act as she had all week, but she forgot how to do anything of use.

Wynter palmed her lower belly and tugged her back against himself. He was hard as stone, but there was no risk of him using *that* in the tight, suffocating space growing hotter with every harried breath.

He slid his hand downward, breached her undergarments, and dipped into an embarrassing amount of moisture. The guttural moan he rumbled under his breath left her with a sense of weightless beauty, as though she were offering him something more valuable than gold. She drew a squeal inward when his finger skipped across the surface of her swollen core, but her face was as still as the walls pinning them.

Wynter moved lower still, hooking upward and into her with one finger...two fingers...and that was the moment—where sparks erupted before her eyes, her toes curling in her slippers—she almost broke the ruse. Where she almost showed all of Duncarrow what a good girl Imryll of Glaisgain was for Syr Wynter.

Her hips moved reflexively to guide him, but he stopped her with a chiding sound. "Don't ride my hand, Imryll."

"Sorry," she whispered between breaths, imagining her desire melting over his knuckles, his wrist.

"Never apologize for wanting pleasure," he said sharply. With a low chuckle, he said, "When we're alone in your bedchamber, you can ride as much as you want."

"Your hand?" she asked, rising to the tips of her toes as he worked a third finger in. This was it, she thought, the moment she passed out and pitched forward over the railing.

"Whatever you want to ride."

But she couldn't...She was going to be queen...She had to...

No.

That was not who she was.

She was leaving.

She was—

Imryll whimpered at the eruption of pleasure he'd drawn by his fingers dancing inside her. She fell back to the balls of her feet, driving him deeper and threading her pleasure through a tight smile she didn't think she could hold much longer.

Wynter pulled back and turned his ministrations to the swollen bundle causing her distress. He worked two fingers around it, securing her aloft by the waist with one arm when her knees wobbled.

"That's it," he coaxed, driving her closer with every escalating swirl. "Eyes open. Show them all that the queen they bought is not the queen they bargained for."

"I'm no queen." Imryll panted, her jaw clenched as she climbed the mountain he'd set her on.

"Then show them that," Wynter said. His next words felt like an accident, a slip in his careful demeanor, something she wasn't meant to hear. "Guardians, why do you have to feel so fucking good?"

Hearing this lapse in her dark knight was the final spark that thrust her over the edge. Her belly seized, her nails digging against the stone as a dizzying, dazzling wave of pleasure crashed down from her head, plunging through every vein, every muscle, every limb. Her strangled cries never left her throat. Wynter commanded the perfect pace and the most exquisite movements to drain her of every last drop of angst and send it plummeting to the mortar, down through the hall, and into the rocks and earth.

Imryll's breathing slowed. She sagged half on her feet, half in the air, and he held her as the final throes of her orgasm ground her to dust.

She wanted to lean back, to roll her head across his chest and disappear there until her vigor returned.

Instead, she managed to smile, her eyes fluttering closed with fatigue and limbs tingling.

"And?" Wynter asked, his voice low and smoky. She wanted to ride it like his hand, silence it with her cunt and feel it rumbling inside of her.

Imryll tried to use her words, but there *was* no *and*. No *but*. Nothing except a cataclysmic reconnection with herself. A restoration of agency she would no longer squander, not for anything. For anyone.

And this man? Whomever he was? She owed him her gratitude for ripping her out of her malaise. She knew precisely how to repay him, and she would, because it was what she wanted, and admitting that was integral to her transformation.

Her *return*.

To herself.

To Imryll.

Once more.

Wynter shifted behind her with a throaty moan. "How would you like to pass the rest of the evening?"

Imryll guided his hand back into place with a commanding jerk. Stars lit up her eyes the moment his fingers reconnected. She still had plenty of angst left to spend. "I don't want to feel your hand leave until that door unlocks."

THIRTEEN
BIG DREAMS OF LIBRARIES AND LETTERS

Imryll craned her head back, enjoying the wash of her cool, briny hair flowing over her exposed face. Sea spray freckled her cheeks, stung her eyes. The ship bucked and crashed under the stormy tidal pull they'd hoped to avoid, causing some travelers to pitch their last meals over the side. Those who could disappear below deck had.

She opened her eyes to observe the starless sky, bloated with the gray clouds causing all the current problems.

Behind her, crewmen skittered across the slick boards and slammed into equipment, each other. Their screams blended with the sea, angry and lashing. Her awareness of their fear was intentionally blunted.

Imryll had never felt more alive than standing on the tempestuous deck of *The Sweet Yvaine*, Duncarrow at her back.

"Princess! You cannot stand there!"

"Princess! You must take Prince Torian's example and return to your bed!"

"Lady Imryll, you'll get swept out to sea!"

167

Imryll rolled her face forward with a languid smile. They—the nameless, faceless *they* who belonged to the world behind, not the one ahead—had been shouting their warnings at her for hours. They were afraid for her, but not so afraid that they'd force her to stand down.

Besides, she had her dark knight hovering nearby.

Their relationship had grown curiouser and curiouser in the days following the Courtship. Still glowing with the flame of his touch, she'd been ready for more when they returned to her bedchamber that night, but Drazhan had ushered her to bed instead, tucking her in with the words, *You'll make that decision with a clear head or not at all.*

Drazhan. It was a dangerous way to think of a man who others already believed was too familiar with her.

Every day since had been the same: tend the unchanged king and serve at the queen's pleasure.

Every night…

She flushed to think of it. Drazhan, waiting for her outside Torian's apartments so he could escort her back to her own and wait, watching her run through her bedtime regimen with trembling anticipation. Before bed, he'd slide his hands around from the back, waiting for her nod. To the window they'd go, his fingers twisting the angst from her day while she stared at the sea, dreaming of freedom. He'd whisper more illicit words in her ear as she crested the tides of pleasure over and over again.

Good on his word, he'd let her ride his hand until she was spent of the effort and raw to the touch.

But it had gone no further.

Not from a lack of her own desire. She wasn't married—was less than a wife—and the title she did bear had been thrust upon her without consent. The "crown" wrapped around her arm was a shackle, not an honor. After the delirious evening spent in the bretèche with a man she still didn't know how to feel about, she'd emerged with the only clarity that mattered.

She would not be a vessel for the Rhiagains.

Not even for Torian.

As Drazhan had said, freedom came in many forms. The trip to the Easterlands was fate clearing a path. Only fear would prevent her from taking it.

She was bowed over the railing to watch the sea when a familiar sensation seized her.

The first thing I know is I'm somewhere I've never been in any vision before, but the second is that this doesn't unnerve me. Peace steals over me as I watch a little girl with white-blonde hair wield an axe with small, wobbly arms. She strikes the wood at its edge, and someone, a little boy, laughs, but not in cruelty.

He says something to her, but I can't hear it. It's not even the garbled sound of the prior visions. It's the silence I remember from the start. And though I cannot be sure, this alone leaves me with the sense I'm not in Ilynglass but somewhere new.

But it's not the only reason. My shoulders are free of tension. Warmth dances across my heart, mixed with a mirth free of burden. I'm happy. Content. And I'm with people I love, even if I can't quite grasp who they are.

Imryll arced her chest back and swallowed so much air, her lungs burned. The ship returned, the crashing sea spilling up and over the sides, bringing her back to herself.

The vision hadn't been like the others at all. Only in comparison did she realize how unnerved the others had made her over the past year.

It was her first in almost a week. She'd fought the others when they'd tried to sneak through.

She'd forget it soon, without being able to write it down. She'd left her vellum in the cave after Wynter's dramatic confrontation. There'd been no way to sneak back and retrieve it, and even if she could, it would be soaked and ruined from the tide.

"Syr Wynter," she called, her heart slowing to normal. She'd nearly said *Drazhan*. She should stop calling him that in private too, unless she wanted to risk saying it in front of others. "Come stand with me."

Drazhan stepped in beside her. He seemed the only other traveler unaffected by the surge, and she wondered if he'd spent a lot of time on ships. She really knew nothing about him, other than he was from Witchwood Cross, high in the Northerlands.

"Your name is on many men's tongues tonight," he said. "The collective opinion seems to be that you've lost your mind."

Imryll glanced behind them. "I need the fresh air, not their fussing. They seem to realize it now, thankfully."

"Should you not be with your prince?"

"While he loses his belly in a bowl? He wouldn't want me to see him like that."

"Perhaps the comfort of his beloved would ease his discomfort." His cheek dimpled at his own impudence.

Imryll curled her lip with a disdainful laugh. "No, he is quite exhausted of my presence of late. It offers nothing more satisfying than disappointment."

She couldn't quite tell in the darkness, but she thought she saw Drazhan crack a smile.

"Your constitution is strong," he said after a pause. He sounded almost impressed. "Even the crew are not so unfazed."

"Another sign fate stands with me," Imryll said. She hadn't intended to say it aloud. Despite the intimacy between them, she still had no idea if she could trust him. "That is, I was meant to come on this trip to support the prince."

Drazhan smirked. "I know what you meant."

Imryll's core swelled with heat. The timbre of his voice was an instant aphrodisiac. She needed to find a way to control her response to him, unless she wanted to bring great shame upon herself.

"Too many eyes," he whispered, as though reading her mind. "We'll be afforded more privacy in Whitechurch."

Imryll settled with relief. Even the prospect of a night without his touch had left her weak.

He leaned in, dropping his voice even softer. "How bad is it?"

Imryll's eyes rolled back with a groan. "Bad."

"You have your own cabin. You don't need me to cure what ails you."

She swiped her tongue along her lips, tasting salt. Another crash had them both planting their feet for stability. "You're really not staying with me?"

"Janus and I have accommodations just off the galley, with the Rhiagain Guard."

Imryll brushed a hand down her face in a vain effort to clear it. "And in Whitechurch?"

"Commander Ofal tells me I'm to make note of every step you take. To stay *extra* close to my charge. Seems the queen fears you're at risk of running off." With a flick of his brows, he shook his head.

"It was her idea to send me at all."

"You know why."

Imryll rolled her eyes. "To charm Lord Quintus. They could have sent anyone for that. As I understand it, he's not one to refuse an illicit offer, no matter the giver."

"Even a man like him can be discerning."

"As long as his discernment does not overtake his judgment."

He lifted his shoulders in a deep inhale. "What were you writing that day?"

Imryll stiffened. "What?"

"That day in the cave."

"Nothing."

"People don't sneak away to write nothing."

She shrugged. "They do when they're forbidden from writing unless supervised by their scholar."

"Duke Tindahl was your scholar on Duncarrow?"

"We call him Duke Rahn. And he's everyone's scholar. I suspect he got the job because no one else wanted it, but he loves teaching. He has a curious mind, which is discouraged in Duncarrow, but no one gives him a hard time about it because he's a man." Imryll stopped before she said too much. She wanted to understand why Drazhan cared before she revealed another vulnerability.

Drazhan nodded to himself. "He gave you the vellum and ink, didn't he?"

Imryll didn't answer.

"Curiosity is a gift, not a flaw." Drazhan flicked his eyes her way and then back down. "You haven't written since."

"No." Imryll swallowed. The ease of his words felt like a trap she wanted to walk into. "I have not."

"Shame." Drazhan ran a hand down his face and squinted the brine from his eyes. "Where would you have gone, if you'd succeeded in running away that night?"

Imryll laughed as though the question were absurd, but she could never confess the truth: she didn't know where she would have gone, because she knew nothing about the realm beyond what Rahn was allowed to teach them. She had no plan beyond reaching the mainland. "It doesn't matter now."

"It does," Drazhan said, almost forcefully. "You were ready to trade one life for another. You assumed the one awaiting you would be the better choice."

"I didn't know if it would be better," Imryll said, lowering her voice to cloak her shame. "Only different."

He seemed to consider that. "Many would be thrilled to be in your place."

"Then let them come take my place, for I *never* wanted this." Imryll straightened, remembering herself—where she was, who might hear her. She sighed. "You want to know what I write? Stories." Not quite a lie. "Of characters who come to me in my thoughts and demand their tale told."

His mouth hitched at a corner as he looked at her sideways. "Stories?"

"Of course you would make fun—"

"I *love* stories, Imryll," he whispered, sharing with her a con-spiratorial glance. "If more in the kingdom could afford to read them, it would be a brighter place."

Imryll shot him a wary but relieved look. "I agree, Syr Wynter."

"Libraries are a privilege of highborns," he said through a long exhale, "when paper is priced as high as gold."

"Well, I would put libraries in every town if it were up to me," Imryll said. She smiled, imagining it. "Not holed up in stuffy keeps but set along the main road for all to enjoy. Lord and baker alike. Where everyone could come to learn their letters, not just those wealthy enough to pay for it."

"A lovely dream," he remarked. "But a dream just the same."

"And what are we without our dreams, Syr Wynter?"

Drazhan leaned over the deck. His sheathed sword peaked out the back when he bent. The sight of it reminded her of the claws he'd worn the day of the tournament, then never again since. She wanted to see them up close but didn't know how to ask. In one particularly vivid and disturbing dream, he'd used them to give her pleasure.

He angled his head to the side to look at her. Lit by the moonlight, he was no longer dangerous, but beautiful. The ache to kiss him nearly overpowered her resolve, but kissing wasn't a part of their interludes.

Drazhan pointed a finger at the sky. "You call them stars, yes?"

Imryll glanced up with a light frown. "No stars tonight though. The storm has taken them."

"To us, they're the Guardians. The keepers of light and dark, life and death."

Imryll had little education about the deities the realm worshipped, but she was intrigued by the idea of them living in the twinkling lights of the night sky. "But there are only six Guardians, and there are endless stars."

"They live in all the stars," Drazhan explained. "They are sky and sea and land and air."

"Are you a man of great faith?"

"I am a man, and I have my faith," he answered.

"I'd like to know more about your Guardians."

Drazhan peeled back from the railing. His shoulders lifted and fell in a long grapple with breath. "This reliquary your people want to build, to become the gate by which all men must enter to access their faith? Is that how you want to learn about our gods?"

Imryll sputtered, her head spinning from the abrupt shift in his tone. There was no longer warmth in his stance, in him. "But the Rhiagains want to *honor* your gods, Draz…Syr Wynter. The reliquary is a gift to the realm, a—"

Drazhan looked away, shaking with cold laughter. "You really believe that, don't you?"

She did believe it, and had never questioned whether she should. The king had said the Resplendent Reliquary of the Guardians was an extension of amity and love for the people of the White Kingdom, a way to honor their ways, not replace them. Yes, it meant a centralization of faith, but that was a natural progression of society, to have a civilized way of practicing fealty, wasn't it?

"I…" Imryll didn't want to lie, but the cool disgust in his eyes as he looked at her, waiting for her to take back what he clearly perceived as ignorance, left her dumbstruck.

Drazhan leaned back to watch the sky. He raked his tongue against his teeth with a heavy, disgusted sigh. "You think you're so different from them, Imryll. With your big dreams of libraries and letters. But you're just more of the same, aren't you?"

Imryll's chest tightened. She wanted so badly to tell him he was wrong, but then he was gone, disappearing into the melee of men struggling to keep everything aboard *The Sweet Yvaine*.

She stared at the empty spot where he'd stood, wondering how it had gone so wrong so fast.

Torian watched from the stairs without ascending to deck level. He'd made it that far, wobbly and lightheaded, before needing a rest. He'd left his energy in a basin by his hard bed. Only the stability of firm land would restore it.

He recognized Imryll's playful smile. Once, he'd been the cause of it. But had she ever stood so close to him, hips touching, shoulders nudging? Had she ever laughed with him the way she laughed at whatever her wretched knight was saying, as though they were the only two aboard the ship, oblivious to crew and cargo sliding from one end to the other?

His stomach lurched again, but he had nothing left to offer. He squeezed against the wall as men raced down the stairs past him.

The situation with Wynter had been odd from the start, but something had changed—*Imryll* had changed—after the Courtship. She denied anything was wrong, but Torian didn't think anything was *wrong*. Her smile had returned, and her cheeks were again alight with fresh-faced joy. She'd even let her guard down with him, engaging him in easy conversation in his bedchamber while they waited for time to pass, as if they hadn't spent the past few weeks completely avoiding each other.

"Your Grace?" One of the deckhands stopped midstride, realizing who the man was blocking the steps. "Everything all right?"

"Hm? Yes, fine, thank you."

"Can I escort ye back to your cabin? The squall hasnae spent itself, not quite yet."

"I came to check on the princess," Torian said. "But it seems… she's not struggling as much as the rest of our company is."

The man squinted seawater from his eyes and shook his head. "Some are just born for it, I ken. The sea is in their bones, aye? You certain I cannae aid ye, Your Grace? Get ye some soup, some dry bedding?"

"No. Thank you."

Torian had decided to descend when he saw what appeared to be a squabble between Imryll and Syr Wynter break out. Where they'd stood a little too close before, there was an intentional distance between them. Wynter's head shake was full of disgust, his body turning away as he completed it. Imryll looked stricken.

175

And then Wynter was striding toward the stairs. Torian gathered his wits and continued up the steps like he hadn't been staring for minutes. Wynter's flushed face registered Torian only briefly, his bow curt and unfinished as he stormed past without so much as a *Your Grace*.

Torian skipped sideways when the ship rolled over the treacherous tides. The storm was the reason they'd waited until nightfall, but they should have postponed the trip for a calmer day. But his father was diminishing by the hour. The embers of the Uprising were still burning, and the threat of hostile takeover was greater than it had ever been. If Carrow died without a formal alliance, there'd be no predicting what would happen to the crown when he was gone.

Imryll bowed over the railing like she were standing in another world altogether, oblivious to the way the waves tossed men twice her size into barrels and chains. It was her first time on a ship, but no one would ever know by looking at her.

Torian wrapped his cloak tight around his face to fight the rough spray from rain and sea. Imryll let her red hair flap wild in the unrelenting wind, her neck and lower arms exposed in the absence of even a cloak. He saw the outline of her silver circlet through her dress.

His belly churned again when he slid several feet, but he clenched his jaw and mustered his strength.

"Tor." She turned, brushing curls off her face. "You should be resting."

Torian braced against her kindness, wrapped in unintentional condescension. He should be resting *because he was delicate* was what she meant. His delicacy was the opposite of the strong, valiant knight she'd claimed to loathe yet laughed with. Smiled with.

"I'm fine," he replied, insistent. "Really." The sympathy in her eyes bored through the lie. He could see her weighing whether she should mother him or say nothing at all.

For once, he hoped she'd opt for silence.

Imryll slowly nodded and returned her gaze to the choppy sea. "How prepared are you for this visit with Lord Quintus?"

Torian gripped the railing with a desperate breath. "Less than I'd like to be, but my mother and the duke have explained things well enough."

"What was their explanation?"

"That we must get Lord Quintus to agree with sending soldiers to the Isle of Belcarrow, and in exchange, we will build the reliquary in the Easterlands instead of another Reach. That we cannot return without an agreement." When Torian finished, he knew they'd been the wrong words.

Imryll turned, leaning casually against the soaked wood before confirming she'd been asking something else entirely. "I mean, how did they explain *my* presence?"

"You're my First Chosen," he answered carefully, his chin upturned in the start of a frown. "It's good politics for a leader to bring his wife."

Imryll's eyes flicked downward and then back at him. "But I'm not your wife, Tor."

"It's no different to me," he said. Desperation threaded his words, but he didn't know how to shed it. "I…I would have rather you be my wife than my queen, but that's not the way of the Rhiagains."

"It doesn't matter how you feel. Your feelings have no place in matters of the crown." Her words were cold, but her tone was not. She sounded almost sorry for him before she exhaled through her nose with a soft, resigned sigh.

Torian inched closer, both of his hands on the railing. He clenched when the ship was tossed, but Imryll didn't budge. "Is there something you know that I don't?"

Imryll smiled with half of her mouth only, turning back to watch the black waves curling in the night. "I'm to 'charm' Lord Quintus, to help him see the favorability of what we offer."

"Charm?"

She laughed, but the sound was buried by the roar of the storm. "There's only so far I'll go for this crown."

For you, he added in his head.

Torian cringed in horror touched with shame. Why did his mother's callousness still manage to catch him by surprise? "I would never..." His voice cracked. "*Never* ask nor expect...You know that."

Imryll tensed before she softened. "I know. But if you're going to be king, you can't go into situations like this without knowing what others are thinking and plotting. The queen wouldn't suggest anything that would compromise the crown, but I suspect her idea of it is different than mine. So I'm telling you now, I'll play along, but my boundaries are my own, and I won't cross them. No matter how it may affect the outcome of the deal."

Torian swallowed, nodding in place of an adequate response. What he wanted to do was assure her he had the negotiation well in hand, Lord Quintus's agreement to the terms a foregone conclusion.

But the truth was he was scared witless.

Their hold on the crown was tenuous, and without the arrangement, it might not even exist in a year.

"Imryll..." He tapped the slimy wood. He didn't know how men hardened themselves to a life at sea. There was no part of him that could. "I saw Syr Wynter marching back as though you two had been in a row."

Imryll hid her surprise poorly. She shrugged and forced a laugh. "He's a volatile man. I cannot claim to understand him."

Torian's heart sank. She *was* hiding something. "You seemed to have been getting on lately. Friendly even."

Imryll traced her tongue along her bottom lip. "I don't know that we could ever be friends. He's hard to like, even harder to know." She spun toward him with a grimace. "There's something I need to tell you before I lose the courage. I just don't quite know how."

178

Torian's pulse pounded behind his eyes. His flesh pebbled with the possibilities that might soon become reality for him. He nodded to urge on her confession before she changed her mind, but the captain approached with two of the Rhiagain guards.

"Your Grace. Princess." He braced against a surging spray before speaking again. "I'm afraid I'll have to ask you both to retire below deck. It's simply too dangerous, and my men are pre-occupied with keeping the ship from taking on too much water. I cannot spare a single one to look after you, and I'll not have any trouble on my watch."

"Of course." Imryll nodded at him, at her feet, and at the sea. "Forgive me, Captain. It was selfish of me to be out here, worrying you and your men."

Torian glanced from Imryll to the captain. He murmured some kind of agreement and waited for the captain to leave so Imryll could finish her confession.

"Good night then, Tor," she said and leaned in for a chaste peck on his cheek before letting the captain escort her to the stairs.

Torian stared after her. He wanted to follow, but she hadn't invited him. He wasn't even on her mind at all, he realized, only the source of her remorse.

Whatever Imryll had been ready to tell him would break his heart. Of that, he had no doubt.

But he wouldn't ask her again until the Easterlands deal was signed.

Drazhan turned the day over to his meditations, ignoring Janus's frenzied, slick-booted pacing. The guard had been muttering—a conversation he aimed at Drazhan, despite receiving no response— about Prince Torian's safety for the past hour, as though one of the deckhands would slit the man's throat while he slept.

Well.

But Drazhan couldn't make a move against Torian on the trip, which was nothing more than an inconvenience to his plan. A detour.

The king's illness had thrown unexpected chaos into the situation. Carrow was more closely guarded than ever. Even if Drazhan managed to slip into his bedchamber unnoticed, there was little joy to be found in smothering an infirm man in his sleep.

He needed father and son together, for Carrow to be of clear mind when he absorbed the words of the man who had been only a boy when the king had had his father and brother executed—the king who had ordered the horrors the Rhiagain Guard had inflicted on the men, women, and children of Witchwood Cross.

If he was robbed of the chance…

No.

Carrow would recover.

Evil men always did.

"His ship, his rules? Does he really think the king will be pleased to hear we weren't allowed to do our jobs because lowly *laborers* thought it was safe enough?"

"Those laborers are too busy saving our lives to be plotting murder." Drazhan whistled in through his teeth at his short-sighted error. He'd wasted words. That was what happened when men sought validation under the guise of conversation. And he'd played right into it.

Imryll. It was her doing.

He'd wasted more words on her than anyone else in years.

"Are you jesting now, Syr Wynter? The prince's safety is humorous to you?"

This *is why it's better to say nothing.*

Drazhan lowered down from the wall. "I offer pragmatism in place of panic."

Janus snorted. He pulled both hands down along his face and then slammed one on the wall. He was a slight man, not at all what one envisioned for a prince's personal guard, but his dagger work was rumored to be divine. "Pragmatism does not keep men safe. It weakens us to danger. You beat out almost five hundred other men, and you want me to believe it was pragmatism guiding you?"

"Unless you wish to sleep on top of the prince, there's no room for you in his cabin."

Janus stared at him for several moments. Then he laughed. "I told them we should have taken a bigger ship. A longer voyage, yes, but a more practical one."

Drazhan steeled his jaw. He'd chosen his fate by engaging. "We'll reach port before they even wake." They'd have already been docked in Whitechurch if the storm hadn't delayed them.

"How? How did you win the top prize, Wynter?"

Drazhan was done answering.

His mind had become too jumbled to return to his meditations.

Instead, his thoughts traveled back to the source of his disorder.

Imryll. Imryll. Imryll.

He could have had her already, checking off one-third of his plan. She was desperate for...*something*. But that desperation stayed him.

She was no different, no better than the men she wanted to flee. A petulant child weary of being told what to do.

His reticence was more nuanced than sympathy.

To coax her into anything she wasn't ready for and couldn't claim to want, with the full force of her mind and reason, would make him no better than the king who had left a stain on his homeland.

From the beginning, Drazhan had been firm with himself: Imryll would have to choose. He could influence her choice, but he would not make it for her.

Rare anger flushed through him, his mind still stuck on their earlier conversation. The question of how she could be so naive was the wrong one to ponder, but rather why he expected any different. Weakness had overtaken him. He'd enjoyed—too much—giving her pleasure, watching her come undone under his touch. It

Sarah M. Cradit

had motivated him to hear her speak her desires aloud instead of burying them. To feel her shame slip away, no longer embarrassed by her desire.

But Imryll was a Rhiagain.

Perhaps not by blood, but it was no accident she'd been chosen to be the next queen.

Forgetting it would be his downfall.

In the end, did it matter if it was Drazhan Wynter who bedded the princess and destroyed the legitimacy of the crown, or Lord Marius Quintus?

It did not.

Better for him if Quintus finished what Drazhan had started.

One less complication in his plan.

One less distraction.

FOURTEEN
THE SYLVAN KINGDOM

The blinding morning sun obscured Imryll's view from the dock. She could make out the barest hints of the castle in the trees Lord Quintus was famous for—a dark shadowed outline glowing at the edges, from the first break of dawn's light. It all seemed so far away, like they could walk forever and they'd still never get there. Nothing on Dunc'arrow was half as far.

But the *trees*. Nothing could have prepared her for seeing one in person, through her own eyes. The green, the leaves of all different sizes and shapes and colors, bowed in the morning breeze with a melodic rustle that connected the entire shoreline. *Trees* she only knew from her hazy visions, or from Duke Rahn's crude sketches, and neither had done them justice.

A wondrous, dizzy feeling rushed up at the realization this was only the first of many such discoveries. The first of firsts.

She was wobbly on her feet when her boots struck the dock. She had to pause and close her eyes, to gather herself before moving into place. Torian ran his knuckles up and down her spine while she regained her breath.

Imryll smiled to show him she was fine. She caught the profile of Drazhan staring stubbornly ahead.

Syr Wynter, she corrected herself. All their progress…undone in a single conversation.

Clarisan stretched beside them. Her presence on the diplomatic mission would be curious to others, but Imryll understood her inclusion perfectly: Clarisan had the right blood to be loyal, but any ambition would die before it took life. A voyage so far from Duncarrow was a ripe opportunity for power grabs from the competing dukes, and Torian's authority must stand on its own. No one had to know his bastard sister was guiding him from the shadows with her wicked cleverness.

Two dozen Rhiagain guards disembarked behind the prince and his small group, filling in to their right and left. She'd thought when they left that it was too many, but now, standing on the horizon of a great big world, she wondered if they'd brought enough.

Janus shot a sharp glare at Syr Wynter and then turned it into a tight smile for Imryll. "Princess, can I send ahead for an attendant to escort you up to Arboriana?"

"An attendant?" Imryll brushed her hands down her dress and drew another deep breath. Her arm beneath the circlet throbbed, but she wouldn't be seen adjusting it in front of others. "No, I'm fine, Janus. I'll be glad of the walk after a night at sea."

"If Syr Wynter will not escort you—"

The dark knight stepped to her side and jerked his elbow outward. Imryll eyed it in indignation, but it was clear no one would move until her delicate sensibilities were dealt with.

Mumbling a groan, she looped her hand through the crook of his elbow, spreading as much distance between them as the connection allowed.

Torian watched them with a murky look. Clarisan stepped forward and swirled her finger in the air, motioning for everyone to get started up the hill.

Imryll glanced warily at Torian. He already led with the awkwardness of someone wondering why no one else had first. He couldn't rely on Clarisan when meeting with Lord Quintus, or he'd never earn the lord's respect.

Before they could get started, a line of men emerged from the horizon, cresting the hill. They were mounted on horses, though she'd never seen one of those before either, except in her visions of Ilynglass. But it was the garish plumes bobbing from their heads that had her staring, open-mouthed, as the Easterland men slowly exited the shadows of light and came into view.

They wore crimson and gold, the latter hitting the sun and creating shards that further blinded the Duncarrow travelers. Even the horses were bedecked in the brilliant colors, and they moved in perfect formation, their legs rising and falling in coordinated time.

One man broke the line and rode ahead of the others. Janus held his arms out, indicating those from Duncarrow should stay back.

Red and gold overtook Imryll's vision as the individual drew near. His tall form blocked the sun, revealing to Imryll the most dazzling man she had ever laid eyes on.

He fanned his own gaze over the small retinue, but it was on Imryll he paused his assessment. With his attention locked on her, he dismounted, ignoring Torian altogether.

The man's mouth curled in interest. His green eyes had a soft, languid blink to them, and when he smiled, the sharp slant of his cheekbones made a pleasing line.

"Princess Imryll, I presume?" He held out his hand.

She could only stare at the line of rings, jewels that glittered in one shiny blur.

"Lord Marius Quintus. But I would love for you to call me Marius."

Imryll released Wynter and stepped forward to take Marius's hand. His easy grin disarmed her, and she immediately understood how the kingdom was so enamored with the charismatic lord.

She shook it off and smiled. "Lord Quintus, it's a pleasure to make your acquaintance, and we are much obliged for the invitation and hospitality."

Marius's eyes hung on Imryll long enough for her to shoot a cautious look at Clarisan. Then he nodded, lifting her hand to his mouth. His moist lips lingered atop her flesh, sending an uninvited chill shooting through her.

Marius dragged his gaze down past Imryll's hips and back up once more before he slowly turned to face Torian. He paused before lowering into a bow. "Your Grace. You'll forgive me for greeting your beautiful queen first. We must always put the women in our lives first, for they are the heart and soul of our land and our people. Would you agree?"

Torian shifted in what must look to others like discomfort, but Imryll recognized it as anger. He made an irritated hacking sound and urged Marius back to his feet. "Yes. Of course. And Imryll is a rare woman whose presence would still any man's senses."

"How fortunate you are," Marius said.

Torian smirked. "You have no idea."

"Hmm." Marius swung his gaze between them, tapping a hand on his thigh. Imryll's eyes were drawn downward at the shimmery movement, mesmerized by the detail in his cloth armor. "I have not yet taken a wife, but perhaps in the presence of the princess, I might find the standard by which I will define my requirements."

Imryll knew she was blushing. She felt first Torian's and then Syr Wynter's eyes on her, as though she had any control over the very forward man who was to be their host for the next week.

Clarisan cleared her throat in annoyance.

"That is a lovely thought," Torian said. His mouth puckered, forming his next words. "But there is only one Imryll, and she is mine."

"A rather uneven partnership then, Your Grace, when she must share you with three others."

"Four," Torian tersely corrected.

"Four." Marius nodded, impressed.

Imryll managed a civil smile, but irritation tingled in her hands flexing at her sides. She didn't know Marius, but Torian? He knew better than to engage in a contest of how far they could swell their chests. To do it at her expense, when she could do nothing but play along, was cruel.

Clarisan clearly sensed it too, but she wouldn't correct her brother in front of Lord Quintus.

Imryll waited impatiently for Marius to guide them up the hill and away from the discomfort of the appendage-measuring contest, but he wasn't done.

"Though, I hear that the king's chosens may choose for themselves when their duty is fulfilled," he said. A soft chuckle rolled off his tongue. "I, for one, would love to see the sort of man the princess prefers in her bed when *choice* is on the table."

Imryll held her breath through the pressure that followed. Some of the guards shifted their hands to their swords, but no one moved, awaiting the word of the one person with the authority to decide the moment.

Clarisan clucked her tongue once.

Torian laughed and clapped a hand on Marius's shoulder. A dozen exhales sounded around them. "Indeed. Shall we continue on?"

Marius nodded, but his eyes shifted toward Imryll and stayed there. "You must be thoroughly spent after a night in that storm. I'll show you to your individual apartments, where you can both take whatever time you need to restore your vigor."

Torian grabbed Imryll's arm like an animal claiming a mate. Instinct almost made her yank it back in recoil.

She refused to meet the searching, apologetic gaze he passed from the side.

If she was expected to spend the duration of their Whitechurch trip as the subject of inappropriate sparring between two powerful men, she wouldn't make it any easier for the one who should have known better.

Torian had heard the Quintuses lived in the trees, but he'd assumed it was a colorful way of saying they took their residence in the forest instead of in town. But Arboriana, the Quintus stronghold in Whitechurch, was built *into* the trees, a kingdom of spires and stairs and lights that towered as high as the forest itself. Marius used the word castle, and though it didn't look like any castle Torian had seen in the picture books from his instruction, he couldn't deny the miniature fiefdom demanded a name worthy of its rare beauty.

Balconies were wound in solid gold, like cages. A dozen… No, a hundred—no, *more* rooms had been built into colossal trees, which had grown together to forge a sylvan kingdom. Bridges connected platforms, joined in the middle by hints of a long staircase.

He was unqualified to record the many wonders, so he stopped trying and focused his effort on attempting to not look like an uncultured fool.

Torian wondered if there could ever be common ground between two men so different.

Imryll was adrift in her own wondrous awe. She'd released his arm before she ascended the grand yet terrifying staircase—that wound them up into another world—and gravitated toward the enigmatic Marius, hanging from his words. The bold lord brushed too close to her in response, whispering his explanations for just the two of them. He took advantage of her pointing to fold her hand in one of his, and there it stayed.

Syr Wynter matched their pace from several steps behind.

Janus must have sensed Torian's agitation. "She makes a fair politician, our princess. Does she not, Your Grace?"

"She's convinced me, anyway."

"His Grace King Carrow was ripe with wisdom when he fore-saw her importance to this pivotal moment for Duncarrow."

"As is so often true of my father." *She's punishing me for what I said on the dock. But how far will she take it?* "Yet it will be words that sway this lord, Janus. Not a pretty face."

"You underestimate a woman's value," Clarisan said as she moved ahead of them.

Torian started up another set of stairs when a Quintus guard, bedecked in more feathers than most birds possessed, stepped out from a landing ahead. The height of his plumage was nearly that of Marius himself, and Torian gleaned it must be a sign of hierarchy.

"Steward Oakenwell, Your Grace." The man bowed far more respectfully than his lord had. He was young but grizzled with duty. "Lord Quintus has asked that I show you to the sumptuous apartments he's prepared for you. The finest Arboriana has to offer. They're even more spacious than the lord's own."

Torian watched Marius lead Imryll farther into the treehouse castle. With a breathy, desperate rasp, he readied a polite refusal, the need to follow Imryll and Marius more powerful, but then he remembered what she had said. What his mother had said.

Secure the deal by any means necessary.

Torian swallowed the bitterness that followed. It burned his throat. His heart.

If Imryll wants to be another man's whore, then I have four more awaiting me in Duncarrow.

He didn't mean it.

He absolutely meant it.

If he wasn't careful, he'd lose himself between those competing sensations.

If he did, he'd lose her too.

Imryll spun around the open room with awe. Everything, *every-thing* was new. The bed was plumper than her own, the furniture made of all hues and types of wood—wood felled and milled in the Easterlands, in their own territory. Even the basket full of colorful fruit held her in thrall.

Leaves from the forest swept in through the billowing curtains. She wanted to roll in them, to feel something new brushing her flesh.

She raced up the small set of steps to the balcony, but when the world surged into view, she fell into a sliding halt with a startled gasp. They were far higher than she remembered climbing. The marble stone flooring threatened to rush up, and folding her hands to her chest, she backpedaled straight into Marius's arms.

He chuckled and slipped a hand onto the low curve of her back, urging her to return to the open air. "It's perfectly safe, Princess. The railings are made of stone, and the trees we live in boast the hardest wood in the realm."

Back in the room, Syr Wynter cleared his throat.

She'd almost forgotten he was there.

Marius urged her closer to the railing. Imryll allowed it because she was tired of being afraid. Fear was the reason she wasn't already free.

He moved behind her and slipped his palms atop her wrists. With his head over her shoulder and his lips dangerously close to her cheek, he spread her hands down opposite sides of the railing until they stopped naturally. His warm breath whispered along her jawline.

The man was bold. If Syr Wynter weren't standing several feet behind them, he might be bolder.

Imryll would indulge his harmless flirtations, but there were lines she'd never cross.

With a polite nudge, she put some distance between them and stepped away from the railing. "Thank you, Lord Quintus, for the generous escort. I am quite tired, though, and will happily take you up on the offer to freshen up."

Marius nodded, sweeping his eyes over her. "I'll have a place set for you at dinner. Beside me, if it pleases you."

Imryll returned the nod. "It does."

Marius hesitated before he left. As he passed her, he brushed his fingers along the tips of hers and departed without another word.

Imryll didn't move until she heard the door open and close again.

She turned, and Wynter was standing at the base of the steps.

"You have something you want to say?" Imryll demanded.

He snorted and looked away. She caught his eyes rolling before he hid his face.

"Pity they didn't shove you with the other guards here too," she muttered and blew past him. Her arm ran into his on the way, and it was like smacking a stone wall. She winced through the shock of pain and pretended it hadn't fazed her at all.

"Disheartened my presence precludes you from receiving the grand tour of Lord Quintus's hard wood?"

"*What?*"

"My charge is to preserve your chastity. Had you forgotten?"

Imryll's mouth hung wide in a silent laugh. "Are you...You cannot be serious...Ah, but you are. You really are two different men, aren't you? One can't be held to account for the actions of the other, is that it?"

Syr Wynter shrugged, still facing away. He fingered a tall bureau in the corner. "I provided a healthy outlet for your over-flowing frustration. The sanctity of the crown inheritance remains intact."

"My..." Imryll couldn't speak. There weren't adequate words even if she could. She exhaled through her nose and tried again. "Are you jealous? Is that what this is?"

"Is that your first thought anytime someone suggests your behavior needs evaluation? Are you at all acquainted with self-reflection?"

"*My* behavior?" Imryll's cheeks surged with heat. She pointed an arm at the door. "But it's acceptable for a man who does not even know me to act inappropriately? When I search for polite balance in my response to his lack of propriety, *I'm* the one whose behavior requires evaluation?"

Wynter leaned against the bureau. His hands braced at his sides, his shoulders pinching in the back. The cut of his upper back muscles peeked from beneath a slip in his cloth armor. She wanted to run her hands over it, to ease his shirt down over his shoulders and press her face to the flesh revealed.

Even with his sudden shift to cruelty, she wanted him. It shocked her to realize that if he ordered her to disrobe and bend herself over the table, she'd be done before he even finished the command.

"It will not serve you to climb so easily into his bed." Wynter's voice was low, clogged with restraint. "He will not respect you."

"And…And you do?" she asked, stepping closer. "You speak to me of freedom, and…and release, and to be unafraid of who I am and what I want, and then when I try to have a normal conversation with you, I say one wrong thing, and suddenly your loathing for me returns. Everything else forgotten."

"I live only to serve you. Your Grace." Condescension dripped from his tone. He looked back over his shoulder, but his eyes were locked away from her. "There is no *everything else.*"

Imryll shook her head slowly as her disbelief caught up. He'd been playing games with her all along after all, waiting for her to want it so badly, she could think of little else. Waited until she'd started to care for the strange dark knight, so he could crush her in the same malice he'd met her with in the arena.

Octavyen had once told her, *Believe someone the first time they reveal themselves.*

She'd been a fool, but it wasn't too late. Drazhan Wynter wouldn't even matter in a few days, as long as she didn't fail at her bid for freedom.

He was a distraction, when what she needed was a conspirator.

When the king sends his son on a diplomatic mission, and he will…you use that. You do whatever you need to do to convince some powerful man to whisk you away. You'll do whatever you must to convince him, and you'll succeed.

Tasmin was outrageous, but she was right.

She was always right.

Imryll inhaled a deep breath and remembered who she was.

Why she was there.

Imryll had her powerful man. Her conspirator.

She just had to convince him to help her without losing more of herself.

FIFTEEN
QUARRELING LOVERS

Torian smacked a palm against the wall, then recalled it with a painful splinter. He checked to see if Clarisan had seen, and as usual, she had and looked not even slightly sympathetic to his plight.

Wearing a predictably sardonic look, she perched on the arm of a blood-red chaise, her arms crossed. "Would you like to tell me what that was?"

"I shouldn't have hit the wall." Torian yanked the splinter from his hand with a wince and a groan. "I was just frustrated."

"I have no concern for a wall, least of all one part of a tree fort."

Torian lowered his hands and wilted against the wall with a drained exhalation. "I'm not proud of how I acted with her. If I could do it over, I would."

"Then do better the next time," Clarisan said.

There wasn't a hint of coddling in her tone. Throughout his life, she had been both his sister and his mother, but he finally saw she was offering something more valuable. Godivah had been wise to send Clarisan, even if the two women didn't get along. But it was another blow to Torian's confidence in his ability to reign. If he couldn't manage a negotiation without his sister puppeteering him from the background, how was he going to lead an entire kingdom?

"What you need…" She pushed off of the chaise and stood tall. "Is to approach this first meeting with Lord Quintus as a man rested. A *new* man, one who does not resort to jealous sparring with another simply for flirting with his concubine."

"I hate that word," Torian said with a scowl. He shook his head. "Don't use it around me and definitely not around Imryll."

"Concubine? I can go back to calling her an incubator, if you prefer," Clarisan replied with an impertinent grin. "Father and Godivah aren't here, so there's no need to use pretty words to cover our ugly truths. I have empathy for what Imryll is going through. Her family's social standing may have risen, but her individual worth is now equitable to how many healthy children she'll bear you. Oh, and how well she can do this without conveying even a hint of dissatisfaction with the empty life others call a blessing."

Torian balked at her stark assessment. She wasn't wrong, but he *loved* Imryll. Her discontent was understandable, but he wanted her to continue doing the things she loved. He didn't want to get in the way of her happiness.

All he asked was to be a part of it.

"Ah," Clarisan said through a short laugh. "I see my words have affected you. They've turned you defensive. You love her, right? So it exonerates you from any role in what has been taken from her?"

Torian's mouth gaped. "Isa, it was not my choice to take anything from her! I had nothing to do with it. I'm as much of a pawn here as she is."

"Do you hear yourself? Our future king calling himself a pawn." She snorted. "Don't let your subjects hear you, or it'll be over before Father's corpse has finished cooling."

196

"You have a foul mouth."

"Truth tastes foul to those who feast on lies."

Torian rolled his eyes and moved toward the open balcony. Gauzy curtains swept in with a breeze that was much lighter and more welcome than the harsh sea gusts that could take a man out with the tide on Duncarrow.

He ran a finger along the soft fabric, then gave it a tug. It was thin, yet strong. He couldn't tear it with his hands alone. It was the small things, like that, that rooted the fears he tried to shake. There was so much he didn't know about his kingdom.

Torian inhaled the air wisping into the room. It had an earthy tang, like a soft spice, and it filled him with peace. "All right. You obviously have something to suggest, so let's hear it."

"I do," Clarisan said. "But will you hear it?"

"I asked, didn't I?"

"Unlike the dukes, I have nothing to gain in helping you, other than seeing you thrive. Even your ruthless mother recognized as much."

Torian closed his eyes when a gust of leaves blew over and past him. "I'm listening."

"To start, you need to be kinder to Imryll. None of this is her doing. She didn't ask to be First Chosen, and she certainly didn't ask to be a dangling carrot for a debaucher lord. She's doing what the queen commanded her to do, and making her feel worse than she already does will only put more distance between the two of you. But...nor will it serve you to be angry at Quintus for *taking* said carrot. We are not here to change the natures of men. We're here to play to them and find middle ground between us."

"So I'm..." Torian winced. "I'm supposed to sit back and watch him seduce her?"

"What's more important to you? Imryll's behavior or leaving here with a signed agreement?"

Torian laughed through a rough exhale. "You don't want me to answer that."

197

"Then let me ask it another way." Clarisan's boots clicked on the floor as she approached. "Which is more important to the crown?"

Torian toed his boot into the step. He did it again, harder. "So what do I do then?"

"You act as though you're perfectly happy he enjoys Imryll's company. You smile. You laugh. Sparingly, of course. You explain your sour countenance earlier as a lack of sleep, but you do *not* apologize. Kings don't apologize. Then you take control of the conversation, because beyond his immediate attraction to Imryll, Quintus sensed confidence and power in her, and he gravitated to it. He needs to see it in *you*. Father would want them all to fear you, but you are not a man who inspires fear, so your goal is respect. Through respect, you convince Quintus the deal is the only way to ensure his favor to the crown and that it will provide unmatched mutual benefit." Clarisan finished her speech with a long sigh. "Can you do that?"

Torian nodded, though he had no idea if he could either watch Imryll hanging off another man *or* feign having a drop of diplomatic skill.

I can't, but I have to.

"Splendid," Clarisan said. Relief hung beneath her words. "They'll be coming for us soon, so let's start from the beginning."

Imryll had to find a way to conceal her awe. All her gaping and gasping and sighing, at each wondrous discovery, revealed a vulnerability she couldn't afford. Her escape depended on her ability to blend in.

More magnificent trees lined the path, a shaded amphitheater shimmering with the song of birds and insects. All manner of emerald undergrowth swarmed around the roots, covering the forest floor in a canopy of green hues. Flowers grew wild and wherever they pleased, in so many dizzying varieties, it made her wish she'd have more time to herself, to write them all down. They were so much more beautiful growing wild than plucked and dying, strewn across the cold stones of Duncarrow.

But she wouldn't need to write them down. The kingdom was her world now—or would be when she escaped. Lord Quintus was leading them to the stables to learn to ride, and Imryll was an eager student. Leaving on horseback would be far more efficient than leaving on foot.

The guards ahead came to a stop in front of a large wooden building. Imryll and the others slowed as they approached, waiting for the guards to open the double doors.

"I so loathe both the winter seasons. Even here, in the land of eternal spring, there's just not nearly enough color," said Marcelina Quintus, Marius's younger, unmarried sister, as she stepped in behind Marius. Imryll had soured immediately upon meeting the beautiful woman, who had the men in their company—Drazhan and Torian included—turning their heads. Her magnificent crimson gown, with layer upon layer of skirts, left Imryll feeling underdressed.

"Lady Quintus, there is more color in this swath of forest than all of Duncarrow," Torian said, his voice cracking like a teenage boy. "A beauty matching your own."

Marcelina grinned, fluttering her lashes. "How you flatter me, Your Grace, when you have brought your own treasure."

"I am undeniably fortunate and yet still humbled in your divine presence," Torian responded with a flush that had Imryll even more annoyed. Marcelina was to Marius what Clarisan was to Torian, a cunning adviser directing the power moves. Imryll had seen it immediately, but Torian was too smitten for clarity.

Marius stepped to Imryll's side, brushing one hand against her waist from the back. He craned his head her way as he said, "I fear my ulterior motive has been revealed. Should I even bother denying I brought my sister to occupy the prince so that I might plot my own occupation of the princess?"

199

Drazhan glowered at Marius from the doorway. He hadn't once looked at Imryll on the walk to the stables, but he'd spared plenty of glares for the lord of the Easterlands.

Imryll flashed a bright smile at Marius. "You are bold to assume I am so easily conquered, Lord Quintus."

"Marius." His voice was a low, hissing whisper in her ear. "To you, always Marius."

Clarisan met Imryll's eyes with an arched brow and then buried a laugh.

Marius broke away to join one of the guards, who then passed his directions to the others. The guards retreated into the stables and returned with six horses. Marcelina pleasantly explained the basics of horseback riding. Mount from the left, heels down, back straight, and confidence intact. Imryll hardly understood the rest, descriptions of walking, trotting, and galloping, but Torian was following Marcelina's instruction with rapt attention.

Imryll eyed the tall, mahogany beast chosen for her. Enzi was a stunning creature, with eyes as deep as the sea. Imryll reached a tentative hand toward her muzzle and the mare snuffled in surprise but allowed the gentle stroke.

Her heart melted. Other than birds and fish, Imryll had never seen an animal in the flesh before. Brushing the soft fur of a majestic horse was more magical than anything the sorcerers could conjure.

"Imryll?"

She snapped out of her daze and saw everyone else had already mounted. Fear pounding in her chest, she gazed up at Enzi and forgot everything Marcelina had said.

Marius started to dismount, but Drazhan was quicker, dropping to the ground and marching to Imryll. She shrank back against Enzi, and Drazhan tightened his mouth in brief but damning judgment, took hold of her waist with both hands, and swung her up into the saddle with one powerful swoop.

Imryll, breathless, watched him call for his own horse. He mounted, grabbed Enzi's reins and wrapped them in his fist, and led her out of the stables at his side.

"I'll escort the princess from here," Marius said behind them. "Syr Wynter?"

"That's not necessary either. Imryll and I will ride together," Torian stated.

"Ah, I think our royal knight is on to something, men. There are three untested riders with us today, and we should pair them with riders of experience. You and the prince have much to discuss, brother, and I'm quite looking forward to getting to know Lady Clarisan." Marcelina winked at Marius. "You'll have plenty of opportunities to occupy the princess in the coming days."

Imryll didn't know which was worse: riding beside a man who hated her, a man who was punishing her, or a man who was determined to bed her before the trip ended.

She glanced at Drazhan, still holding Enzi's reins, but he stared defiantly ahead.

"You can let go," she said but knew he would not, and she wasn't disappointed.

Torian clenched to stay in the saddle. The very idea of riding such a beautiful creature was appalling but also terrifying. It would take only one buck for him to go flying into the brush. And what if he took the horse with him and landed underneath? Marius had made a point to assure him men didn't die *that* often on horseback, but the implication was clear: it happened often enough.

He wondered how Imryll was faring behind him. It had been hard not to grin at the glare she'd given Syr Wynter when he'd snatched her reins like she were a petulant child. It was far better than the laughter and soft swats he'd witnessed on the ship.

"You like my sister, Your Grace?" Marius sat bone-straight and confident. His chest arced with the curve of his rigid spine. "You fancy her?"

"Fancy her?" Torian asked. Even the welcome breeze didn't cool the heat exploding in his cheeks. "No, Lord Quintus. That is not…She is, of course, lovely, but I have my own…"

"Problems?" Marius grinned.

"That's not the word I would use."

"Five concubines." Marius whistled an exhale. "I won't deny the fantasy of it, but how does a man keep them all satisfied?"

"They're not concubines. They're chosens." Torian winced at the weak defense of his words. He kept his eyes on the path but felt Marius's knowing grin clawing from the side.

Marius pointed an arm ahead. "You see that?"

All Torian could see was more dense forest.

"Ahead is the border of Whitechurch. It's an arbitrary line on a map, because all of the Easterlands belongs to me. We're not the largest Reach, but we are the wealthiest. Our land produces everything we need, and we're the claimants of magic and education, with both the Sepulchre and the Council of Universities sitting in our domain. I already have all I need."

Torian brightened at the switch in topic. Fresh off Clarisan's imbued wisdom, he was ready with the right rebuttals.

Marius shook his head. "But I brought you out here to enjoy the *real* magic of the kingdom. The beauty and endless bounty of nature."

"Your land *is* beautiful," Torian said. He rolled his sweaty palms against the leather reins and tightened them. "Your generosity will not be overlooked by the crown. I will return with stories others will struggle to believe, for all their wonder. And it's a perfect backdrop for us to discuss our business."

"Business can wait." Marius waved his hand around. "I've heard Duncarrow is a dull and lifeless heap of rocks. I brought you here to enjoy something different."

"And I do, but—"

"Pleasure comes first," Marius said with a bemused sigh. "Tell me more about Princess Imryll."

"What?" Torian's hands went numb. "Lord Quintus, I believe there's a been a misunderstanding. Imryll is my..." *Your what? Your possession?* He rolled his dry lips inward. "She has come as my companion. Our relationship may be built on a different tradition than yours, but she is no less committed to me."

Marius flicked a look behind them. "Does this commitment include her guard?"

"I don't understand."

Marius grinned and winked before rotating in his saddle, a feat Torian was certain he himself was incapable of. "Princess, are you and your knight faring well?"

Torian heard no response. He dared not move for risk of falling off entirely.

"Ah. Well I see you are in strong, capable hands. Perhaps Syr Wynter will consider releasing you sometime before we return. Riding is *truly* freeing." Marius turned back. "Your Grace, am I understanding correctly that your Queens' Guard is there to satisfy your...*chosens* so that you do not have to be in five places at once?"

Fire returned to Torian's face. "You misunderstand completely, Lord Quintus."

"To fluster them then? Perhaps to ready them for you?"

"I'm sorry?"

Marius quirked his mouth into a grin. "So you have not observed the princess and her guard behaving like quarreling lovers?"

Torian nearly dropped the reins. "That is not a fair assessment." *Even this infuriating stranger sees it.* "Their relationship is designed to be close...intimate even. That is *not* the same as what you are suggesting."

Marius lifted both of his hands. "Was I not supposed to mention it?" He lowered them and leaned over his saddle toward Torian. "Is it a secret? I can keep secrets, Your Grace. I rather enjoy them."

Imryll flicked her gaze at Syr Wynter's hand, still holding her horse's reins. His attention was aimed forward, held in place by stubborn purpose. He rode in silence, and she was grateful for it. She had nothing to say to him anymore. He wouldn't be her problem for much longer.

She could still feel his handprint on her hips…his—

No. *No.* There was a thin line between hate and desire, and she'd never want a man who could so easily waver between the two.

Before she left forever, she'd tell Torian everything. She'd tried, on the ship, but the captain's interruption had snapped her from her daze long enough to realize she couldn't burden Torian until he'd made a successful deal with Lord Quintus. The least she could do was not make it harder.

Imryll listened to the conversations ahead and behind her. Marius handled Torian effortlessly, while Clarisan and Marcelina playfully sparred. She only caught pieces of each conversation, enough to know Torian was woefully outmatched and Clarisan had finally met someone capable of holding their own against her.

The Quintuses had started the game long before Torian and his retinue pulled into port.

Even if Imryll wanted to ride up and bail Torian out, her dark knight had her wrapped in his fists like a gaoler.

It was just as well, for Imryll needed her full wits to map the path in her mind. Marius had said it was one way out of Whitechurch, but she hadn't fully grasped what that could mean until he stopped at the town gates and pointed.

Freedom.

It wasn't just a dream anymore. She saw the potential stretch before her, set between the golden gates that she'd remember forevermore as the sigil of liberty. She'd leave in the middle of the night, when everyone was asleep, and ride until she was swaying in the saddle. She didn't even need to know where she was going. Her knowledge of the realm was grossly inadequate, but *anywhere* would be better than Duncarrow.

By the time they'd realize she was gone, it would be too late.

Imryll stroked Enzi's mane with a grin. She bit her lip to bury a laugh and felt Syr Wynter's scrutiny wash over her from her right. She refused to look up and give him the satisfaction.

Whatever power he had over her was gone.

For the first time in her life, Imryll had a way forward, and there was nothing—no one—capable of stopping her.

Torian was still figuring out how to safely dismount when he watched Marius rush to Imryll's side and hold out his hands. She looked only slightly unsure, flashing a look at her knight—her *knight*—before pulling her leg over the side and falling into the lord's arms.

Marius held her a second too long. Marcelina laughed and rolled her eyes at Clarisan, a little inside joke that only made Torian angrier.

Marius dusted his hands down Imryll's arms with a slow smile. "Next time you'll ride with me, Princess. I don't think you need anyone holding your reins anymore, do you?"

"I do not," Imryll answered. She made a polite step to the side, out of his reach. "And I would like that, Lord Quintus."

"Marius. You wound me with formalities."

"Marius," Imryll said. The word rolled off her tongue like something forbidden.

Torian started to speak up, but the sight of Syr Wynter's hard look stayed him. The knight's mouth wrinkled, his eyes pinching at the corners. His glare was trained on the lord who had already overstepped his place with Imryll.

Wynter's protectiveness should have made him a valuable ally for Torian, but Torian knew better.

Syr Wynter wasn't dismantling Lord Quintus in his mind from a place of duty.

He was sizing up the man who was threatening his claim.

Clarisan stepped to Torian's side. "I know what you're thinking," she whispered. "Let it go. For now, let it go."

205

"Tonight!" Marius exclaimed with an enthusiastic hand clap. He waved Steward Oakenwell over, who had just joined them. "You're all invited to a private supper in my quarters—the six of us and Francis here, who tells me he'd love to get to know Lady Clarisan better."

Oakenwell looked at Clarisan briefly before lowering his gaze to the side.

"We'll be discussing business then?" Torian asked, moving away from his sister before he could see her reaction to the Oakenwell revelation.

"Of course, Your Grace." Marius looked at Imryll. "And then we'll reward ourselves with even more pleasures."

SIXTEEN

A WILLING DISCIPLE

Drazhan was relegated to the back of the room, shoved into a corner with Janus and several of the Rhiagain guards. Oakenwell hovered nearby, his hand on his sword hip as he excitedly explained his role as head of the Quintus Guard. The Rhiagain guards and Janus looked impressed, but Drazhan didn't care.

He wished he could apply the same indifference to watching Marius Quintus handle Imryll like a collectible doll. The cheeky lord had set a place for her at his left. The sisters made small talk across the table about trees and flowers and seasons, while Torian took the chair opposite Marius.

Drazhan was close enough to hear the conversation, not close enough to sever Marius's arm at the shoulder.

Janus's laughter from whatever story Oakenwell was telling died as he leaned in. "Ease your instincts, syr. It's all part of the plan. The queen sees the wisdom in it, and His Grace the Prince agreed to it. The lord would never go far enough to incite a war."

Drazhan doubted the prince had agreed to it.

"Besides," Janus said, "the princess is like an explosive that could detonate with the right pressure, isn't she?"

Drazhan said nothing.

"Cheer up." Janus clapped him on the back. "Relax. Now that the food testers have gone, eat! Our presence isn't even needed, so take the night off." He waggled a finger. "Go wherever it is you go in your head when you tire of speaking to people."

Drazhan shifted his eyes toward Janus.

"You think I don't know you disappear from time to time?"

Drazhan was debating a rebuttal when he caught Marius running his fingers up and down Imryll's half-bare back in slow, lazy strokes as he charmed the table with a story about his recent trip to the Northerlands to hunt mythical snowbeasts. Imryll's shoulders pinched back in response, but the lord didn't stop speaking or caressing.

Something hard and dangerous clenched inside of Drazhan.

"I'm inclined at this point to agree with the majority on this one. The Northerland men made them up to protect their little raven sorcerers in the mountains and keep foreigners away." Marius shook his head. "They needn't have bothered, for the cold was enough to send me home!"

Everyone laughed, except Torian and Drazhan.

"Surely it cannot be as cold as Duncarrow and the cursed wind that takes men to sea," Clarisan said. She fingered the base of her wine glass.

"There's wind, Lady Clarisan," Marius said, his voice lowering in tone. "And then there's *snow*."

"Brother exaggerates greatly," Marcelina said with a long-suffering sigh. "We get snow here in the Easterlands as well."

Marius's hand stopped moving, but he left his fingers in the middle of Imryll's back. "I'm sorry, Marcel, have you been to the Northerlands?"

"No, nor do I care to," she replied with a smirk at Clarisan. "We have all we need right here."

"Their snow is not our snow. The men of the north must be part beast to be able to survive it. For most of them, it never goes away." He shuddered. His hand spurred to life again, causing Imryll to twist.

Calm. Steady. Lord Quintus can finish what you started with her. It's all the same if you arrive at the same ending.

Imryll's squirming continued, though more subtle. She'd turned her discomfort to her feet, tapping her slippers against the legs of her chair.

"Perhaps, then, there is an even more compelling reason for the crown to ally with the Easterlands and not, say, the Northerlands. Or the Westerlands." Torian's careful smile appeared, but his eyes remained orbs of ice. "Or even the Southerlands, though they would, of course, be a last resort."

Clarisan flashed her brother a warning look. "What the prince is trying to say—"

"What I said is what I meant. We're here to discuss the joining of our guard, and the building of the first religious institution in the realm. As Lord Quintus already has the monopoly on magic and education, perhaps he already has more than enough." Torian pushed his glass out and folded his hands atop the table.

Clarisan choked out a breathy exhale. She drained her wine and shifted her eyes toward her lap.

"Ah, there you are, Your Grace. I thought you were all pleasantry, no sting." Marius extracted his hand from Imryll and leaned in.

Drazhan breathed out. *Either meditate or join the guards' trite discussion.*

"I can employ whatever tactic you prefer, Lord Quintus, but I'm here to either form an alliance or eliminate the possibility of one."

Imryll's back straightened. She shifted her attention from one sparring man to the other.

"Is this your first negotiation, Your Grace?" Marius asked. He sank back in his chair, holding his hands out. "I can only assume so, from your eagerness to move right to the unpleasantness of legalities and contracts. But here in the Easterlands…Nay, in most of the realm, a man seeks to understand another man before jumping into bed with him."

Marcelina snickered.

A deep-red flush clawed up from Torian's neck. Drazhan wondered if Janus had seen it, if he even cared, with how caught up he was in Oakenwell's stories.

"Into bed?" Torian dragged his palm down his chin. "Seems to me it's my wife you're trying to jump into bed with."

"She's not your wife, Your Grace." Marius lowered his hands to the table and cocked his head toward Imryll. "Are you, Princess?"

Janus stopped laughing. He turned toward the table, coiling tight.

"Shall we start over?" Clarisan asked. Her voice shook. "This wine is—"

"Imryll." Torian gripped the table's edge and started to stand. He hovered, his nose flaring and eyes wide. "We're leaving."

"This is not good," Janus murmured. Oakenwell had ceased his storytelling, and the other guards were staring too.

Imryll's feet stopped pattering. She ignored Torian's demanding stare and spun in her chair toward Marius. "I feel we owe you an apology, Lord Quintus."

"Imryll!" Torian slapped his hands on the table.

"Tor," Clarisan whispered, cautioning.

Marcelina watched the tense exchange with increasing delight.

Janus went for his sword, but Drazhan waved a hand low to stay him.

Imryll fixed her stare on Marius. "I know we have come to you with what, to us, seems like a deal no man could refuse. I thought the same before we set sail for the Easterlands. When you are as sheltered as the prince and I have been, your perspective is limited to the rocks and shore that have set the boundaries for your entire life."

"Imryll. Stop speaking. We're leaving. *Now.*" Torian stood and waved a furious hand toward the back of the room, snapping his fingers. "Janus!"

"Tor," Clarisan said again, less fearful. She watched Imryll with a curious look.

Marius trailed a finger along Imryll's shoulder, but she snaked a hand up and clapped it atop his. She peeled it away and set it on his other hand.

"Not so sheltered that I would mistake your lust for anything more flattering," Imryll said. "I was brought here to entice you, but I want to be sure our expectations are aligned…" She drew a short breath. "I have no intention of jumping into bed with you, Lord Quintus."

"Marius."

"Marius," Imryll said with a slow smile. "But I *will* apologize on behalf of the crown."

Drazhan shifted, listening raptly.

"Imryll, what are you *doing*?" Torian demanded. "Janus!"

Drazhan sliced another hand low. He flicked his eyes toward Janus's, but the other man already understood the better choice was to wait.

"I'm listening," Marius said. He glanced at his sister and then back at Imryll. "Have a seat, Your Grace. I would like to hear what the princess has to say."

Clarisan communicated with her brother in quick, hard facial tics. He lowered to his chair, but perched on the end of it with a furious glare.

Imryll cast a glance at her lap and then back at Marius. "I thought we were coming here to bestow a great honor upon the Easterlands. But someone close to me explained things differently, and it opened my eyes. I am not so set in my beliefs that they cannot be changed."

"What is she doing?" Janus whispered.

Drazhan pressed a finger to his mouth and inched closer.

211

"The Guardians belong to this realm, and we have not...Well, we have not spent adequate time understanding them, or you. And yet we want to build an institution in *our* name, to honor *your* gods. I see the audacity in this choice now, and I would like to amend our offer."

"Imryll, you have no...You cannot..." Torian blubbered in angry confusion.

"Princess, perhaps we should discuss this and reconvene later," Clarisan said.

Imryll kept her eyes on Marius. "We will build the reliquary here, Marius, but it will become a place of learning as well as worship. Duncarrow will send their own children for education so that future generations do not possess the ignorance of the present one. We will partner with you on every detail." She wrung her hands in her lap. Her chest swelled with a sigh and she continued. "As for me, I am a willing disciple of whatever tutelage you are willing to offer me."

Drazhan held his breath. He saw others do the same, but their reasons were not his.

Someone close to me explained things differently, and it opened my eyes.

Marius rolled his head back and to the side, studying her. He nodded to himself. Silence blanketed the room, covering the anticipation of everyone watching Marius and Imryll negotiate.

"Then allow me to reciprocate your candor and honesty, Princess," he said at last. "I never intended to sign this deal, for the very reasons you've just stated. I invited you and your prince here so that I might meet our future king and queen and size them up." He reached forward and fingered one of Imryll's curls. "I'm still deciding who our king will be, but he has chosen a most impressive queen."

"My words come with no expectation of a return compliment, Marius."

"The only true compliments are the ones given without expectation," he answered. "And I like what you said, Princess. Or can I call you Imryll?"

"You may not," Torian said through clenched teeth.

"For his sake," Marius said with a curt nod and a wink, "let's stick with princess. I like what you said, and that respect for our culture and beliefs is front of mind for all my people. I'm interested."

Torian settled into his seat, nearly slinking off of it. Clarisan exhaled.

Drazhan realized his heart had softened toward Imryll, and he forced the weakness back where it belonged.

Someone close to me explained things differently, and it opened my eyes. She didn't mean it. She was just cunning enough to know she could use it to get what she wanted.

"I'll want to see Belcarrow first, of course," Marius said. "The few Rhiagain guards you've brought with you are impressive, but I need to see their training camp, the conditions they live in. The Quintus Guard dine like kings and sleep as well as princes. They are gods here, in their own way, and I would not send them anywhere that did not meet these standards."

"*We* don't sup like kings, and we sleep on cots," one of the Rhiagain guards muttered.

"Of course," Imryll said. "Just as we needed to see your land to know if it was the right fit for our build, we invite you eagerly to ours."

"I'll send word to Duncarrow," Clarisan said. "We'll begin preparations."

Torian should have been the one speaking but wore the defeated, stunned look of a man who had just returned from war.

"But I do have one more condition of my own," Marius said.

Imryll gestured for him to continue.

He planted a finger under her chin and tilted it. "Tomorrow, we are holding a ball in your honor. But I find I cannot bear to watch you in another man's arms while you fill his head with your delectable wisdom. So you will spend the night in mine."

Clarisan clamped a hand atop Torian's before he could leap forward.

Drazhan ground his boots against the stone floor. *This is what you wanted.* A storm brewed in his chest. *Let it go.* His heartbeat pulsed in his eyes. *Let it go.*

"Marius, I am not—" Imryll's words were clipped by Marius's thumb brushing along her mouth.

"Not like that, Princess," he said. "I simply mean that for the few hours we are all dancing and laughing and eating in front of all of Arboriana, you are mine." He leaned in and pressed his lips to her cheek. "And I am yours."

Torian's head shook. His mouth parted as he clearly readied a rebuttal, but Imryll was faster.

"I accept," she said. Her fidgeting hands, buried in her lap, brought Drazhan back to the day in the Sky Dungeon.

"Wonderful." Marius released her and sat back. "Time to eat."

Torian cut to the right without even a good-bye, following his guards to his apartments. He hadn't said a word since supper, but his rigid posture, flaring nose, and flexing hands spoke for him.

Let him be furious, Imryll thought, watching him storm off. He'd almost thrown away his entire future because he couldn't keep his emotions under control. To save the deal, she'd had to set aside her own.

She'd saved *him,* and all he cared about was his childish jealousy.

Imryll huffed and went to the left, following Drazhan across the bridge to her own apartments. When they stepped inside, she kicked off her slippers and released a long, hard breath.

She followed it with a laugh. The force of it caused her to sway, and she braced herself on a post. She didn't know where it had come from or why, only that it felt right, a release of energy she wasn't supposed to have.

"I suppose you're proud of yourself," Syr Wynter muttered. He unlatched his sword belt and laid it beside the chaise he'd claimed as a bed.

"Ah, more wisdom from you? I've had about all I can take." Imryll released the post and brushed past him and into her sumptuous bedchamber.

A shadow fell over her, and she turned around and saw Syr Wynter standing in her doorway, his hand propped on the frame.

"I'm not in the mood, Syr Wynter." She growled her words through clenched teeth. Too many emotions competed for priority, with no clear winner: angst, fear, loathing, sadness, regret. She had nothing left to give him or anyone. All she wanted was to race to the stables and leave with Enzi and never look back, but she had to stay through the celebration to keep Lord Quintus happy, for Torian's sake.

Syr Wynter flicked his tongue to the corner of his mouth and shook his head in disgust. Then he lowered his hand and left.

Dark heat rushed up from Imryll's feet. Impulse forced her to follow him, and she stormed into the sitting room, where he was staring at the balcony curtains.

"Is misery and loneliness all you know?" she asked. Her voice rasped, her energy depleted.

He didn't respond. She couldn't see his face to know if her words had landed.

"You know all the right ways to hurt me," she said and nodded to herself with a deep, rumbling laugh. "So let's find yours, eh?"

Silence.

"Is it your honor? What if I said you had none?"

Nothing.

"Hmm, your skill then? We already know you can do magic. Did you glamour your way to winning the top guard position?"

No reaction to that either, except the twitch of a finger.

"Shall I insult your mother?"

215

Her dark knight shifted from one foot to another.

"Your sister?"

Syr Wynter's shoulders lifted, stiffening.

"Getting warmer, am I?"

He opened and closed his hands. Turned. The storm in his eyes when they met hers made her want to retreat. "Now I understand why your prince won't touch you."

Imryll recoiled. "You speak like a man wounded."

He narrowed his eyes and stepped closer to her. "What would you know about wounds, Princess?"

"I know you were listening the night of the choosing." She pressed on even though everything inside of her screamed to walk away, to leave him to his misery. "So I know you know it was me who couldn't fulfill my duty."

"Should your failure surprise me?"

Imryll thrust a hand toward the door. "I will not defend myself to you, Syr Wynter. But I am either…" She braced against a swell of emotion threatening to steal her words. "I am either a chosen who cannot rise to duty or one who just saved the Rhiagain crown because the prince could not rise to his. When a man decides his own fate or steps up when others could not, is he given the same appraisal? Are his actions called failures?"

He shook his head at his feet with angry bemusement. "You don't think I know what you were doing in there?"

Imryll held her hands out. "Can there be another interpretation than the one I just offered? Did we not come here to sway the lord to our needs?"

He crossed his arms and moved his gaze to the wall. "You can't stand that I saw you for who you are. It's not enough for you to be one of them. You have to pretend you're not."

"What?"

"Don't act stupid, Imryll. You're a lot of things, but you aren't that."

The cold use of her name kept her from responding right away. "Everything I said was true." She steadied herself with a deep breath, running both of her hands through her thick hair. "We aren't born with all the right knowledge. I can't change what I've learned thus far, but I can continue learning. What you said last night, it...I've never felt so ignorant, so small. But it made me want to do better. To be better." Imryll took several bold steps toward him, enjoying the wince pulling at his cheeks when she neared him. "*That* is the difference between you and me, Syr Wynter. You assume you already know everything there is to know. I'm painfully aware of just how much I don't."

Syr Wynter closed his eyes. The cords in his neck flexed. "Just go to bed."

"Go to bed?" Imryll burst out laughing. "Says the man who followed me when I tried and stood in the doorway glaring!"

"Go. To. Bed." ·

Imryll folded her hands over her chest with a smirk. "No."

He rolled his lips inward, then outward. "Go to bed, Imryll."

"You want me to go to bed, *Drazhan*? Say it to me like you did in the Sky Dungeon. In my head."

His mouth parted again before closing. "No."

"Why? Did it scare you when you discovered I can hear you?"

"Go to—"

"*Make me.*" Imryll's heart pounded as soon as the words were out. The hard flash in his eyes when he snapped his head upward doubled her fear.

Syr Wynter stormed toward her and scooped her into his arms before she could get away. She wiggled and swatted but was no match for the bulging muscles pinning her legs, curved under her back and over the side of one breast.

He marched her into her bedchamber and tossed her onto the bed, where she rolled once before drawing up on her hands and knees in horrified indignance.

Syr Wynter's eyes met hers in silent challenge. She held his steeled gaze, panting through her bewilderment. What would he do if she clambered back out of the bed? If she planted herself in front of him and dared him to try it again? Would he pin her to the bed, hands over her head, exhaling the heat of his filthy words against her neck? Would he…

Imryll buried the fantasy. It belonged to the past.

The present offered only confusion.

And a dark knight who had *almost* hidden the desire in his eyes before hardening them again.

"Bed," he said once more and then was gone, leaving her alone to process whatever had just happened.

The screech of a large, loud bird woke Imryll. She slithered under the covers, which caught on her sweat-covered skin. It wasn't from heat, not with the gentle breeze coming through the wispy curtains providing the perfect temperature.

With her pulse humming, she looked around the dark room that was not her own. It took a moment for her to remember where she was and why. How far from Duncarrow she was, and how close to freedom.

Syr Wynter hadn't bothered her again, which was both a relief and not. His physical presence made her feel safe, even if she couldn't trust him.

Imryll spotted a pitcher of water across the room. Her throat prickled with relief, but before she could leave the bed, her head swam with the woozy promise of a vision. She tried to fight back, but she was too tired to oppose the takeover and had only enough time to sigh.

I'm cold. Very, very cold. Colder than I've ever been on Duncarrow, but it's more than that. It's a different kind of cold. It's settling into my bones and threatening to never leave. My fear tells me there isn't enough fire in the realm to warm me from this.

I'm standing in a courtyard. I don't recognize it. Men are working, making things with their hands, their tools. Their breaths swirl in the air, but they're bundled in furs so thick, they don't seem to notice the cold.

I look down and see myself wearing the same, fur woven into more fur woven into leather. It's so thick, I cannot see my feet.

My attention is called to the left, to a covered area filled with hay. A child is there. A boy. He beckons me, and I have no control of the body I'm in, so I follow.

The boy cannot be older than thirteen or so. As I approach, I see we are of similar height, me being a hair shorter, which means I am either a smallish man, an average woman, or a child myself. My gut tells me I am the last.

The other boy speaks to me. He digs a sword out from where it is stuck in the hay and uses it to point farther into the covered area. I don't understand, but whoever I am follows anyway.

The other boy leans over a barrel and withdraws another sword. It's dull, the metal flat and lifeless, but he hands it to me, hilt first. It's so dull that gripping the blade didn't even break his skin. I take it, and from the authoritative nod he gives me, I know what this is. He's teaching me. From the raised flesh on my arms and the chill passing down my spine, I sense I am afraid but also excited. Something flashes through a mind that is not my own: I've been waiting for this.

He's still speaking, but silence is all there is. He seems annoyed with me as I stare at the sword but don't raise or swing it.

Then he throws his own sword into the hay and raises his fists. I cannot hear the challenge that comes from his mouth, but I read it in his narrowed eyes: if I will not fight with a sword, I must learn to use my hands.

I back up until I hit the wall. Something about this request scares me far more than wielding a sword, and hot tears burn my eyes. I don't want him to see this, but he's walking over now, and there's nothing—

Imryll pitched forward in a desperate, rocking gasp that tore through the quiet.

In the other room, Syr Wynter's boots hit the floor with a thud.

She sorted the room into items—bureau, cloak hook, table, chairs—until her breathing slowed and her mind returned to

219

reality. Unlike her other visions, this one had been harder to leave. It met her resistance and pulled her in anyway, then kept her longer. She even *wanted* to stay, to know why the boy was afraid… what the other boy would do about it.

Like her last vision, nothing about it felt like Ilynglass.

But it must have been, for Imryll belonged to that world, not this one.

She closed her eyes and tried to fall back asleep.

SEVENTEEN
A SPLENDOR OF LIGHT AND SOUND

The courtyard was stuffed full of revelers. Hundreds, Torian thought as they descended the Golden Stair with his sister, Imryll, and their guards. He caught small peeks of the festivities on the way down, but then he saw there were far more celebrants swelling past the courtyard, beyond the gleaming gates of Arboriana.

They were faces he didn't know, but they all knew him. Watched him in wonder. Bowed in reverence.

When he reached the bottom, he glanced the way they'd come, wondering if it would feel any more familiar, but it was still a stunning confusion to his mind how they'd built an entire castle into the broad trees of Rushwood Forest.

The assault to his senses felt like a barrage of arrows raining in from all sides, a splendor of light and sound. Luminescent orbs by the thousands were strung into the trees, lighting the otherwise-dark night. Sweet, beckoning melodies strummed from massive stringed instruments larger than the musicians playing them, all children.

The Quintus colors appeared everywhere, from the crimson velvet centering every step to the gold spun through chairs, tables, and poles. Dozens of couples danced across stones littered with red rose petals dipped in glittering gold.

It was excessive. Stunning. All of it was designed to awe the Duncarrow visitors.

Marcelina stepped beside him in a radiant dress resembling ice after a wintertide squall. She was unfairly beautiful, like her brother, possessed of exquisiteness beyond what one person required. The Quintus siblings were orphans, but Torian had seen the paintings of the late Lord and Lady Quintus, who themselves had set a high bar for attractiveness. Neither Marius nor Marcelina were married, but Torian had no doubt they'd find a partner just as gorgeous to continue the pattern.

How was he supposed to compete against men like Marius? Like Drazhan, who was similarly stunning in a way that felt more foreign than the sorcerers skulking the halls of Duncarrow.

If he were looking for sympathy, he'd be in short supply, especially where his sister was concerned.

I tried to be kind, Tor, but that clearly hasn't worked. So I'll say it another way. Grow up. Be a man. Imryll did what you could not, and punishing her for it would not only be abhorrent but illogical. The pretty lord wants to dance with your First Chosen all night. Let him. He wants to fuck her, ah, then we have a problem. Until then…Be a man. No. No, be a king.

Clarisan peeled off with Steward Oakenwell, hand in his as they moved to join the throngs of dancers. Torian caught her delighted giggle when she passed, and it almost pulled one from him too. When had he last heard his sister giggle? Had he ever?

"Well? Your assessment, Your Grace?" Marcelina stretched a hand to her opposite arm and drummed her thin fingers against the sparkled fabric of her dress.

"Are there words for such beauty?" Torian said, lighter than he felt.

"In the Old Languages," Marcelina said smoothly. "But your father prefers we have one central language, and so, naturally, we chose the least imaginative one."

Torian tilted his head toward her. Unlike his mother and father, he only knew the realm language, which was true of everyone else in his generation as well. But not even the elders spoke the language of the old sceptre. He'd only heard it in whispers or the occasional cursing. "Do you not think a central language leads to less confusion? Better communication across the realm?"

Marcelina's delicate mouth curved into a smile. "Of course it does. The king is infinite in his wisdom."

Her sarcasm lashed him, but the feeling wasn't entirely unpleasant.

"Shall we dance, Your Grace?" she asked. Her dark eyes fluttered in anticipation.

"I, uh…" His shoulders clenched when Imryll and Marius appeared at his other side. Imryll wore a smile so big, he couldn't discern the meaning behind it. But as he drank the rest of her in, dragging his gaze over the emerald gown that swept down off her shoulders, lifted her bosom, and exposed her soft tan flesh, it was no longer desire he felt but the returning sting of rejection.

Imryll turned toward him with a deferential nod. "I was hoping you and I might dance before I have to fulfill my promise to Lord Quintus."

Torian held up his arm linked to Marcelina. "I have my own dance partner."

A light dimmed behind Imryll's sparkling eyes. "Ah, of course. Lady Marcelina."

"Princess," Marcelina replied with a curtsy.

"Later then?" Imryll's voice lowered to a whisper. "Can I come to your apartments tonight?"

The offer filled him with heat, but reality cooled the sensation. Others around them would take her words the way he *wanted* them to take them, and that was the problem. She didn't want to be with him. She wanted reassurances, to know things were all right between them after she'd practically thrown herself at Marius and humiliated him in the doing.

That's not fair. It's not fair and you know it.

Nor is a broken heart.

Torian straightened and projected his voice loud enough for not only their present company but anyone in the vicinity. "That's generous, Princess Imryll, but your services will not be needed tonight. If you'll excuse me."

Torian led Marcelina down the rest of the steps with a jerk that almost pulled her off her feet.

They fell into formation when they reached the courtyard. One hand held Marcelina's, the other scooped around her back. He moved the two of them farther and farther from the others, stepping faster than the rhythm called for.

"Are you all right?" Marcelina asked, peeling away a bit. "Your Grace?"

"Fine," Torian muttered and pulled her back in. "Better now."

"May I make an observation?"

Torian caught Imryll, led by Marius, wearing a look so crestfallen, his heart broke again.

"You're punishing her," Marcelina said. Her small hand twitched in his tight grip. "For serving you."

"You and Clarisan are too similar," he muttered. He lost sight of Imryll but spotted her guard disappearing into a group of dancers near the refreshment table.

"Your sister is wise, Your Grace. She can be a good counselor to you. Here in the Easterlands, women are placed in leadership roles, some even having titles in the peerage they earned themselves, not from a husband or father."

"How progressive."

"You don't agree?"

He did agree but felt far too foul to be reasonable. "If Imryll wants to throw herself at your brother, I'll not stop her."

"Throw herself? But..." Marcelina shook her head. "Forgive me, Your Grace, but I thought you brought her for him."

Torian pulled his attention back to her.

Marcelina clipped her exhale. "You have five chosens. You offer one as part of the deal. We were surprised it was your First Chosen, of course, but it only emphasizes your willingness to negotiate."

"Marcelina, what are you suggesting?"

"The king sent word ahead of your arrival, outlining the terms of the agreement. We already knew before you made your offer."

Torian let go of her waist to mop the sweat beading around his temples. "What offer?"

"The reliquary and a chosen, in exchange for a thousand of our men sent to Belcarrow to begin training immediately."

Torian caught Janus standing off to the side. The guard nodded. Torian tried to nod back, but his head swam with confusion.

No.

Betrayal.

"The king offered one of my chosens to Lord Quintus?"

"Well, not *forever*." Marcelina giggled nervously. "But for the duration of this visit, yes. And also for any visits my brother makes to Duncarrow."

"With the expectation…"

Marcelina stopped dancing and stepped back. "Did you not know?"

"Of course I knew," Torian murmured, flustered and blubbering his words, which never turned to anything coherent. "I just…I don't think the princess knows."

"Well, she'll know soon enough, won't she?" Marcelina pressed toward him again. "But don't worry yourself too much, Your Grace. My brother would never cross a line. He would never do anything the princess did not consent to. He's a gentleman, not an animal."

Her words should have eased him, but they didn't, because he couldn't predict what Imryll would want anymore. Everything he thought he knew about her had been wiped away after the Choosing.

Marcelina's sweet breath, which smelled faintly of cinnamon, warmed his neck. "Let me take this from your mind, Your Grace." Her lips grazed his flesh, causing a throb between his legs. "By morning, I'll have solved at least some of your problems for you."

Imryll was mesmerized. Everything from the way the stars danced in the trees—not stars but magic, Marius explained as he led her to the center of the courtyard—to the scents of rich meats foreign to her constitution…to the music, softer and lovelier than what they'd heard from the coastal Southerland band brought to Duncarrow. It sounded like the voices of the gods themselves—or the Guardians, but she felt a stab of shame even thinking about them.

Marius stopped and pulled her close, one hand laced through hers, the other looped around her waist. She was gawking at the sights and sounds when he began stepping in time to the trill of the large instruments. Imryll recovered her footing and tried to follow his lead through the dance, which was close enough to how she'd danced with her brother that it softened the edges of her nerves.

Imryll looked up and into his eyes. He smiled down at her and flicked a circular nod toward their surroundings.

"Do you like it, Princess?"

"Do I like it?" Did she *like* it? How could anyone not like beauty? It was excessive, but not enough to mar the way sound and color blurred into magic.

"The Easterlands are known for their showmanship," he said with a short laugh. "The other three Reaches are far more practical. But is there not joy in beauty? Does this not fill your lungs with air and your heart with gladness?"

Imryll watched Marius speak, the way his eyes sparkled as he ran through his assessment of the night he'd put together for them. He'd been aiming to impress, but more was there. He loved his home. His people. His customs. He seemed to want her to love them too.

Her eyes caught first Torian dancing with Marcelina and then she saw Drazhan, coiled with tension as he leaned against a column with his arms crossed. Neither man was near enough to remind her of her failures.

Tonight, at least, she could be whomever she wanted.

"Tell me about your beloved Whitechurch, Lord Quintus."

Marius's grin broadened. "You want to know about my home?"

She glided in his arms as he swept them through the center of the courtyard. Although she was aware of the eyes following their movements, for once she didn't care. "If you're inclined to tell me, yes."

He screwed the corner of his mouth into a playful smirk. "Then you'll need to start calling me Marius, Princess."

Imryll laughed and shook her head. "What will others think if I'm overly familiar with you?"

"Would it be so wrong for them to believe a woman enjoys my company?"

"You know it isn't that simple."

"Nothing is," he said, nodding in agreement. "But I hope you know, Imryll, that no matter the choices others have made on your behalf, you are no one's possession. You don't belong to the prince, nor even the king. How can you, when they won't even call what you have a marriage? When they won't even bind the prince to you under the eyes of their gods?"

Imryll was too taken aback to speak at first. She took a moment to gather herself. Nothing he'd said was novel; everything was a mirror of her own thoughts. But though this man was not her enemy, she couldn't be sure he was her ally either. And she wasn't a springtide maiden, oblivious to the dangers of men and their questions. "We all have our customs," she said, deciding to land somewhere safe.

"You defend this one, yet I sense it bothers you too," Marius said. His palm was warm and comforting, nestled into the curve of her lower back.

"No society is a paradise, Lord Quintus."

227

He grimaced at the use of his formal name but picked up his smile again. "No, but should that not be the aim of any leader?"

"Above security? Prosperity?"

"Is there no intersection?"

Imryll shook her head. "Of course there *could* be, but a leader must prioritize the safety and perpetuity of his people before he can address their happiness."

"You say that with confidence," Marius said.

Imryll again checked for both Torian and Drazhan. Neither had moved out of sight. "Everything has a priority. And without a population to make happy, what is happiness but a fleeting ideal that has roots without soil?"

"Do you enjoy philosophy?" Marius cocked his head. She saw in his earnest eyes that he wasn't mocking her.

"I would if I could get my hands on more books," she said boldly. He'd probably offer to send her some, but she wouldn't be there to receive them.

The reminder of her imminent freedom sent a thrill of excitement rippling from her head to her feet.

"So," Marius said with a nod, his eyes to the side in thought, "if I'm to understand your meaning, although you are evidently unhappy about being the prince's concubine—"

"*Chosen*," Imryll stated, correcting him. She hoped it was the last time she had to defend it.

"Chosen," he said with an impertinent grin that said he knew he'd gotten under her skin. "You accept the pragmatism of the arrangement because the need to expand your population is greater than the happiness of the one who has been asked to give up her own desires to see it done?"

"Something like that," Imryll replied. She was struck with the powerful sense that Marius *would* help her if she asked for it. She'd been working up the courage for that very thing. But his circular words, his delight in leading her into traps, made him no different than the other men in her life. What could he offer her beyond a bigger, prettier cage?

She had to do it herself or not at all.

"Sacrifice for the greater good," Marius mused aloud. "Selflessness is valuable in a society that seeks to decide futures for others."

Imryll did another sweep across the courtyard, but she couldn't find Torian. Drazhan was still standing in the same spot but was alert, fixated on something in the distance.

"What's wrong?" Marius asked. His hold on her tightened slightly. "Have I upset you?"

"No. No, you have a right to your opinions, Lord Quintus. I lost myself for a moment is all." She shook her head and searched for a smile. "You were going to tell me about Whitechurch."

"You mean the most profitable city in the whole realm?" he asked, with a twinkle in his eyes. "Well, you already know the universities are here in the Easterlands, and the Sepulchre, of course. But our capital also hosts the kingdom's guildhalls. I can take you to see them if you'd like. All the blacksmiths, silversmiths, clothiers, armorsmiths, they all pay their dues to Whitechurch. In turn, we provide them with the latest research, methods, and—"

They both started when Janus slid in beside them with a wild look. Steward Oakenwell was a pace behind him.

"Janus?" Imryll asked. She again looked for Torian, but he was still missing.

Drazhan joined Janus and the steward.

"Continue dancing, Princess," Janus said. He turned a grimace on Oakenwell and then Syr Wynter. "Lord Quintus. Please."

Marius locked his gaze with hers. Reflecting was the same confusion she felt.

"Listen carefully," Oakenwell said, pretending to look elsewhere. "We've detected a threat against the prince's life."

"What?" Imryll cried. She stepped back, but Marius reeled her in with a tight head shake. The flicker of fear in his eyes set her own ablaze.

"Everything is fine, Princess. We escorted the prince and Lady Marcelina back to his apartments, where they are well guarded."

Imryll buckled in relief. "And the assailants have been apprehended?"

"Not yet," Janus said. "It's why we've come to take you both upstairs as well. We need to be very inconspicuous, but we cannot waste time either. Let's go."

"But if Torian is safe—"

"The threat is not only against the prince," Oakenwell said, with a firm, impatient look. To Marius, he grunted, "The Goldtails again."

"But we imprisoned their leader months ago, Francis. I thought we agreed this was over."

"Goldtails?" Imryll asked. She caught a sudden movement from Syr Wynter.

"Realm loyalists. Anti-Rhiagain. Gold is the opposite color of purple," Marius murmured. He nodded at Oakenwell. "Lead us."

Imryll broke away from Marius right as Janus erupted with geysers of blood. She gasped and skittered back, straight into Drazhan's arms. He pinned her there while she watched in horror as Janus fell to his knees and then pitched forward.

Steel rang out. Screams followed. Oakenwell swung his sword down on the man who'd cut down Janus, and the rest of the world exploded in violence.

"My sword!" Marius cried, his hands slapping his hips. He paused his frenzied gaze on Imryll. "I didn't wear it tonight."

Syr Wynter handed his over. "Take Stormbringer. Go find Lady Clarisan."

"What about you?"

"I don't need it." He tucked Imryll tighter under his arm and nodded into the melee. "Go."

"The princess—"

"I have her."

Imryll's legs gave out as she tried to follow the insanity. She couldn't move, and she didn't want to, because everywhere she looked was blood and screams and terror.

She saw Marius reach Clarisan and rush her up the steps.

Janus dead at Imryll's feet.

Three men wearing the Rhiagain violet bleeding out in the courtyard.

A head rolling across the stones.

And from the corner of her eye, she watched claws gnashing through air, through flesh. More screams rent the air, mixed with the vigorous grunts of Drazhan, who had taken down at least two men already without letting her go.

Imryll whipped her attention to the claws. Claws, yes, that was what they were. It was all they could be, long and sharp and deadly, swirled with red and indigo light. One set crashed through the belly of a man. The force lifted Imryll from her feet.

She looked down, panting, and saw the other set cradling her belly.

Claws.

Where hands should be.

Stormclaw.

They weren't weapons at all.

They were—

"No. Like this," he tells me, but I'm not listening. I don't want to do this, and he knows it. I see in his eyes that he's battling my resistance, but also that he won't give up.

The boy fists his hands again and swings one into an uppercut.

"I'm not like you," I say, and I hope it's true. I can't reach into the memories of whomever I am, but I feel the history driving my fear. The absence of details makes it no less real.

"Do you want to find yourself bloodied in a ditch again? Is that it?"

"No," I say. "No, it's why you're here. You're the fighter."

It occurs to me there's sound. Not silence, not garbled noise, but clear, crisp sound.

"I won't always be here," the boy says with a hard, sad look at the hay. "And I won't be with you at the Hunt—"

Claws tore the air. Blood ran down her face, into her eyes. She felt the viscous trail sliding under her dress, pooling where Syr Wynter's grip was tightest.

Imryll was ripped from his arms with enough force to send bile into her throat. She thrashed and kicked, but another man joined her kidnapper, and in moments, they were running away with her.

"*Drazhan!*" Her scream was cropped by an elbow dug to her throat.

Drazhan growled, his mouth gaped wide in bloodlust as he swung his arm and then himself backward. It stopped in unison with the scream of the man who had pulled Imryll away. Wynter spun and sent a whirlwind of knives into the other one, knocking him from his feet.

Imryll dropped into a crouch. She fought a harsh wave of dizziness from all the movement, all the blood, and—

"What would Father think?" the boy asks me.

"Father already knows I'm a failure," I say. Now I wish I could reach into my memory and know the history behind such a tragic phrase.

"I wasn't born knowing how to do this. I practiced. I learned. I pushed myself through sweat and tears and blood, and I persevered. I survived."

"I'm not you," I say again, using pride as a front for disappointment. "And I never will be."

"Imryll. *Imryll!*"
She was shaking. No, something was shaking her.

"That would be failure. Giving up. Letting the world decide your future instead of you."

"You sound like Father." It's not a compliment.

"Do I? Good. Good, because he knows—"

"Imryll!"

Imryll, you need to listen to me. You need to hear my words. Wake up.

Imryll's knees gave out, but she didn't fall. She was suspended in midair, blood choking her vision, running down her chin and into her mouth. She sputtered and twisted away from the hold, but nothing happened. She didn't move. She couldn't.

Her world upended once more as her legs came up. Drazhan swept her into his arms and burst into a sprint, zigging and zagging through the carnage and leaping over bodies. She turned her face to his chest and tried to breathe, but the cloying copper of blood—blood everywhere—choked her and turned her attempts into tearful screams.

"I have you," he said, panting. "I have you."

"You know what your problem is, brother?"

"Am I allowed only one?" Cynicism drips from my tongue like a bitter draught. I know he's right, but it makes me more determined to fail, not less.

The other boy, my brother, snorts. "Your problem is you look at the world and think you need to mimic what others do. That if you cannot, then you're useless. But the men who have changed this world started by finding a new way. Their own way."

"I don't want to change the world."

My brother sighs. He gestures at the bin. "Then pick up a sword, and let's have another go."

"She's in a trance." Marius leaned over the bed with his hands stretched toward Imryll's face. One of the attendants cutting the blood-soaked dress from her flashed him a scandalized look, and he recalled his hand. "Did you hear me?"

Drazhan stood a pace behind the lord, his arms crossed high over his chest. It was one of the many things he was doing to regain control. He exchanged words for thoughts. Meditations were out; he had to be present.

"Are you seeing this?"

Drazhan craned his neck in a stretch before his muscles could tighten again. His hands were a bloody mess, but he paid no mind to them. It was the blood on Imryll that had his undivided attention. It had congealed in her red curls, crusted along her temples and jawline. It formed the shape of incomplete handprints on her cheeks—*his* handprints. Her gown had borne the brunt of the gore, enough that he couldn't discern whether any of it was hers. He needed the attendants to get the damned dress *off* of her so he could check for wounds.

They cut it away in strips and carried the dark, heavy pieces to a basin and dropped them in one by one, exposing Imryll inch by inch.

"Knight? Wynter?"

Drazhan pointed a nod at the bed. Short of telling the lord to fuck off, the best he could offer was a reminder to watch and listen.

And was *she* listening? Was it a trance or was it something bigger, something worse?

He recalled the way she'd been torn from his arms. The unbridled terror in her eyes as two men had carted her away. *Drazhan!* He cleared his throat and swallowed. *Drazhan!* Whether her desperate cry of his name or his own disconcertment had caused it, he'd done something he'd sworn to himself never to do again.

Drazhan had reached into her mind to calm her.

Imryll, you need to listen to me. You need to hear my words. Wake up.

But she hadn't. Wherever she'd gone, he couldn't reach her.

One of the attendants, her hands covered in blood, sopped Imryll's brow with the back of her sleeve and shook her head at Marius. "I know you said we can't leave until it's done, my lord, but we have no more clean rags. Both basins have run red."

"Then go get more!" Marius commanded, swatting the air. "Go get more, and find out what the bloody Guardians is happening. I need to know Prince Torian is safe, and my sister,

234

and…Find Oakenwell, find…Find *someone* who knows what's going on."

"Yes, my lord." The attendant didn't hide her relief. She whispered to the others, and they skittered behind her and left.

"Go on with them," Drazhan said to Marius. "I have her."

"Leave?" Marius gawped at him. "She shouldn't be alone right now. Look at her."

She's not alone. "She's resting."

"Resting?" Marius reached a hand up and roughed his hair with a fevered laugh. "Right. Right, resting. Not in a trance then?"

Drazhan twisted his mouth into a scowl. *Trance* didn't feel like the right word, but he knew one thing.

Imryll wasn't resting.

She wasn't there at all.

And he'd never find her again with the half-crazed lord mumbling and flitting around the room like an injured bird.

Drazhan! The terror in her eyes…the desperate plea in them, for him—him alone. She'd known he *could* save her, but *would* he?

In her still, filth-caked face, he found no answer.

Drazhan angled away.

For the next hour, he watched from the other side of the room as the attendants finished with Imryll. Her hair was pulled through rags. They stripped her bare and cleansed her flesh. The young women cast suspicious eyes on the men, wondering why they didn't leave or even turn away when the last of the destroyed cloth was peeled away, but they said nothing.

Drazhan had seen her nude before. Sometimes when he touched her—when he *used* to touch her—she enjoyed herself more when unencumbered by the restriction of her elaborate gowns.

He knew the valley of her waist by heart. The smooth expanse of her belly. The hills that sloped into hips, swelling into an ass he'd cupped in his waking hours and dreamed of in his meditations. In his mind, he saw himself standing behind her in front of the window, pulling her hair away and over the front of her shoulder so he could graze his lips along the graceful slope of her neck.

The memories made him sick in juxtaposition with how wilted and damaged she looked lying in her un-waking stasis.

Marius curled next to her in the bed like a grieving lover. The urge to send him sprawling to the floor was almost too great for Drazhan to ignore.

Imryll. Where are you? He inhaled through his nose, chastising himself. Never again, he'd said, and he'd made a liar of himself twice since.

But there was no response. Not a twitch.

Imryll. Imryll. Imryll.

He closed his eyes but didn't sleep.

The attendants left.

Marius disappeared and reappeared. He murmured something about checking on the prince.

He shared news upon his return, but Drazhan didn't care. He didn't care about the weak little prick who was supposed to be the future of a kingdom he knew nothing about. He didn't care about his clever sister or Lady Marcelina or any of them.

Men had died tonight. Good men. All because someone had wanted the prince and his family dead—perhaps as much as, or even more, than Drazhan himself.

Drazhan hadn't thought much of Janus, but the loss weighed on his heart. He'd *seen* something was amiss, and his hesitation cost Janus his life.

And Imryll...

"Syr Wynter? You in there?"

Drazhan's eyes fluttered open to the sight of an agitated Marius snapping his fingers in his face.

Marius stopped and rolled back with a snort. "You're more beast than man, aren't you?"

Yes. Yes I am.

"I've called an emergency meeting with my council. I need to go, but I'll be back as soon as I can." He swung his gaze over his shoulder to Imryll. "At first light. I don't believe it would be prudent to put everyone from Duncarrow in one room, not until we understand the situation and what risks are still out there. I can't send more guards here or station them outside the door. It would be like hanging a sign telling assailants precisely where to find our royal family." He caressed his chin, darted his eyes to the left and right. "I saw what you did tonight. You can protect her? Without help?"

Drazhan nodded, though he doubted Marius had *really* seen, or it would be fear in his eyes, not hope.

Marius sighed at Imryll. She hadn't stirred at all. "I never expected…on my watch, here in Arboriana…" He dug a fist against his sternum. "Neither of you leave until I've confirmed we have all the suspects apprehended and there's no further danger. You understand?"

Drazhan nodded once.

"I need verbal confirmation, Syr Wynter." He closed his eyes and spaced a breath through clenched teeth. "Please."

Drazhan wet his bottom lip with his tongue. "Yes."

Marius bobbed his head in an overlong nod and then left.

Drazhan pushed to his feet and bolted the door behind him.

He looked back.

Imryll slept on.

He hastily tended his own wounds before she could wake and ask him more questions he wouldn't answer. His injuries were nothing too troublesome. Mostly superficial.

Wood screeched on stone when he dragged his chair across the floor and dropped it into place several feet from her bed.

Close enough to hear her soft, uneven breaths.

Not so close that the scent of her could stir more than duty.

He tilted his head back and returned to his meditations.

I'm standing on the hay-covered barn floor, one hand on the hilt of another rusted sword.

I'm also climbing a mountain to see the oracle.

My mind rips me between both places, back and forth, back and forth, but neither vision advances. I am forevermore stuck with my hand on a sword I don't want to swing and my gaze on the top of a mountain I'll never reach.

I'm dizzy. I'm sick. I want to return to myself, but none of my usual tricks work. I'm stuck here, in a form of purgatory.

I surrender to the constant shifts.

What else can I do?

My hand is on a sword, my feet on loose stone. On. And on. Until I've felt both scenes so many times that I wonder if neither vessel made it further than this, and I'm left reliving their final moments over and over.

But I know this isn't true because Oldwin is there, and Oldwin makes it to the White Kingdom.

More sickness. The smell of blood. Screams.

Imryll, you need to listen to me. You need to hear my words. Wake up.

I know this voice, but it's too far away from the two locations demanding my constant presence.

I feel the old, cracked leather of the hilt that had once, perhaps, been a great weapon. Or maybe it never had. Maybe it came from the discard pile of an apprentice blacksmith.

My eyes squint at the sun, still present enough to blind the path up the mountain. The oracle still feels so far away, but never more so than now, when I can't take a single step.

Imryll. Where are you?

"Here!" I cry out, but neither my brother nor Oldwin hear me. My brother eyes the sword bin with heated urgency. Oldwin and the others have their gazes pointed exactly where I do. I'm whomever they believe me to be, not Imryll. In here, I'm never Imryll.

I never realized how much that would upset me until I couldn't return to myself.

Fingers wrapping around old leather. Feet dusting atop loose soil.

I watch the scenes a hundred times.

238

Anxiety turns to annoyance, which turns to peace.
And then my brother says, "Go on then. It's time."
Oldwin says, "Final push."

Imryll turned her head on the pillow. Her lips moved in soundless replies to the last things said to her. But she wasn't standing on hay anymore, nor climbing a mountain. A breeze blew into the room, carrying remnants of the sweet-and-spicy flora of the Easterlands.

She was in the bed she'd slept in only once before.

She connected the fact to everything that had happened since then. She'd risen late, and a midday meal had been sent to her apartments for her to enjoy alone.

No, not alone.

With the lord. With Marius.

He'd talked. She'd listened, searching for ways to keep him satiated without sacrificing herself—for information that could contribute to the success of her escape.

Then they'd danced. He'd flirted and she'd…Well, she'd demurred, hadn't she? The whole time she'd been excruciatingly aware of everyone watching. Of where Torian was and Syr Wynter was and—

Imryll inhaled a shaky breath. She slapped both of her hands onto the blanket for purchase and scraped her way to a sitting position.

Boots slapped the floor, causing her to cry out.

"You're awake." Drazhan.

"Where…" Imryll felt blood trickle down her neck, and she clasped both of her hands there, but the flesh was unsoiled. Her mouth tasted of copper, but her tongue swiped clean lips.

Drazhan shoved to his feet and paced away from the bed. "What do you remember?"

"Nothing. I don't remember, I…" Imryll's hands slid down to her chest and back to the bed. A swimming sensation overcame her, and once more, she struggled to breathe. "Lord Quintus and I were dancing."

"Yes."

"And I saw Torian." Imryll's voice scratched. Her swallow was painful. She looked at the bedside table for anything to quench her thirst, but there was nothing. She cleared her throat. "And then he disappeared."

Drazhan stopped moving. He crossed his arms, faced away. "Go on."

"I don't want to." Fear crept into the spaces around her, the air dancing across her clammy flesh. "Where's Torian? Where's Lord Quintus?"

"The prince is in his apartments with Lady Marcelina. Lord Quintus is dealing with the situation." He unwrapped his arms and turned halfway. "Where did *you* go?"

"Where did I go?" She repeated his question as though she didn't understand, but the sharp, peeling leather still scratched her hands. Her feet were still rooted to the rocky path.

"I know you remember." Drazhan's tone shifted, becoming angry, impatient. "Weak people disappear, Imryll. You are not weak."

She had an urge to laugh, but it wasn't stronger than the one to curl into a ball and cry. It wasn't stronger than her desire to disappear again.

"Why do you care what I remember and don't?" Imryll retorted. With every second, she became more rooted to reality, leaving her visions behind. She couldn't feel the sword anymore. Her feet brushed soft linens, no longer shoved into boots. "Where is everyone?"

"I already told you."

"No," she said, pulling herself higher. "No, you said Torian was in his apartments with Lady Marcelina, which would be a scandal he cannot afford. And that Lord Quintus was dealing with the situation. What does that mean?"

"You know what it means." He slapped a palm on the wall, startling them both. "Dammit, Imryll, you are the most maddening…"

Imryll wanted to defend herself, but first she needed to understand what had prompted his annoyance, which was far more advanced than his usual snorting and glowering.

"Why do you care?" she asked again, as her thoughts struggled to reconcile the gap in her recollections of the evening. She'd seen Torian, and then…Then he'd disappeared. He'd disappeared, and Wynter had disappeared, and Janus…

Blood spurting from his throat.

Swords ringing.

And…and…

Imryll sucked in a scream. She clambered against the headboard, practically climbing the wall as Drazhan watched, doing nothing. Saying nothing. His face was devoid of emotion beyond rapt interest.

"There you are." Drazhan crossed his arms again. "Welcome back."

"Janus! Janus is dead?" Imryll squinted her eyes repeatedly and tossed her head as she battled the rolling return of the night. "I need to go to Torian." She ripped the blanket aside and leaped onto the floor. "Take me to the prince."

Drazhan lifted his brows and turned away again. "I cannot."

"You cannot?" Imryll patted the thin chemise someone had changed her into. She scanned the room for something else to wear, something proper.

"Until your lord returns—"

"He's not *my* lord—"

"Until he returns," Drazhan said, in the same tone people used to placate a child, "and confirms the danger is subdued, we stay here."

"What danger? What *happened?*" Imryll continued searching for something to wear and found a heavy, violet cloak bearing the Rhiagain sigil, crossed swords. She didn't know who it belonged to and didn't care. She slipped it on, grunting as she pushed her arms through.

"Janus told you what happened, right before he was slain in front of you."

A hard knot traveled from her chest into her belly. She'd known Janus her whole life. Could he really be dead? Murdered? "Why are you…Why are you acting like this? So flippant? Like it doesn't matter?"

Drazhan took a single step forward. "When the fighting broke out, you went somewhere."

"Went somewhere? What does that mean?"

"In your mind. You disappeared."

Imryll snorted. "I did not." She turned her face to keep him from reading the lie.

"I want to know where you went."

"I didn't go *anywhere*—"

He stormed across the room and grabbed her by her shoulders. "Don't. Lie. Imryll, I *called* to you."

She tried to tear away from him, but she was stuck in place, iced over.

Imryll. Where are you?

Her eyes darted at one of his strong hands, still cupping her shoulders. His knuckles were white, red, white. The same flush lived in his cheeks, spidered through his eyes.

"Where did you go?" He released her and coiled his hands back to his sides.

"I…" Could he read minds too? "Why?"

"Why?"

"Why are you asking me these things? Why do you care if I disappeared somewhere? Why does it matter to you?" Her voice choked with a sudden rush of emotion.

His jaw snapped together. "Because I'm your *guard*, and it's my job—"

"Job!" Imryll laughed. The sound caught the breeze and evaporated. "You don't really expect me to believe that you care at all about your *job*?"

"Why would I compete for a full year if I didn't care? Give up my life?"

She shook her head, open-mouthed. Her arms swam in the too-big cloak that she realized, too late, probably belonged to him. "I've been asking myself the very same thing since the day you came into my life, Syr Wynter."

He rolled his mouth into a sneer. "I don't have to explain myself to you."

Imryll forced a dry smile. "No. Nor do I." She tried to step past him, but he blocked her way. She breathed deep and said, "I'm leaving. You can either follow or stay. I don't care either way."

Drazhan lowered his gaze and propped his hand against a post. Something drew her eyes to the way his fingers wrapped around the wood. How long and lean they were, like…

Like claws.

Imryll stuttered back, her bare feet slapping stone as she desperately fought to put distance between them.

"Imryll?"

"You…your hands…" Her belly soured. The room spun.

"My hands?"

"They're not hands! That's not the word for them. They're…" Imryll turned and braced against the wall, fighting a wave of nausea. *Slicing through air. All the blood.* "Stand down, Syr Wynter. I'm leaving, and if you even try to stop me…" She couldn't finish. Razor-sharp claws slashed through her mind, splitting her between past and present.

"You're safest here."

"I do not feel *remotely* safe with you." Her chest rose, crashed, and rose again.

He tilted his head to the side. "You're alive, aren't you?"

"Claws!" she screamed. The word used the last of her breath and seemed to steal his air as well.

His mouth clapped shut, and his eyes narrowed.

"They were claws…your hands…They were actual claws, like a beast…Oh, gods."

"They weren't *claws*, Imryll. They were fist weapons. The same weapons from the tournament." He structured his words in careful precision. "And you were upset, scared—"

"No—"

"Out of your mind, enough to disappear somewhere for *hours.*"

Imryll thrust herself forward a step. Her heart raced nearly out of her chest. "They were real, actual claws, Drazhan! I saw them, I *felt* them!"

He recoiled at her use of his name. "You need to go back to bed. You're clearly still in a delirium."

"Then show me! Show me the weapons. Where are they?"

"No. You're acting irrational and—"

"I saw what I saw. *I saw what I fucking saw!*" Imryll licked her dry lips. She blinked through phantom tears. She *should* be crying. Fear should have hobbled her by now, leaving her entirely at his mercy.

But it hadn't.

Imryll breathed just as heavy. Her heart still sped dangerously close to bursting.

Something else, however, had shifted. She was too exhausted to define it. But she understood it enough to know what must happen next.

Imryll curved her mouth into a smile. "I do need to lie down again." She tapped her dry throat. "Do we have water? Wine?"

The immediate relief rolling over him, settling him, was all she needed to see to trust her senses. She'd seen exactly what she thought she'd seen. What it meant…why…how…Those things should matter, but they didn't.

Because Imryll had seen the way forward.

Away from him. From the Easterlands. From Duncarrow. From everyone and everything that had held her back, lied to her, shaped her, groomed her, or used her.

The worst night of her life so far had also provided her first real chance to leave.

"There's wine. I'll bring you some." He nodded to himself and crossed to a part of the room covered by shadows.

"Thank you." Imryll moved back to the bed and slipped in, but she didn't remove the cloak.

She'd say what Wynter wanted her to say and do what he wanted her to do, but when he fell into his brief period of respite, lost momentarily to wherever it was he went, she would make her move.

"Take that off." Wynter flicked a hard nod at the cloak as he passed her a mug of wine. "You'll strangle in your sleep."

You'd like that, wouldn't you?

"I have a chill," she said. It was true. Her back rippled with fresh excitement.

Wynter watched her for a long, hard moment and then grunted.

He returned to the sitting room.

Imryll guzzled the wine and shoved the empty mug onto the bedside table.

She slipped down under the covers, still shaking, and waited.

EIGHTEEN
ANGER IS THE HAMMER

Drazhan listened to Imryll pretend to sleep.

He watched her slip into the sitting room, her eyes darting around the room in wild fear. She dodged the bands of moonlight like a cloaked assassin but jumped at thunder rolling through the storm as it rippled through the forest.

With ginger steps, she fluttered around the room, shoving random, mostly inane items into a travel satchel she'd found hanging with the cloaks. The apples were prudent. The empty candlesticks—sans candles or fire implements—and the blot of ink were not.

Every few steps, she glanced his way. If she'd have stepped a touch closer…paid even slightly more attention to the shadows… she'd have noted his eyes had been open the entire time.

Imryll passed her gaze once more around the room. She drew a shaky inhale before locking her attention on the door.

Drazhan knew what she was thinking. The bolt was loud. There was little chance she could throw it back without sending the shrill sound rippling across the apartments.

Go on, Princess. Of course I'll hear it, but it won't matter because I want you to go. I want to see how far you'll take this childish bid for freedom. You'll be lucky to make it past the courtyard after what happened tonight, but even an hour without the oversight of your chastity guard is an hour no one can be sure you weren't with another man.

Drazhan fisted his hands. He'd nearly sent the words into her head. Such carelessness was why he needed to stand down. There was no logical reason for his reticence other than his nerves firing through a prospective win, in the plan that had been almost half his life in the making.

If he failed in the end, it would not be because some spoiled princess had gotten under his skin like an infected splinter.

Go on. He practiced more caution with his thoughts, guarding them within the fortress of his own mind. *Go on, Imryll. Throw the bolt.*

She did. The little delighted gasp she buried in her hands afterward almost made him smile.

Drazhan forced the sound into the same place where he'd tucked images of her lost to the throes of pleasure. He'd successfully suppressed memories of how the smooth velvet between her legs had felt pinched between the pads of his fingers. The muted cries rolling from the back of her throat when he'd slipped half his hand inside her, stretching her, as they both imagined how much more delicious it would be when it was no longer his hand.

He ground his palm against his crotch with an annoyed grunt. *Don't forget what happened next. When she showed you who she was.*

Imryll yanked at the door and darted outside while he was wrestling with his thoughts.

Drazhan leaped to his feet and started after her. With a glance at the stormy sky beyond the curtains, he snatched his own cloak from the rack and followed her.

He kept a careful distance as she moved down the steps, her hood pulled low over her face. The cloak wasn't the one she usually wore. It had been left there, presumably by someone in the

Quintus household, and was similar to the purple garment Imryll had worn to Whitechurch but not the same.

Marius, true to his word, hadn't left any guards outside her apartments. She caught some incredulous glances in her Rhiagain colors, but it was that very thing that kept them from stopping her.

Imryll reached the broad steps of the courtyard and nearly slid across the wet stones. She pinched her cloak tighter to brace against the heavy assault of rain and wind and adjusted the satchel higher on her arm, but her hesitation was short-lived. She wrapped her arms tight, lowered her head, and continued on, heading west through the courtyard.

I just want to make sure she's really, truly gone, he told himself, hoping it was true and she wasn't still invading her way into his sympathies.

Imryll reached the stables and looked to the right and left but never behind her. He knew if she had even a suspicion he was there, she'd confront him.

Drazhan didn't follow her inside. He watched from the other side of the doors, hidden, as she skimmed the row of stalls. *Working up courage,* he thought to himself, until she opened one near the end and guided out the same mare she'd ridden before, Enzi.

Imryll ran both of her hands down Enzi's snout and pressed her mouth to where her hands had been. Her whispers were obscured, but Enzi snuffled in happy rejoinder.

She moved to the rack and hoisted a saddle, then carried it to Enzi. Her uncertain pause had Drazhan rolling his eyes. Of course she wouldn't know how to saddle a horse. She could hardly dress herself.

Drazhan slipped under the awning and waited for her to decide she'd gone as far as she could with her reckless plan.

Minutes passed. Five. Ten. At twenty, he was moving to peek inside when a flurry of hooves and grunts had him ducking into hiding again.

Imryll flew out of the double doors on Enzi's back. Mud whipped up and slammed into the doors with a barrage of squishy thuds, and she was gone.

Let her go. It's done.

Drazhan ground his jaw. He ran his fist against his leg. Groaned.

He flashed a dubious glance in the direction she'd disappeared. She wouldn't last long. She didn't need to. The future was no longer in his hands.

Let her go.

Drazhan whistled in through his teeth and rushed into the barn to pick his own horse. *Let her go.* He picked the first one that looked alert and buckled the saddle in less than a minute. *Let her go, you fool.* He mounted.

The Goldtails could still be out there. He'd follow her as far as the border of Whitechurch, and his conscience would be clear.

He gathered the reins in his hand and turned the horse around. With a grunt, he spurred the horse into action and headed into the night in the same direction Imryll had gone.

Drazhan caught sight of her again when he cleared the path separating Arboriana from Whitechurch proper.

Her cloak snapped in the wind. She could barely keep mounted, almost falling off from one side and then the other. She was practically climbing Enzi's mane to stay up.

The tumultuous din of the storm allowed him to draw closer, and he saw the culprit: the saddle buckles had come undone. She'd probably not secured them properly to begin with.

It was a matter of time before she fell or flew.

A sinking feeling twisted Drazhan's gut. An experienced rider knew how to adjust to danger. How to brace with one arm. To tuck the head and chin down. Where to take the impact to be able to walk away.

She's not your problem. This is not your problem.

Imryll screamed when a branch smacked her and knocked her sideways in the saddle. Drazhan clenched and narrowed the distance further. She screamed again, stabbing the air with raw fear. Enzi came to a mud-spattered halt, her hooves inches from the drop-off at the edge of the path.

An eerie silence followed. Enzi backed up but then went utterly still. Rain spattered the earth through a crack of lightning.

Drazhan drew closer. He became near enough that he slowed his horse to a walk. He pressed aside the branch that had hit Imryll and what he saw choked his breath.

Enzi was alone. No sign of her rider.

His eyes flicked to the drop-off. It was too dark to see whether what stretched beyond was a ravine or something deeper.

"Imryll?" Drazhan dropped to the wet earth and stepped to the edge. He peered over. Though he couldn't see the bottom, the height of the trees was a good indicator of how far down the land sloped. Twenty feet until the first outcropping, then another twenty or so to the bottom.

Far enough that if she were safe, she'd still be screaming.

Drazhan looked for something to grab hold of. A cluster of roots caught his eye, and he wrapped his fists through before swinging down over the side of the cliff wall. The land sloped enough for him to find unstable footing, and he half slid, half ran the rest of the way, using the brush to slow him from a fall.

He squinted to adjust his vision. A canopy of trees blocked what moonlight the storm clouds hadn't covered.

He heard the distant sound of horses neighing.

"Imryll?" Drazhan couldn't see anything but darkness. She wasn't where he'd landed, which was a good sign. It meant the thick brush on the cliff wall had broken her fall and changed her trajectory. He stepped carefully over moss, patches of branches, and fallen logs. "Imryll, say something so I can find you."

Rain muted everything. A flock of birds returning to the dark sky startled him, but he barely registered a sound. He inched through the forest like a blind man.

Death of the First Chosen would also put an end to the Rhiagain succession. It won't matter if the others produce sons when

251

she's gone. The superstitious fools believe the next king must come from her.

He imagined finding her dead in a bed of leaves and moss and fought the black wave cresting up from his chest.

Imryll. Please.

A sputtering cough drew his focus to his left. It stopped before he had a clear direction.

Again. Do it again.

Moaning broke through the batter of rain. It disappeared again but not before he'd locked onto the sound.

Drazhan crashed through the undergrowth, dodging fat raindrops filtering through the needled trees. He spotted her several feet ahead, lying on her side and facing away.

Relief ripped the cage from his heart. He flew forward and landed on his knees in the wet brush.

"Imryll. Imryll!" He rolled her onto her back. Her face was covered in dark mud, but it didn't hide the blood around her mouth. "You foolish girl. You stupid, foolish—"

Her eyes fluttered open, but barely. "Draz—" A cough interrupted her from finishing the word.

Draz. Only one person was allowed to call him that.

Say it again.

"How badly are you hurt?" he asked. It wasn't the right question. She wouldn't know the answer. Nor would he until he got her out of the ravine and to safety.

"I don't..." She trailed off. Her eyes moved downward. "My arm."

Drazhan lifted her wrist, and she screamed again. He eased it back onto a bed of leaves. "It's broken. What else?"

"I don't know," she whispered, wheezing. Her tongue darted out, licking away blood and mud in the same swipe. "Why are you...What are you doing here?"

He couldn't answer. "And the other arm?"

"It's...no. I think it's fine."

"Can you stand?"

252

"Maybe." She winced through an attempt to sit. "Maybe not."

"You're certain the other arm is fine?"

She nodded.

Drazhan stood and moved to her other side. He knelt and slid an arm under her. "Does this hurt?"

She shook her head.

"Your broken arm. I need you to pull it up onto your chest."

"No. No, I can't—"

"You *can*."

Imryll whimpered through the attempt, but she managed to droop it over her torso.

He hooked his other arm under her legs and hoisted her into his arms. She cried out with a start but settled against his chest with a garbled sigh of relief.

Drazhan adjusted her to a more secure position in his arms. She was heavier than he remembered, but rain had turned her garments into a weight.

Imryll started to shake. She rolled toward him and buried moans into his cloak.

Drazhan looked up. All he saw was darkness and trees, but his sense of direction was sound, and he moved successfully in the direction of the ravine wall. When he reached the slope, he searched for something to use as leverage.

"There's no way." Imryll sniffled. Her breath shuddered. "You have to leave me and go get help."

Drazhan scooped one of his arms all the way under her, from shoulder to hip. With his free hand, he patted the wet earth until he found a root system to take hold of. He tugged. Solid.

"Drazhan. Listen to me."

"Listen to the princess who ran away without a plan and almost got herself killed?" Anger was the hammer that crushed fear. Honor demanded he come to her rescue. It had to be that, because he couldn't comprehend the alternative.

"I didn't ask you to follow me."

"And where would you be if I hadn't?" He cleared his throat to seal the crack. "Where would you be, Imryll?"

Her laugh was hoarse. "Was it not you who told me freedom came in many forms?"

Not like this. "Hold onto me with your good arm."

Drazhan stretched his hand to as high on the root as it could go. His arm strained as he lifted them up onto the first narrow shelf, where he could regain purchase. He adjusted her and reached higher, digging the toes of his boots into the wet earth one by one, using the root to climb. Imryll's grip on his neck was so powerful, he couldn't look up to see how much farther it was to the top, but her tight, fractured breaths told him it didn't matter. Seconds, minutes, *hours.* His muscles screamed for the reprieve he wouldn't allow himself until she was safe.

Drazhan felt a nuzzle on his head and looked up to see Enzi. He almost laughed.

With one final grunt, he lifted Imryll onto the grassy edge and climbed out of the ravine and to his feet.

He afforded himself a moment to catch his breath but also to take measure of the situation. The rain hadn't let up, and the path was even muddier now. The horse he'd borrowed was gone, probably returned home.

Enzi's dark eyes watched him. Her saddle hung off the side of her by luck alone.

Drazhan looked down at Imryll. She was no longer crying. Her expression was stoic. Inquisitive.

"We need to take your cloak off."

He expected her to argue, but she nodded. "It's heavy."

Drazhan turned away and went to work on Enzi's saddle. "I saw a chalet in the woods when we rode through here during the day."

"What's a chalet?"

"It's like…like a cabin."

"I've never seen one of those either."

"A cabin is—"

254

"I know what it is," she said quietly. "I've just never seen one."

Drazhan inhaled through his nose. He drew his soaked hood back. "We'll go there."

"To the chalet?"

"I can't take you back like this." Oh, but he could. And if he showed up with her in his arms, muddy and broken, it would be enough.

"Oh." Imryll used her good arm to push herself to a seated position. "Are you hurt?"

"What?" Drazhan released the final saddle buckle and looked over his shoulder.

But Imryll had passed out in the grass.

He checked the buckles once more and returned to Imryll's side. She was starting to come back around, but it would be better for her if she didn't. The ride would jostle her arm and whatever other injuries she hadn't been able to articulate. Until she was warm and clean, he could do nothing to help that.

Drazhan sighed and scooped Imryll back into his arms. He laid her over the front of Enzi's saddle until he was mounted and rolled her back against his chest. He looked down and straight into the slow blink of her glossy eyes.

He buried the ache in his chest and returned his gaze to the path ahead.

Drazhan clucked his tongue, and Enzi reared to life.

The chalet was an abandoned monastery. The realm was littered with the hollowed relics, a plague growing worse as the curse of the Rhiagains swept the kingdom. They were the old homes of the Guardian Keepers, monks who provided abbeys for the devout to come give modest offerings. Monasteries had been intentionally simple places, because true faith didn't need gold to thrive.

It brought him back to Imryll's artless promotion of the Rhiagain quest to commandeer the Guardians for their own nefarious purposes.

Drazhan looked down at the woman dangling in his arms—the one he'd been so determined to corrupt that he'd made her the most important aspect of his mission, setting aside the real reason he'd traveled to Duncarrow. Her red curls bounced as he carried her, the only signs of life. Her hair, buried within the oversized cloak when she fell, had escaped the mud. Drazhan had draped the cloth behind the saddle after he'd rolled her out of it.

He almost regretted it. All she wore underneath was the thin shift the attendants had dressed her in after the trouble in the courtyard. It was soaked to transparency from the rain, but the cloak had done its job keeping the mud from spreading to anything underneath.

Drazhan glanced back at Enzi. He'd found a dry spot for her under a dense section of the forest canopy. He should tether her, but it wasn't necessary. She wouldn't leave Imryll. He'd seen animals bond to men and women, and Enzi had undoubtedly bonded to Imryll.

He shifted Imryll to a more stable place in his arms and kicked the door open.

It sprung wide with ease, revealing a large open room. Dust and cobwebs bounced off the moonlight, which streamed in from a series of windows near the ceiling. What few furnishings remained were hardly serviceable. A table and chairs, a couple of divans, and a musty stack of blankets were all he had to work with.

He started for the blankets, but a shadow gave him a start. He was preparing to shift Imryll again and draw his sword when he saw it was just a large bearskin tacked to the wall.

Drazhan shook his head. He went over and ripped it down, using one hand and both feet to smooth it out across the floor.

Careful to land her on her good arm, he knelt, and Imryll gently tumbled out of his arms and onto the bear's pelt. Before he stood, he moved her broken one onto the fur in a relaxed, natural pose.

She stirred but didn't wake.

Drazhan went back outside and said a short prayer that he'd find what he hoped. There'd been no stream nearby, which meant there had to be a cistern. There was no reason the monks would have taken it when they left, but it was possible they'd dismantled it so none of the usurpers could make use of it.

One of those usurpers is asleep inside.

The thought wasn't as vindicating as it had once been. Imryll had been a surprise from the moment he'd laid eyes on her in the lyceum, and every moment since had chipped the edges of his loathing, softening him in a way that was unacceptable. Weakness, he'd called it, because that was what it was.

She was his weakness.

But nothing about that scared him more than her dying on the pelt.

And until he could get his hands on her and listen to her body, he couldn't rule it out.

The cistern was set back a hundred or so feet into the woods. He rifled through a stack of useless, hole-filled buckets until he found two that were passable. When both were full, he returned to the chalet.

He made a fire in the hearth, though with what few sticks and logs remained inside, it would die before the night ended. There was no dry wood to be found in the storm still pounding the earth outside.

He unclipped his sword belt and laid it across the table. His cloak he hung from a hook, though it would take more than that to dry it out.

In the stack of blankets, Drazhan found some thinner linens. He grabbed them and tossed them onto the edge of the fur. With one last pass around the chalet, he decided there was nothing else he could use and went to Imryll's side to start the long task of cleaning her up.

He removed her gloves and boots and pulled one of the buckets closer. Leaning in, he checked the strength of her heartbeat. *Strong enough.*

Drazhan dipped a linen in the water and began with her ankles. He worked upward from there, traveling over her knees, along the sides of her hips, and up across her belly. He was careful to keep his touch from veering anywhere provocative, but sex was the furthest thing from his mind. He'd already cleared it, readying himself for what he needed to do—what he would do, for her, despite the terrible risk to himself.

He ended with her broken wrist, placing it in his low palm and dabbing only hard enough to clear the dirt.

Drazhan fell back on his heels and regarded his work. Her fingernails were stuffed with dark crescents, and he'd missed streaks on her shins and neck. Blood caked at the edge of her temples and along one side of her chin.

But in the absence of a proper bath, it was the best he could do.

He shuffled on his knees back to her side.

Am I really going to do this?

Drazhan closed his eyes and flattened his hands.

Yes. I am.

He pressed them to her nearest limb—her leg—held his breath, and listened.

Her arm is definitely broken. One of her ankles is twisted. Bruises were along her backside, across her shoulders. There's bleeding in her abdomen, but nothing alarming. She hit her head hard enough to knock her out—once near her chin, the other just above the nape of her neck— and it's why I keep losing her.

He pitched back in a hard exhale.

He understood the work ahead. It could've been worse. He didn't *have* to heal her. Nothing she'd endured was bad enough that it wouldn't eventually heal on its own.

It was the head wound that worried him. He'd seen good, strong men lost to rest after suffering what seemed to be an inconsequential injury. And she wasn't waking. Even after the hard, jostling ride.

You can still leave her. There's still a way out of this.

No, he couldn't. And there wasn't.

He had magic twice over, both kingdom magic and Medvedev. His mother had been a quarter Medvedev, which made him only an eighth, but even that was strong enough to imbue him with powers he had to willfully suppress to keep from exposing himself.

Drazhan stretched his hands down and over her flesh, whispering his intentions to her unconscious form. Color returned to her legs and spread upward, outward. Her mouth parted in a soft groan, her chin jutting when her head fell back and dug into the fur.

He stopped, listening again.

Curious.

She seemed to be…*helping* him, even in her unconscious state. Her self-healing matched his work, doubling his efforts. Only strong magic could be so effective, and if he believed Imryll, she claimed not to know she had magic at all.

But that was a problem for later. The more immediate one lay before him, vulnerable, waiting for him to finish.

Minutes stretched to hours as he continued his work, his whispering…moving his palms across every inch of Imryll's flesh, leaving nothing to chance. He didn't think about the questions she'd rain down on him when she woke healed and confused, or the ones he needed to ask her about the same thing. Nor did he dwell on the explanation others would demand when he showed up with her in the morning in her nightshift and naught else— enough to sow the doubt he'd come for but no longer felt quite as passionate about.

When it was over, Drazhan moved to the door, swaying on his feet.

He opened it and let the cold, wet air rush over him as he waited for Imryll to wake.

NINETEEN
YOU CAME FOR ME

Imryll's dreams were full of familiar but confusing images. Of reticent boys with claws for hands and endless journeys up mountains. She wished the flashes from the cold, wet gulch could be dismissed as dreams, but she knew better. Enzi had spooked, Imryll hadn't reacted quick enough, and she'd flown through rain and air. What she didn't remember was landing.

She remembered Drazhan though. At first she'd thought *he* had been a dream, but he'd pulled her mind back to the living with his intrusive telepathy and then he'd hauled her body to safety. The last thing she remembered was lying on the grass, her eyes slowly closing as she watched him secure Enzi's saddle.

Much had clearly happened since. She was warm, for one. The large, unruly fur she lay on was only part of it. A fire crackled somewhere nearby. The smells of the place were less welcome, sour and musty from disuse. The roof above was still solid, but the wood was old, from another era.

Imryll winced before she shifted, but her arm didn't hurt any-more. Only a distant ache remained in the spot where it had

261

fractured. Her head swam with a dizzy spell, but *that* pain was gone too. What remained was the throbbing discomfort of having slept too long.

She glanced to the left and the right. Whatever the place had been, it wasn't that any longer. Only a table and chairs were to her right, and a divan to her left—no, two divans, but one was rotted in the center.

Moonlight drew bands across the floor. Across her belly and legs. She glanced up and saw the source: a handful of smallish windows along what would have been a second floor, had they built the place that way.

What had Drazhan called it? A chalet. The word sounded far too ornate for something so barren and forgotten. But she was safe and...

Healed.

Completely healed.

Only phantom pains lingered.

Drazhan.

It all came back to him.

It always did.

Imryll filled her lungs and gave herself a moment to let that wash over her.

He had healed her. With magic. There was no medicine capable of the transformation she'd been through. Even magical healers were not as thorough, or so she'd read in the pamphlets Duke Rahn had had his students read as part of their Duncarrow youth curriculum. Healing took multiple sessions. With breaks in between. Time.

The moon's position indicated it couldn't have been more than a few hours.

Healing. Claws for hands. Telepathy. What else wasn't he telling her?

Imryll started at the shake of boots on the floor. She started to cover herself, but there was already a blanket lying over half of her. It was moth-eaten and slightly damp but still mostly in one piece. She tugged it into place.

Drazhan's shadow cut the light from the fire.

"How do you feel?" His voice lacked inflection. He could have been talking about anything. To anyone.

"Tired," Imryll replied. She coughed to clear the rasp from her voice. "Confused."

He walked away but returned moments later with a chair. He plopped it onto the wood next to the pelt and sat. "Your arm?"

"It feels fine." Imryll tried to look up at him, but the moonlight washed out his features, surrounding him with an eerie glow. She sighed and turned her gaze back to the tall ceiling. "Too fine."

"Are you aware you can heal yourself?"

She tried to laugh but coughed instead. "Me? I've never healed anyone or anything in my life."

He watched her in careful consideration before he continued. "If you tell anyone I healed you, I'll tell them what you did tonight."

The urge to jump and confront him wasn't as strong as the pull to stay still. "Have I told anyone about your telepathy, Syr Wynter? Your hands that turn into claws?"

"They're weapons, Princess."

"Oh, they're weapons all right," she said with a bitter snort. "Weapons that don't come off. Like *claws*."

"You need rest." He pitched forward, starting to stand, but settled back. "And your head?"

"It's almost like I wasn't thrown from a horse at all." Imryll turned onto her side to face away. It wouldn't have been possible only hours ago. But then, neither had freedom. She'd torn off like the foolish girl Wynter had said she was, and she'd paid for it. If he hadn't come along, she might have died in that ravine. Unable to walk, to stand, to climb out. Starvation was a terrible way to go, people said. She'd nearly found out for herself.

"I've been thinking of the right story to tell. You wanted to ride, to clear your head of the bloodshed from the courtyard. No one has to know about the bag you packed...poorly."

Imryll bunched her arms under her head and scowled at the door. "You must want something from me in exchange for this lie."

The resulting silence almost made her turn around. "I don't want anything from you."

"Why would you lie for me?"

"The truth would make me look inept."

"But you're not. You followed me."

"Yes."

"Why?"

"You're my charge."

"Save your hogwash for someone who doesn't know better." Imryll returned to her back. "You don't give a whit about your *charge* or being a knight." She rolled her once-broken wrist in the air. "Or any of this."

Wynter didn't respond.

"Why you bothered to compete at all is a mystery that disturbs me more with each passing day. For if it wasn't the honor or the challenge or loyalty to the crown, what does that leave?"

Her dark knight pushed to his feet. He sighed before speaking. "We need to return soon if our story is going to hold any water."

She rolled to her right side and propped herself up on one arm. "I can't make you tell me your secrets, Syr Wynter, but you owe me one answer at least."

Wynter turned away and walked toward the table. "My horse ran off, so we'll ride Enzi together. Your boots weren't damaged, but they're full of muck. I suggest we leave them. You won't want to wear them as they are."

Imryll swallowed the lump in her throat. She inhaled a steadying breath through her nose. "You will tell me, Syr Wynter, why you came for someone you so obviously *hate*."

Wynter stopped moving. He reached for a chair and gripped the back with one hand. "I don't hate you, Imryll."

"No?"

He shook his head.

"What then? What do you feel for me?" Only after did she realize what she was asking.

Wynter scoffed. "Nothing."

"You *came* for *me*."

"As I said, you're my—"

"Don't you *dare* repeat lies when you hold me to a higher standard," Imryll retorted. She sat all the way up. The blanket fell away, and she made no attempt to cover herself. "You have made your disgust for me quite clear. You had a chance to be rid of me. You could have let me leave."

Wynter hung his head with a dark laugh. "You wouldn't have lasted a day out there. You had no gold. No *map*. No survival skills."

Imryll matched his laugh. "So you do care."

"Don't put words in my mouth."

"Why not, when your own are so intentionally bewildering?"

His grip tightened on the chair.

"You came for me, even though I didn't want you to."

Wynter rolled his fist hard enough, she thought he might snap the entire chair in half.

"You came for me," Imryll said again. She rose to her feet and took a step forward. Why was she pushing him? He must be wondering the same thing. She didn't care what he thought or felt, and the indifference was reciprocal, so *why* could she not stop? "You came for me, and I am absolutely furious that I'm not already hours away from this place, but you came for me."

"Dawn will break soon."

She moved closer to him. "You came for me, Drazhan."

A groan started low in his throat. He released the chair, and it went toppling.

Imryll reached an unsteady hand toward him. Drazhan spun around and clasped his fingers around her wrist, his breath shaky and his eyes wild. She exhaled a breath, and he inhaled it. Her lips parted, and his rolled inward with a bracing sound.

He dropped her wrist and gathered her into his arms in an effortless lift. She had only enough time to gasp before he crushed his mouth to hers and lashed his tongue, demanding entrance. His lips were softer than she'd expected, but his kiss was exactly as she'd imagined it would be: a hypnotic command of strength and darkness. She wrapped her legs around his waist and then locked them at the ankles when he clawed at her, sending a delicious pinch of pain straight to her core.

Drazhan released a choking breath and broke the kiss, but he didn't let her go. He rolled his forehead against hers with his eyes closed, gathering himself.

Imryll angled her face downward and looked up at him. She jerked her arms tighter around his neck until he opened his eyes again. "Don't stop, Draz," she whispered. She swept her mouth back to his and locked him into a kiss that was even better than the first.

"Don't say that." Strain cut through his gruff tone. He kissed her again and then slammed his mouth shut with a throaty groan. "Don't ask for things you don't understand."

"I might not know a thing about surviving in this realm on my own. I may be naive about anything beyond the rocky isle I was born on," Imryll replied. She kissed the corner of his mouth to slow the wall he was constructing right in front of her. "But I know what I want. Because of you, I know how to ask for it."

"Fuck," Drazhan hissed and carried her to the table. He set her down with a soft thud, trailed more kisses along her chin, and sucked the hollow of her neck on the way to her chest. He tore her chemise down and cupped his mouth hungrily to one breast, sending a sharp wave of pleasure straight to her head.

One hand strummed down her arm, but he stopped when his fingers hit the circlet the king had derisively called her crown. She felt him brace right before he yanked it down her arm and flung it into the fireplace with a shattering crash.

She gasped in dazed delight. Her arm throbbed where the silver had been. They'd punish her, but she was past the point of caring.

266

Imryll arched her back to show her approval of his brazen act, and he rewarded her by thrusting two fingers inside of her. She cried out in gratitude and bucked to drive him deeper, because it wasn't enough. It was never enough.

He devoured her nipple, raking his teeth against it, and switched to the other, dividing his attention equally. Imryll threw her head back and rode the force of his hand, gasping through the jolts as the friction sent her back and forth across the wood.

Drazhan reeled with a heaving breath. He withdrew his hands, ignoring her protesting moan as he turned his gaze on hers and locked it there with an insatiable glare. She blinked, trying to read the moment, to help guide it toward the conclusion she'd wanted so badly, since he'd first spoken his intentions to her in the lyceum.

He hooked her legs over his arms and tugged, dropping them over his shoulders. He raised her higher until he had what he wanted. Imryll closed her eyes in anticipation, but nothing could have steeled her for the shock of his tongue brushing against her throbbing sex. She pressed a scream through her teeth.

"You taste so good. Too good." He moaned, burying his face deeper as he lapped ravenously from end to end, sending her hurtling up a dangerous, delicious path that promised an exquisite descent. She locked her legs behind his neck to show her approval.

His mouth formed suction over her swollen nerves, and she dug her nails to the table at the wild surge of pleasure that coursed through her in determined thunderclaps. He sucked harder, his fingers digging against her ass and lower back as he rocked her against his mouth with unrestrained urgency.

Imryll cut her nails in deeper and squeezed her eyes closed as she screamed her release into the empty room. He locked her in a vise she was unable to squirm away from, forcing her to confront her desire—her vulnerability—as she spasmed against his swirling tongue.

Her throat constricted as the waves subsided. It took so much longer to return to herself than when he'd used his hand, and she was desperate for a break. She focused on her breathing, but Drazhan didn't let go.

"Not yet," he murmured, reading her mind. He returned to his ministrations, climbing her back up the same mountain, cresting a higher pass.

"I can't," she whined, but it was a lie, and she came again in seconds, shuddering over his face with another desperate wail.

Imryll tried to sit, but he yanked her back to his mouth. She stumbled over another weak protest, but it was pointless to pretend she couldn't come all night under his skilled tongue. She was surrendering herself to the inevitability of it when he pushed two fingers inside her again.

Yes, she said in her mind, because her mouth was busy trying to swallow air. He buried his fingers to the knuckle and moved them apart, stretching her.

Imryll gulped and raised her ass higher. She couldn't even form thoughts between the twin assaults of his mouth and hand, and her breathing arrested when he spread his fingers so wide, she thought he might split her down the center.

She heard the buckles on his trousers clang when they hit the floorboards.

"If you want to take this cock, Imryll, first I need to know you can handle it."

And she came again, crashing against his tongue. With his hand open inside her, she felt all the ways her body responded to the orgasm, tightening over him in hard, tight contractions. His greedy tongue had made her so wet, his fingers were forced out with every clench, but he won the battle each time, sliding them back into place.

With an open-mouthed groan, Drazhan took a half step back. He passed his forearm along his mouth to clean it and lowered her legs but caught them at his waist.

His cock throbbed against her opening. She bit down with a whimper, nearly coming again, yet he hadn't even touched her.

Drazhan slid his tongue along his bottom lip and sucked in. His tongue flitted in, out. His crown pulsed against her slit, going no farther.

"You said all I had to do was ask." She moaned, wriggling to collect more of him. "I've asked enough to wonder if you meant any of what you said that day."

"I also said you'd be writhing on my face begging for more, didn't I?" He gripped her thighs tighter.

Imryll choked out a laugh. "Is that what you want? For me to beg?"

Drazhan jumped his hands farther up her thighs. "I think you just did." With a throaty groan, he shoved inside.

Imryll closed her legs at the shock of his size, but he nudged them back open with his forearms and drove his thick cock all the way in. She throbbed around him, still working through the jolts of her last orgasm.

He met her eyes and stopped moving. The longer he was motionless, the bigger he felt, swelling and filling her until she was squirming for relief.

"You want me to stop?" he asked. A devilish smile tickled the corner of his mouth.

"No, no," she said, burying the last *no* in a desperate whine.

"Tell me what you want then." His cock twitched, sending her head back against the wood.

"I want this."

He slid out an inch. "Tell me what you want."

"I want...you."

Another inch. She almost cried.

"I want..." Imryll bit down on her lip so hard, she tasted blood. "I want you to fuck me, Draz. I want...I want you to fuck me so hard, I'll be stranded here because walking is impossible. I want you to..." She blinked away a tear. "I want you to want me as much as I want you."

"Imryll." He grunted her name and then crushed toward her with one hard thrust. Then another. He watched her through every one, as though expecting she would change her mind.

She wouldn't.

Now that Drazhan Wynter was inside her, she was never letting him leave.

"Don't be afraid of breaking me." She moaned, twisting against the wood. "Be afraid of not and wishing you had."

That did it. Drazhan yanked her legs back, dragging her along his cock. He gripped the underside of her thighs and bucked her over him in long, full thrusts, urging her legs wider with every encouraging cry she sounded.

He fell down over her, dragging them both up the table. He snaked a hand forward and grabbed her face, then angled it down so she could watch him fuck her, stretch her. *Tear me in two,* she begged, afraid he would—more afraid he wouldn't.

"I didn't think you could take me." He panted, controlling his pace, but his red face and corded neck betrayed how difficult the restraint was. "But you're taking me so good, Imryll."

"You've underestimated me from the moment you met me," she said, tightening to show him just how well she could take him. Her eyes rolled back, exploding with stars, when he met her challenge.

"I knew you were a good girl." He grunted. His jaw hinged tight, and she felt him tighten. Fear flashed in his eyes, and he pulled out and spilled across her belly.

Imryll looked down at the mess and a terrible, forbidden thought flashed through her mind. She wished he hadn't panicked and pulled away, so she could feel the force of his desire for her, before it was gone.

Drazhan reached for a blanket and wiped her off, but before he could re-dress, she crawled across the table and wrapped her arms around his neck. He caught her legs and went sputtering back across the floor, recovering his balance right before they fell.

He lowered her toward the pelt, but she shook her head and nodded at the fur. Fiery understanding danced in his eyes, and he bit his lip as he adjusted down onto his back.

Imryll pulled her hair out of her face and straddled him. Before she was even in place, his thumb was pressed between her legs. Despite how sensitive she was after four rounds, she still lit up under his touch, tottering precariously close to the edge.

Drazhan reached his other hand between them and positioned his cock against her core. He waited.

Imryll braced one hand on his chest and lowered herself onto him. She held her breath through taking him in a second time, which was both better and worse, as she was so delectably sore from how he'd risen to the command to break her.

Once she'd taken him in, Drazhan brought his hand back to knead her breasts, tucking forward to nip and suck as she guided them both toward another release. She rode him with the same full strides he'd given her on the table, enjoying the way his eyes rolled back…the way his thumb stalled when she went faster.

She exploded once more, panting through stunned disbelief. He was right behind her, his hands on her hips to lift her away before he released inside her. She almost stopped him, but with her emotions running high and the angst of the evening living on the edge of every one of her thoughts, she knew such recklessness shouldn't be decided until she had a clearer sight of the future awaiting her.

He spurted his release on himself and when she was done, Imryll leaned forward to take some of it onto her tongue. The sound he made when she did was animalistic, and she knew he'd be inside her again.

She grinned and he spun her around. She landed on her hands and knees as he crawled up from behind. He cupped his hand around her neck and lifted her chin, and in one move, he drove into her sensitive, swollen core.

Imryll slammed back onto him. Pain mixed with pleasure, becoming something so exquisite, so perfect, that even the thought of the sun breaking through the night sky and announcing a new day made her want to cry and beg the gods for more time.

In the morning, she would accept her fate and return to the role she was born to play. To the cage others had been building her entire life.

Tonight, the cage door was open.

Tonight, she belonged to Drazhan Wynter, and he belonged to her.

Tonight, she had a taste of the freedom she knew would never be hers.

Imryll woke squinting. Where the moonlight had provided gentle illumination, dawn's sun was blinding. The harsh light caught thousands of tiny dust particles, and what had seemed like a quaint, abandoned cabin in the night was a horrific tableau of insects and grime.

She shifted to prop herself up, but a strong arm tugged her back into place. Her face landed on a warm chest, and she smiled against Drazhan's taut flesh.

Her first thought was *What have I done?*

The second, *When can I do it again?*

What she didn't feel was guilt. Not about Drazhan. Not about the swollen ache that made it hard to even close her legs.

Even as she accepted her fate with numb resignation, the resentment just under the surface came to a boil. Everyone from her mother and father to the king and queen—and yes, even Torian— had feasted on excuses to subjugate her. Of all of them, she wanted to understand and forgive Torian for his treatment of her since the choosing, but she was tired, bone tired, of worrying how her behavior affected others when no one gave her the same courtesy.

Drazhan's mouth swept against her scalp. He mumbled something into her hair, and his warm breath brought her back to the hours before. She slid over him to relive even a whisper of that pleasure before they had to go.

Before they had to convince the others she was safe.

Fine.

Unchanged.

The first two would require only creative storytelling. The last was a lie.

Drazhan was already hard for her. His cock twitched against her, and he gazed up at her with a tired, dreamy look. "Last night wasn't enough for you?" He grinned.

Imryll shook her head. How could she say what she was really thinking? That she could bear the spiders and grime and dust and seclusion of the place if it meant staying, with him, forever?

"Was it enough for you?" she asked, timidity creeping into her voice.

Drazhan cupped her hips and lifted her over his cock. He reached a hand between her legs first, to check if she was ready, and she was. She enjoyed the rise of his brows when he confirmed it.

He pursed his mouth and pulled her back down with a deep moan. Imryll clenched as though reopening a wound, but it only took seconds for her to adjust to the size of him, the shape of him. Like fitting into a mold.

Drazhan had been right after all when he'd claimed his cock would ruin her for all other men.

He released one of her hips and ran a calloused palm against her lower back. The touch bordered on tender, and she grew wetter from that, somehow, than the deep plunge of him or the twist of his fingers between her legs.

She came so quickly, it had Drazhan bracing to stay his own finish.

When he was close, she pressed a hand to his mouth and shook her head. She pulled off him and crawled backward and down and took his cock in her hand. She looked up and into his stunned—elated—eyes and devoured him, filling her mouth with a subtle sweetness, a different taste of the pleasure he'd given her.

Drazhan screamed and bucked off the pelt. A barrage of hot seed pierced the back of her throat in hard, constant spurts. She had to swallow twice to keep breathing.

When he was finished, she fell back on her heels to watch him recover.

Drazhan's chest rose and fell with his slow pants. He lifted his hands off the fur and beckoned for her through his exhaustion. Imryll crawled back over him, and he tugged her into his arms.

He tucked a hand under her chin and raised it. Their eyes met. He held the gaze before kissing her. Tasting himself. Tasting her.

Imryll nestled against his chest. Drazhan's hand fell into place along the outside of her arm, sweeping back and forth.

"Did you sleep at all?" she asked. Her voice, breaking through the remnants of passion, didn't belong. She regretted asking.

Drazhan shook his head. He inhaled a deep breath. "I never do."

"I know, but…I thought…"

He kissed her forehead. "I couldn't risk you running off again."

Imryll frowned against him. "I see."

"When I saw you…in the ravine…" Emotion choked his voice, taking the rest of his words.

Imryll sighed and draped an arm over him. "I'm sorry."

"For running off?"

"For scaring you."

"But not for running off?"

"I don't know…I don't know what to feel about that," she said, the start of a confession. "All I wanted was to be free to make my own choices, but last night…Last night I chose something for myself, and I've never felt more alive." She looked up at him. "The first time I even knew what the word meant was when you touched me in the bretèche, Drazhan."

He made a soft sound, and she pictured the smile that followed.

"You're not…" Imryll nibbled her lip. "I need to know that you're not…That this isn't…"

"Isn't what, Imryll?"

"A game," she said. "I need to know that *I'm* not a game to you."

"What do you want it to be?"

"I don't know," she admitted. "But not that."

Drazhan gave her back another quick rub and peeled away. "We have to get back. If they weren't already searching for you, they will be now, and with daylight arrived, they'll find this place without much trouble."

Imryll sat up and crossed her arms over her bare chest. In the light of day, she was aware of her nudity, of the many acts of sex that had transformed her into someone else. She had yet to discover who that was, but she unwaveringly knew that Imryll of Glaisgain belonged to no one.

Not Torian.

Not Marius.

Not the crown.

Not even Drazhan.

"Your nightgown is dry. The cloak is still a mess, so we can come back for it later." He tossed her chemise at her. "You went for a ride. You got caught in the storm. I found you and tried to guide you back, but you were afraid of the thunder, so we found a dry place to wait out the storm.

"I'm not afraid of thunder."

"Do you have a better story?"

She shook her head.

Drazhan re-dressed, facing away. She tried not to gasp when his back came into full display. It was covered in deep, long scars. Old ones. Claw marks.

And then his shirt came down, hiding it all once more.

She wanted to ask, but he would loathe the question…and maybe her.

"Men think women are the weaker sex. Playing to that assures believability."

Imryll shimmied into her nightgown with a snort, trying to put the sight of his back out of her mind. "That's why men are unfit to rule."

"I didn't say I agreed," he said.

"No? You revere women, do you?"

"Yes. I do." Drazhan turned as he buttoned his shirt. "The women I've known have all been pillars of strength. They hold families together and are the lifeblood of society. Men cannot be the men they need to be without them."

"What a shock it must've been for you to come to Duncarrow then."

"You think the women on that rock aren't strong?"

"I think they're powerless."

"They feel that way across the entire realm, I suspect. It doesn't mean they are."

Imryll turned away to hide the flush of emotion rising from her chest. She didn't know where it had come from, but it felt like the weight of things unsaid, and the fear of returning to a world where whatever had passed between her and Drazhan would shift from the realm of magic to the cold blast of reality.

Where Drazhan's fickle moods decided his treatment of her.

Where she was still expected to charm the lord of the Easterlands and, eventually, bed the prince of the White Kingdom.

Drazhan's arms folded around her from the back, enveloping her in a cocoon of warmth and protection. "I'm sorry too."

Imryll craned up to kiss him. "For what?"

But he didn't answer.

TWENTY
PROTECTIVE. COMMANDING. MINE.

They're entering the courtyard now, Your Grace.

Torian had never been more relieved to hear words in his life.

He stood at Marius's side, flanked by the Rhiagain Guard, now led by a man named Evos. Evos was Janus's replacement. It hadn't even been a full day since Torian's lifelong bodyguard had been murdered, and already someone was standing in his place as though always having been there.

Marius wore a barely concealed smirk. His sister's matched. In the hours Torian had spent with Marcelina after the crisis, he'd made two observations.

She was disgustingly gorgeous. If she'd offered herself last night, he wouldn't have refused.

And she was as dangerous as a hurricane.

Torian had sensed they were about two rounds of witty barbs away from matters escalating when a Quintus guard had come to inform Evos that Imryll had gone missing.

And so had her knight.

Torian watched them ride up the path with a slow gait. Imryll was in the front, riding astride, Wynter with one hand on the reins and the other on…her. His arm draped around her from the back like it was the most natural thing in the world. It lacked the tautness of decorum, of duty. Of *decency*.

There's something I need to tell you before I lose the courage.

All she wore was an oversized blouse that could only belong to her guard. Torian clenched all over at the sight of her bare feet dangling to the side. Her red curls were matted and wild, telling a side of the story Imryll never would.

Marius rushed forward when Torian didn't. He held out his arms, and Imryll hesitated before jumping into them. She tossed a half-eaten apple into a bush just before the lord fawned over her, his hands dancing along her face and hair as though she'd been gone years, not hours.

It felt like years. It might as well have been.

"What happened? Are you all right?" Marius crushed her to his chest and squeezed his eyes closed. "We were so worried."

Torian met Wynter's gaze as the man dismounted and handed the reins to a young attendant. He caught a flash of the man's bare chest through a gap in his cloak.

Wynter's mouth twitched. His eyes shot briefly upward before moving away from Torian altogether.

I should have listened to Imryll when she said he was trouble.

"I just needed some air," Imryll said. She peeled away from Marius in a daze.

"She went for a ride," Wynter said. He angled himself to create distance between Imryll and Marius. He wasn't even trying to hide his protectiveness, which went well beyond professional. Did no one else see it? "I followed her, she ran into some trouble, and we decided to wait it out somewhere dry." He flashed a quick grin at Imryll. "The thunder unsettled her."

She returned the smile and lowered her eyes. "It was foolish of me to think I could take off alone when I hardly know how to ride. I'm sorry for any worry I caused."

Marius divided looks between them. "Well, you're safe, and that's what matters. Right, Your Grace?"

"Right," Torian whispered. His gaze stayed on Imryll. A violent chill shuddered across his flesh despite the humidity of the post-storm morning. When their gazes connected, he saw another kind of storm brewing in her eyes, and he knew.

He knew.

You have no right to be angry. She doesn't belong to you. She never asked for this.

But it wasn't Imryll he was angry at.

It was his mother. His father. The traditions that had forced them into such a terrible situation, destroying anything pure that had once lived between himself and Imryll.

"Tor," she said, snapping him out of his ire-filled haze. "I need to change into something decent, but then can we talk?"

"Talk?" Torian shook his head. "Yes. Yes, that would be good." He glanced up at the bizarre sylvan castle that reminded him how unprepared he was for anything at all. "Shall I come to you, or would you like to come to me?"

"I'll come to you." She accepted Marius's cloak and moved ahead of the group before starting up the stairs.

Marius shook his head at her bare feet. "I don't even want to know what happened to her boots, Syr Wynter."

"No," Wynter said in agreement. "You don't."

Imryll flung off the cloak the second the door was closed. In the next, Drazhan had her in his arms and backed her against the nearest wall.

She whimpered when she connected with a commanding thud. He panted into her chest, holding her aloft with one hand under her ass and unbuckling his trousers with the other. In one fluid move, he cupped her ass in his palms, lifted her, pushed aside her undergarment, and buried himself inside.

Imryll closed her eyes and threw her head back to cry out. He stole the sound with the crush of his mouth, the intrusion of his tongue drawing her back. His movements were both hard and fluid, cruel and beautiful, as he thrust into her with the force of a storm, unselfishly caressing two fingers between her legs to bring her with him.

He dipped his head between her breasts, exposed through the gap in his shirt, which he'd buttoned around her himself when they'd realized her nightgown was a loss.

She tightened her thighs against his waist and trapped her moans in her throat, where no one but Drazhan could hear them.

He slapped a hand to the wall above her with a grunt, driving even harder, his pace chasing his desperation. She could swear his fingers had turned to claws, boring into the wall, and rather than scaring her, the idea excited her. But it was the sight of his eyes rolling back in submission that sent Imryll sailing over the edge. She pitched forward in his arms, bit down on his shoulder, and rode her pleasure through the tide of unrelenting thrusts.

"Fuck," Drazhan whispered and stumbled back, spilling into his cupped hand.

Imryll regained her footing. She pulled the thin fabric of his shirt down over her thighs and watched him breathlessly recover.

Drazhan's gaze lifted to hers. His mouth twisted in a playful smile, and then he disappeared into the privy. He returned moments later with clean hands.

"Sorry."

"You're sorry?" Imryll's muscles contracted in happy repose, dizzy from the sudden shift in motion. A welcome buzz traveled across her flesh as she tried to return to the real world. "So I *shouldn't* confess I wish you'd carry me to the bedchamber and do it again?"

His eyes flashed wide. He swallowed and looked away with a stilted laugh. "Not if you want to leave this room in one piece."

I don't want to leave at all, Imryll thought, but she had to. Speaking with Torian was a must now that her relationship with Drazhan had escalated.

Drazhan shed his filthy clothes and tore through his satchel for something clean. Imryll took a deep breath and went into the other room to do the same. She allowed herself a few extra moments to dip a rag in cold water and clean the spots on her skin Drazhan had missed in the dim light of the chalet. When her hands traveled over the empty spot on her upper arm, she winced in anticipation of the inevitable trouble it would bring.

When she was dressed, she came out and found him decent as well, one hand propped on a windowsill as he looked out.

"I have to go see Torian."

He nodded over his shoulder.

"I know you need to come, but I'd like to speak with him privately."

Drazhan turned halfway. "What will you tell him?"

"The truth," she said. "What else?"

His mouth twisted in a hard coil. "He'll punish you."

"I haven't done anything deserving of punishment," Imryll said. "And I don't intend to stop."

Drazhan smirked and turned back toward the window with a short laugh. "Good girl."

Imryll tilted her head. "I can't tell if you're trying to seduce me or praise me."

"Aren't they one and the same?"

That's a good girl, Imryll.

Her cheeks filled with a flush. "Fair point."

"Be prepared for him to ask you to stop." He gazed out the window and pulled his other hand to the wall to join the first. He seemed to be almost defiantly avoiding the balcony, only several feet to his right. Being able to read these subtleties in him, when he was otherwise completely closed off emotionally, felt like progress.

"He can ask," Imryll said. She didn't dare move closer to him, or they'd be rolling around on the floor like animals. "But my days of bowing to the command of men are behind me."

Drazhan's windowed reflection showed his tight grin.

"He can set me aside as a chosen. He can banish me. He can even throw me in the Sky Dungeon—"

Drazhan spun hard. "He even *thinks* about trying, and he'd be dead before he reached the first stair."

Imryll lowered her gaze to her feet with a laugh. She loved this side of her dark knight. Protective. Commanding. *Mine.* It astounded her how much had changed since the day in the lyceum. "He won't. He'll be upset with me, and maybe he'll ply me with some speech about what we used to be to each other as children…but he won't hurt me. He knows I was forced into this arrangement. He knows I never wanted it. And if he were me—"

"He'd fall in line without question because he's *weak.*"

The venom underlining Drazhan's words took Imryll out of the moment completely. "I know you don't like him, but—"

"I don't have to like him. I'm not his guard." He lowered his face to the side so she could no longer make out his expression in the window.

"He's a good man, Draz. He's just inexperienced. He doesn't know how to navigate the roles he's inherited, and we all thought… We all thought he'd have more time."

Drazhan didn't respond.

Imryll sighed. "You understand why I prefer you to wait outside his apartments while I speak with him?"

"For you," he grumbled. "Because you asked."

Imryll resisted rolling her eyes. If he knew she could hear his jealousy so openly, he'd have done more to hide it. "Thank you. Now let's go before I lose my nerve."

When Imryll left Wynter in the hall, Torian's last thread of hope snapped. All that remained was to fill in the details, to replace them with what his imagination had already knit together.

Torian nodded at Evos to join Wynter.

"Just outside. No farther," the guard said. Torian heard the words in Janus's voice. He couldn't believe the man was gone. Torian's shadow would never cast the same shape without him.

Imryll closed the door and turned with a deep inhalation. She closed her eyes as the outbreath settled over her.

"You fucked him," he accused.

She didn't blanch or look away. "Yes," she said with a soft nod. "I did."

Torian scrunched his face in pain and spun away with a heaving, choking breath. There was knowing, and there was *knowing*.

"When did it start?" he asked, wincing at the wall.

"Last night was the first time, but…but it really began the moment I met him."

"The night of the Choosing…when you wouldn't come to my bed…"

"That's not why." Imryll took a few more steps into the room. "You're my friend, Tor. My oldest. And until that night, I thought you were the dearest too."

Torian spun, open-mouthed. "That's not fair. How dare you—"

"Not fair?" Imryll asked. She shook her head as she closed the distance between them. "Not fair, Torian? You would speak to *me* about what isn't fair?"

Torian sputtered a nonresponse. His cheeks flushed with heat, shame, and pain alike. He'd seen himself handling the conversation far more deftly and with less obvious emotion, but how had he ever convinced himself that was remotely possible in reality, when all he could see in his mind were the same torrid imaginings of Imryll writhing under her crude knight?

"*Me*," Imryll said. "You knew who I was before the Choosing. You knew what I wanted. What I *needed*. Then the king tells you that you can have me, and it was as though it kindled a different light in you. Where instead of my Torian, my *friend*, you became just like the men you swore to never be like."

"I thought you wanted to leave Duncarrow," Torian said weakly. "Not...not fornicate with your guard."

"I do want to leave," she said. Her gaze traveled to the side. "But I want him too. It would be pointless for me to pretend I don't—and a lie, and I won't lie to you." Her shoulders lifted, then fell again with another hard breath out. "I'm sorry for not telling you sooner. I wanted to tell you on the ship."

Torian swallowed and lifted his chin. "I remember."

"Then I thought," she said, "it would be better to wait until we had Lord Quintus locked into agreement with us. I didn't want to distract you with anything that might jeopardize the plan."

"How magnanimous of you."

Imryll stormed forward, which sent him stumbling back a step. "I have had to debase myself before that man to help *you*."

"Help all of us," he feebly tried to retort, but he was wrong, and she was right. He just didn't know how to bring his heart around to the truth.

"The way he touches me..." Imryll grimaced. Her hands fisted at her sides. "The way he'll *keep* touching me before the ink is dry. You can either support me in trying to save your crown or you can shame me for it, but I won't be your whipping post for the well of your confusing emotions. Friends are supposed to want the best for each other. I'm stepping beyond what makes me feel safe to help protect *your* future. Can you not understand that's all I ask of you when I want you to respect my desire to be my own person and not a man's concubine? Not an extension of a man who says he loves me, but only under the conditions of his choosing?"

"I do love you," Torian said. He kicked his feet on the floor. "But how...How can you be sure you're not just *his* concubine?"

"I can't," Imryll replied with a sad laugh. "All I can do is feel freedom in knowing that whatever we are to each other, I chose it."

"And last night…" Torian chided himself for being too weak to finish his question. It was then his eyes caught sight of the way she was caressing her arm, and he noted there was no longer a raised outline of a circlet. He didn't have the heart to ask about it.

"I was running away. At least that's what I thought. Draz—Syr Wynter, that is…He—"

"Draz." Torian flicked his tongue against his bottom lip. "It's fine, Imryll. I want you to be open with me."

"He made me see how foolish and incomplete my plan was." She finished with a sorrowful sigh. "I thought I could stay until the end, but then watching Janus…everything…" She buried her face in her hands.

Torian's chest cracked to see her sorrow. Was this not the love she spoke of, the kind where he could care for her unconditionally? Where he could understand her pain and not contribute to it?

He went to her and gathered her in his arms. She wilted against him, and for a moment, he forgot where and when they were, remembering how it had been when their problems were no more complex than what game to play in the courtyard.

Torian kissed her scalp and rubbed her back. "I know."

They held each other in a comfortable, familiar silence that made his heart ache even more for simpler times.

"I'm so sorry about Janus, Tor. And the others we lost. I'm just so sorry."

"He once told me…" Torian rested his chin atop her head as he held her. "He once told me the only honorable way for a prince's guard to die was in defense of his prince. I've thought about it a lot over the past hours."

"And the men who did it?"

"Lord Quintus wants to speak with us all after breakfast to discuss what they've learned in the intervening hours." Torian released her. "But he believes the threat has passed."

"Thank the gods." Imryll wiped her red-splotched eyes with the backs of her hands. "It could have been *you*."

Torian lowered his eyes. "Actually, they now believe it was you the thugs were after."

"*Me?*"

"There's a rumor you're carrying the heir." He laughed. "If only they knew."

Imryll turned away, one arm draped over her belly.

"I'm sorry," he said quickly. "Imryll."

"Don't apologize. I just didn't realize how hard that would hit…feeling like I've failed a mission I never signed up for."

Torian froze at the words that finally quieted his racing heart and allowed his mind to take the wheel. "Imryll…Can we just go back?"

She spun around. "What?"

"Can we just go back to who we were before the Choosing? Before we were *both* set upon these missions neither of us had any choice in? Is it even possible at this point?"

Imryll's guarded expression dissolved. Her eyes welled with tears. "I miss my friend, Tor."

He chewed his bottom lip. "I miss mine too, Ryl."

"And the rest?"

Torian gathered his courage and approached her with a smile he hoped would one day feel natural again. "If you can do what you've done to protect me, I can find the same resolve and support you."

"You mean it?"

He nodded. He did mean it. Perhaps only in that moment or until his courage gave out, but how could he let her do what she'd been commanded to do by the queen, knowing how it hurt her and not be willing to swallow his own selfish pain to accept what she'd been telling him all along: that she loved him but not like that?

Imryll flung her arms around him, choking back tearful relief. "I would love nothing more than to go back, Tor. I've really missed you."

"Well, I'm back. And this time, I won't muck things up between us."

Imryll struggled to lock her eyes on Drazhan, but she knew where he was. His presence wrapped around her from behind, a warm promise.

Marius had assembled the same group of men and women who had been in attendance at supper the night before. Aside from the somber mood holding tight to all of them, the other difference was the number of guards. Evos and Drazhan disappeared in a thick sea of mostly Quintus guards. Twice as many were stationed outside in the hall and landing and down the Golden Stair.

Torian could barely keep it together. He drummed his hands on his knees, which bounced out of time. When Marius commanded the door be shut and bolted, Torian abruptly stopped, then started again.

Imryll guessed his nerves came from a mix of their difficult conversation and the looming unknown of the unsigned agreement. But only one of those matters would be resolved when they set sail for Duncarrow in the morning, several days ahead of schedule.

"I'll keep this brief," Marius stated. He moved his gaze around at his guests. "Your Grace, we're making good time on readying your ship, and you could leave as early as this evening, if it is your preference."

Imryll's skin was covered in raised flesh. Once she boarded that ship, her opportunities for escape dwindled to practically impossible. But was it even what she still wanted, when all she could think about was the way Drazhan's muscled thighs felt spreading hers? The way he'd pushed sweaty, matted curls off of her face and kissed the spot where they'd lain?

Had one night with a man really weakened her resolve so much?

"It is, Lord Quintus," Torian replied. His voice sounded small. Imryll wished she could help him. "We thank you and your men for the hasty preparations. We would have liked to avail ourselves of your hospitality a few days longer, but…"

"And you will, sir, when you next return to Whitechurch."

"An invitation we accept with gladness in our hearts," Clarisan said. A smile followed her words, but her eyes were locked on Francis Oakenwell, who flushed and pretended to be interested in his hands.

"We'll return the favor in a few weeks, when you come to Duncarrow," Torian said. Imryll looked over in surprise.

"And what an honor it will be, the first lord of the realm invited by our king." Marius folded his hands with an easy smile. "As the princess lived up to her end of the agreement and spent most of the night in my arms… at least until events made it impossible… I agree to come to Duncarrow, where we will together sail to Belcarrow to inspect the training grounds of the Rhiagain Guard so that Oakenwell can obtain confidence his guard will train at the best camp in the kingdom. If everything is as you say it is, you can expect my men to arrive in springtide. We'll break ground on the reliquary at the same time."

"A perfect plan," Torian said. He wrung his hands under the table.

"A productive visit, in spite of the terrible turn." Marius's exhale made a whistling sound. "Which is what I've called you here to discuss, to provide an update on all we've learned and the measures taken."

Torian nodded. He didn't seem to notice the intense stare Marcelina had trained on him.

"As suspected, our assailants were part of a disheveled but highly radical group called the Goldtails. They are anti-crown, anti-regulation, anti-border expansion…anti-*everything*, except chaos. They tolerate us because we keep taxes low, respect local governments, and incentivize farmers to produce more so fewer people starve. They know it could be worse."

Clarisan's mouth curled in derision. "Tolerate *you*? Are you not the lord of the Easterlands, Lord Quintus?"

Oakenwell shifted to restrain a grin.

Imryll didn't know what had happened in the hours she was away, but she was positive *something* had happened between those two.

Marius ignored the question. "But when they learned of Your Grace's visit, we began to hear whispers of stirrings."

Imryll couldn't stop herself. "You heard whispers, Lord Quintus, of *stirrings* and did not see fit to warn us?"

He trained a hard grin her way. Darkness twinkled in his eyes. It lasted only a moment, but she saw straight to the heart of the man, and what she saw gave her a chill: an equal capacity for cruelty and kindness, with the ability to shift from one to the other in an instant. "If I warned everyone about every whisper a lord hears, we'd do nothing but wait to be attacked."

"But we didn't have to wait," Imryll retorted. "We *were* attacked. We lost good men."

"We did," he said, nodding, "but the ones who matter are sitting at this table due to the skill and guidance of men like Steward Oakenwell, who sprang into action before more blood could be spilled."

"Did you just imply…" Imryll, incredulous, inched back in her chair.

"Imryll." Clarisan shook her head from Imryll's right.

"All respect to your new lover, Clarisan, but to imply the men we lost didn't matter is beyond what I can keep quiet about." Imryll twisted her jaw, losing the battle between holding her tongue for the crown's sake and using it to stand up for Janus and the others. "Janus was a good man. An excellent guard. The others who died to protect us were also good men—men who gave up having wives and children to serve their king."

Marius lifted his palms in surrender. "Princess. It would cut my heart if I thought you believed me to be so heartless as what you've described."

"I have tried to hold my tongue, brother, forgive me," Marcelina said, breaking her silence. "But there is not a cruel bone in your entire body. You have mourned for these men. You hardly slept. But to dwell on it puts us all at risk."

Imryll's anger brimmed to the surface, but a glance around told her she was alone. Everyone watched her, waiting for what she'd say next, but none of them were going to back her words. No one—not even Torian, only half-present in the moment—shared her horror in the way Marius had treated their casualties like acceptable losses.

Except Drazhan.

She caught him in the corner of the room. He gave her a somber nod, but on the down sweep, she saw something in his eyes that made her want to cry.

Pride.

"I am not so imaginative as to describe something I hadn't just heard you say, Lord Quintus," Imryll replied. She tucked her shoulders back and sat straight. "But our losses are not your concern, as you've said. We will pay appropriate respects to the dead when we return to Duncarrow."

"That isn't what I said—"

"It is," Imryll stated. She inhaled a shaky breath. "Please, continue with your brief so we may prepare for our return."

Marius's gaze lingered on her for several more agonizing moments. The others shifted, no one apparently knowing the right words to restore peace.

"The Goldtails are vanquished," he finally said. He turned back toward Torian but flicked his eyes once at Imryll, a sign she took to mean he wasn't leaving her words alone, just giving them rest. "We have a hundred of their heads lining the approach from the Whitechurch gates to Arboriana, lest any stragglers get further ideas about coming after their future queen and her unborn child."

"Imryll," Clarisan said at her side with a soft laugh. "What a blessing."

Imryll didn't correct the misguided assumption or address Clarisan's knowing jab. She pointed her focus at the space between Marius and his sister.

Drazhan cocked his head.

"Vanquished, as I said. There are no more risks to any of your persons, royal or otherwise."

"And yet we are practically choking with guards," Imryll muttered.

"Peace of mind," Marius said. "That's all I've come to say. A supper invitation is extended to you all, though I have no expectation of anyone accepting under the circumstances. Take your rest and then I'll see you to your ship."

"Thank you, Lord Quintus." Torian stood after everyone else had. "We appreciate your swift response."

Marius bowed. "Your Grace."

As everyone began to shuffle out, he raised his finger. "Ah, but I'd like a few moments alone with the princess. Imryll, do you mind staying?"

Imryll trapped a breath between her shoulders, turned, and nodded with a forced smile. "Of course."

Marius looked over her shoulder. "*Without* your guard. You may join the others on the landing, Syr Wynter. Thank you."

It took a few minutes for everyone to leave. Imryll allowed herself a quick shared glance with Drazhan. His eyes were full of violence. For one tense moment, she thought he would refuse the command, but she nodded to tell him it was all right, and he calmed enough to follow the order.

But nothing was all right. Marius wanting her alone meant that whatever he planned to say—or do—wasn't fit for the eyes and ears of others.

Torian's easy departure surprised her the most. The entire trip he'd allowed himself to be led by a lesser man, and Marius's request to meet with her alone was shocking. But all he did was nod, flick a quick look at Imryll, and leave with the rest.

"I can smell it on you, you know."

Imryll realized she'd been staring at the closed door. "Sorry?" she asked without turning.

"The others might believe your story, Imryll, but I know better."

She watched him step up onto the balcony and disappear behind the thin curtains.

"Come stand with me. It's a beautiful day."

Imryll rolled her shoulders in a shiver. The last thing she wanted to do was stand next to him, but it became clear to her how he had been such an effective leader. Marius was a confusing, enigmatic combination of charming and devious—difficult to trust and skilled at drawing people in anyway.

She took a deep breath and joined him.

"You've said in your days here that you're surrounded by beauty, but this is nothing, Imryll. The leaves and blooms you see are just the most hearty, strong enough to last through the cold months. Some say the Guardians designed our forests to be beautiful in all seasons, not just the woefully short springtide." He gestured around. "But if you saw the Rushwood in full bloom, you'd know this is but a small consolation for what's coming."

Imryll found a spot on the balcony a few feet away. "To someone who has lived their entire life around nothing but rocks, a single leaf is a wonder."

"Did you enjoy the imported blooms we sent for your celebrations?"

She nodded slowly. "Yes…though once plucked, it's no longer a bloom, is it? Its life is already over, taken from its life-giving stems and roots for a few days of enjoyment by those who will discard it the moment it begins to wilt or lose color."

Marius grinned from her left. "Are we still speaking of flowers, Princess?"

Imryll spun and propped her hip against the stone railing. "The longer this takes, the greater the chance my guard will come barreling through the door."

"He's very protective of you, Syr Wynter."

"He takes his charge seriously."

"And what is his charge?" Marius swept his gaze over her. "Do you think the king had *fucking the future queen* on his list of duties when he brought the knights to Duncarrow to compete for you?"

Imryll fought the flush rising in her cheeks. Any reaction would be confirmation. "The king doesn't make it his business to share his intentions with anyone."

"Before or after he took ill?"

Imryll tensed. That was two things Marius knew more about than he should, but the king's health was a far more dangerous piece of knowledge. "We all catch our share of chills on cold Duncarrow."

Marius cocked his head. "Is that why he sent his inept son to broker a deal that determines the future of his crown?"

Imryll scoffed, shaking her head in disbelief. "You are dangerously close to speaking treason with your words, Lord Quintus."

"Treason is determined by the one in power. Unless I come to the crown's aid, the Rhiagains will not be in power much longer, will they?"

Imryll steadied herself with a deep breath. The silence was louder than the breeze carrying leaves away from their branches. "I ask you again. Why am I here, and why alone?"

He tapped the railing and closed his eyes, letting the breeze finish before opening them. "I know what you did last night and why."

"I needed—"

His dark eyes burrowed into her. "I know what you needed. And you got it. Part of it anyway." He dragged his hand along the stone as he came closer to her. "Does the prince know?"

"You're speaking nonsense." Imryll shook her head. "You're insinuating things that—"

Marius leaned in. "I know you tried to run away, and when you failed, you spent all night underneath your knight in an abandoned abbey. Before you waste precious energy on denials, Wynter wasn't the only one who followed you last night. My men were there too. For all of it." He rolled back and grinned. "I can't fault you for either endeavor, Princess. Your knight is a delectable man whom even *I* wouldn't turn out of bed, and from what little I know of Duncarrow, being trapped there the rest of my life seems a worse fate than death."

Imryll fisted her hands. Her nose flared.

Marius noted both with a short laugh.

"What do you want from me?"

Marius reached forward and cupped her cheek. "Can I kiss you?"

"No." Imryll recoiled out of his hand.

"What if I said I was going to anyway?"

"I'd scream."

"And who would hear you? A thousand men loyal to me and only a dozen loyal to you?"

Imryll backed farther away. Fear turned her vision to a sky full of stars.

Marius's mouth spread into a broad grin. He held out his hands in mock surrender. "It was only a question, Princess. I'm not that kind of man."

"What. Do. You. Want?" Imryll pressed her words through clenched teeth. Moments before, she'd been afraid Drazhan would burst into the apartment, and now she wished he would.

"A better question is what do *you* want? What do you want me to do with this knowledge I have of what you did last night?"

Imryll's face cooled. "The prince already knows about Syr Wynter. I told him everything."

Marius's brows jumped in surprise. "What a bold choice. How did he take it?"

"As he should have." Imryll crossed her arms over her chest. "Seeing as I had no say in becoming his First Chosen."

Marius slowly nodded, his eyes down and to the side. "Fascinating. And he knows you were going to run off and never look back?"

"Torian and I were friends before any of this. It's no secret I wanted to leave Duncarrow and have a life on the mainland."

"Fascinating," he said again. "Truly. And the king? I take it he knows all of this?"

Imryll paled. She began to say one thing, but nothing came out.

"As I thought," Marius said. He turned back toward the forest. "You asked what I want. Well, I wanted your truth, and now I have it. If we're going to be partners, there can be no lies between us."

"Partners?" Imryll swallowed. She dug her hip into the stone.

"Nothing has changed, has it? You still want to leave?"

Imryll shouldn't tell him anything. The voice of reason in her head screamed at her to say no more. But in a few short hours, she'd be on a ship back to Duncarrow. She'd leave the mainland behind and, with it, her best chance of escape.

"I'll keep your secrets, Imryll of Glaisgain." Marius studied her. "In exchange, when the time comes, you'll return to the Easterlands with me and become my wife."

"Your...what?" Imryll bounced back another few steps. "You cannot be—"

"Serious? Oh, but I am. I am. I can see the thoughts whirling in your keen mind, and I suspect you've already guessed correctly. The days of the Rhiagains are coming to an end. The rise of the Quintus crown is just over the horizon." He shrugged. "It's not as though you're actually married now, is it?"

"You would..." Imryll's throat locked. Beads of sweat spread across her chest and back. "You would overthrow the king? And you'd *tell* me this, knowing I'm returning there tonight?"

"I don't have to overthrow a dying king, Imryll. I just have to wait." Marius moved closer again. He reached for her hand on the railing and covered it with his. "You want freedom? You'll have all you want here. I need a wife and children, and if that wife comes from Duncarrow...Well, you can imagine how the realm would perceive that union. For those like the Goldtails, the end of the

Rhiagains would be enough. For the royalists, the joining of our houses would satisfy their desire to worship foreign kings."

"How is this…" *Better than the life I have now,* she almost said, but the answer was already clear. She would be surrounded by beauty. She'd have more freedom than she had on Duncarrow. She had no desire to bed Marius, but it would be for the sole purpose of having children, and while Imryll had always struggled to see herself as a mother, it was only because she didn't want to raise children in such a cold, lifeless place.

But that cold, lifeless place was her home. On that rock lived everyone she loved in the world. It was one thing to leave, and another to know leaving would cause their lives to be upended. Or worse.

"Go on. Ask your questions."

Imryll didn't answer. She was still working her mind around the insanity of Marius's proposal.

"You're worried about your family."

"Among other things."

"When the king dies, the crown will crumble. It won't be a war, or even a fight. The end will come quietly, without fuss. Torian is the last Rhiagain, and he's no threat to anyone. We both know you're not carrying his child." He shook his head. "I have no desire to hurt anyone. A peaceful exchange of power is possible."

"Possible, but not certain."

"Do you want me to promise not to hurt the prince?"

Imryll thrust her hands out. "I want you to promise not to hurt anyone!"

Marius lifted his shoulders. "For you, I can make that promise."

Imryll couldn't believe she was talking about *treason.* But she hadn't been able to shake her unease about the Goldtails. Marius might dismiss them as rebel insurgents, but many shared their view. Tens of thousands of lives had been lost in the Uprising because the realm didn't want to submit to foreign kings—and the war clearly wasn't over. What if saving the crown had been the wrong goal all along?

"This is a lot to take in," she said. She didn't want to commit to anything. She didn't know what was right or wrong or what side she should be on. Her personal desires mixed with her loyalty, turning to mud.

"Of course it is. If you gave me an answer here and now, how could I trust it?" He stepped forward and took firm hold of her shoulders. "I'll see you in Duncarrow in a few weeks. You can give me your answer then."

She wanted to say she already knew her answer, that she'd never, ever consider trading one cage for another…that what he proposed was the worst kind of sedition and she'd tell the king the second she returned, no matter what repercussions came down on her when Carrow learned of her behavior.

But in her flustered confusion, she only nodded.

Marius turned her and aimed her toward the stairs. "Go on then. As you said, we wouldn't want Syr Wynter to break the door down."

Imryll took each step in a daze, fighting a sway. She descended the stairs and kept moving by instinct alone.

"Oh, and, Imryll? There'd be one condition that's nonnegotiable."

Imryll turned.

"You'd have to agree never to see or speak with Syr Wynter again." He held up a hand when she started to rebut. "And I suggest making the cut now, because if I find out you're carrying his child, the deal is off, and I can't promise *anyone* on Duncarrow will be safe. Not even you."

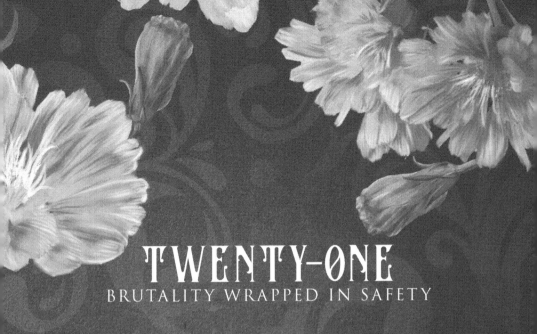

TWENTY-ONE
BRUTALITY WRAPPED IN SAFETY

Drazhan breathed a short sigh of relief when the door opened and Imryll finally came out. Another few minutes and he'd have barged in, no matter how it looked. He didn't trust the slippery, pretty lord or his equally pretty, slippery sister or even Oakenwell, who seemed honorable enough, but honorable men didn't debase themselves with lesser ones.

Marius lingered at the door. He brushed his hands on Imryll's shoulders before raising one to the edge of her jaw and tilting it as though readying for a kiss. Imryll's arms hung straight down at her sides, a sign of her disconnection with the lord's overfamiliarity, but she let him run his thumb along her soft flesh with a languorous haze in his eyes that meant only one thing from a man.

She was playing the game the disgusting crown had set for her. Unlike her simpering prince, Drazhan wouldn't punish her for it.

Drazhan curled his toes in his boots. Twitched his sword hand out of a fist to keep himself from instinctively drawing steel.

His hands flamed in darker response.

Marius ran his thumb along her lip, tugging it to expose the soft, damp flesh beneath. It was the move that made Imryll duck away with a sheepish grin and move to Drazhan's side.

"Good afternoon, Lord Quintus," she said, breathy and flustered.

"Good afternoon, Princess." Marius bowed low, winked, and backed into his apartments without breaking his gaze.

Imryll sagged when the door closed.

"He's bold." Drazhan urged her on. He needed distance between that man and his own anger—distance from what shouldn't upset him at all, but had.

It's just sex. There's nothing wrong with taking pleasure from a conquest.

"He is." Imryll trailed her words with a contemplative exhale, and he realized she was intentionally hedging her words.

"Too bold, even for a lord." Drazhan's palms warmed from the center, the heat spreading to the first knuckle of his fingers. *Not here.*

"He hasn't met a boundary he couldn't cross yet," she replied, her face pointed ahead as they descended one level on the stairs.

"Is that your way of saying he crossed yours tonight?"

Imryll stopped midstair and pivoted toward him. "Are you really asking me that, Draz?"

Drazhan looked around and then back at her. "You grow careless, princess."

She recoiled, straightening. "Torian has always called his guards by their first names."

Drazhan lowered his voice to a terse whisper. "Torian isn't *fucking* his guards, is he?"

Imryll scoffed in disgust and continued on without him. He fell in behind her and stayed that way until they reached her apartments, where he entered ahead of her to sweep the rooms for danger.

He beckoned her in when he was finished. As she closed the door behind her, she rolled her eyes, which he caught as she was turning.

"Are you going to tell me why he wanted your guard to leave the room?" Drazhan fought to keep the edge from his tone.

"I didn't realize talking was a part of our relationship." Imryll quipped, but there was no humor in her expression when she brushed past him and entered the bedchamber.

"As your guard—"

"I know, I know. Every detail, right?" Imryll undid the clasp on her cloak and hurled it across the room, where it smacked into a wall and bounced off the floor. She winced at each consecutive sound and dropped onto the end of the bed.

Drazhan felt something fray within him. A thread was all it was, but it was enough to whittle his self-control down to nothing. "Did he...Did he hurt you, Imryll?"

Imryll lowered her head and shook it.

"Did he threaten you?"

"Why even ask? If he did, so what? What would you do, Draz, march back there and wave your claws at him with a mighty roar? Scowl and brood and grunt in the corner?"

Drazhan balked, tensing. "He *did* threaten you."

"No." She bowed over her knees, her red curls falling over the sides like a curtain, veiling her face. "He just did what the men in my life have always done—*tell* me what my future will be. Like I should be grateful for whatever consolation is at the end of the games they play, moving me across the board like a pawn with only one purpose."

He wanted to push harder, peck at her until her resolve crumbled and she told him what she was holding back. But even the thought of it made his stomach turn after listening to her speak of how the men in her life had treated her.

No matter what his initial impetus had been for seeking her out, Drazhan refused to treat Imryll with such gross disrespect.

Everything he had done—would do—must come with her full consent and enthusiasm.

No, had *done is right. It's done. Return, finish with the king and prince, and* leave.

Taking Imryll to bed even once more would be the same as admitting that his desire for her had grown bigger than his thirst for revenge.

"Nothing to say to that? Of course not." Imryll's voice choked with emotion. She rolled back and swiped at both eyes. "Our ship will be ready in a few hours, and I know I won't get much rest on the ship—"

Drazhan towered over her, his shadow consuming her on all sides and stretching behind her on the bed. She fell back on her hands, her jaw parted in alarm that didn't match the flash of excitement in her eyes.

"You really want to sleep?" he asked, his voice husky, the way he knew she liked it. *Just this last time,* he told himself. *For her. To take her mind off her distress.*

Imryll rolled in her bottom lip. Shook her head.

Drazhan's cock roared to life. He held her gaze as he unbuckled his sword, enjoying the way her eyes widened with every lash of the belt. With his eyes still on her, he backed away and set it on a nearby table.

She followed his movements in charged silence.

"Here's what's going to happen," he said as he returned to the bed and her. "I'm going to eat that pussy until I'm satisfied and then I'm going to fuck you until both of us will be walking diagonal when we board the ship."

Imryll's throat jumped with a hard swallow.

"Nod if you understand," he growled.

Imryll bounced her head in vigorous nods.

"Lie back."

She didn't move right away. She only stared at him, wearing a look of shock mixed with longing.

"Don't make me say it twice."

Imryll swallowed hard again and started to ease back, but Drazhan dropped to his knees and hooked his hands over her thighs and yanked. She fell back in a whimper and then made another, louder, more desperate cry, when he ripped her undergarments off instead of tracing them down her legs like a gentleman.

Because Imryll didn't want a gentleman. She wanted a dark knight who roared and clawed and left no survivors. She wanted brutality wrapped in safety, and he would give her that and more.

Imryll bunched her dress up over her waist, but Drazhan didn't wait for her to finish before burying his face in her. He groaned through the welcome, moist heat of her arousal, delirious in the knowledge he was the only man alive capable of making her so wet so fast. It reminded him of how she'd tasted the night of her choosing, like lavender and raspberry oil.

Imryll twisted through the hard flicks of his tongue. She tried to close her legs, whining that it was too much, but he pried them back open with his elbows, and her moans swelled in urgency.

She came fast, bucking and clamping her thighs around his head as she screamed and thrashed in ecstasy. He gave her no time to recover, ignoring her pathetic pleas that she couldn't come again.

But she did come again. Twice. A third time and then a fourth, each more vocal and turbulent than the last. Imryll had the blanket gathered so tight in her hands, her fingers were as white as snow. Her slick desire coating the inside of her thighs and covering his face and hair, Drazhan wished he'd met Imryll under different circumstances, that they could indulge their fantasies together until they grew weary of it, oblivious to the hard realities calling them back.

He rolled onto his heels. Imryll released the blanket with an exhausted but satisfied sigh. From where he knelt, he saw her bunched dress rise with each hard breath. She gleamed from his skilled tongue, and he knew she was ready to take him.

Sarah M. Cradit

Drazhan climbed to his feet. "I want you out of this dress in less than a minute," he ordered and went to work removing his own clothing as he watched her scramble to obey.

She stood before him, naked, looking up with her wide doe eyes that made him want to fuck her so hard, they couldn't flare any wider. She still hadn't said a word other than the desperate cries she'd made when he was eating her.

He ran his tongue along his bottom lip and then the top one to drink up the last of her wetness. Her mouth tightened, her eyes threatening to roll back as he continued his cleanup, using the backs of his hands to wipe his face down.

He was tempted to slip his tongue inside her mouth so she could suck on her desire, but there was something else he wanted more. Something *she* wanted more.

Drazhan seized her by the hips and spun her. She gasped at the sudden turn and again when he bent her over the end of the bed, one hand on her neck, the other stroking his cock.

"You take this cock so well, Imryll. But you haven't taken it all the way yet."

"How...How is that possible?"

He released her neck and his cock and planted both palms on opposite ass cheeks. He spread her wide, and she moaned in delighted shock. Her glistening core was ready for him, but he wanted to stretch all the way to the end of her.

Drazhan swung his hips and his crown brushed her entrance, causing her to buck up and back. He came to a stop when he'd lined himself up just right and then buried himself in one hard thrust.

Imryll squealed and arced up off the bed, but he wasn't even all the way in yet. He spread her wider and drove in deeper, stretching her more than ever before. She threw her head back with a deep, guttural moan, one hand slapping the bed, the other stretched above her head like a cat clawing at the air.

"Is it too much for you, Imryll?"

She shook her face against the blanket.

304

"I want your words."

"No." She panted. She squirmed underneath him, trying to get away yet trying to take more. "No, don't stop, Draz."

Every time she'd said his name like that, *Draz,* it turned him into a brute with no self-control, no sense of right or wrong or good or bad. It was *Draz* who fucked her so wildly, he wondered if he'd transformed into a beast entirely. It was *Draz* who dragged himself out, slowly, then in, slowly, only so he could slam himself against her and earn one of her girlish whimpers as his reward.

One of those girlish whimpers pushed him headlong into the abyss, and he started to pull out to finish on her ass when she turned her face over her shoulder and shook her head.

"What?" he asked, breathless, pumping his cock slower.

"I want you inside of me when you come."

Drazhan's knees threatened to buckle. "No, Imryll, that's—"

"Yes," she insisted. Her eyes glossed with wanting as she tilted her ass at him. "Yes, Draz. Unless you don't want to."

You have no idea. "Do you know what you're asking?"

She bit her lip and nodded. "I want to feel *all* of you. Every last drop."

Every last drop had him pressing one hand on her lower back to brace, using the other to slide back inside. He didn't need any time to bring himself back to the edge because he'd never left. He curved his hands around the edges of her hips and thrust back in just as his cock erupted, filling her with *every last drop,* just as she'd asked for.

Drazhan waited until his last spasm to back away. The sight of his seed dripping out of her, mixed with her own arousal, sent blood rushing to his head. The urge to collapse was almost as strong as the urge to keep fucking her.

Imryll rolled over. She sat up and slid to the end of the bed and hopped off.

Drazhan watched her for any sign he'd hurt her, but the only emotion he read in her eyes was longing.

She snaked her arms around his neck and craned her head back. "I guess I wasn't so tired after all." She raised up onto her toes and kissed the corner of his jaw. "That's how I want it every time. All of you, every time. Nothing less."

Drazhan nodded, even though tonight had to be the last of it. It *had* to. For the sake of his mission. For her sake as well, as he could already see that through the cloud of delirium, she was developing feelings for him, and hurting her was never part of the plan.

"We still have a few hours," she whispered. Her hands wound through his hair at the back. "It would be a shame to waste any of them."

Drazhan lifted her into his arms. "I may be a lot of things, Imryll," he said as he carried her back to the bed. "But I'm never wasteful."

My arms are sore. No, not just sore, bone tired, like I've swung them for days straight. I can hardly move either of them, but everyone around me is looking at me with strange pride, as though I've just won a contest.

I'm in the same place—world? I don't know—as my last few visions, as the boy in the barn, but I'm no longer in the barn. I'm standing in a frosty courtyard surrounded by men in heavy furs and solemn faces, but I only recognize one of them.

My brother nods approvingly. "There's no such thing as being ready for this, but you've trained well, and you've come a long way. I believe your odds are better than most. Better than mine, when I did the Hunt."

In my head, I have capitalized the Hunt because of how others around us are murmuring about it, about their own turn at the Hunt. It's an event, this much I know, but my instincts tell me it's not hunting as most know it.

"Everyone chooses a different strategy, son." A man approaches and claps me on the shoulders. He wears the same pride as my brother, and

in the man's eyes, I see what is almost a reflection. If he's not my father, then he's something close in blood relation. "But seven days is a long time to keep running. You didn't train to run. You trained to fight."

"He will," my brother says, almost stepping between us. He seems annoyed with the man, who I think may be my father, but I don't understand his annoyance yet. "What matters is that he comes home to us."

"No. That's not all that matters." The man grimaces. "As you well know from your own shameful showing." He walks away.

My brother's gaze follows the man. He looks sad, like he's the one who has failed our father when I'm fairly confident it was me. The looks on the faces of the other men seem to confirm it.

"It's all right. He doesn't mean it," my brother says.

We both know he does. I just don't understand this situation enough to know why.

The other men filter out of the courtyard until it's just my brother and me. He kicks at the frozen earth, clearly searching for words.

"I don't care what he says, brother. If you see the white wulf barreling down on you, you either run or play dead. Honor has no place in the Hunt. What good is honor if you're dead?"

I don't know why I say it. I'm not in control. "What if I want to kill the wulf?"

"What?"

"What if I want to kill him? What if I don't want to run, to hide?"

My brother's face erupts in horror. The slow shake of his head is almost devastating.

Instead of responding, he pulls me in for a hug and crushes me against his chest.

Imryll awoke to the welcome poke of Drazhan's nocturnal erection. She noted his hand resting on her bare hip. A soft snore.

The man never slept, but he was sleeping.

With her.

In her bed.

But if they were sleeping, then…

She started to leap from the bed in alarm, but Drazhan's hand on her hip tightened, pinning her.

"We still have a half tick before they'll come for us," he murmured into the pillow. She heard him roll his face on the soft fabric, and he snapped her tight against himself, practically impaling her. "Your trunks are packed."

Imryll was still in two places. The emotional tug of the vision had her wishing she could go back and learn more about the Hunt—and the fate of the boy whose memories she kept visiting. But then she was grinding her hips back, ready for more of the man who had torn her apart in the night, piece by piece, and had put her back together as someone else.

Drazhan's hand traveled the valley of her waist and slid around her, over her belly, and farther down. "One last time," he said with a short thrust. He didn't need to prepare her. She was still ready from the last…still full of her desire, of *him*.

"One last time," she said back, threading each word between sharp cries as he took her from behind. But there was something so clinging and desperate in the way he clutched her, flesh pinning flesh, sweat providing the perfect slip to his movements.

"Imryll," he whispered, the last word to leave his tongue before he came.

As Drazhan grunted into her matted hair, filling her, a pang of sadness washed over her.

One last time to Imryll meant the end of their wonderful but confusing interlude in the Easterlands.

But she couldn't help but feel as though it meant something far more final to him.

TWENTY-TWO

IMRYLL. IMRYLL. IMRYLL.

Imryll ran her fingers along the gold flakes etched in the title
of the book Marius had given her as her parting gift. It was
called *The Long Wintertide*, and though she'd only read the first
few pages, she already understood his intention in giving it to her.

The story was about a man who had been separated from his
family and forced to survive an entire wintertide in the unforgiving northern forests. His family had believed him dead the
entire time—mourning him, etching his name on a funerary
marker. His wife had moved on, marrying a widower, and his
children called the new man *father*. He returned to a world that
had moved on.

But he'd survived. Against the odds.

She'd hidden it in her trunk, fearful of what anyone in
Duncarrow might think about her having a realm book in her
possession.

Imryll replaced the book under a dense pile of fabrics and
locked the trunk. It wouldn't keep anyone out, but it would reveal
if someone had been in her things.

They'd been back in Duncarrow for mere hours, and already the queen had summoned her. She fell back on her heels with a prolonged yawn. Much-needed sleep would have to wait. A bath—twice as needed, as she'd had no opportunity to clean herself after her hours with Drazhan, followed by the damp conditions on the ship home—would have to wait.

She turned to see him watching her. He didn't grin or even scowl. His lack of warmth matched his strange distance on the voyage back, and she didn't yet know what to make of it.

"I'll just change before we go," she said. Her gaze lingered on his, searching for a sign of the enthusiasm he'd showed in Whitechurch. *That* Drazhan would be bartering with time, would already have her in his lap for a quick interlude.

He leaned back against the wall and crossed his arms. Looked away.

And Imryll remembered that, no matter how wild and intimate and personal the past couple of days with him had been, she didn't really know Drazhan Wynter at all.

Imryll sat across from Godivah at the modest table in the queen's chambers. The table was the only modest thing about the room. The apartments were larger, more sumptuous than the king's, something Imryll only realized as she sat in pained silence, waiting for the queen to speak.

Her mother and father sat to her left and right but hadn't said a word to her, nor met her eyes once.

Mortain hovered near the hearth, propped against it like he were about to tell a story. It hadn't occurred to her what a relief it had been to be free of him until she caught his icy eyes scrutinizing her.

Drazhan was somewhere. She felt him, though she couldn't see where he'd settled himself.

Godivah tapped her fingers along her arm, her eyes cast to the side like she was waiting for another guest, but no one else came.

She inhaled a long breath through her nose and then directed a steely gaze at Imryll. "I understand you made quite the impression on Lord Quintus."

Imryll looked first at her mother, then her father, but both were still avoiding her. "Forgive me, but I'm not certain of your meaning, Your Grace."

"I'm not trying to trap you into saying something untoward. I told you what the expectations were, and you followed them, and because of this, we now have a confirmed visit from Lord Quintus and his men a fortnight from now."

Imryll exhaled her relief.

"I want to offer you a rare compliment, Imryll."

Imryll cocked her head slightly in surprise. "Ma'am?"

Godivah drew a sip of her wine. She swilled it around in her mouth for several excruciating seconds before swallowing and forcing a smile that didn't quite fit her face. "You somehow managed to entice the man without bringing shame to your husband or the king. There's a fine line between flirtation and seduction, and it is nearly impossible to stay firmly in the middle."

Imryll briefly closed her eyes. Her thoughts traveled to her arm, bare under the puffy sleeves of the gown she'd chosen to hide its absence, and she realized the queen didn't yet know she'd lost her circlet. If she had, she'd not be so gracious with her "compliments." "That was my hope. I let him enjoy his time with me without offering anything I shouldn't."

His *offer, on the other hand...*

"Indeed," Godivah said, nodding. "You got us this far, and we thank the gods they stood with you."

Imryll nodded her thanks.

"And so this makes you the precisely perfect person to bring our agreement with the Easterlands to conclusion." Godivah reached forward and snagged an empty goblet. She filled it and pressed it across the table with her fingertips, toward Imryll. "Go on, drink."

Imryll stared at the wine with the first pang of horror. The queen didn't serve anyone.

She forced a grateful smile and sipped as commanded. Sensing eyes on her, she glanced over and saw Mortain wearing a stony look, but it wasn't for Imryll.

It was aimed at the queen.

"By now, we'll assume you're with child, and so your role in this deal should be without fuss."

Imryll cleared the remaining wine from her throat. "Your Grace?"

"You are with child, are you not?"

"I…"

"Well, we at least agree you have been lying underneath my son long enough that either you're carrying his child or you're barren?"

"Yes," the duke answered for Imryll, with a warning peripheral glare her way. "We agree, Your Grace."

"But…" Imryll swung her attention between her mother and father. "Forgive me, but I'm not certain that's a fair assessment."

"If I say it's a fair assessment, it's a fair assessment," Godivah said, wearing a look that dared Imryll to challenge her supremacy. "So, as you are either already with child or never will be, you will offer yourself to Lord Quintus for the duration of his visit, or until the agreement is signed."

Imryll stopped breathing.

Drazhan's buckles clanged from a corner.

Mortain tapped his bony fingers on the mantel.

Her father cleared his throat. "In case it was unclear—"

"It was clear enough," Imryll said, choking on the last word. She spread her palms over her knees, trying to find her calm. "With respect, Your Grace—"

"If you're preparing any form of rebuttal, Imryll, it comes with disrespect," Godivah replied. "You are First Chosen. You have a duty to protect this crown, same as I have. Each of us came into our roles in the middle of upheaval. Uncertainty."

Imryll couldn't help but pitch forward. "I *know*, which is why I acted beyond my own level of comfort to sway Lord Quintus to our case. I did things that left me feeling dirty and used, and—"

"Imryll." Her father shook his head in tight strokes. "That's enough."

"May I perhaps be of some counsel on the subject?"

Everyone turned toward Mortain at the shock of hearing his voice. He was a constant, a presence in all meetings that mattered, but silence was his way.

"Cursed Meduwyn," Godivah muttered, quiet. "The matter is decided, Mortain."

"Statistics tell us a woman's fertility cannot be a foregone conclusion until a full year has passed. We cannot know if the princess is with child, and if we cannot know, we cannot put the First Chosen and the future of this crown at such risk."

Godivah ground her jaw in circles. "Have you any children, Mortain?"

"Yes," he replied, prompting even more shock from everyone watching the odd exchange. "And if you're preparing to use my gender to exclude me from this matter, it would be folly. No one requires female anatomy to know what statistics tell us."

"If I have need of a statistician, I'll send for you." Godivah spun back toward Imryll and the others with a look of such thorough annoyance, it made the duke frown in alarm.

"Statistics are unemotional," Mortain stated. "Unlike people."

Godivah slammed her palms on the table, making everyone jump. "I said the matter is decided, Mortain! Leave us!"

While the duke and duchess watched the queen's tantrum, Imryll's gaze followed Mortain's reluctant departure. Far more interesting than an unhinged woman acting unhinged was the unflappable sorcerer and the dark wave that flashed in his eyes. Pure hatred etched the lines around his eyes, the set of his jaw.

A smile worked its way onto his face. "Of course. I'm due to visit the king."

Godivah didn't seem to catch the meaning in his parting words, but Imryll had. The queen would not have dared to speak with Mortain as she had if the king were around. Mortain obeying her command was no victory for her.

The door clicked closed.

Imryll's dread returned.

She tried to catch her mother's eyes, but the duchess hadn't stopped cowing to the queen.

"It's decided." Godivah shoved back from the table. One of her hands trembled. "You will visit Lord Quintus's bedchamber as often as he asks for you. You will do whatever he wants, whenever he wants it. And since you seem to be so concerned with the future of this crown, Adamina will be joining the prince in his apartments each night until a second heir is on the way." Godivah coiled her hands to her sides with a rattle of jewelry. "Should any of this still be upsetting or confusing to you, I understand you know your own way to the Sky Dungeon now."

Imryll, Drazhan, the duke, and the duchess were ushered out of the room in seconds. It slammed and bolted behind them.

Imryll spun toward her mother, then her father, but the duke's eyes narrowed with a darkening look that silenced Imryll's objections.

"This is not up for debate, Imryll. You'll do it." Duke Drushan drew a bracing inhale. "And if in a year's time you have a child who looks like the lord of the Easterlands, then it will still be a Glaisgain sitting upon the throne one day, and I can live with that."

He nodded and stormed off, with Melantha shooting one last helpless glance at Imryll before she followed him.

Imryll stared down the empty hall. Her chest caved. She almost reached for the only man who could give her comfort, but something in his eyes stilled her attempt.

She looked down again.

Drazhan sighed.

"What?" she asked. "Are you surprised?"

He rolled his tongue along the inside of his lip and laughed, a dark, bitter sound. "No. I'm not surprised."

Imryll thrust her hands outward. "That's all you have to say?"

Drazhan glanced past her with a hard look. "Not here."

"They just commanded me to be a man's whore!"

Drazhan grabbed her arm, marched her to the end of the hall, and pulled her around the corner. "Trying to get yourself thrown in the Sky Dungeon?"

Imryll swallowed a sob rising from her throat. "I thought you'd kill any man who tried?" She lowered her face to hide the stinging rush of tears. "Or do you only feel that way when you're in my—"

"Imryll!" Drazhan hissed her name, whipping his head to the left and right in panicked swings. "I said *not here.*"

"I thought you reserved ordering me around for the bedroom?"

Drazhan's eyes widened, swelling with his chest, his shoulders...all of him. Then he turned from her and slammed a palm to the wall with a rumbling, frustrated grunt.

He stayed that way, his hand pressed to the stone, his shoulders lifting and falling. Imryll wiped her eyes, trying to make sense of how quickly, once again, everything had shifted between her and Drazhan...how she seemed to be witnessing his attempt to drive her out of his head.

His heart.

She sniffled and held her head back and high, despite that he couldn't see her woeful attempt at confidence. "Well. There's an alternative to being the man's concubine. Marius made me a more-than-fair offer before we left—"

Drazhan whipped around, rage swimming in his eyes. "*What?*" The word bounced off the stones.

Imryll shrugged and blinked her remaining tears away. "I'd rather bear a man children as his wife than his mistress."

His head shook wildly. "You are *not* marrying Marius Quintus."

"Why not? Why shouldn't I accept the best offer I'll ever get?"

"There's nothing...*nothing* good about this offer, or that man."

"What other option do I have?"

315

"Not that." His mouth drew into a scowl. "Not *that*."

Imryll rolled her lips in, shaking her head. "You made it quite clear to me I have no chance whatsoever of surviving on my own in the kingdom." She pointed down the hall. "I won't be a prince's concubine…his broodmare. But the wife of a lord? With the freedom to travel, to do as I please, to *breathe*?"

"That man would choke the breath from your lungs to fill his own."

Imryll jammed her tongue to the roof of her mouth. She started to answer, but all that emerged was a strangled cry that made her spin away from him in shame.

There were so many things she wanted to say, but every one of them positioned her for more heartache.

"I have to fuck him anyway. Might as well marry him too," she spat and stormed away before she could decipher whether her words had left him hurt or indifferent.

Imryll.

Imryll.

Imryll.

Drazhan flattened his hands against the cloudy windowpane, failing every attempt to sink his thoughts into meditation. Tension rippled from his shoulder to the tips of his fingers, prompting the almost-numb tingling that would lead him down a dangerous path. One that ended equally in shame and salvation.

Neither ending felt right. He'd *earned* his claws, becoming one with the creature he'd bested. The alternative would have been death, but maybe it would have been preferable. Certainly more honorable.

What are you doing, Draz? What's really going on? It was his sister's voice, but it wasn't her. He hadn't truly heard Aesylt in his head since before the massacre. He'd give anything to feel the soft intrusion of her sweet voice cutting through the slow-moving glacier of his own dark thoughts.

You've won, Draz.

One down, two to go.

Move on, before you drown in whatever this *is.*

He cast a glance over his shoulder. Imryll was finally asleep. She'd lain awake for hours, staring at the ceiling or turning from side to side in frustration before eventually succumbing to exhaustion. She hadn't said a word since their fight in the hall. Nor had he.

He *had* won.

All he had to do was claim the victory.

Kill the king.

The prince.

Tell all of Duncarrow what he'd done to the First Chosen.

Destroy the last of their hope for a Rhiagain future.

Avenge the pain the crown had caused the people of Witchwood Cross.

Caused *him.*

Drazhan lowered his hands from the window and watched Imryll sleep. Her mouth moved in soundless confrontation. Sweat stained her forehead, matting her hair. Fresh tears ran along the path of dried tears. He'd been the cause of at least some of them.

His heart lurched.

He quickly turned away.

Let it go.

Let it go.

Let her *go.*

She's nothing.

Nothing to you.

Nothing at all.

Drazhan looked down in a sudden flash of pain. His fist mindlessly ground against his thigh, but his hand had begun to shift into a claw. Blood ran down his pants and was pooling on the floor, trailing into the mortar between the stones.

"Fuck." Drazhan searched the room for some linen to throw down. If Imryll woke before he returned, she'd undoubtedly see the blood, panic, and try to follow him.

Follow him to the king's bedchamber.

Drazhan dropped the linens with a heavy breath.

How long had the idea been there, waiting?

At the late hour, the king would have only the guards outside his bedchamber. They'd likely be sleeping as well, confident no one would be awake to witness their dereliction of duty. A guard's role was largely ceremonial on an island no one could sneak onto.

If they were awake…Well, it would be nothing to knock them out.

But if *that* were to happen, his next stop would have to be the prince's bedchamber because his secret would be exposed. Making it off the isle alive would no longer be a viable ending. All chances of it would die when his secret did.

Drazhan realized he didn't care.

It had to be tonight.

One way or another, he was leaving Duncarrow before it took even more from his soul.

He watched another hour pass, afraid Imryll would wake. But waiting any longer would be as good as confessing he'd lost his resolve—lost his appetite for the vengeance his family and people were owed.

That could never happen.

Drazhan slipped out quietly to make his way down the series of halls and eventually turned into the king's private one. He passed guards half-asleep—or all the way—in front of the other apartments. He met no resistance, nor did anyone even take notice of him heading to a place he didn't belong.

Drazhan didn't slow to steady himself when he rounded the final corner. If he wasn't ready, he'd never be.

His prediction about the guards turned out to be part right. One slept, hunched halfway out of his chair. The other was still standing, his head nodding back along the wall as he fought off his own fatigue.

Drazhan hastened, his sword hand already moving across his body to draw steel, when the half-asleep guard bobbed back to life.

"Oh! Syr Wynter." He blubbered against his hand to clear the spittle from his mouth. "What time is it?"

"Late," Drazhan answered. His hand hovered just above the hilt.

"Everything all right?" He narrowed his eyes, one hand coming up to scratch his head.

Drazhan calculated his options. Their chances of success.

He grimaced in overdone annoyance and said, "It's nothing to worry about. But I'm afraid I need to tell the king directly."

The guard's eyes widened. He nodded at his sleeping companion, then turned toward Drazhan with a glazed look. "You have a message for the king, you say?"

"Confidential."

"Ahh. Who from?"

"*Confidential.*" Drazhan stepped forward. He put on what he hoped was a look of weary camaraderie and said, "You know how it is. I'd much rather be sleeping, but…"

The guard rolled his eyes with a short chuckle. "Do I ever. Haven't slept in…eh…" He tried to do the math on his hands but gave up.

Drazhan nodded. His heart tickled, a sign his nerves would follow, but he willed it to remain calm. "Well, I've got another few hours before I can turn in. Why don't I take your place when I'm done?"

The man balked in surprise. "In exchange for what?"

"Nothing."

"You'd do that?" Suspicion entered his voice, but it was also clear he was talking himself into the offer.

Drazhan snickered. "Either that or watch the princess sleep."

That drew a laugh from the guard. His suspicion dissolved faster than it had appeared. "And Declan here? What of him?"

"Don't need two men to guard a sleeping king, do we?"

The guard didn't hesitate. He roused his friend, who put up even less resistance, and they ambled off down the hall, mumbling their gratitude.

Drazhan exhaled slowly.

He was alone, but the guards knew him. They knew he was going to see the king. It wouldn't take long to connect Drazhan to the crime.

Not a moment to waste then.

Drazhan slipped into the room.

A fire blazed in the hearth. Grotesque snores cut through the otherwise-silent room.

Drazhan approached the bed and allowed himself a quick study of the man. Before coming to Duncarrow, he'd only seen the king from afar. He'd locked the image to his memory, using it to fuel his rage, to focus on the training required. He saw the man's face in his sister's hollow stares, in the remnants of a town that had been razed under Carrow's order, to make an example out of Ezra Wynter and his family to anyone else thinking of standing up to the usurper king.

But Carrow, a once fierce and forbidding figure, had become an outline of skin and bones under the thick quilt covering him all the way to his chin. His mouth quivered with his snores, age spots painting his face like terrible art.

What vengeance could there be in smothering an infirm man in his sleep?

It doesn't matter how he goes, as long as he's gone.

But it did matter. If it didn't, Drazhan could have pooled his wealth and hired the task out to someone else.

It had to be him.

He had to avenge his father and his older brother, Hraz. And his people, still rebuilding their town and lives. How could he face Aesylt and tell her there'd been no moment of reckoning for the ruler who had left her alive to tell the story of the Witchwood Massacre? That he'd simply...died, never knowing that Ezra Wynter's son had come to even the score. The prince he could kill quietly, for his only crime was who his father was, but the king...

No. It had to be tonight. No more excuses. No more hesitation.

He was either a man of his word or he was a man of his failures.

He could not be both.

Drazhan stretched over the bed, leaning past the king's blubbery sleep sounds to procure one of the dozen pillows cradled around his head. He let it hover over the old man's face, and with a single shake of his head, he—

Imryll's cry started as a scream and curdled into a whisper. "What are you...*Drazhan!*"

Drazhan dropped the pillow and rushed toward her. He drove her into a corner. "What are you doing here?"

Imryll gaped at him, flushed and wild. "It's you who needs to explain yourself!"

"*Keep your voice down.*"

"You were..." Imryll bounced her glance between the still-sleeping king and Drazhan. "You had a pillow. You were..."

Drazhan sucked in hard through his teeth. He planted a hand on the wall and rolled his head back to release the breath. Anyone...*Anyone* else could have found him and he'd have killed them to protect his secret long enough to finish.

"Draz. Why?" She reached a hand up and yanked his face down to look at her. "*Why?*"

He tore away, his heart racing faster than it had when standing over the king. "I don't have to explain myself to you."

She shook her head slowly. He felt the sadness in her eyes like a stab to the chest. "You've demanded *my* truths without ever offering one of your own. You've..." She squeezed her eyes closed. "I really don't know you at all, do I?"

Drazhan's hands burned with another problem he couldn't afford. "I never *asked* you to know me."

"No, that's right. All you wanted was to bed me. To *break* me." She spread her palms against her face and dragged them downward.

He looked past her to confirm the king hadn't woken. Not that it mattered. It was over. Imryll would run straight to her father or the queen, and it wouldn't be enough time.

"No…" He almost said it wasn't true, but wasn't it? "Who will you tell first then? Your father? Your best friend, the prince?"

"Who will I…" Imryll lowered her hands and gaped at him. Her bottom lip twitched. "You think that's why I'm here? To catch you and turn you in?"

Drazhan whipped his hands out to his sides. "I don't know why you're here. I don't know why you followed me."

"You really don't know?" Imryll's expression caved. "I had no idea what you were up to tonight, but I knew it was nothing good. I *felt* it, because whatever else is true between us, I can sense you. I can…*feel* you, and it's why I couldn't sleep. It's why I waited for you to leave so I could finally understand you, understand why you're here, what you want—"

"Stop." Drazhan backed up a step. "Imryll. Stop."

"You think I'm here to tell on you, Drazhan?" Imryll narrowed the gap between them. "I'm here to keep you from doing something that will get you killed." She said the rest through clenched teeth. "I'm here to keep your head from joining the others rotting on pikes for crossing this family!"

Drazhan drew back. "So you're not here to keep me from killing the king for any moral reason," he said, watching her flinch at the confession, "but because you don't want to see me punished?"

She nodded through a shuddering breath.

"Why?"

"I—"

"*Why?*"

"I don't know what you want from me!"

Drazhan stormed forward and grabbed her by the shoulders. "I want you to stand for *something*. I want you to care about a

322

calling higher than yourself, to look beyond the putrid stone walls of his cursed keep and see a world that has been made worse by the same man whose life you just saved! But you're a spoiled, self-ish girl, who can only see to the end of her own problems. And you want to know why I never tell you anything about myself? About my purpose, my *reason?*" He released her. "What would be the fucking point?"

Imryll paled. She backed away slowly until she hit the wall, tears spilling in fat drops down her cheeks. She flattened her hands against the stones, gulping in breaths.

Then she ran.

Imryll shed her cloak halfway down the hall, enjoying the soft, damp plop it made when she offered it to the stones. Her night-gown, soft and billowy, hit just above the ankle, and she didn't need to hike it to stretch her legs and run the way she used to as a little girl: all legs, no fear.

When her feet connected with the muddy, pebbly ground outside, she paused for only a moment to consider she was bare-foot. No one ever went barefoot on Duncarrow, not even chil-dren, because they lived upon a serrated nightmare that could take everything from them in an instant.

Fear was the second thing Imryll shed.

Though her soul felt aimless, she knew exactly where she was going. She batted rain from her face as she flew across the court-yard and then shimmied down onto the rocks that had been for-bidden to her all her life. Her mind registered Drazhan yelling behind her, unable to match her speed; it noted the undersides of her feet were already a mangled, bloody mess.

If she ran fast enough, maybe it would be enough to leave her shattered soul behind too.

She slid along the slick, uneven surfaces of the boulders that lined the coast, her cries strangled by the surf of a tide on its way in. Drazhan had been wrong the day he'd told her she'd drown if she stayed in her cave. If she stayed where she was comfortable, perhaps, but she intended to climb all the way up, into the darkness, for the first time.

Playing it safe had kept her from living at all.

If he'd taught her nothing else, it was that.

The cumbersome rocks gave Drazhan a chance to catch up, but Imryll was still faster, her bare, bloodied feet a better match for the slick surfaces than his boots. When the shoreline appeared around the bend, Imryll leaped onto the gravelly sand with a wince, but she didn't slow. She kept moving until she found the spot under the columns. She shimmied up and allowed herself a moment to catch her breath.

Her thoughts had no cohesion. *Drazhan. Claws. Regicide. Mistress. Secrets. Vessel. Pleasure. Love. Lies. Hate.* Incomplete ideas flooded her mind, competing for space. Dark dots of exhaustion blurred her vision, and she saw again the climb up the arduous mountain. Another blink and she was the boy preparing for the Hunt.

But her visions were just more things vying for her attention. More ways to hurt her, to break her, to keep her pinned into a world she'd never felt wholly a part of.

Imryll threw her shoulders back, swallowed a breath of briny air, and started to climb. Each step marked the farthest she'd ever been, a challenge to both her past and future. *Secrets. Pleasure. Claws. Draz. Lies.* How had she allowed herself to become so snared by a man whose only aim had been to use her? He'd told her that day in the lyceum what he wanted. He didn't even have to work for it. She'd given it willingly. Freely. Easily.

Given *everything* to a man with no honor.

"Imryll. Wait."

Tension started in her belly and rippled up into her chest. "Leave me alone. I won't...I won't tell anyone what I saw tonight. Just leave me alone."

"That's not...Come back down."

She shook her head, though he couldn't see her.

Drazhan responded with leather striking stone, gathering purchase. He grunted and pushed on. "Stay put."

Imryll tried to climb higher, but the firm simplicity of his command had her rooted. She realized she'd never stood a chance against it. Everything dark and dangerous in that man called to everything broken and searching in her.

"It's not safe," he said when he was close. He sounded almost tender, but she knew better than to trust any kindness he offered.

The chill from the night's storm caught up to her. A deep, ferocious shiver started in her lower back and radiated outward. Once she started shaking, she couldn't stop.

Drazhan's strong arms gathered around her from the side. She collapsed against him and allowed him to guide her back to safety in a mix of loathing and need. What a fool she must look to the man who only had to open his mouth to gain her obedience.

They reached her usual spot, but he kept moving them toward the drop that led back to the beach.

Imryll shook her head as she mouthed the word *no*. She strafed away from him, tripping over a rock, but he snaked a hand out and caught her arm before she went sailing into a bed of jagged stones.

She found her footing and ripped loose of his hold, leaping into a small enclave before he could stop her a second time.

"I can't do this with you anymore," she whispered, straining through the rawness in her chest and throat. Now that he was no longer holding her, rational fear returned to remind her of how dangerous he truly was. "I knew there had to be more to your being here. I knew it wasn't about honor or duty or any of the nonsense the other knights like to bandy about, as though it means *anything*."

Half of Drazhan's face was shadowed. "You need to leave here before the tide comes all the way in."

"Why do you care?" Imryll's voice returned to her. She slapped her chest with her open hand. "Why would you even follow me after what you said to me back there?"

"I want to know why you lied to me." He regarded his arms with a strange look and then crossed them over his chest.

"*Lied* to you?"

"You said you stopped me because you didn't want to see me punished. And we both know that's a lie, Imryll, so why did you say it?"

"Why did I..." Imryll backed up another step, catching her bare foot on a rock. Drazhan started forward just as she stuttered back, but the cave wall broke her fall. "You really...You really believe that?"

Drazhan glowered from the shadows. He shook his head with a scoff.

"Is it so hard for you to..." Imryll tapped her throat to clear it. Her tears ran unabated, mixing with remnants of rainwater, leaving her weak and wounded. "Is it so hard for you to believe I care what happens to you? That I care about you?"

"Yes!" Drazhan thundered. The boom of his voice echoed, making her jump.

"Why did you really come to Duncarrow, Drazhan?"

"Same as the other men."

"You're the liar," Imryll accused. She pressed one hand to the wall and waved the other at him. "You came for the king. You came for the king, and you...You *used* me to get close to him—"

Drazhan snorted. "How small your world is that everything is so simple to you."

"There's nothing *simple* about any of this! I don't need to know why you want him dead, because half the kingdom shares your desire. Your reason doesn't matter."

"Which is why you'll never survive in our world, Imryll. Because it does matter. It *does*..." He shifted forward, clenching his jaw. "It matters. It matters to me. To my people. To the dead left in this craven usurper's wake. To the survivors who don't know how to move on from the day that changed *everything* for us."

Imryll swallowed. She found more solid footing. "He killed your people?"

326

Drazhan's head shook in wild passes. "I'm not talking about this with you. You're not worthy—"

"*Worthy?*"

"You're a child, Imryll. A—"

"And the claws?" She pushed on, fighting a hard swoon, exhaustion catching up. "The *magic* you carry in your hands?"

"You really don't—"

Imryll burst forward with a scream that stunned him into silence. When the bouncing echoes faded, she gathered the frail threads of her calm and said, "You've always been wrong about me! I may not be as sophisticated and worldly as the women from Witchwood Cross, but at least within my dreams lives a desire to be." She roughly swiped at her face to clear more tears. "Maybe I wouldn't understand…but maybe I would. All I know is…" She cupped her hands to her face to stifle a sob. "All I know is when I saw you standing over the king with a pillow, it wasn't the king I was afraid for. I saw you falling out the window in the Sky Dungeon, just like the old man, and everything inside of me was ready to fight to prevent it."

Drazhan's chin dimpled. He squeezed his eyes once. "I'm nothing to you."

Imryll lowered her eyes. Tears spattered the rocks. "If you're nothing to me, Draz, then why does my heart feel like it's been ripped out of my chest still beating?"

Drazhan's hands fisted at his sides. His bottom lip twitched. He grunted ahead of his words. "You have no heart."

Imryll shook her head, wondering how she'd let herself get so attached to him…why she'd allowed him to take her apart and put her back together, over and over. "You take such joy from wounding me."

"And yet the score is not anywhere near even when measured against the wounds inflicted upon my people by *your* king."

"He is not my king!" Imryll shrieked. "He made me the plaything of his son, stole my autonomy, and now wants to sell me to a lord. What makes you think *any* of that inspires loyalty?"

327

Drazhan laughed bitterly. "I never said you were loyal. That would take a level of honor your people aren't capable of."

"My people? Do you allow yourself to be judged by the actions of others like you?"

"All we're doing is talking in pointless circles. Come *on*, before the tide forces the issue another way."

"Why do you care?" Imryll asked. Her gut felt like it had been run through and hollowed. Even her tears lacked meaning. She'd been drained of everything. "You got what you wanted from me."

Drazhan threw his shoulders into a shrug. "I don't care. But if I leave you here, I have no reason to be at Duncarrow anymore, do I? And if I have no reason to be here, then I can't finish what I started."

"What you started…" Imryll filled her lungs as a cruel wave of understanding washed over her. "Ruining me…That was part of your plan. Wasn't it?"

Drazhan kicked his boot into a rock. His eyes followed the action. "You want me to deny it?"

Imryll sobbed into her open hands. She smeared her cheeks and faced him again. "No, I want you to say it. I want to hear *you* say it. In *your* words."

His throat bobbed. He looked past her when he spoke. "I wanted to fuck you, and I fucked you. There's nothing more to it than that." He slammed his fists against his outer thighs, his jaw straining. His gaze was still fixed on some point beyond her. "How could there ever be? You're a concubine of the usurper's son. Flesh to be bartered by men vying for power. You're *nothing* to me. You could never mean more than nothing to me."

Imryll ceased breathing. The blood in her face plummeted toward her feet, reminding her of the lashes across her soles that suddenly began to throb and burn. A stabbing chill rocked her off balance.

She exhaled the foul breath trapped in her chest. A light, dizzying sensation stole over her, but she pushed it down because he'd already feasted upon enough of her sorrow. She would give him not an ounce more.

She gathered the last of her resolve to steady her voice. "I'll keep your secret, Syr Wynter." Her bare toes curled on the wet rocks. Pain constricted her chest. "I'll never tell anyone what I saw tonight. But in exchange for my silence, you will not speak to me unless silence is unavoidable. You won't even look at me unless it's with lowered eyes. And when your foul business at Duncarrow is done, you will leave here, and you will never *ever* come back. Never *ever* speak of me, let alone think of me." She braced herself between two walls, ready to bolt as soon as her words were out. "And if you renege on this promise, then mine is forfeit as well, and you'll have to *kill me* to keep your secret safe."

Imryll scrambled over the rocks, leaped over the cave entrance, and dropped onto the rocky sand with a painful slide. She'd need a healer, but if Drazhan Wynter touched her again, she'd scream and never stop screaming.

She ran as hard as she had before, but Drazhan held his distance when he followed. She turned once to see if he was behind her, but he'd slowed his pace to a brisk walk.

Imryll hit the stones of the keep with a guttural groan of relief but kept running. They'd hardly been gone long at all, and already the keep was bustling with the aftermath of the noise they'd made when they'd left.

She earned many curious gazes but ignored them. Horrified exclamations sounded around her, about her feet leaving a bloodied trail that told a tale she couldn't speak of, now or ever. She didn't stop when she hit the stairs, nor when she turned onto her floor and barreled down the hall, limping on two mangled feet.

She spun around a corner and ran straight into Mortain. He wrapped his firm hands around her arms and eased her back, righting her.

"*There* you are," he said. The worry in his voice rang genuine, but she was too distraught to process her confusion on top of it. "My gods, Imryll, what *happened* to you?"

Imryll could only shake her head. There weren't words. She didn't want there to be.

Aghast with horror, he gaped at her feet. "Come. Let me take care of this for you."

Imryll reeled back in surprise. The sorcerers never offered healing to the mortals of Duncarrow. But the thought of him touching her bare feet sent a harder chill than the storm outside had produced. "I'll be fine. Thank you. I need to—"

Her gaze caught a familiar face coming down the hall. Worry etched between Torian's brows as he melted at the sight of her.

Torian nudged Mortain aside and flung his arms around Imryll, wrapping her in a hug so warm and real and wonderful that she wished her heart had been content to live there always. So much would be different.

He pulled back and brushed his hands along her face on both sides, clearing rain and tears and hair. "Imryll, I was so worried. When they said you were screaming…"

Screaming? Had she been?

She couldn't remember.

Everything, from the moment she saw Drazhan holding a pillow above the king's head to the final words she'd left him with in the cave, felt blurred into another reality altogether.

"I'm all right," she assured him, trying to smile. "I'll tell you later."

"You'll tell me now," Torian gently countered. He cleared her forehead and kissed it. "Because you're staying with me tonight, where I can look after you. Because I know you, Imryll of Glaisgain. You are not all right. And if I can't fix it, I can at least be there to prevent it from getting worse." He nodded at Mortain. "Please let the guards know Imryll has been found, is fine, and there's nothing more to the matter. I'll send for you when she's ready for your healing."

A flicker of rage passed over Mortain's eyes, but it was gone so fast, Imryll wondered if she'd imagined it.

He grinned. "Of course, Your Grace." He bowed and left them.

330

When Mortain was gone, Torian dragged his gaze over her with more head shaking, sighing through his examination. "It was *him*, wasn't it?"

Imryll started to pretend she didn't know what he meant, but she nodded in surrender. She bowed her head when more tears burned her eyes, but those were not for Drazhan.

They were for Torian.

For his kindness.

His love.

Both, he'd given willingly, and she'd closed her heart to those gifts, unable to accept them. Unable to accept a life she hadn't explicitly chosen.

"Come on, Ryl. Let's go." He gathered her in his arms and guided her to his apartments. "You'll stay with me tonight. You'll stay as long as you need. And if he comes here looking for you, all he'll find is a locked door."

"Thank you. I don't know what to say."

"You don't need to say anything." He craned sideways to kiss her drenched scalp. "I'll take care of you."

A guard opened Torian's door and he stretched his arm, indicating she should go first.

Imryll felt the sting of someone watching her. She glanced to the right and saw Drazhan at the end of the hall.

Glaring.

Seething.

She squeezed her eyes clear of tears, held her head high, and entered the room.

Drazhan's belly clenched with each breath out. He watched Imryll enter Torian's room. Saw the prince's hand at the small of her back…the elated relief in the young man's eyes as though he'd just won a long contest.

The door closed. Drazhan didn't follow. He'd never be allowed in, and so be it. Severing whatever had grown between him and

Imryll was an exercise in absolutes. There'd been nothing halfway about their passion, and there could be nothing halfway about abandoning it.

Drazhan traced Imryll's bloody trail back down the hall, ignoring the icy stab in his chest when he thought of the pain she must be in—would stay in unless someone healed her.

Voices came from all sides, asking him things he didn't hear, didn't care about. A raw, unbridled heat roared behind his ribcage, in the place where his heart had once lived, and if he opened his mouth, he couldn't be certain it wouldn't be flames in place of breath.

Imryll. Imryll. Imryll.

He slammed the side of his fist into a wall when he reached the stairs. He flew down in a dizzying race to outrun all the things he'd done and felt that were counter to his mission. To leave them behind and reclaim his resolve, reclaim *himself.*

Drazhan burst into the rainy night. The urge to fall to his knees was vigorous, almost instinct, but he fought it—fought the ache across his shoulders and the flame kindling so high within that his throat burned with the promise of combustion.

Winded, he looked around, searching for release. The tiny isle had never felt so suffocating. He'd never before considered how the sea clawing in from all sides could drive a man to madness. How he might already be halfway there himself.

He marched to the opposite direction of the courtyard, away from the living, from the imprint of moments and memories. When he reached the rocks at the back end of the keep, he continued until he had no choice but to climb or go back.

Drazhan climbed.

He climbed until he could no longer do so without using his hands.

He climbed until his hands turned to claws.

He climbed until there was nowhere left to climb.

When Drazhan reached the top, he pushed to his feet, wavering for balance. He pumped his fist to his chest to clear the evidence of his failures—the ache, the fire raging out of control, its flames licking the backs of his eyes and burning down the center of his tongue. He gazed into the rough swells of the sea that had brought the cursed Rhiagains into his world.

The sea that had brought *her* into his bones, becoming one with the marrow, the sinew and blood and cartilage, and—

Bracing through a shaky breath, he raised his arms so he could see the swell of red and blue swirling the clawed digits where his fingers should be.

He curled them toward his palm in a waving roll and then thrust them down and to his sides with a scream. It burst from the hollowed-out places where his organs used to pump blood and life into him. He thrust his chest forward to deepen the sound, competing with the crash of the sea that had ruined him not once but twice. He screamed louder, demanding to be heard, but there was no sound capable of drowning out the tumultuous waves slamming against the rocks.

Drazhan roared like the beast he'd once bested with his bare hands as a boy.

He roared until there was nothing left.

And when he was done, Drazhan Wynter gave his knees permission to buckle. His hands followed, and there he crouched, hunched and panting, until dawn broke.

THE ILLUSION
OF CHOICE

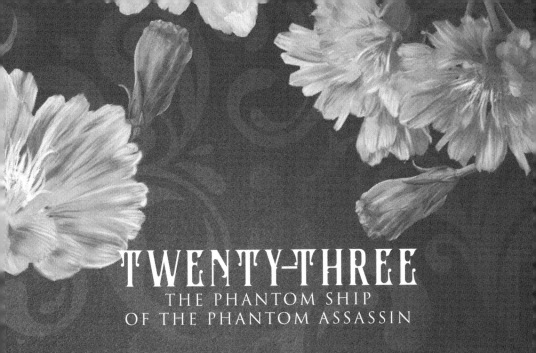

TWENTY-THREE
THE PHANTOM SHIP
OF THE PHANTOM ASSASSIN

Ofal refilled their mugs one by one. Even Drazhan's, though when the commander wasn't looking, he'd just pour it into the dirt like the previous three fills.

He caught Blackfen staring at him. The bowman nodded once and tilted his mug in reverence. Drazhan attempted a politic grin, but he'd lost that skill, same as he'd lost his connection with his meditations. Throughout the small celebration, Blackfen had watched him as though he knew the internal battle Drazhan waged with himself, while Owen flicked his confusion between the two.

Even the shitheels, Waters and Garrick, had kept their snickers and barbs to themselves for the evening. Waters stole glances across the hours, wearing nothing more offensive than somber respect, but Garrick seemed almost afraid. Every time he returned from filling his mug, he pushed his log a little farther away.

"This is why…" Ofal slurred, as drunk as the rest of them. He hid a belch in the crook of his elbow. "Pardon me. I didn't see it

337

at first. I just didn't see it. I—" He belched again, his cheeks filling with the effort.

Waters and Garrick exchanged disgusted smirks.

"I didn't see the *need* for you knights," Ofal said, finishing his words with a proud grunt. "When we have thousands of perfectly good men in the Rhiagain Guard."

Here we go, Owen mouthed with an eye roll at Blackfen.

"But I never imagined any man could sneak onto Duncarrow and escape notice. And they did, Guardians deliver us. They did." He turned his glossy eyes on Drazhan. "Our king would have been taken from us if not for your heroic actions. Our princess..." He closed his eyes, overcome. "I'm not too proud to say I was wrong. You men are warriors. Syr Wynter, you are a hero."

Mugs clinked. The others mumbled similar venerations.

Drazhan tightened his mouth and raised his own ale. It was the best he could do.

Everyone drank except Drazhan, who only pretended.

Garrick slammed his mug on the ground and ran his arm against his face to clear the foam. "Aye, but what I cannae ken is *how* did that ratsbane make it onto land unnoticed? Where did his ship go? I come from the land of ships, lads. Ships cannae *hide.*"

The other men chuckled.

Ofal smiled through obvious annoyance. "You are always the last to comprehend a matter, Syr Garrick. The scoundrel sank his ship to avoid notice. Never intended to escape. He came to take our king from this kingdom, to...to defile our princess, and then let us run him through with swords." He shook his head. "Then he denied us that privilege by leaping into the sea like the coward he was."

"Says him," Garrick said. He nodded at Drazhan without turning his eyes toward him. "Anyone else see this?"

"The rest of you were sleeping, as I recall," Ofal said with a haughty quirk of his mouth.

"Took 'em a month to find the scoundrel's ship," Owen said. "That's why we're only just now drinking to it."

338

"Aye, convenient, that. There are a thousand ships on the floor of the White Sea. Ye ken anyone would know friend from foe?" He continued to avoid looking at Drazhan. "Just have to take his word for it, do we?"

Owen shot to his feet. "Say what you mean, but only if you're prepared to defend yourself against the lot of us."

Garrick snickered. "You've been suckin' Stormclaw's cock since training."

Blackfen was up and subduing Owen before the man could react.

"Say what I mean?" Garrick tucked his chin in and chortled. "Oh aye, you sure about that? You really ken the others want me to repeat the rumors? Aye, about how our brave knight here has been fuckin' the same princess they claim he saved?"

Blackfen released Owen. His hand moved to a dagger sheathed at his waist.

Drazhan didn't speak. The first celebration had been bad enough, but the "discovery" of the phantom assailant's ship had dragged it all up for another round, weeks later. But Garrick's crude claim sent fresh rage blooming within. Without his meditations, Drazhan had no effective defense. He was forced to feel every word.

"Men," Ofal said, stumbling to his feet. "This is a night for celebration. Leave your quarrels out of it. As for rumors…Only women and old folk indulge in them."

"He ain't denying it," Garrick cried, waving his arm like a flag.

Waters groaned into his mug.

"He doesn't *have* to deny it," Blackfen said. He took a step forward. "Why should he even acknowledge such an abhorrent, nonsensical charge?" He spat at his feet. "And on the night we honor him? Jealousy does not become you, Garrick. Not at all."

"Nonsensical, aye? Then let's hear him say so. If it's all rubbish, 'tis a simple thing to clear up."

"Garrick," Ofal warned. His eyes were wide, alert, sobering him in an instant. "That's enough."

339

"You call them rumors," Garrick said, continuing, "but even stone walls cannae disguise everything. We gonna call all those attendants, who heard them, liars now, just because they ain't highborn?"

Drazhan trained his attention on the swirls in the dirt but failed to keep it there. Flashes of Garrick's smug face crept in. He wrenched his hands around his mug, the only thing keeping them from becoming fists.

Or claws.

"And are *you* going to fall so low as to put the word of strangers above the word of your fellow knight?" Blackfen challenged. "You know this man. You know his honor." He scoffed, shaking his head at Owen and then Ofal. "We've already indulged this too much."

"If he'd speak at all, maybe I'd trust him," Garrick replied. He lifted his shoulders in a violent shrug. "But innocent men donnae let accusations lie uncontested."

Ofal poured out the remainder of his ale with a regretful sigh. "Syr Blackfen is right. It's late. We've all had an ale too many. Let's—"

"Not fucking her anymore though, is he? They say the princess's bedchamber has gone cold and quiet since that night." Garrick tore his mouth into a feral grin. "Lovers' spat, aye?"

Drazhan inhaled through his nose. He kept his chest still to keep the flames from building. *You're nothing to me.* Bile tickled the back of his throat. *You could never be more than nothing.*

"Something I've been dying to ask." Garrick went on, his eyes flashing with growing excitement as he fed off the energy of each word. "Does it taste different?"

Owen started forward. "Another word, Garrick."

"Royal cunt." Garrick enunciated the last letter. "Was the princess's any sweeter than a realm whor—"

Drazhan roared like a bull and charged. The last thing he saw before barreling into Garrick was the man's horrified eyes, the flicker of miscalculation. They hurled to the ground, Drazhan's fists coiling and landing in blows he didn't stop to count. Garrick screamed beneath him, but the sounds blended with the screams of the other knights, and Ofal, none of which had any power over him.

His assault came to a sudden halt when his arm was caught midair. He looked back, snarling, and saw Blackfen and Owen both restraining him. But it was their eyes…Their eyes reflected awe—fear—as their startled gazes darted between whatever they saw on his face and the claw where his hand should be. There could be no mistaking them for fist weapons when they'd *seen* him shift.

Drazhan's cyclone of rage died to gentle wind. He rolled back off of Garrick, his claws becoming hands once more, and ripped out of the other men's grasps.

He stumbled back in the dirt. Garrick turned his bloody face to the side as he tried to push up onto his knees. Waters and Ofal moved in to help.

Drazhan slowed his breaths. With every rapid beat of his heart, he allowed himself to take in another detail: the edge of Garrick's mangled face, the horror brewing in Waters's flinty glare, the questioning gazes of the two who were the closest he would ever have to friends, and the abject confusion in Ofal's face as he weighed what had happened and what to do about it.

"Well…uh…" Ofal trailed off, looking not at Drazhan but slightly to the side. "That's enough for tonight, boys."

Waters and Ofal helped Garrick to his feet. Owen followed after, shaking his head at the ground. Only Blackfen lingered.

"Wynter," he said. "*Drazhan.*"

Drazhan looked up at him. He didn't know why. He didn't know anything anymore. The king was still alive and guarded more heavily than ever before. His appetite for killing the prince had dulled, as he'd watched Torian care for Imryll in the way Drazhan could not. He was a man without a clear mission, unmoored and sinking like the phantom ship of the phantom assassin.

"What was that?"

Drazhan tightened his closed mouth and shook his head off to the side.

"You're coming apart, my friend," Blackfen said. "I won't say this in front of the others because Garrick was out of order. He's always out of order. But I've heard the same things. About you and the princess. And I've *seen*, with my own eyes, how you both go out of your way to pretend you're not following each other's every move. The jealousy in her eyes when you even look at another woman…The same emotion lives in yours when she's with her prince." He exhaled. "I can't tell you what to do, but there's no joy to be found in this for you. None. There isn't a world where she can be yours, Wynter, and if you don't cut this thread now, you'll be dangling from it the rest of your life."

Tasmin smiled patiently at the shaky-handed attendant pouring the tea. Imryll had often been amused by Tasmin's outwardly easy way with everyone, when on the inside, she was brimming with annoyance.

She exhaled with a brow wag when the attendant left. "New one?"

"They got rid of the others after…" Imryll gazed off to the side.

"Right," Tasmin said. She brought her tea to her mouth for a dainty blow. "Of course they did. Well, they're always skittish when they've spent so many months in isolation."

"She's fine," Imryll said. It was a lie, a comfortable assurance in a time when she had none. Malyse, the attendant, was homesick, and if she wasn't shaking, she was crying. Of course she was. It was cruel, what the Rhiagains did to bring young women to Duncarrow, so unless Imryll had a visitor, she usually dismissed the girl and served herself.

But Tasmin was a truth sniffer, and before she could lift her brows once more and call her out, Imryll corrected herself. "She's not fine, Tas. She's sick about being here, as everyone who comes to Duncarrow is. When I think about the realm chosens, locked away in their rooms…" She trailed off. "I know we're told the workers come willingly, to serve, but…"

Tasmin made a soundless laugh. "Please tell me you don't still believe that."

Imryll shrugged. She pushed her tea away and flopped back. "I don't know what to believe about anything anymore. Even simple, commonplace things I've accepted as truth feel like they could just as easily be tidy deceptions. It wouldn't surprise me at all to learn everything I've ever been told is a lie."

"That's very fatalistic. Even by my standard."

Imryll scoffed. She watched steam float off the surface of the dark liquid. "Forgive me if I cannot summon any optimism."

"Nothing to forgive," Tasmin said gently. "You've endured a lot since becoming First Chosen. Madly, the most challenging of those times has little at all to do with the Choosing itself. Is it still so hard between you two?"

Imryll knew Tasmin meant Drazhan. After that horrid night, she'd needed someone to confide in, and Tasmin was the only one she trusted to tell the whole story.

Well, mostly the whole story. She'd left out the part about her dark knight trying to murder the king.

A king who, though bedridden, was still very much alive.

Imryll pursed her lips and kept her eyes on the wispy trails. "He ignores me. I ignore him. He no longer insists on being in every room I'm in, and he stays outside my door, except at night."

"That sounds far too neat," Tasmin said with a quick grin. "Especially as I have eyes myself and have observed precisely how the two of you 'ignore' one another."

Imryll folded her hands over the table and leaned in. "Please tell me you're being cheeky and aren't serious."

"I'm being both, actually," Tasmin said. She sipped her tea, sighed at the end, and set the cup back in its saucer. "And if I can see it, you can be certain others have." She nodded at Imryll's arm, which she'd kept covered at all times. "You need heavier sleeves if you don't want others to know the circlet is gone. Tie a rope. Something."

Imryll glanced down with a start. She'd been cautious in her choice of gowns, and so far no one had said a word to Imryll about the missing circlet, not even Torian, who she'd seen mentally note it on more than one occasion. But if Tasmin could see it, then others would too.

Or perhaps they had.

The past month had been one dizzying blur.

She floated through her days in a trance, offering a smile when one was required and speaking when spoken to. She spent her evenings with Torian, and they were her singular release from the shackles of propriety. They laughed together, even slept in the same bed some nights, but Torian respected her desire to maintain a platonic relationship. They'd kissed a few times, and she'd allowed his hands somewhere only one other man's had been, but she wasn't ready for more.

She wasn't sure if she ever would be, but it didn't matter. Because running underneath the surface of every happy moment was the knowledge Lord Quintus would arrive soon. His ship had been delayed several weeks due to weather, but the weather would clear soon, and there'd be nothing stopping him from setting sail for Duncarrow.

The queen had doubled down on her plan, going so far as to discuss the needed "preparations" for Imryll when they offered her as a gift for the man securing their crown. Imryll wondered if Marius still had mutiny on his mind, though the king was still alive. For now.

"Well," Imryll said with a weary shrug. "It won't matter much longer."

Tasmin's smile faded. "Have you decided what to do?"

Imryll shook her head.

"You already know what I think."

"That I should embrace his indecent offer?"

344

"Yes," Tasmin said. "You might not realize it, Imryll, but you *are* in a position to bargain with the man."

Imryll snorted. "How do you suppose that is? At least when I was valuable to Torian, I had the crown to keep Marius from getting too familiar, but now? Now, I've lost *any* bargaining I had, Tas. He has no reason to agree to any ask I make of him."

"You said he was a reasonable man."

"He's certainly not the *worst* man, and it seemed like he was serious about helping me. But that was before the queen decided to hand me over to him without a fight."

Tasmin folded her hands out. "You won him over in Whitechurch. You can win him over again."

Imryll laughed. "You are far more optimistic about my prospects than you have any business being."

"*Realistic*," Tasmin said, emphasizing the word slowly. "No matter how it may feel now, your options are far greater on the mainland than they are here. When they find out you're not carrying Torian's child and have been the plaything of Marius Quintus, there won't *be* a place for you here, Imryll. And with Syr Wynter fooling about with Ada—"

"*What?*" Imryll practically came out of her seat. "Draz and Ada?"

"Draz?" Tasmin shook her head. "You're utterly lost for him, aren't you?"

Imryll was too stunned to respond.

"I thought you'd have heard as well. I'm sorry." Tasmin sat back. "Really, there's been rumors for a couple weeks and…Gods, Imryll. I've really put my foot in it."

"But Ada…She wouldn't…Godivah just started Adamina's preparations, for Torian…"

"Just like you were prepared?" Tasmin stretched across the table and reached for Imryll's hands. "You must forget him. He was good for your bed, but he's broken your heart, and he'll break it a hundred times more if you let him."

Imryll lowered her eyes. The old ache in her chest reignited. It shouldn't hurt. It did anyway. "He didn't break my heart."

"If you say so."

"I do say so."

"I didn't mean to reopen a wound." Tasmin squeezed her hands. "Truly. I'm sorry."

"You didn't." Imryll shook her head to clear the tears. She couldn't afford them anymore. Like her other weaknesses, they belonged to the past, because they would only choke her future. She looked up at Tasmin and forced a smile. "I'm just overwhelmed with everything. I'll be fine. It's like you said. I have more options than I realize. I'll consider them and be ready when Lord Quintus arrives."

Drazhan waited until Tasmin Farrestell reached the end of the hall before he entered Imryll's apartments.

She was sitting at her tea table, her eyes glossed over with a bewildered expression. But when she saw him, her gaze lingered a beat longer than it should have before she snapped back, wiping her eyes, and shot out of her seat.

She spun away and crossed her arms, like she had every time she'd seen him since the night he'd crafted the irreparable rift between them. She reached a hand to her face in swiping motions and waited for him to retreat to his corner.

Drazhan commanded himself to continue to the next step in his routine, to leave her alone so she could return to whatever it was she was doing.

But his feet didn't move.

Imryll sniffled. Turned halfway. "Why are you still standing there?"

Drazhan didn't know how to respond. He flexed his swollen, battered hands at his sides instead.

"Were you with her?"

Drazhan shifted in place. "With whom?"

"*Ada.*"

Ah. He had not been with Ada. Not that day, nor ever. It was Ada herself who started the rumor, knowing it would hurt Imryll, and Drazhan had done nothing to perpetuate nor deny it.

Imryll's strained laugh was low and muted. "Of course you were. Because that's what you do."

Tension rippled from his feet into his torso, across his chest. He grimaced through the urge to defend himself. It was almost more powerful than the fortress he'd built to keep her out.

"I hate you," she whispered.

Drazhan cleared his hoarse throat. "You should."

"I wish we'd never met."

"I wish that too." *More than anything,* he added in his head, leaving the thought to settle with the lump in his throat.

"I..." When her voice broke, something inside Drazhan broke with it. "Please just...go."

Go where? he almost asked, but there wasn't a simple answer. She wanted him gone from her room, from Duncarrow, her life. And every day he couldn't oblige the request was another arrow in his tendons, another useless emotion hobbling him from the mission he was no longer confident in his ability to complete.

He wrung his mangled fists, lingering hardly another second before turning and retreating into his corner, where it was safe.

348

TWENTY-FOUR
REALITY CRUSHES
EVEN THE PUREST INTENTIONS

Torian lay on the bed, skimming the book Imryll had brought back from the Easterlands. She'd pulled the divan to the window and drawn her knees to her chest, her head tilted against the glass. Neither had spoken since the morning. They passed the hours that way as they waited for the inevitable news that Lord Quintus had safely docked.

He was lost for words. What could be said to make anything better? She was nursing a broken heart, which he had no power to heal, and stuck as his chosen until she was handed over to Marius, without any consideration for her feelings. Torian had no power over any of it. His mother and Duke Drushan were the de facto rulers until the king either died or miraculously rose from his sickbed. Carrow had always tempered them both, and in his absence, they carried on in a way clearly indicating they believed their newfound status would be permanent.

When Torian had dug a little, in a particularly heated conversation with Godivah, she'd confessed it was Drushan's idea to offer Imryll to Lord Quintus. *You can trust a man, Torian, who would sell his own daughter for advancement. There's no line he wouldn't cross to please you.*

Or do you trust him because you're fucking him? He couldn't say it, of course. He'd never so much as raised his voice to her. But if the rumors were true…

Rumors also explained Imryll's particular melancholy. She denied there'd been love between her and Wynter, but even the thought of him with Ada had sent her into a dark spiral. What he *wanted* to do was face off with the knight who had treated Imryll so carelessly, but he stood no chance against Drazhan Wynter—neither the warrior nor the man.

Torian read the same page for a sixth time. His eyes kept traveling toward Imryll, huddled around herself like a lost cub. His heart broke for her. He respected that she could never love him, not like that. But it didn't mean he didn't live for their occasional kisses…or that he didn't dream about the time she'd let him slide his hand beneath her undergarment.

His cock treasonously throbbed under the blanket at even the thought.

They were slowly finding their way with each other, but he'd never know where it might lead because she was about to become the property of another man. Godivah had never forgiven Mortain for strongarming Imryll into the First Chosen role. She'd always wanted Ada. And with Imryll out of the way, Ada was who she'd have.

Torian wondered where that left his realm chosens. He hadn't seen them since the Week of Feasts. According to his mother, they were sequestered in their apartments until Ada was pregnant, then they'd be summoned as well, one by one.

Not if Father dies first. My first act as king will be to send them home.

"Tor?"

Torian jumped. The book fumbled forward and flopped closed.

"What are you thinking about?"

"What am I thinking about?" He bunched the blanket to create a fort of concealment around his erection.

"You have a very stern look on your face. I can't read it."

He pivoted and saw she'd unfurled, both of her bare feet planted on the floor as she watched him with a mix of curiosity and concern. "You know me. Champion wallower."

Imryll's face brightened in a grin. "The very best."

Torian flushed and lowered his gaze. Her smile had done nothing to quiet his desire, but if he was being honest, he'd been hard in her presence since they were thirteen. He'd never been in control of how he felt about her.

Imryll pushed the chair back and made her way to the bed. Torian quickly shoved the book to his other side to make room for her, but in doing so, the blanket slipped, and a quick note of her gaze said she'd seen.

She slid under the covers and propped her arms under her pillow, watching him. "Don't blame yourself for what's about to happen. You're a pawn as much as I am. But when you're king, you can do better. You can be better." She withdrew a hand from the pillow and laid it over his cheek. Torian pressed his own hand atop hers. "You *are* better. Don't forget that."

Tears burned his eyes. He pressed his forehead to hers to hide them. "I won't know if I'm better until I'm doing the job. Perhaps my father said the same thing once, when he was my age. Reality crushes even our purest intentions."

"No," she whispered. She nipped her teeth on his nose, drawing a shocked laugh from him. "No, Tor. That's just the excuse men make for being weak, so they don't have to stand in account for their crimes."

A surge of bold courage seized his words. "I can still stop this, Ryl. My mother isn't the king. She's just…"

Imryll smiled sadly. "His chosen?"

"That's not what I meant."

"I know." She drew a deep breath and then kissed him on the mouth. "I know."

351

She hadn't commented on his gallant proclamation. They both knew who he was. Who he wasn't.

"What is it?" She slid her hand down his face and tilted his chin. "What else is going on in this head of yours?"

Tiny dots of shame peppered his cheeks. He didn't know whether the bulge in the blanket had sold him out or if she really could read him. She used to read him. He used to soak those readings up.

"You can tell me," she said, watching him from her pillow. "You already know my darkest secret."

But could he tell her? Was it fair? It had been his idea to return to their old friendship and forget the sexual expectation, but the kissing and touching the past weeks had worn him down. Now that he'd had a taste of her touch, he wanted so much more.

"Tor?" Imryll reached for his hand under the blanket and squeezed. Their conjoined fingers brushed his cock by accident, and he jolted. Her eyes widened. "Ah."

Torian quickly shook his head. "I can't control how my body responds, and I don't…I don't expect whatever *he* thinks is going to happen." He smiled, trying to make a joke of it.

Imryll's expression darkened. "I've confused you."

"No." He squeezed her hand and slid closer. "No. Not at all. I've…Ah, well I've enjoyed our kissing, and…and the touching, but I know it for what it is. I'm happy just to breathe your air for a little while."

"Breathe my air? Even though I've had garlic with my breakfast?"

To prove his claim, Torian leaned in and drew her into a kiss, the kind with tongues—his favorite. He ended it with a flourishing whip of his tongue and grinned. "You still taste like Imryll."

Something unreadable flashed in her eyes, but it was gone before he could decipher it. "You still haven't told me what's on your mind."

It would be unfair to tell her the truth. But would deception not be worse, especially when she'd been so open and honest with him?

"I...don't want you to hear these words and ascribe expectation to them." He clasped their hands tighter with a rough squeeze. "I have none."

Imryll nodded.

"But as we approach this awful day ahead, when I have to watch you walk into a life I can't save you from..." Torian cast his eyes downward. "And I think of my own days ahead, when I'll be expected to perform for Adamina, to create new life..."

"It's all right," Imryll gently urged.

"I realized today how hard it will be to let you go. For me to *be* with another woman when I always dreamed you would be my first."

Imryll's hand went slack in his. She inhaled slowly, eyes closed. Torian started to panic, regret replacing any peace in his confession, but she opened her eyes again.

"Is that what you want, Torian?" Gone was her soft-eyed gaze. In its place was something darker, dreamier. "Even with everything you know about me? How I feel? With everything we know about our futures?"

Torian didn't hesitate. "Yes. Even now. *Especially* now." His head shook. "But I'm *not* asking you to do this."

"I'm asking if this is what you want," Imryll said, sighing. "We'd be wrong to ascribe any meaning beyond the sentimental, but..."

Torian's flesh pricked with heat. She was *considering* it. Rationalizing it. Planning it. "Imryll—"

"Are you sure it's *me* you want now?" She looked him in the eyes. "Are you sure, Tor? Because you already know you're not my first. We have between us years of friendship but also heartache and angst. Ahead of you is a life that won't include me. Are you sure?"

353

Torian swallowed and nodded. He realized she'd said nothing about her own wants, but they both already knew he wasn't among them. She could never feel for him as she had for the wretched Wynter. Perhaps even Marius lit something in her that called to a place Torian would never find. Whatever she agreed to, whatever was about to happen, it came from a place of love, but not lust.

It would be enough for him.

Imryll rolled onto her back. "Come here," she said, beckoning him with one arm.

Torian pushed onto his knees and climbed over her. He didn't know what to do next, but she took the decision-making from him when she crushed his head toward hers in a fiery kiss that had him recalibrating his breath's rhythm.

She clasped one of his hands and guided it between her legs. Torian's heart thumped, knowing it was his turn to lead. In his hesitation, her hand found his cock, and his vision burst with stars of pleasure.

In his fantasies, she'd taken him into her mouth. Nothing sent him into a wilder frenzy than the idea of her throat moving as she swallowed all he had to give. He'd imagined the stretch of her ass as he took her from behind. The curve of her hips, where he'd nock his hands for purchase and find the right strokes to have her screaming his name loud enough to wake all of Duncarrow.

But none of it had prepared him for the way she looked up at him, her heart beating in her neck as she waited for him to make the next move.

Torian fumbled with her gown. Pulling it up high enough was no easy feat with all the tulle and layers, and she had to help him, through awkward laughter, before they finally got it bunched around her waist.

He breathed slowly. There she was, the love of his life, ready to take him, and he was so afraid of disappointing her.

Imryll nodded. It was all he needed. She understood. No matter what happened, she understood.

Torian reached for her undergarments and found the band. He tugged them down, and she lifted her legs into the air for him to extricate them from her feet. When she did, he saw the underside of her, the place he'd only touched with his hands.

He brought her legs back to the bed and climbed over her again, terrified he wouldn't know how to perform the most basic, most innate act of all men and find his way inside. But Imryll was there to help him again. She circled him with her hand and guided him to her core, nestling his cock into a thatch of hair.

Torian braced his hands on either side of her head and pushed in, surprised at the resistance. The sensation of her tight flesh sheathing the tip of his cock was too much, and he had to stop, to breathe, before he embarrassed himself.

Imryll's anticipating gaze was enough to give him the courage to push all the way in, fighting the difficulty of the narrow passage. He went until his hips stopped him from going farther, but she spread her legs wider, and he found there was still more to go.

Torian moved his hips in short thrusts, and her head fell back on the pillow. He was already ready to explode, and he would only have one chance to get it right.

Imryll bit down on her lip with every thrust. It made him want to go faster, and he did, for the joy of seeing her respond.

"Is it good? Does it feel good?" He panted, falling into a quicker pace he knew he couldn't maintain for long. He didn't know what she needed to achieve her own pleasure from the act, but he assumed what he was doing was it and kept thrusting.

Imryll nodded, her lip still docked between her teeth as she jerked back with each thrust. "Yes. It's good, Tor."

He dropped his forehead to hers and went faster, desperate to hear, at least once, the sound of her crying out for him. She wound her arms around his neck, down his back, and lifted her hips to urge him on, but she didn't moan or whimper, as he'd heard women did when lost to the throes of pleasure.

But she was finally a little wet, which was another sign, other men had told him, of a woman getting what she needed.

Torian sat up higher and hooked her thighs under his arms, so he could watch his cock sliding in and out of her, smoother once he'd worked it in. The visual validation of years of fantasies had his toes curling and his balls tightening.

Imryll hooked her hands into the bedsheet. He pitched forward over her with a groan as his seed left him in spurts, his cock jerking into a finish of what he'd only just started.

Torian shuddered against her in a bewildered haze. It was over before he'd even learned what to do.

He rolled onto his back, winded. He wanted to ask her if she'd come too, if it had been as incredible for her as it had been for him, but he was afraid she'd say no. He wouldn't have the experience or skill to fix it.

Those were Torian's final thoughts before he succumbed to the heady call of sleep.

Drazhan waited with Blackfen on the dock. The task was beneath both of them, but the queen wanted Adamina to be there to greet Marius, and Drazhan was dismissed whenever Imryll was alone with Torian, doing Guardians knew what.

Imryll didn't want Torian. Whatever happened in that room, it wasn't anything to get worked up about.

Sometimes he had to remind himself she was no longer his concern.

Wind whipped the port, sending Adamina into a frenzy as she batted her hair and dress into place without success.

"This cursed isle. Can we not build things to block the wind?" Adamina muttered. Her feet danced in irritation. "How am I to greet a visiting lord, looking like *this*?" She thrust her hands toward her head.

Blackfen flicked the briefest eyeroll at Drazhan before turning back to watch the sea.

"Neither of you want to answer?"

"Not especially," Drazhan muttered.

Blackfen chortled.

"The lot of you both!" She sputtered hair from her mouth. "And you, Syr Wynter, why are you even here?"

"The princess locked him out," Blackfen said, hiding an impertinent grin.

"Locked you out? She doesn't like you listening in on their lovemaking? Or was it the prince who slighted you?"

Blackfen's gaze shifted to the side in alarm.

Drazhan was a stone wall.

"Ah, well, the rest of us are certainly weary of it." She snorted, still struggling with putting her hair back into place. "All day, all night, rutting like wild animals. And I wonder…Is it really necessary to *scream* like that? I daresay it's more appropriate for combat, but what do I know?"

"Lady Adamina, perhaps another subject?" Blackfen suggested, affecting a pleasant, placating tone.

"You aren't insinuating I'm gossiping, Syr Blackfen?"

"Ah…No, my lady, only that—"

"Good," Adamina said, the word ending on a sharp lilt. "Because it is not *gossip* when Syr Wynter is her personal guard. And as you tell me all too often, Blackfen, a guard must know *everything* about their charge's life, down to the most minute detail."

Blackfen's jaw tensed. "I did say that, my lady. But is it not the princess's business to share these details with Syr Wynter?"

Adamina twisted with a haughty head shake. "Well, she won't be the princess much longer, will she?"

Blackfen's gaze shot to Drazhan, but he'd convincingly returned his attention back to the pointlessness of ship-spotting.

"Did you not know?" Adamina's laugh sounded more like a trill. "Imryll will be relinquishing her role as First Chosen as soon as the queen hands her over to Lord Quintus. Whether he'll take her back to the Easterlands or not is really up to him, but

357

once he's had her, well…How could she ever show her face at the prince's side again?"

Drazhan crossed his arms, shifting his weight. Even if he could still access his meditations, her shrill voice would slash through them like a dull-edged dagger.

"But I suppose you don't care, do you?" Adamina went on. "According to the rumors, you've already moved on to something…better. Sweeter."

"Lady Adamina," Blackfen cautioned.

"No rational person would believe them, seeing as I have a shadow of my own who will stand and swear to my purity. Of course, Imryll isn't exactly *rational* about you, is she, Wynter? Though…I *might* be swayed to put truth to whispers, once I'm carrying the prince's child." Adamina stepped in front of Drazhan and swept her eyes over him. "Yes. I think I could manage that. Assuming you're still here at all when your charge gets sent to the Easterlands like a wh—"

Drazhan thrust his hands at his sides to keep from throttling her. A low growl emanated from the back of his chest, and her eyes enlarged with fear.

Blackfen stepped between them. "That's enough. Both of you. Please."

"See, Farradyn?" Adamina stepped to her guard's side with a simpering grin. "I told you he cares."

Drazhan eased his hands. He retreated. "Any woman who speaks like this about another woman is not their friend, Lady Adamina. Consider this when you pretend to be."

He pivoted away just as Blackfen called, "I see it! There's the ship."

Drazhan stepped closer to the edge of the dock with a squint. His heart sank.

"Wynter, you'll alert the prince?" Blackfen asked.

"Me?"

"The princess is with him. I just thought…"

"Right." Wynter marched away before Adamina could make another petty charge.

Imryll didn't sleep. She watched Torian instead.

He'd passed out as soon as he climbed off of her. His prideful exhaustion quickly turned to gratified snores she didn't have the heart to interrupt. He lay with one leg draped over her, his entire backside exposed.

It had been impossible to smooth her dress back down with the way he was lying, so instead she'd carefully lifted it over her head and discarded it on the floor in a heap.

Her heart hadn't stopped racing.

Had she done the right thing?

She'd been asking herself that for the past hour. Every answer was different, exposing new fears and inadequacies. He knew her love for him was not the same as his love for her. He knew she would be leaving soon, without him, and that even if she stayed, there could never be more between them.

He'd wanted it anyway, and she'd given it to him.

The throb between her legs remained wholly unaddressed. She'd tried so hard to put memories of Drazhan aside, but she couldn't help remembering how he'd made her pleasure his priority, refusing to go further until she was soaking wet and begging for him.

The last gift she'd give Torian was believing it had been as good for her as it was for him.

Imryll could still dull the ache. Torian slept like the dead. She wouldn't wake him with the subtle movements needed to bring herself over the edge.

But if her hand even brushed down there, it would remind her of someone she had to forget.

Torian's leg shifted upward, gliding over the area she'd been trying to avoid. Maybe if she moved her hips a little, just enough…

Imryll swallowed. No. Not like that.

She pursed her mouth in a grimace and tried to think of something else. Instead, her mind was tugged violently forward into—

I've never known cold this terrible. Such soul-deep hunger. Fear has my heart pattering in my chest, driving me to exhaustion. The fire I'd kindled died at some point, and for some reason, I haven't stirred it back to life.

I'm the boy again, and I'm alone. But the world around me has changed from one I recognize. Here, wherever I am, I'm not safe. I have no brother to cushion my failures, nor a father to remind me of them. No hay or courtyard or comfort.

A violent shiver racks my starving body. The all-consuming thought of food makes the hunger so much worse, and I don't understand why I don't just eat *something, how it came to be that I'm cold and alone and starving close to death.*

Then it occurs to me.

This is the Hunt.

I'm hiding from the wulf, but I told my brother I wanted to kill the beast. Was it misplaced idealism? Have I already killed him?

No. If I did, I'd be home by now. And I know I haven't been home for a long time.

A noise startles me. I fall off the rock I was sitting on and turn toward a cave entrance. It's then I see him: the wulf. I've never seen one before through my own eyes, but I am the boy, and the boy has seen many.

I quietly reach around for something. A weapon, perhaps. Yes…the sword my brother tried to train me with. I see it lying propped against the damp, stony wall, useless at this distance. I wonder if I've gotten any better with it.

But I have no time for wonder. The wulf bares his fangs, lifts his shoulders, and—

The door slammed open.

Imryll didn't even have time to sit before Drazhan burst through, his cheeks stung with wind and exertion.

His eyes locked on hers before they swept down to register the scene. Torian's nude leg was folded across her nethers, which she'd not yet had the time or ability to clean up after their brief, unsatisfying union. Her exposed body was pinned beneath Torian's.

Drazhan ripped his gaze away and trained it across the room. He reached a hand out and gripped the doorframe. "Tell..." He grunted and cleared his throat. "Tell the prince that Lord Quintus has arrived."

Imryll had no opportunity to respond. The next sound she heard was Drazhan's boots crashing back down the hall.

362

TWENTY-FIVE
SOMEONE WORTH HAVING

Imryll paced her bedchamber, counting the seconds between breaths. She couldn't afford to lose focus or she'd get sick again, and she'd already turned over her stomach three times. She hadn't even had nerves this frayed when she'd been preparing for the Choosing.

Drazhan had one leg casually propped up onto the back of a chair, the other looped over the first, his eyes closed. Not once had he asked if she was all right when she was retching over a bowl. All he did was drop a stack of linens on the floor beside her before retreating back to his corner.

Sickness had already caused her to miss greeting Lord Quintus and his retinue in the banquet hall. Malyse went in her stead, to give Imryll's regrets, and upon return, she spared no detail recalling the varied reactions to her message. Predictably, the queen and Imryll's parents were livid, tripping over excuses and apologies to Lord Quintus.

More unexpected was Marius's reaction.

He ignored them, my lady, and sort of turned, like this. She'd mimed him clutching his chin and angling away. *He seemed worried. And then he looked right at me and asked if you were going to be all right. I said of course you would be, but I don't think he believed me.*

There's nothing wrong with me, Imryll had told her, trying to assure her new attendant, but her words ended in a bowl that Malyse reached forward to empty, running one hand down Imryll's back.

No, my lady. I don't think there is either.

After, she'd dismissed Malyse for the evening. The girl was reluctant to leave, but she eventually did.

Imryll slumped against the wall near her privy and dabbed a cloth wrung with cold water along her forehead and chest. She'd never been so sick in her life, but she'd also never been under so much stress. And she had plenty more to look forward to.

A vision tried to sneak in and take hold, but she braced her hands on the floor and forced it back with a weak grunt.

Imryll wilted against the welcome, cool stone, panting. She needed water, but even that wouldn't stay down.

She caught Drazhan staring at her, but when their eyes met, he swiftly lowered his.

He jumped when someone knocked on the outer door. He answered it with one hand near his sword belt. If she weren't so miserable, she'd have rolled her eyes.

The door flung open, knocking Drazhan back a step. Marius flew in, his eyes flaring in concern as they swept over her before he fell to a crouch at her feet. Drazhan ushered the lord's guards back into the hall before shutting and bolting the door.

"Imryll," Marius whispered with a long, soft sigh. He cupped her cheeks with a crestfallen frown. "You really aren't well, are you?"

Hot tears sprang to her eyes at the first genuine show of tenderness for her illness. She tried to dip her head, to hide them, but he held her face firm, his mouth opening and closing without actually speaking, and then he planted tender kisses against both sides of her mouth. She winced, knowing how disgusting she must look and taste, but he showed no sign he felt that way.

"Let's get you cleaned up." Marius scooped an arm under her from behind and pulled her back to her feet. He helped her to the broad chaise on the other side of the room, glaring at Drazhan on the way. "Have they all left you like this? Alone?"

"I'm fine," she insisted hoarsely. Mortification replaced her relief. Not only had Marius Quintus seen her in such a pitiful state, he knew no one cared enough to help her. "It will pass."

"They told me you were unwell and couldn't come to greet me. You know what I said?"

Imryll shook her head. She cradled her belly, freshly raw from the disturbance of moving.

Marius brushed sweaty, matted hair from her face and smiled. It struck Imryll how gentle he was being, away from his comforts, his people. Instead of mingling with the nobles, he'd come to look after her, when there was nothing for him to gain in doing it except angering the crown. "I said I came here to see the princess, and so that's where I'll be if you need me."

Imryll licked her dry lips and laughed. It sounded raspy, like her words. "You really didn't have to, Marius."

"Ahh," he said, beaming. "Finally."

She looked up.

"Usually I have to beg you to call me by my name."

Imryll glanced at her hands, joined in her lap. She became aware of how thin her shift was, how she'd had no time to even grab a robe. But the lord's eyes didn't veer anywhere inappropriate. They stayed fixed on hers. "I call a man as I see him. And you coming here..." She coughed into her thin sleeve. "You coming here is the behavior of a man, not a lord."

Marius laughed in mock offense. "Can I not be both?"

"Men are always more one than the other. The two things are conflicting, not complementary."

"You really think so?"

"I've spent my life surrounded by nobles."

365

"Well…man, lord. Whatever I am, I won't leave your side until you're better."

"No. You have important business here. I'll be fine." With a chill, she thought of his plan to overthrow the Rhiagains, but he wouldn't make a move until Carrow was gone.

Marius cradled her head in his hands and then slid them back to the nape of her neck, where he combed through her hair to smooth it. "Can we trust him?"

"Who?"

Marius flicked his head toward the corner.

Imryll laughed bitterly. "I know something about him that's far worse than anything you could say."

Marius raised a brow. "But will he be jealous? I know what he is to you."

Imryll lowered her eyes.

"Or was," he amended, followed by a gentle sigh. "I see no reason women shouldn't indulge the same enjoyments men do, though I'm admittedly relieved to see you've wisely ended it."

"What he thinks or does not think is of no concern to me. What were you going to say?"

Marius wound his hands further into her hair. "You said something untrue, even if you didn't realize it."

"Oh?"

"I did come to Duncarrow for you, Imryll. I'm indifferent about the alliance. About a reliquary or guards or any of it. None of it offers me anything I couldn't obtain by other means, and I know it's the crown that stands to gain, more than I ever could." He exhaled hard. "I promised you in Whitechurch that I'd sign the agreement, and I will, if everything in Belcarrow is as promised. But I could have sent Oakenwell for that. Wouldn't be the first time business of the Reach kept me from travel." The corner of his mouth twitched. "I came in person for *you*."

Imryll rolled back, causing him to release her. "You don't even know me."

"I find when people make this claim, it's because they fear the opposite."

"To you, I'm nothing but an object of desire. Like I am to all men. To…" Her gaze traveled fleetingly to Drazhan.

Marius shook his head. "The day you docked on my port, yes. I won't deny it. But when you sat at my table and defied your prince to speak your truth, it became more. The Rhiagains dangled you as an enticement, but it wasn't until that day when I understood the real enticement was to *know* you, in the way I suspect very few do."

Imryll crossed her arms over her chest. The sour sickness in her had dulled, replaced by an odd tingle permeating her flesh, drawing inward. His claim spoke to a long-dormant part of her, a piece of her girlhood that had died with the rest of her misplaced idealism. They were the words she'd wished Drazhan would have said, even once, to know she'd been more to him than a conquest.

But it would've been just another lie from him, in a sea of them.

"Come back with me, Imryll."

"Marius…" She'd been hoping he'd forget the offer he had made in Whitechurch, move on to some new amusement.

"Forget the Rhiagains, and your miserable guard, all of them. They don't care about you. They will grind you into dust for their own gain, until there's nothing left," Marius said. He ran his hands down the backs of her arms. "Come to Whitechurch, Imryll. Not as my mistress. As my *wife*. My equal."

"Your equal?" Imryll scrunched her face to hide her shock.

"You met my sister. Did she seem to lack in any freedoms? Did I ask her to mind her tongue?"

Imryll didn't answer.

"Whitechurch is not Duncarrow. I want to *know* you, Imryll of Glaisgain. I want to know you in a way no one here ever chose to. Your joys, your sorrows." He buried a devious grin by looking down. "And yes, your desires."

Drazhan made shifting sounds from the corner, but Imryll hardly noted them. It felt good not to care about him, what he thought or felt. She hoped he could hear it all, every last word. *You may not think I'm worth much, but someone does.*

"What if..." Imryll fought another wave of bile.

Marius was quick to his feet and returned with a mug of water. She smiled but shook her head, and he set it down.

"What if my idea of freedom doesn't involve marriage?"

Marius leaned back. "You base that idea on what you know of marriage, which is not the same kind I offer."

Imryll shook her head. "And you mistake my point by assuming it's the customs of marriage that are the deterrent, and not the natural confines consistent with any lifetime bond, especially one chosen from desperation."

He nodded. "Let the crown think what they may of my accepting you as my prize, but between us, there's only honesty. Openness. You can live the life of your choosing in Whitechurch, and perhaps with time, you may decide that life includes more of me."

"Not as your wife?"

He beamed a grin. "I'd like to think I can win you over, with enough time."

It was the best offer she would ever receive, a powerful man willing to give her everything, asking almost nothing in return except an open mind.

But the offer was too good to be true. Why would a man lusting for power rescue a princess and risk a war, unless a war was precisely what he was after? Everyone in the Easterlands answered to him. Who would ever defend her if he reneged on his promise? She had no friends in the realm, no allies. Marius could lock her in a cell for the rest of her days, and no one would lift a finger to stop it.

Her alternatives were dim. She could remain in Duncarrow, and be thrust aside as a failed chosen once it was revealed she wasn't carrying a child for Torian. Or she'd be sold to the next person they needed to court for power, someone who might be a lot less accommodating than Marius Quintus. She'd lost any leverage she had once possessed, and she lacked both the experience and the cleverness to outmaneuver any of it.

Imryll closed her eyes and nodded. "What you told me that night in Whitechurch…I won't agree to that."

"No." Marius looked down. "That part of is off the table. For now. But I won't deceive you, Imryll. I haven't lost sight of the objective. I actually did come here for another reason, not just because my sister would be exceptionally disappointed if I didn't come home with the woman I can't stop going on and on about." He looked up with a smile. "I also wanted to use this opportunity to learn. So that one day, I *will* be ready, and when the day comes, you'll have to be ready with me. As my equal. So I have as much time as that will take to convince you this is the best thing for the entire realm. The *only* thing."

"Whether you want this days from now or years from now…" She lowered her voice to a whisper. She didn't recognize the sound…the way she was actually *entertaining* what he had to say. "Even a drop of blood spilled will be more than I can condone."

Marius shot forward and kissed her. He tilted his head down with a guilty grunt. "Forgive me. I should have asked first."

Imryll leaned forward to return the kiss, but she remembered the foulness in her mouth and pecked his cheek instead. Gratitude waited below the surface, but he hadn't earned it yet. She had to trust him first.

"Is that acceptance?"

Imryll lifted her shoulders in a sigh. Was it? Should it be? She'd give anything for someone with more wisdom to come tell her what to do. She had options, but they were just boxes of different sizes. Perhaps the one Marius offered would be so big, she'd rarely have cause to reach the sides, but that didn't mean it wouldn't have them. "I don't know. You'll be here five nights?"

He nodded.

"Can I have until your final night to give you an answer?"

Marius nodded with a hint of a smile. "Of course. Sadly, we know neither the queen nor your beloved Torian will put up a fuss on your behalf, as they expect you to warm my bed every night I'm here. You'll come to my chambers each night, or me to yours, and we'll…talk. I'll tell you about the Easterlands, about anything you want. No one will know that's all we're doing. Otherwise…I suspect they will punish you, Imryll."

Imryll's heart sank because he was right.

"And your guard? You remember what I said about him? You sure you won't be too troubled to leave him behind?"

Imryll burst into laughter. "Gods, no. No, that is done. Professionally *and* otherwise. I'll be glad to finally be free of him."

"Good. I was trying to find a diplomatic way to remind you he couldn't come, but it seems that won't be necessary." Marius grinned. "I have to go, Princess. Any longer in here and they'll realize you *can* stand me, and that I've gained far more than they have in the deal. Wouldn't want them asking for more." He moved to his feet and gathered her to help her rise as well. "Will you be well enough for dinner tonight?"

"I have to be, I think."

"Rest then." He pecked another kiss, this time on her cheek. "And if you aren't feeling up to it, I'll return after dinner and stay with you. I'll even stay the night if you'll allow it…as friends, of course."

"I'm already regretting this," Imryll said, trying to smile. "I'll see you this evening."

Marius lifted her hand to his mouth. "I'll be waiting."

When he was gone, Imryll stared at the door in a daze.

"What is it about you that otherwise-rational men can't help making themselves look like fools to save you?" Drazhan stormed into the privy and slammed the door behind him.

Torian didn't appreciate the way the duke and duchess of Glaisgain had arranged the tables for the feast.

Usually the Rhiagains shared one table, looking out upon everyone else, but Melantha had put the smaller tables into storage, replacing them with longer, sturdier ones. She'd lengthened the royal table to stretch nearly wall to wall and built a mirrored one facing it, but from twenty or so feet away—far enough that no conversations could be heard from table to table yet close enough to see the subtle ways people leaned in to pass messages and whose feet brushed whose, both evidenced by the way the cloths moved near the floor.

One table for the Rhiagains and their confidants.

One for Lord Quintus and his.

Except, Imryll was sitting at the Quintus table, at Marius's right, like a wife.

Between the tables, couples danced the carole, weaving back and forth in a confusing chain, further obscuring any reading Torian tried to conduct on the situation brewing at the Quintus table.

Quintus openly doted on Imryll. Feeding her bites from his plate, provoking laughs…Torian wasn't close enough to see her eyes, to know how much was an act or whether any of it was real. His logical mind told him *of course* it was an act, because Imryll was wary of the man at best. But Torian's heart was more confused than ever, since she'd given him the one thing he wanted most in all the world.

No, what he wanted most in all the world was something he'd already resigned himself to never having.

She did it for you. Because she loves you.

She pities me.

She loves you. And that was her good-bye. Because you are too weak, too cowardly, to stand up to a mother who has no right to be running the crown in your father's absence. The duke doesn't respect you. Who are you, if not the prince and future king of this realm? Or maybe you've forgotten, so mired in your self-pity.

Adamina leaned in, brushing her shoulder against his when she made her approach. "Imryll is handling this all exceedingly well, would you not say?"

371

"Ada," Torian groused with a deep sigh. "I told you, her name—"

"Princess, yes, yes. Though certainly not for much longer now." She shook her head with a dainty scoff. "Even if the queen changed her mind, all of Duncarrow has seen the man handling her like she's already his mistress." She tilted her head with a devious grin. "Is she?"

"Stop," he ordered. "Of course not."

"How sure can you be?"

Sure enough to know it's not pretty boy Marius she's in love with. "This isn't appropriate, Ada. What if the other..." Torian glanced down the row, but the other three chosens were locked away in their rooms, on Godivah's orders. Yet another failure he lacked the spine to right. "The princess is in a challenging situation right now and is handling it with grace. How would you feel, if you were her?"

"I wouldn't be," Ada said, pinching in her chin with a surprised quirk of her mouth. "She's in this position because she has displeased the queen."

Torian clenched. It was another reminder, perhaps even an intentional one on Ada's part, that Torian was only powerless because he refused to seize it. *No wonder Imryll could never love me.* "The queen has never particularly taken to Imryll for some reason. But she *chose* her—"

"No," Adamina said quickly. "*She* did not. The sorcerer chose her. Mortain chose her, and the queen has never gotten over it. Then you add in the nasty business with her guard—"

"Ada!"

"It's almost a game to watch them pretend not to look at each other, to count the scowls and sighs and huffs. Either they don't care if everyone knows or they're too caught up in their own little world to notice." Ada fluttered her head and shoulders. "Our poor queen. Everyone blames her."

Torian's face surged with heat. "Rumors are beneath you."

"Rumors? Nothing I've said is a rumor, Your Grace. I have eyes. And if you'll forgive me for saying so, you do as well, and I'm quite sure you've seen this all yourself. Whether you're in denial about it..."

Beads of sweat dripped into Torian's eyes. He caught glimpses of Imryll through the weaving dancers. While she seemed engaged in whatever Lord Quintus was saying, her eyes were fixed on a distant spot. Torian couldn't follow her gaze without drawing Ada's keen attention, but he didn't need to confirm what he already knew. "She is still the First Chosen, our princess, and it is unbecoming to speak of her the way you are."

Ada cocked her head and grinned. "So you *do* know. Did she tell you? Or...Or did you *catch* them?" Her eyes lit up.

Torian's belly clenched. "I will not dignify that with a response."

"Does Wynter watch, when you and Imryll..."

Torian grimaced and pointed his annoyed gaze forward.

"I haven't decided whether I'd like Blackfen to watch us when it's my turn." Adamina tossed her words out with a light huff.

Torian scoffed and turned back toward her. "If your guard watches, it will not be out of some perverse pleasure. And no, Wynter is not there...He hasn't...no."

"Hmm." Ada looked pleased with herself. "You've now confirmed a second rumor for me, Your Grace. The court feared you and Imryll had *not* consummated, but you have. For her sake, I hope she *is* with child when she goes to the Easterland playboy's bed, because it will be the only thing that can save her now."

Torian released a long, slow breath. Imryll appeared and disappeared amid the shifting dancers. Each time she came into view, she was drinking more wine.

"I'd like to dance, Your Grace."

Ada's words prompted him to glance to his other side, where both his mother's and Clarisan's chairs were empty. Godivah had been there only moments before, but Clarisan's had been abandoned for some time, for she and Oakenwell were busy stepping in time with the other revelers on the dance floor.

"I don't have the appetite for it tonight, Ada." Torian emptied his wineglass.

"Then you will not be cross if I dance without you?"

Torian gestured toward the floor. "Don't let me stop you."

Drazhan watched Imryll drain goblet after goblet of wine, wondering why no one stopped her. She'd been sick all day and shouldn't even be at the celebration. She was only making it worse for herself. Worse for him too, for he'd be the one who had to hear her retching and moaning long into the night.

But while she might be entertaining Quintus's bold offer, Drazhan noted the tight winces when Marius touched her, the slight draw of her mouth when he leaned in for a whisper. Imryll *was* attracted to him. Drazhan had seen it the day they'd landed in Whitechurch, and he could see it now. Every woman in the hall struggled to keep their eyes off of Quintus.

But she couldn't wait to be rid of him.

What Drazhan didn't know was whether she was stubborn enough to follow Quintus to the Easterlands anyway.

Drazhan was still thinking about it when Adamina blocked his view with the top of her head.

He looked down at her.

"Syr Wynter, would you indulge me in a few rounds of the carole?"

Drazhan leaned in to hear her better. "Excuse me?"

Adamina rose to her tiptoes. As she did, she pressed one hand to his chest and looped the other around one of his shoulders. "I asked you, syr, if you'd like to dance."

Drazhan scoffed. He flexed his jaw into a surprised scowl. "I don't dance."

Adamina hadn't released him yet. The pleased look she tossed over her shoulder explained why.

Imryll stared their way. Her mouth quivered, her wine suspended mid-drink.

"Are you really going to refuse a chosen, syr?"

"I have my own."

"Your own? What an interesting choice of words." Adamina threw her head back with an overdone giggle, still hanging from him. He wanted to pry her away, but it seemed she wanted him to, to create a scene.

He groaned and braced into his response. "If I'm dancing, I can't keep an eye on the princess. Do you see Blackfen dancing?"

"Blackfen is a stick in the mud."

"If he's a stick, I'm an entire trunk."

Adamina's eyebrows shot upward at the same time her mouth widened. "An entire *trunk*, you say. How lucky for Imryll."

Imryll's goblet spilled, sending wine all over the table. Marius was quick to jump up and tend to it, while she stared, wan-faced, at an empty corner.

Drazhan peeled the young woman off of him. "Find someone else."

Adamina dropped back to her feet in a pout, but Drazhan was done entertaining her nonsense. He watched Imryll push away from the table, while Marius and a cluster of attendants cleaned up the mess. She backed away with the same empty stare and bolted out of the room with an unsteady gait, disappearing between two pillars.

Drazhan brushed past Adamina, ignoring whatever rebuttal she'd offered. He jogged down the side of the room until he reached the same pillars and slipped out.

He slowed when he picked up the sound of Imryll sobbing. But it was the other voice that had him ducking behind a row of potted palms.

Tasmin.

"I don't want to talk about it, Tas." Imryll belched into another sob. "I need...I want...I'm going to..." A retching sound followed.

Tasmin squealed. "What in the name of the gods, Imryll?"

"I've felt poorly all day...It doesn't matter...I need my bed."

"You need some water, and perhaps a physician."

Drazhan leaned out and saw Tasmin looking around the empty hall.

"I need to magically sprout wings, so I can fly so far from Duncarrow, I don't even recognize myself anymore." Imryll stepped sideways, tripping over herself. She laughed, but the sound ended with a hiccup, and both of her hands clamped over her mouth in alarm.

"You're drunk, love. Let me get you back."

"Everyone's drunk, Tas. Isn't that the point of a fete?"

"Not so drunk they missed the hopeless looks you and Wynter flung at each other all night."

"Wynter?" Imryll snorted. Another sob followed. "You're mistaken. He hates me, Tas. *Hates* me. He came here to…" She hiccuped again.

Drazhan's heart seized.

"He never cared about me. He only pretended to, so I'd fall into his arms more easily. And I did, didn't I? You were right. I was just someone to fuck."

Drazhan's eyes closed.

"*Lower* your voice!" Tasmin sighed. "I'm sorry, darling. I am. I know it hurts. But let's finish this in your apartment."

"He let me believe…that I was someone worth having. That I was someone…" Imryll stumbled, but Tasmin caught her before she fell. "Someone who could be more than a concubine of men."

Drazhan gripped the wall. No words had ever left him so hollowed. He summoned the last of his will to keep from going to her, crushing her to his chest, and insisting she hear the way his heart had forgotten how to beat in rhythm.

Because of *her*.

"Oh, Imryll." Tasmin was crying too. "I wish I could take this pain from you."

"You can't," Imryll cried. She sniffled against her bare arm. "No one can. Just like no one can tell me it's going to be all right. Because it's *not* going to be all right, is it? I told Marius tonight at supper I'd go with him to Whitechurch, even though I know at least half his promises are lies. As soon as I get there, he'll have me in his bed, night after night, until he tires of me, which won't be long, I'm sure. A man like him has options a woman like me does not."

"You accepted?"

"Isn't that what you told me I should do?"

"It is, but…never mind. Don't listen to me. I'm a little drunk myself." Tasmin's laugh was forced.

"He told me he wants me in his bed before he leaves. He said…He needs a show of faith from me. To…to prove I'm not going to run when we land in the Easterlands."

Drazhan's hands began to sting. To feel the swirl.

"How…How does that prove anything? You could still run."

"I could, but…but once he's had me, he said, I will be…" Imryll hiccuped again. "Marked."

"He's going to *mark* you?"

"No, he didn't say *that*, exactly. It was implied, because others will know I…I belong to him, and no one in the Easterlands would steal from their lord. There will be nowhere *to* run, Tas."

"He *said* this?"

"Well, he made it sound far more romantic and chivalrous, but…" Imryll retched again.

"Gods. We *really* need to get you back. Come on."

Drazhan stormed out from his hiding spot, startling Tasmin into releasing Imryll. "I'll see that she gets back." He swooped in and lifted Imryll into his arms before she could protest or make a bigger scene. She squirmed and cursed but was too drunk to fight.

"You…" Tasmin's eyes narrowed. "You will *not*."

Drazhan brushed past her and started down the hall.

"You let her go!"

"I will *not*," Drazhan called back without stopping.

"Put me *down*," Imryll said through gritted teeth, wriggling and swatting at Drazhan all the way down the hall. "Put me down, you lying, murdering, claw-handed thug!" With all the nobles in the Great Hall, there were few around to see the display, but she didn't care anymore. Let them all see how Imryll of Glaisgain had been *ruined* by Drazhan Wynter.

Drazhan held tight all the way to her apartments. He wore the same resigned expression for every grueling step and jolt. Even when she tried to leap *over* him, inadvertently planting her breasts across his face, he betrayed nothing.

When they stepped inside, she took advantage of him distracted by bolting the door, and she skittered out of his arms in a move so ungraceful, not even sobriety could have saved her from sprawling herself across the stones.

She peered up at his towering form. A hand stretched toward her. She sneered and spat, clambering away backward on her hands and feet.

"Suit yourself," he muttered and turned away.

Imryll stumbled to her feet. She crashed against the bedpost, rolled, and drunk-stepped to the wall. She stole a moment to breathe—or try to anyway—but Drazhan's dark judgment stung her from across the room. It lived in his slowly narrowing eyes, his self-satisfied grin...the way his neck corded in delight of her distress, that same joy traveling to his hands fisting at his sides.

Imryll wiped her face across her arm and straightened. A dizzy spell had her nearly missing another step, which caused him to lunge forward, but she cackled to show him she was *fine,* perfectly *fine.* Nothing could possibly be amiss with the future Lady Quintus of the Easterlands.

Drazhan watched her in heavy silence. Gloating. Loathing. Enjoying all of it: her downfall, her drunkenness, and even her earlier sickness, which was coming back, she could feel it. Soon. *Yes, you ruined me, and I hate you, I hate you, I hate you.*

She waited for him to look away, but he didn't.

Imryll sniffled, a gross mix of tears and wine and sweat and shame. A bitter grin found its way across her dirty face and she let it grow, fester, as she reached behind her neck to undo the clasp on her dress. Her mother had sent it for the evening. *Easy off,* the attendant had said, because everyone knew Imryll would be spreading her legs for yet another man tonight. All their problems solved with the dip of a lord's wick. Praise the gods.

Her silver gown dropped to the stones in a whoosh.

Drazhan's mouth parted quickly, then closed.

Imryll didn't collect the dress. She made no move toward the nightgown left on her bed, nor the many robes hanging all over the room. She stood, nude and defiant, waiting for him to decide the appropriate punishment.

Because at that moment, Imryll was most definitely *not* a good girl.

"Put that…" Drazhan cleared his throat. It moved in a deep bob. "Put that back on."

Imryll folded a hand over her hip. She curved her mouth to perfectly form the word "no."

"*Now.*"

Imryll laughed. She lifted her chin. "No."

Drazhan shifted his weight. One palm scraped his mouth while his eyes bulged and then narrowed. "You're drunk. And you're acting like a child."

"A child?" Imryll looked down at her breasts. She pursed her lips in a frown and twisted both of her nipples between the pads of her fingers. "I don't recall having *these* as a child."

Drazhan huffed a jumble of unintelligible words and started for the bed. He gathered her nightgown in his fist and held it out, his arm fully extended. He shook it. "Take it. Now."

Imryll released her nipples and flattened her hands, then she smoothed them down her belly and crossed them just over her hips. "But you're right. I am a little drunk."

"A little?" Drazhan scoffed in disgust. His arm shook her nightgown again. "You're humiliating yourself."

"Oh, we're a little too late for that!" She laughed and switched her hands, which traded places on her hips. "All of Duncarrow knows how easily I spread my legs for my dark knight." She closed her eyes when a swoon hit. She stuttered sideways.

"Imryll?"

She sucked in a breath and opened her eyes, batting them. "Is that *concern*, Drazhan? Or have you just realized none of my attendants will be returning for hours, so that leaves *you* to clean my bile?"

"You think I'm afraid of some vomit?" He tossed her night-gown at the bed. It missed and landed on the floor. "Go to bed, before you really make a fool of yourself."

"I hate you." She seethed, pitching forward.

"I know. Go to bed."

Imryll backed herself up until she smacked against the wall with a gasp. She spread her arms along the wall and lifted her feet, one at a time, then pressed her soles to the cool stone, moving her legs wider apart with each change.

She closed her eyes, and for a moment, she was somewhere else. She was in the chalet again, but it was different. The fire was well-tended, and there was food and water, and the sense she was home was so elating, it transcended happiness and became pure, raw desire.

Imryll worked her hands between her legs with a feral moan that sent her to the tops of her toes. She heard Drazhan mutter something just as carnal under his breath, but he might as well have been miles away.

Drazhan marched over and thrust his palms against the stone on either side of her. "You think I care that you're pleasuring yourself? Like an exhibitionist?"

"I'm not thinking about you at all," Imryll lied, crunching her teeth to her bottom lip as she ascended to a place where there was no room for the business of men. Where the deep ridges of Drazhan's cock had not molded her into the shape of one man alone, and her arousal had nothing to do with the heady waft of his breath as he held his position, awaiting her answer.

With every flick of her middle finger, she felt Drazhan tighten the makeshift cage he'd surrounded her with. His breaths came quicker, hotter, scaling with her own as she stretched higher onto her toes in a futile attempt to climb right out of her skin.

Imryll's mouth fell open with a whimper when she crashed, boneless and swaying. Before she could fall, she was impaled by two of Drazhan's strong fingers, driving up and into her, lifting her nearly off her feet.

"Pretty fucking wet for someone who hates me so much," he charged, spreading his words between thrusts.

"What do you think made me so wet, Draz? My hatred for you is the only thing that gets me off anymore."

She shivered and came all over his hand, twisting to take in more, to release more.

He raised his other hand to her cheek, in a move so gentle, it took her momentarily out of the wonderful, freeing moment. When he removed it, she felt different. It took her a moment to understand he'd eased her inebriation. All she felt were the exhausting remnants of a hangover.

She pushed his chest with one hand and tugged his shirt with the other until he removed both of his hands. Pulling, swatting, moaning, crying.

"You in your right mind now?" He inhaled a hard gulp of air.

"I won't blame the wine for my behavior, and neither should you," she said, issuing a challenge. "Should we repeat the past few minutes again now that I'm sober?"

"Imryll." His jaw twitched.

She glared through an impertinent, dangerous grin. *"Draz."*

Drazhan hoisted her, then carried her to the bed and threw her with a bounce far gentler than his intentions. Imryll rolled her head back and squirmed, still making sense of the room spinning when she turned to the side. Sounds split through her bewilderment, steadying her surroundings but not her heart. The crack of his belt, the fall of his pants. The one, final grunt of surrender

Drazhan allowed himself before he flipped her legs over his arms and drove into her.

Imryll laughed and reached between them, circling the base of his cock with her thumb and forefinger. She squeezed, which made him thrust harder, knocking her hand loose and sending her inching back on the bed.

"Is this what you want?" His fingers dug into her hips so hard, it stung. "To be fucked like someone's prize?"

She shook her head back and forth, nearly choking on her spit when she laughed harder. "I hate you so much." She moaned, and seconds later, she exploded with stars when he hit a spot that had her bucking and clenching.

"Fucking hate you more," he murmured through a clenched jaw, riding the movement of her muscle spasms. "Fuck, Imryll. Damn you."

Imryll grasped hold of his shirt and used it to pull herself toward him. She yanked his face toward hers, both of them bouncing with the delicious violence of his deep plunging. "You can say…whatever…you want…" Imryll threw her head back and came again.

He gritted and bore down harder.

"But we both…know…you're mine."

She released him and flopped back with a stilted sigh. It ended when he lifted her legs even higher, sliding in so deep, she couldn't discern pain from pleasure. Her eyes closed in surrender, but she opened them, just for a moment, and she was almost certain his hands, wrapped around her ankles, had turned to weaponized digits, surrounded by warm red and cobalt light. The trail of blood running up her calf made it even more real.

A torrent of warmth flooded into her, jerking his cock, spilling his weakness into her where she could turn it into her strength.

Drazhan's cries echoed off the stones. They clung to the foggy panes and seared her flesh.

He stumbled back and dropped to his knees on the stones, his head bowed.

Imryll drew her ankle in. She *hadn't* imagined it. Where his hand had been, on her left ankle, was a puncture mark. Blood coated her ankle and pooled on the bed.

Drazhan looked up. First at her, then at her foot. He climbed forward, his eyes wide with alarm, and grabbed hold of her ankle. He brought it to his mouth and suckled the wound, his throat moving as he swallowed her blood.

Imryll realized she was touching herself again, and she came before she could even make the climb.

When he released her, her ankle was healed. Clean. Smooth.

Drazhan wiped the blood from his mouth and pushed to his feet. "Please go to bed."

Imryll breathily nodded. He nodded back, securing silent confirmation.

He lowered his head, shook it, and retreated to his corner.

384

TWENTY-SIX
THE WEAK MEN
OF THE FRAGILE MONARCHY

The sea voyage to Belcarrow was only a few hours long, but the fog and freezing rain had the captain suggesting they return to port and try again the following day. Duke Drushan shut it down quickly, and unless Torian wanted others to think there was division in his inner circle, he had no choice but to pretend he felt the same way.

Every day we delay is a day that man gets time with his thoughts. And this is a man who thinks highly of his own revelations, Duke Drushan had said, pulling Torian aside once the matter had been settled. Torian noted the man hadn't added *Your Grace*, and he wondered if it was a sign of the future awaiting him.

Torian had been anxious about the lord of the Easterlands arriving at Duncarrow with Carrow dying in his own bed, but everyone around him, including the dukes, acted as if Torian were already king—even Godivah, at least in front of others. Behind closed doors, she wielded her commands like lashings he was too inexperienced to dodge.

385

Clarisan, when she wasn't exchanging girlish glances with Oakenwell, was in on the charade too.

It was almost as if Carrow weren't withering away at the end of a dark hall.

The ship was a smaller, faster vessel than *The Sweet Yvaine*, and the below-deck quarters were small and cramped. With several of the dukes milling about like vultures, Torian couldn't leave them to court Lord Quintus without him. They'd already quietly sent Marquess Octavyen and his wife to the Westerlands for a secret negotiation, in case the Easterland deal fell through.

"Lovely day for travel," Duke Rahn said as he stepped to Torian's side. Torian looked over and saw the man's smiling mischief. Rahn Tindahl was the only duke Torian liked. He was young and had lost his family on the voyage to Duncarrow, arriving as a little boy who had, overnight, become both the head of his Noble House and the last of his name. Clarisan said no one had known what to do with the wide-eyed, precocious boy who loved learning, so they cultivated that joy in him, and when the next generation of Duncarrow was born, they turned it over to Rahn for the children's compulsory education on realm matters. Indoctrination was more like it, as the curriculum was decided on and approved by the king, but Rahn always found ways to make learning entertaining.

Rahn, at almost thirty, had yet to marry and rebuild his house. Torian had always sensed an undercurrent of contempt in the duke, a derision for the totalistic ways of Duncarrow. Like Imryll, Rahn would have been happier roaming freely on the mainland. It was Rahn who had treasonously encouraged Imryll's forbidden writing, something known only by Torian and Tasmin.

Torian forced a laugh. "Can't let the Easterland lord spend another day without spreading ink, I suppose." Quintus should be in a prison cell for failing to protect his future king, but he'd managed to spin the situation as further evidence of why the crown couldn't afford not to have powerful allies.

"The princess all right?" Rahn nodded at Imryll. She'd been pitched over the side of the ship for over an hour, Marius glued to her side with a hand running constant strokes up and down her back. Drazhan hovered nearby, pretending not to be distressed.

Torian hadn't stopped thinking about his own night with Imryll, but every time a fragment of those few minutes flashed across his mind, he couldn't help but wonder how it compared to the way Drazhan had turned her inside out.

"She was feeling poorly before we left. I should have insisted she stay behind."

"The sea doesn't agree with everyone."

"She did better than the rest of us on the trip to Whitechurch," Torian muttered. The thought clung to him as though he should think harder, dig deeper. "So well, even the crew was surprised."

"Indeed?" Rahn nodded with a thoughtful look. He squinted at the sea spray coming over both sides of the ship. "How can I serve you on this visit, Your Grace?"

Torian startled at the question no one else had asked him. "Thank you for asking. But as long as Admiral Pettigrew and Major Smithwick have the camp in order, there's nothing to do but hope Lord Quintus is in a more favorable mood than the weather."

"And the princess?"

"What about her?"

Rahn lowered his eyes with a brief smile. "Forgive me. It's not my place." He bowed lightly. "If I can help at all, Your Grace, you need only ask."

Drazhan was glad to be finally docking after the rough journey to the Isle of Belcarrow. The small island had only one purpose, one single port—manned, at all hours, by armed infantry. The men populating the Belcarrow encampment weren't from Ilynglass, nor even Duncarrow, but the kingdom. No one knew for sure how they were selected. Some said a competition, like the one the Knights of Duncarrow had gone through. Others said it was forced conscription.

Drazhan had not heard even a single word whispered about contests or honor, but he *had* watched men disappear from their beds in the middle of the night.

Much like the camp's inauspicious start, the matter of exact population numbers was also dubious. Depending on who was asked, it was either several hundred or tens of thousands. Scanning the sea of crushed-together tents and the tight cluster of barracks in the middle, he couldn't fathom how the Rhiagains intended to double their ranks.

There wasn't much else to the cluster of land. The only colors to be seen, other than the red-and-violet flags bearing the Rhiagain crossed swords, were various shades of gray.

Drazhan followed Imryll and Marius down the gangplank. Imryll swayed to create distance between herself and her benefactor, but Marius, either oblivious or bold, narrowed it each time, and looped an arm around her waist to keep her from wandering too far. He reached over to straighten her hair, matted by wind and sea spray. Drazhan caught a glimpse of her colorless cheeks and sunken eyes.

He'd attempted to heal her while she'd slept, but whatever was wrong with her, it couldn't be assuaged by magic. She shouldn't be there at all. She should be back in her bedchamber, resting, not the prize in a political game.

The urge to toss her over his shoulder and sail away was powerful.

"It took us nearly five years just to clear the rocks and make the land livable," Duke Drushan was saying. He walked backward as he addressed the group. At his side, the prince looked lost. "Another five to bring everything here and build what you see."

"Impressive," Marius said drily. "Though not what I expected."

"What did you expect, Lord Quintus?" Imryll asked. Her heavy-lidded eyes blinked as she tried to smile. Even with how sick she'd been—and despite her vapid father's intentional ignorance to her condition—she was still trying to help Torian.

"Well, it's all…" He screwed his mouth into a frown and fluttered his hand around. "Rather gray and lifeless, no?"

"Color. We can add that," Drushan said, nodding at his groom, who was taking notes.

"Who lives in the tents?" Marius asked.

"Privates mainly. Some low-ranking officers," Drushan said.

"And the barracks?"

"Commanders. Our major and admiral."

"Hmm." Marius nodded, moving his gaze slowly across the tent sea. He squinted into a gust of wind. "So you take men from home and family, promise them the rather dubious pronouncement of honor, and give them…canvas?"

Nervous laughter tittered through the crowd of men on both sides of the negotiation. Drazhan loathed Quintus too much to give him credit for what was a rather daring—and apt—observation.

"Is this not the way in all societies, my lord? Men work and aspire for what other men have?"

"A system of gradual rewards. What do these men get for advancing their skills?" Oakenwell squinted his face. "Bigger tents?"

Drazhan coughed to keep a grin at bay.

Drushan reddened. "Well…yes."

Duke Fenring, Adamina's father, stepped forward. "But of course, we are here to understand what traditions the men of this realm hold dear, so that we may travel down a path of continuous improvement."

"I have to be candid," Marius said. He kissed the side of Imryll's head and walked slowly forward, his hands looped at his back. "This would be a most wretched backslide for any man I agreed to send here. They live like princes in the Easterlands, while this would make even our prisons feel cozy."

More laughter.

"Our men are well fed." Drushan's nostrils flared. He twitched his eyes. "They know what an honor it is to even be here, to—"

Imryll, throwing glances around at all the men, stepped forward. "What my father is trying to say is that this arrangement has served us well. But the Easterlands is, as you know, a paragon of our realm. We stand to learn so much from you, Lord Quintus, and we would appreciate any wisdom you might offer. We will use it to make Belcarrow the best training grounds the kingdom has ever seen."

"Of course, love." Marius brightened with a slow smile.

Drazhan allowed his fist the fantasy of punching him.

"If that is your intent, to bring me here to guide you toward an ideal encampment, you'll find I'm quite agreeable to that."

Drushan grumbled something to Fenring about Imryll *knowing her place.*

Fenring ignored him, observing Imryll with keen interest. "Shall we introduce you to Admiral Pettigrew and Major Smithwick so we can begin the tour and assessment?"

Marius turned to face Imryll. "You're unwell. Will you stay behind, catch your breath?"

Imryll nodded in clear relief.

Marius looked past Drazhan and flicked a hand toward Evos. "Please escort the princess back to the ship and find her water and a place to lie down, while Oakenwell and I meet with the leaders."

Evos bowed.

Drazhan watched Torian, waiting for him to take control—or even pretend to—but he hung off to the side with a defeated look.

"Oakenwell and I would like to meet with your major and admiral alone, without the constant intrusion of men trying to sell us something that's quite different from what we need it to be. Duke Rahn, you'll join us though?"

Rahn glanced nervously at the other dukes and then nodded.

"Your Grace, you don't mind staying back?" Marius asked. It wasn't a question but a challenge.

"I should look after the princess anyway," Torian said.

Drazhan scoffed at the concession of weakness.

The men disappeared.

Drazhan followed Evos and Imryll back onto the ship, but Torian was soon at his side.

"Wynter," he said and then repeated it to be heard over the hard wind. "I thought you and I might talk."

Drazhan pretended not to hear. He pushed ahead and leaped down from the gangplank and onto the deck.

"Syr Wynter. I *know* you can hear me."

Drazhan tensed but kept walking.

"Please. Are you really going to reduce a prince to begging a knight? Does everything have to be difficult with you?"

Drazhan flicked his eyes upward in annoyance, sighed, and turned.

Torian's face lightened in relief. He looked so pathetic, Drazhan almost felt pity for him, but there wasn't room for something so kind for the son of a genocidal monster. "I thought I might ask you how you felt about Imryll leaving with Lord Quintus."

Drazhan rolled his tongue to the side of his mouth and shrugged with one shoulder.

"Oh, *please*. I *know* you have thoughts. I know how you feel about her."

Drazhan's brows lifted.

"And I know you know that I know." Torian chuckled at his wordplay, but it was joyless. "Imryll doesn't keep things from me. No matter what does or doesn't exist between us, deception is not part of it."

Drazhan inhaled through his nose, debating whether it was worth responding at all. Torian had asked the wrong question. It wasn't Drazhan's job to guide him where his father had failed.

"I thought you might...use your...*words*..." Torian wrinkled his nose in repugnance. "To convince her not to go."

Drazhan forced an unexpected laugh. "Are you not the prince of this realm?"

"It's complicated. Far too much for me to explain to you."

"Complicated." Drazhan crossed his arms over his chest and squared his stance. "What's so complicated, *Your Grace*, about a prince who lets his mother tell him what to do, and can't find his voice amidst weak-minded nobles trying to preen for a man even less important than they are?"

Torian balked with a heavy step backward. "Well, you are not mincing words today, are you?"

Drazhan charged forward, enjoying the scared widening of Torian's eyes, the retreating tuck of his chin. "No, but they are *wasted* on a man who would ask a *guard* for help when he already has the answer."

"It's not that simple," Torian said, shaking his head back and forth in short whips. "If I refuse, he leaves without signing the agreement. I have nothing else he wants."

"So that's it then." Drazhan pursed his mouth in a hard sneer. "That's her worth."

"But if *she* says no…then Lord Quintus must respect that."

Drazhan raised a hand, and Torian skittered back. Looking into the weak man's eyes summoned the image of Imryll lying under the prince, awake and unsatisfied, as he snored away, oblivious that the woman he cared about had needs of her own.

But as Torian cowed, Imryll left Drazhan's mind altogether, replaced by the memory of standing in front of the dual tombs of his father and brother. Of Aesylt's tiny hand wedged in his as she stared, emotionless, a husk of her former self. She hadn't cried. Not a tear. Tears were insignificant for the little girl who had watched her father and brother slain and then looked out the window at the ruins of her village. What were tears for the child who was left alive for the sole purpose of telling a story there were no words for?

I swear to you, cub, Drazhan had said that day, kneeling in front of her lifeless eyes. *I won't rest until the men responsible are dead and the Rhiagain rule is reduced to rubble and ash.*

The rage that had brought Drazhan to Duncarrow flamed in his hands. Torian quaked, stepping toward the ledge and almost falling overboard as he gaped in dawning horror of the transformation happening to the knight.

There was no one around to save him. The crew was below deck, enjoying a break. Everyone else was on land.

This is it. The opportunity you've been waiting for. Take it, and be done with him.

Drazhan took another step forward. He imagined the seconds ahead, throttling the life out of Torian Rhiagain and tossing him over the side like discarded waste, just as his father had ordered to be done with Ezra and Hraz Wynter when the Rhiagain guard had dragged them from their beds and executed them in front of their people. As had been done to so many others in Witchwood Cross, for daring to defend their own land and people.

Do it! Do it now, or accept you never had the mettle for the mission.

"Wynter?" Torian gripped the railing. In that moment, he looked more boy than man, his sins no greater than naivete or cowardice. He was not his father, nor the men who'd sacked the village. He'd only been a child himself when it had happened, as innocent as the ones slaughtered in Witchwood Cross, slain for being the children of those loyal to the Wynters.

Fuck.

Guardians curse it all.

Drazhan dropped his hands to his sides with a violent grunt. His claws retracted, his digits returning to fingers. "Is it any wonder, princeling, why Imryll accepted such a hollow offer to begin with when she's surrounded by weak, craven men more concerned with holding together their fragile monarchy than her own life?" Drazhan swept his judgment over the prince. "Perhaps she's better off leaving. At least the simpering lord *pretends* to care."

Drazhan left Torian and hustled below deck before he changed his mind about killing him.

He moved through stowage, slapping away nets and dodging crates until he saw the makeshift cot Evos had made for Imryll.

The guard held the back of her head steady as she drank from a wineskin. It sputtered out the sides of her mouth and down her dress, but she nodded her gratitude through tear-filled eyes.

Whatever afflicted Imryll, it was killing her. It was bigger than heals, than magic, and as long as she boarded that ship with Lord Quintus in a few days, no one cared that it would be the end of her.

Drazhan's fingers clawed at the thick web of an old net as he inhaled the damp, mildewed musk of a hold not fit for a prisoner, let alone a young woman so sick, she couldn't even hold her head up.

Imryll.

A fist closed around the cage holding sentry around his heart, snapping it.

Imryll. Imryll. Imryll.

He started forward, but Torian brushed past him with a hard elbow and rushed to Imryll's side. She folded into his arms like a broken doll, and Evos peeled away to join Drazhan.

"Something is very wrong with the princess, Syr Wynter," he said with a heavy breath.

Drazhan closed his eyes and could feel her head roll along his chest as he cradled it. He saw her eyes look up at him, her fear disintegrating at the realization she was safe and where she belonged, with him.

He forced the image away and tapped Evos on the shoulder before leaving.

TWENTY-SEVEN

LONG MAY HE REIGN

Imryll turned her head away from the soup Duchess Teleria held at her mouth. The stench of the heady broth curdled her stomach.

Tasmin sighed, her hands wrapped around her waist as she paced on the other side of the room.

"I can't," Imryll whispered, hoarse. Opening her mouth made her want to retch. She held both of her hands over it to suppress the urge.

"You have to eat *something*, dear." Teleria set the bowl aside and traded it for the cool rag she'd been using to mop Imryll's face. "You'll only get sicker."

"She knows, Mother," Tasmin said with gentle annoyance. "It isn't Imryll we need to be saying this to. The queen—"

Teleria shook her head tersely. "It goes without saying. And there are ears everywhere."

"But the Meduwyn could heal her! Mortain has healed her before."

"Tas."

Tasmin snorted and dipped a fresh rag into the second basin. "And trust me, if there were ears everywhere…" She didn't finish.

Imryll sat up higher in her bed. "Where's Drazhan?" She lacked the stamina for modesty and wondered if it was even worth trying anymore. Everyone already seemed to know about her sordid affair with her knight, and she was no longer the favored chosen.

The women exchanged careful looks.

"I'm sure he'll be back soon," Tasmin said with a strained smile. "We know he never leaves your side for long."

Imryll leaned back. Sweat dripped into her eyes, so she closed them with an exhausted exhale. Hearing others speak of the way Drazhan tended to her sharpened a pain that had become so acute, she could no longer deny what it was.

Love.

She was in love with Drazhan Wynter, but he didn't feel the same. She was no better than an addiction to him, one he hadn't expected on his quest for vengeance but also one he couldn't afford.

What a pitiful fool am I.

"Another physician then," Teleria said. She reached for her own wineglass and tossed it back. "Something."

"Lord Quintus will have brought his own," Tasmin said, brightening. "I'll send word right away."

"That's a very good idea, daughter."

"He won't want Imryll to suffer needlessly."

"Protecting his investment," Imryll muttered. Sickness mixed with her exhaustion, clinging to the bone-deep weariness she feared she was stuck with forever.

Where had her bitterness come from? How had she changed so much in mere months?

The door flung open. Tasmin jumped, while Teleria rose to her feet so fast, Imryll thought it must be the king himself, returned from the brink of death.

It was only Mortain, his face as still as ever and his hands folded over his flowing black robe, giving the impression he was merely a docile servant and not a creature powerful enough to bring the kingdom to its knees.

The Farrestell women didn't seem to know how to greet him.

Imryll couldn't decide how to react either.

"Leave," he commanded the women with a flick of his wrist. His tone stirred their stubbornness, for they both bristled, talking over each other in an attempt to tell him they weren't going anywhere.

"Your commitment to the princess is honorable and noted," he said evenly. He bounced his icy gaze between Tasmin and Teleria. "But I've come to ease her where you have failed, and if you do not leave, I can and will find ways to make that choice unpleasant for you both."

Teleria whipped back in defiance.

Tasmin scoffed. "Look here, sorcerer—"

"It's all right," Imryll said. Before the Choosing, she wouldn't have been caught alone in a room with Mortain for all the gold in the realm, but he didn't scare her anymore, and she wondered if it was because she'd grown braver or if she simply had nothing more to lose. "Go on. He's not here to hurt me."

"There's no reason we can't stay while he heals you."

"Tas, really. Duchess. Go to the ball with the rest of Duncarrow, where you belong."

"You know I don't care about a stupid ball," Tasmin replied.

"You do," Imryll said with a weak smile. "Please look in on Torian for me. I fear Marius will take advantage of him if I'm not there to soften the blow."

"If it's what you want," Teleria said, glaring at Mortain. "Come, Tas. We'll check in on Imryll in an hour, to be sure her needs have been adequately met in our absence."

Mortain didn't move or avert his rigid forward gaze until both women had left. When the door boomed closed, it lighted him into motion and he glided toward the bed. He took the chair Duchess Teleria had vacated.

His flesh was preternaturally pale, beyond his usual pallor. His skin pulled taut when he smiled—or what he seemed to think was smiling. Mortain smiled like someone who had seen it on someone else and wanted to try it out.

But when he took one of her hands in both of his, there was warmth. In his flesh. In the easy way he held her, as though he knew she was strong but did not want to add to her pain.

"Your guard tried to heal you. Twice," he said. He rolled both thumbs over the top of her hand, massaging her flesh over her bones. "And he failed. Twice."

It was a double surprise to Imryll—that Drazhan had tried, but more so that Mortain knew Drazhan had magic—but she didn't react. His velvety touch was hypnotic.

"Do you want to know why, Imryll?"

She started to shake her head but nodded instead.

"Yes." He hitched his cheeks to tug his mouth outward at the corners. "Of course you do. Our curious Imryll."

Imryll's eyes lowered to where he traced intentional circles on her hand, alternating his thumbs in perfect synchrony.

"He couldn't heal you because there's nothing to heal."

She looked up at him.

Mortain cocked his head. "You haven't flinched once as I've spoken of your guard's magic. Why is that?"

Imryll closed her eyes and swallowed to coat her dry, inflamed throat. "What would be the point? Don't the Meduwyn know everything?"

Mortain seemed amused. "Is that what you think?"

"It's what everyone thinks."

"Good." His brows twitched. "I rather like that they do."

"You're saying it's not true?"

"You're asking the wrong question."

Imryll rolled her eyes. "How am I ever supposed to know what the right one is with you?"

"Your claim is abstract and inane. Expanding the scope of your curiosity to cast a wide net when you are only after a simple answer is what apathetic minds do."

She groaned. "I'm tired. Can we please not turn this into another lesson?"

"Are you? Tired?"

"What?"

He released her. "Is that how you feel right now? Tired?"

Imryll recalled her hand. Her breath caught. She *wasn't* tired anymore. Her belly had finally settled. She was thirsty. Hungry.

"I've eased your symptoms, but I'm afraid I cannot cure what ails you. I would hardly call it an ailment at all, though any reasonable being would understand why you might, in your current predicament, consider it such."

Imryll could only shake her head in confusion.

"The same guard who harbors a secret magic, the one you did not seem remotely surprised for me to know about, has left you with child."

Imryll's blood cooled. She pulled away in the bed, half climbing the headboard. "No. That's not...No."

"Not possible? Was that what you were going to say?"

Imryll nodded and shook her head at the same time.

"Because you first consummated your relationship just over a month ago? And it hasn't been enough time?" He gave her a pointed look. "Please don't insult me by asking me how I know."

Her flesh pricked with heat and then cold, then heat again. "Why...Why are you saying this?"

Mortain tilted his head back with a breathy sigh. "I will attribute your frivolous questions to your weakened state and not a depreciation of mind." He looked at her. "Imryll, you are with child. The father is Steward Drazhan Wynter, and you are as ill as you are because the father carries the blood of the wulf within him. And now, so do you."

"Wulf?" Imryll panted the word.

"Four legs. Fur. Fangs. Carnivore. Rather vicious, particularly when starved."

"I know what a wulf is!" Her scream turned into a screech.

"A relief, that. I suppose you haven't lost *all* your faculties." He shook his head. "Tell me about your visions. And for the love of the gods, Imryll, don't play coy. I know you've been having them, and now that I've eased your sickness, I'd like you back to your usual, precocious self. If you don't mind."

"I..." She folded her hands over her lap and looked down at them. It shouldn't surprise her that he knew about the visions too. It would be more surprising if he didn't. "I think...that is, I'm fairly certain I'm in Ilynglass, and that I am...well, one of *you.*"

He grinned. "Spectacular. And?"

"You already know what I'm going to say, don't you?"

"Keep going."

Imryll narrowed one eye at him. "At first, I couldn't hear anything. I could only see. Oldwin was there. And others...like you. But I don't know them."

"Get comfortable saying the word. Meduwyn."

"Meduwyn," she said back with a wry smile. "Other Meduwyn. But then the visions shifted to climbing a mountain, to speak to an oracle. But we never reach the oracle."

"How far do you get?"

"I don't know. Only that it seems impossible to reach the top."

Mortain nodded to himself. "I see. You're not ready to see the oracle then."

"Not ready?"

"Not strong enough. And the boy? The boy and the wulf?"

She hesitated. "Yes. There's a boy and his brother. And later, others. He's training for something called the Hunt. I think...the last time I see through his eyes, he's facing down the wulf."

"So you have not yet seen the outcome of that event." He mused over the words.

"No." A sudden, disturbing memory of the claw marks on Drazhan's back gnashed against her thoughts.

"That's all right. The visions came to you later than I'd hoped. I cannot hold you to the standard I would hold myself." Mortain said the words as though speaking to himself. "But you'll get there. You'll speak with the oracle as *me*, for those are my memories. You'll see the wulf die at the boy's hands, because those are Drazhan's memories. And when you do, this will all become so much clearer to you."

"*Nothing* about *any* of this is clear. Why am I even having the visions? If anyone else on Duncarrow knew—"

"They do not," he stated. "Nor will they. Even if they did, they could never understand who you are. What you are."

Imryll squinted her eyes and winced through her frustration. "Why do you speak to me, always, in such vague terms? Why can we not ever have a frank conversation? You don't speak to others this way."

"No. Why should I speak to anyone as I speak to you?"

"None of this makes *any* sense, Mortain!"

"It all makes perfect sense," he said, maddeningly calm. He lowered his hands to his thighs. "I have other matters to tend. But you will not be going with Lord Quintus to Whitechurch."

Imryll recoiled. "And how am I supposed to get out of that mess when the queen has already bartered me off?"

"I'll deal with the queen." He pursed his mouth. "Vile, wretched cunt."

Imryll's eyes widened. "And the king?"

"Carrow won't be a problem much longer." Mortain lifted to his feet as though floating off the chair. "You'll stay. You'll complete your visions. And then you will know the path fate intends you to walk."

"Fate? Why would I put my belief in something so fickle?"

"Fate does not need you to believe. That's the beauty of it."

Imryll sighed and shook her head. She felt like she'd been tossed around in the sea. "You say you want me to be curious, to understand. But I have never been more confused than I am right now. If you came to provide clarity—"

401

"Clarity for you?" He laughed a dull, hollow sound that chilled her. "Light of Enivera, no. I came for my own, and now I have it." He reached for the door and smiled. "And to ease you, darling Imryll, at least for now." He lifted a hand. "Sleep."

Imryll passed out.

Torian danced with Adamina with the enthusiasm of a dying slug. He was tired of celebrations. Tired of entertaining. Tired of being on display.

Tired of being the prince.

Tired of everything.

Adamina spent the evening filling his ear with gossip, while he watched Lord Quintus sulk at his table, the spot next to him glaringly empty. Torian's mind ran a million paces a second, wondering if Quintus was displeased or pouting because he couldn't flaunt his claiming of Imryll—wondering if Imryll was even all right.

Godivah glowered from the head of the room, boldly assuming Carrow's place on the throne. She wouldn't have dared go anywhere near the thing when he had been well. She was counting on his death and her authority to control Torian.

She already was.

And he was letting her.

"And *I* heard poor Duke Rahn has already asked two nobles for their hand, but they feel he's too old now. But *I* say, why *not* an older man? He's sure to know what he's doing." Adamina shook her head. Her ornately styled hair smacked the side of his face. "But it could be worse. He could be poor Tasmin, who no one wants because of her heathen mother."

"Tasmin is beautiful," Torian replied. "And Duchess Teleria is a capable woman who just happens to be perfectly suited to the role without requiring a duke to guide her."

Adamina snorted. "Maybe she and Rahn should marry then. Perfect match."

"They would both gain from it." Torian grimaced, glad she couldn't see. It would be one more thing for her to pick at. She'd already corrected his posture, reminded him to smile, and chided him for not being talkative...as if she didn't know Imryll was bedridden, possibly dying, while he'd had to come perform for all of Duncarrow and a lord he regretted getting into business with.

She reminded Torian of his mother.

"Your mother came to see me today," Adamina said, as if she'd read his mind.

"Oh?" Torian braced for impact.

"I'll be coming to your bed tonight. She's already ordered the attendants to prep the dressing room."

Adamina's matter-of-fact delivery made him pause to collect his thoughts. His heart twisted. He pulled back to look at her. "So soon?"

"So soon? I should already be full with your child!"

"Hardly," he countered. "Imryll isn't even..."

Adamina laughed. "No? She has many secrets, our Imryll, doesn't she?"

"She's unwell, and I won't indulge you speaking of her like that."

"You'll indulge me later tonight, unless you want all of Duncarrow to hear confirmation of what—or should I say whom—she's been doing each night when she *should* have been warming your bed to build for our future."

Torian forgot how to move his feet, and they stumbled into another couple. Adamina apologized on their behalf before turning an astounded glare on him.

"Is that...Are you..."

"No, Torian, I'm not threatening you. I'm doing what you *should* be doing as the prince of this realm and thinking of the future of the Rhiagain monarchy. Father says it hangs by the thinnest of threads, and if there isn't a child soon—"

"Your father is among the list of men I wouldn't trust to tell me how to put my boots on," Torian snapped. "Fenring, Drushan,

Drummond, they're all the same. They all want to use me to further their own ideas, and if they thought they could get away with it, they'd take my place altogether."

Adamina straightened with a haughty look. Her rouged lips pursed. "Fine. But am I wrong?"

"How can I even think about an heir when Imryll is so sick?"

"Always Imryll!" Adamina's nails dug into his back. She eased off. "She's your past, Torian. Your *past*. Whether you think it's fair or not, it's done. She's ruined. Tainted. Even if she were carrying your heir, no one would actually believe the child was yours. No one with eyes anyway."

"And my father." Torian went on, ignoring her outburst. "My father is...I can't even speak of it."

Adamina hissed in his ear. "It's precisely *because* of your father and the state he's in that you cannot be so careless with the crown!"

Torian balked, shaking his head in lieu of words. Did she not think he'd given himself this same speech? The same rational arguments, designed to separate emotion from pragmatism, to push him into acting like the prince he was supposed to be?

"This is your lot in life," she said, softer this time. "There's no choice here except to embrace it, and if you cannot, then you will forever be the prince who toppled a crown over a broken heart."

When Torian said nothing, she continued. "You *will* be king. Sooner than you should be and sooner than we'd all like, but there's no changing what will be. And if you cannot... Torian, if you cannot get your head straight about it, then the men you claim will puppeteer you will do exactly that." She pulled back again. "I'm not Imryll. But I don't need to be. You need one thing from me, and you can be absolutely certain of getting it."

Torian had opened his mouth to respond when Evos appeared at his side and whispered in his ear.

From the look on Adamina's face, he imagined his own.

Torian frowned. "It seems Lord Quintus is bored of our hospitality and sees no point in waiting until our morning meeting to conclude our business." He squeezed Adamina's hand. With a defeated sigh, he said, "I'll send for you after."

Adamina screwed her mouth into a victorious grin. "I look forward to it." She curtsied. "Your Grace."

No one followed Drazhan. Without the company of a noble-born, he was just another man walking the halls, deserving no notice.

He made it to the prince's short hall without so much as a nod. As expected, the apartments were unguarded. Torian's retinue was too preoccupied with protecting him at the ball, and despite the increased measures after Drazhan's attempt on Carrow's life, there were only so many men they could fit inside the impractical keep.

He spent his doubts on the walk. He'd had two perfect opportunities to dispose of father and son. The first was understandable. He couldn't have predicted Imryll would follow him into the king's bedchamber. But Torian, on the ship? There was no justification for that failure that didn't lead him down a path of deserved self-recrimination.

Drazhan's hesitation had cost him the reward of gratification.

Hesitation was weakness. Weakness had slowed him, but he would dip into the well of strength he'd spent a decade building and finish the job.

Drazhan slipped on his gloves and pulled out the vial given to him by the old poison master in Witchwood Cross. Alchemist Astor had survived the massacre, and his thirst for vengeance was equally strong. Astor had explained the mix of oils, both things Drazhan was familiar with—belladonna and wulfsbane—and not. He knew all he needed to: whether consumed or absorbed, only a few drops would be enough to shut down a man's organs. A few more, certain death, within minutes.

The poison had always been Drazhan's last resort, a reserve weapon to be drawn only if all other methods failed. If *he* failed. There was no pride to be found in using such an underhanded method to dispose of a man, but there was finality.

There would be peace, for his people, only when the Rhiagain crown was ended.

While the keep flurried around the dead prince, Drazhan would draw his last breath taking Carrow's life. He was prepared to feel the thrust of swords running him through when they realized what he'd done. He'd never see Aesylt again, which stung. But he'd left matters in place for her in the event of his death. She was surrounded by competent, loyal men and women, who would help raise her to be a fair and just stewardess, and she'd forever be known as the Wynter who lifted Witchwood from the ashes and returned it to glory.

As for Imryll…

She deserved better than what he'd put her through, caught in the web of his disordered vengeance. The last—and best—thing he could do for her would be to exorcise himself from her life for good.

To confirm he was alone, Drazhan quickly checked the rooms in the prince's apartments.

He searched around for the right vessel for the poison. Wine was out, because the prince consumed nothing anymore without a royal taster going first—and then an innocent man would die.

Astor had said clothing was safest, but only items the target was certain to wear soon. The efficacy of the poison waned from exposure, and after too long, results were unreliable.

Drazhan started toward the prince's closet, stopping when a robe hanging near the door caught his eye. He'd seen Torian wearing it almost every time he'd come to escort Imryll back to her rooms for the evening. It draped, wrinkled from use, a wasteful mass of violet velvet with true silver stitching that could feed a family for a month.

Whispers of doubt slivered through Drazhan's resolve. It had always been the risk of staying so long…seeing the Rhiagains as men and not just monsters. Torian was deplorably weak and insufferable, but he wasn't—

Drazhan blinked hard to expel his cowardice and covered his face with the hood Astor had given him. Then he carefully opened the vial and tapped out several drops onto Astor's poison-handler's gloves. He set the vial on the table, worked the poison into the interior of the garment, and reached to pour out more, until half the vial was gone. He recorked it before he recklessly wasted the rest.

He shouldn't need the other half, but nothing yet had gone to plan. Only a fool would assume the rest would.

Once the poison was back in its protective pouch, he removed the hood and tossed it into the hearth. The gloves were next. He had more of both in his satchel, but if he could keep his head straight, he wouldn't need them.

Drazhan didn't allow himself a final review of his work. Those were the moments that had cost him his victories thus far, and he could afford no more losses.

"For Father. For Hraz. For Aesylt. For Witchwood. For the realm."

Drazhan held the salute of his people and departed the chambers.

"How's Imryll feeling?"

Torian hadn't even finished taking his seat before Marius asked the question.

"I don't know," Torian answered, as one of his men pushed his chair closer to the table. "I had planned to look in on her after the ball."

Marius nodded around the king's office, his gaze never landing on Torian. He was alone, other than a handful of guards. His eyes had the glossy sheen of a man deep in his cups.

"I understand you wish to conclude our business this evening." Torian reached for the carafe of wine to clear his throat, but he had no taster in the room, and his guards would be all over him before he could draw a sip. He pushed his hands under the table to exhaust his nerves another way.

His father would be disappointed to see it, but his father wasn't there.

"Ah, yes. Yes." Marius waved a hand and slumped back in his seat. His eyes closed and stayed that way, long enough for Torian to wonder if the man had fallen asleep. Then he jerked forward. "I agree to your terms, Your Grace. Oakenwell has the list of modifications we require on Belcarrow, but we are otherwise content with the offer."

Torian angled his head. "But?"

Clarisan stepped into the room with an anxious look and closed the door behind her. She stayed by the door, finding a spot against the wall.

"No but," Marius said. He straightened the edges of his crimson vest. "I'm happy to send my men to Belcarrow in exchange for your building the reliquary in the Easterlands. We already have the perfect parcel of land selected for it, in Riverchapel, and we see no reason excavation couldn't start in springtide. You're more than welcome to come see it for yourself."

Torian glanced at Clarisan, who shrugged. Her eyes were full of the same hard caution Torian felt in his gut.

"We're pleased to hear it." Torian cleared his throat. "And if that's all, then I'll have the contract drawn up—"

Marius pitched forward over the table. "That's not all. There's a reason I didn't invite your insufferable mother to this meeting. I don't like dealing with her, nor will other men of the realm. I suggest you find a way to muzzle her, lest she cause you harm you can't recover from."

Torian nodded. "On this we agree."

"And yet," Marius said. "She was the only one with the foresight to offer me something I couldn't refuse."

Torian tensed. Clarisan's deep inhale was the only sound blanketing the otherwise-silent room.

"Imryll," Marius said. "While I haven't availed myself of her during the visit, as your mother had hoped, I have my reasons. Her illness was one, but also, when she left Whitechurch, her absence led to a deeper fondness than simple attraction. I found I *missed* her candid tongue and her lovely smile. I even began to dream of her." He smiled to himself. "Of a future with her at my side."

Torian gripped the seat of his chair and forced himself to nod. "I already know she intends to leave with you."

"Then you also know she will be my wife, the future lady of the Easterlands, and the mother of my children?"

Torian's throat locked.

"Your *wife*?" Clarisan broke her silence when Torian didn't respond. Her usual restraint slipped, revealing her shock and disgust. "Imryll is a princess of Duncarrow. She cannot be wed to a man of the realm. No matter how highborn or respected."

Marius slapped the table with a raucous laugh. "You had no problem whoring her to me, but when I instead choose to respect her with a more honorable offer, *that* is a problem for you?"

"You misunderstand—"

"No, Lady Clarisan. I don't think I do." Marius watched Torian as he spoke. "You have all handled the princess as though she is an object to barter. What becomes of her if I leave without her? Or even if she comes with me but is sent to live freely in a realm she knows nothing of? And you, Your Grace, would allow me to abscond with the woman you love without more than a sad, defeated frown?"

"You dare speak to your prince—"

"It's fine, Clarisan. I want Lord Quintus to speak openly. I wouldn't have it any other way." Torian lost feeling in his hands. He curled his toes so hard in his boots, they cramped.

Marius reclined in his chair. "There's nothing more to say. It's done. Decided. I need a wife who is worthy of siring my children, and if the woman is one I could come to love, then all the better. I *could* love Imryll. In Whitechurch, she'll have the respect she should have been afforded on Duncarrow."

"Imryll will never agree to this," Torian stated, blinking hard through his incredulity.

"She only thinks she has a choice," Marius said with a slow grin. "Whether she's amenable now or later makes no difference to me."

"And if she never is?" Clarisan's cheeks were shot with a red blossom. "If she refuses your offer?"

Marius shrugged. "Do we care?"

Clarisan shook her head with a short, hard laugh. "Have you said that to *her*?"

"A version of it." Marius sighed. "This conversation is growing dull. Does it matter what I said to Imryll? What she believes? I care for her, which is more than anyone can say about most in Duncarrow. She thinks she wants freedom, and she'll have it… more than she has here. And if she thinks she's making the choice, she'll embrace her future all the more." He snorted. "We all know she'll never actually run away from Whitechurch. She learned the hard way what a terrible idea it was, and she won't have her dark knight to come running after her next time."

"And…" Torian blinked hard. "If she refuses, you'll marry her against her will?"

Marius held out his hands. "That's a rather strong way of putting it, don't you think?"

There was more Marius wasn't saying. Clarisan surely sensed it, coiling like a snake deciding whether to strike. The man might care for Imryll, but care wasn't the impetus for his marrying her. It all seemed so clear to Torian in hindsight, the game Quintus had been playing.

Marrying the First Chosen of Duncarrow aligned Marius Quintus for the takeover Torian's father had feared all along.

Tension replaced words, expressions saying what none of them dared. Then the thick silence was broken by a harried guard appearing at the door. He rushed in, unapologetic and red-faced, and whispered something to Evos, whose eyes and mouth widened enough to turn everyone's attention his way.

Evos swallowed and nodded at the guard to leave.

Instead of announcing the news to everyone, he approached Torian and knelt at his side to whisper the words.

"Your Grace, I inform you with the deepest regret that His Grace King Carrow is dead. Your father is gone, and you are now king. The dukes have already assembled in the Great Hall to pass the sceptre to you." He allowed Torian only a few seconds to absorb this before he backed away and said louder, for everyone. "All hail King Torian the First, Unchallenged Monarch of the White Kingdom, Father of our Glorious Realm, and Grand Cardinal of the Resplendent Reliquary of the Guardians. Long may he reign."

Evos caught Torian on his way to the floor.

TWENTY-EIGHT
THE SCEPTRE OF ILYNGLASS

Torian fixed his gaze on a crack rippling down the far wall. There were many of them, in a keep so new it had only begun to settle, but this one was long. Deep. It would need to be filled, and thinking of doing this himself, employing his hands toward something useful, kept him from passing out again as the Sceptre of Ilynglass was shoved into his hand and a crown too big crushed his scalp.

Duke Drushan ushered the other men back and rolled his hand forward in an embarrassing show of fealty that was neither necessary nor desired.

My father is dead.
The king is dead.
I am the king.
Long live the king.

Those were the only words Torian could process, despite the flowery, overdone speeches of Drushan and Drummond and Fenring and the other men vying for favor in a crown at risk of division.

413

The only duke not clustered around him was Rahn, who stood off to the side with a somber look trained at his feet.

It was late—past midnight, or maybe even closer to morning. Torian had no idea. The rushed, slapdash crowning had been thrown together in the moment, with no ceremony to accompany what had been inevitable but still a shock.

Carrow Rhiagain, the man who had saved them from inevitable destruction on Ilynglass, founding a new crown, a new sceptre, was dead. Gone. In his place was a boy who had no idea how to lead a kingdom, nor the desire to.

Torian I, King of the White Kingdom.

It was a blur.

It wasn't real. Not yet.

But it *had* to be, and soon.

When the dukes had exhausted themselves of words, Torian thanked them and said he had something important to tend to.

"More important than sitting down with your council to discuss matters of the crown, Your Grace?" Drushan asked, already testing the waters to see how much Torian would accept of his insolence.

"Whether it's more important is for me alone to decide. Thank you all for coming together so quickly. We will have plenty to discuss when dawn arrives. For now, take your rest where you can."

Torian left before Drushan or the others could test him further. He would fail, if not now, then over the coming days, when his resolve would be stretched and prodded to its breaking point. Where the men would decide whether to follow him or usurp him.

He ignored the flurry of bows and reverence as he rushed down the halls toward Imryll's apartments. He didn't wait for the guards to let him in, instead shoving the doors inward with the force of his weight and stumbling inside.

"Tor?" Imryll emerged from her privy room, securing her robe around her. A quick rush of steam followed her and then died.

414

Her wet curls framed her flushed, troubled face. If she'd have been told about Carrow, she would have greeted him much differently.

Torian ached for a world where he could fold himself into her arms and forget everything.

"Are you all right?" he asked. He should've told her. He *had* to tell her. But all he could think about was how he'd abandoned her. How he'd folded before a man who had outplayed him. Outplayed them all.

She nodded and pointed toward the bench. She sat and waited for him to do the same. "I'm better. How was the ball?"

"I don't care about the ball." Torian shook his head to begin again. "It was fine. Lord Quintus didn't really enjoy himself, but then, he only came for you."

Imryll sucked in a breath. Her cheeks puffed with the exhale. "I know."

"There's something I need to tell you," Torian said. He didn't know if he was even capable of saying the words.

Imryll reached a warm, water-wrinkled hand and laid it atop his. "Can I go first? I fear if I don't, I'll...I'll lose the courage. I can't say it in front of Drazhan, and he could be back any moment." She glanced around before speaking. "I'm with child, Tor. *His* child."

Torian shrank sideways against the arm of the bench. His reaction to her words didn't match how he knew he must be feeling. It sank into the numb recesses of his angst, where his father's death still lingered, waiting to settle. "Are you...Are you certain?"

Imryll retracted her hand. "Mortain confirmed it. And if there's anyone who would know..."

Torian ran a hand along his mouth. His breathing slowed. "This is why you've been so sick?"

"I don't think I'm supposed to be this sick, but...So much of what he said was confusing. I can't make sense of it, so there's no point in repeating it."

Emotion finally caught up to Torian, but it wasn't the one he expected. His face surged with hot anger. It burned its way downward, into his hands. "That man has been inexcusably care-less with you. He…How could he allow himself to sully you like…How…" Torian brought his hands to his face to stifle the choking in his throat.

Imryll shook her head. "We can't blame Drazhan for every-thing. I *wanted* everything that happened. Even after he pulled away…I reined him right back in. I didn't allow him to walk away."

"If you insist on exonerating him, then you cannot take all the blame either!" He bounced in his seat, landing in a position to face her. "*Imryll*. He's older than you, more experienced than either of us. A steward. A knight. A man of the realm. He knew what he was doing, coming here, laying his hands on you, messing with your head."

She squeezed tears from her eyes and nodded some more. "I know that too."

"And for what? To what end?"

Imryll pushed off the bench and paced, her head low and her arms wrapped all the way around so her hands were clawing at her back. "I don't know! I don't know. He never felt anything for me but lust, and now I'm the one left to pick up the pieces."

"Imryll, that man is in *love* with you."

She laughed and unlaced her arms. "Why does everyone keep saying that, as if they know something I do not? When they weren't even there for *any* of it?"

Torian lowered his voice. "Everyone can see how he looks at you. I've seen…I know the look he wears in his eyes."

Imryll looked back over her shoulder without turning. "And why should that matter when his actions have told a different story?"

"I'm sorry," Torian said. His heart ached equally for Imryll as for himself. "I really am sorry, Ryl."

She turned and leaned against the hearth. "Wynter *cannot* know. You understand? He cannot ever know."

"But—"

"*Ever.*" She chewed her bottom lip. "When I get to the main-land, I'll start putting a plan in motion."

"How are you going to do that when you've agreed to marry the man who will take you there?"

Imryll looked up. "I said I would go with him. I never said I would marry him."

He had to tell her, but he didn't know the right words. "Imryll—"

"It won't matter soon anyway. He said if he finds out I'm car-rying Drazhan's child, there's no offer anymore."

Torian folded his hands over his chin. "Imryll, listen to me. He wants you, however he can have you. And the offer he made you? It's no offer at all. It doesn't matter what you say; he intends to marry you regardless. Even if it means against your will."

"You have it wrong, Tor. He—"

"He *told* me this himself, Imryll!"

Her voice lowered to a whisper. "What?"

"He told Clarisan and me *tonight*. He has no intention of let-ting you go. *You* are part of the deal—a deal I have no power over anymore, if I ever did." Bone-deep weariness gnawed at Torian, but he had to tell her what he'd come to say. She had to hear it from him. "He's making a play for my throne."

Imryll went silent, but she didn't look surprised.

"You knew?"

"I knew he had ambitions for it, yes, but…" She looked off to the side, her mouth still parted, but didn't finish.

Torian didn't have the heart to push further. It didn't matter what Imryll knew and didn't. "He won't let you keep the child."

"I know."

"You can't go. You'll never be free there."

"I have to, Tor. Whether I stay or leave, this child is not yours. There's no place for me or them in Duncarrow."

"There's no place for you in Whitechurch!"

She laughed and looked up. A tear slid down her cheek. "I'm beginning to understand there's no place for me anywhere."

"That's not true—"

"But my *child?* I'll find a place for him or her. It will be different for them." Her eyes sparked with passion. "And if Marius Quintus thinks he has power over a princess, well, he hasn't met me as a mother protecting her child."

Torian ran his hands through his hair with a low grunt. "You don't *have* to leave. Not anymore. You don't understand…Gods, there's something I have to tell you. Something's happened."

She looked at him in alarm.

"My father…"

Imryll's face fell. "Oh, Tor." She rushed over and dropped to her knees. Her robe slipped, and his eyes caught a glimpse of what his future could have been like, with her. "I'm so, so sorry."

"Don't…" He brushed her wet hair back off her face. "I don't need comfort. Not yet. What I'm telling you, Ryl, is that my father isn't here to tell me how to rule. My mother has no power over me now. Which means you can and will stay here." He wound a hand through her curls. "With *me*. I'll say the child is mine—"

Imryll tore away, stumbling into a standing position. "Don't you dare finish that thought."

"Why? Why shouldn't I protect someone I love?"

"You can no longer afford not to have an heir, Torian," she said carefully.

"And I would have one! Your son or daughter—"

"If you do this, the Rhiagain dynasty ends with *you*." Imryll's jaw trembled. "I will not have that on my heart. I will not be the reason you throw *everything* away."

"Do you know…"Torian stood. "Do you know that, even now, knowing you and I can never be, I still can't imagine another woman in my bed? That I cannot bring myself to want Ada?"

Imryll shrugged. She blinked more tears away. "If I can accept what awaits me, so can you. Ada will *gleefully* give you as many children as you want." She started forward but stopped. "Don't deny her for the remnants of a dream. She's your future, Torian. I'm your past."

"Imryll..." But what could he say? What would he offer except a lungful of emotion that had no place in a king's life? "You could still stay. I could make you a duchess, make a place for your child here in our court."

She smiled sadly. "I could never accept that, and neither will your subjects. Your wants...They have no place in your life anymore. You can't make decisions as Torian. You must make them as king or not at all." Her shoulders lifted with a breath. "Now, go. Go to her."

"I can't." He whispered the words out of shame.

"You can. And you will. Your men need to see you're taking this seriously. They need to know you won't squander all they helped build."

"What if I wanted to? Squander it? What if I wanted to watch it all crumble back to rocks and dust, like we found it?"

She shook her head. "That's not how power works. It doesn't die or dwindle, does it? It just passes to the next strongest."

Torian felt her slip away with every word. His tenuous grasp on sanity traveled the same path. "Will you at least think about my offer?"

"Yes," Imryll lied. The deception, wrapped in kindness, lived in her eyes. "It's late. I need to rest."

Torian nodded.

He waited for her to change her mind, knowing she wouldn't—not about him leaving, nor any of the rest.

"Good night, Ryl. Everything will be all right."

"Of course," she said with a tight smile. "Night, Tor." She sighed. "Your Grace."

Drazhan heard the news on his way back to Imryll's apartments.

He passed Torian, who paused his hard stroll long enough to level a nasty glare.

Torian, the new king of the realm.

Not for much longer, he thought with a numb thrill.

419

What he *should* feel was vindication. It would come later. He'd shifted to a state of survival, moving through the last steps of a plan ten years in the making. It wasn't the way he saw it ending, but an end was still an end.

He wasn't as disappointed about the king's natural death as he thought he would be. Not having to do the deed himself meant there was yet a chance of him making it off the isle and back to Witchwood, though there was nothing waiting for him but the cool embrace of a life spent of purpose. Aesylt would fare better in the long run without a moody older brother clinging to his past.

Drazhan found Imryll bowed over her hearth.

"Oh," she said with a flick of her eyes to the side. "You."

"Why are you in here and not with the king?"

"I could ask you the same."

"What?"

She sneered. "Ada."

"I…" Drazhan ran a hand down his face. "I wasn't with Ada. I've never been with Ada."

"So you were, what, just wandering the keep?" Imryll broke away from the heat and poured herself a glass of water after eyeing the wine with disgust. She didn't know if he was lying, but that was the problem. She never knew what was real and not with him. "You've really given up all pretense? Not even going to act like you're guarding me?"

"Are you in need of guarding?" He constricted his throat with a wince at her appalled scowl. He hadn't meant the words to sound so licentious.

"No," she said matter-of-factly. "And you are free to continue doing…whatever it is you've been doing. The king is dead now. What's left for you?"

She wouldn't like the answer, so Drazhan provided none.

Imryll rolled her eyes. "Right. Well, I don't care what you do anymore, Drazhan." She disappeared into her dressing room and emerged wearing a cloak over her gown. "I lied. I do care. Don't follow me." She started for the door, but Drazhan's instinctual reach stayed her. She looked down at her arm in fury and ripped away.

"I'm still your guard. For now." Drazhan squared his stance, effectively blocking the door. "Where are we going?"

"*We* aren't going anywhere," she spat defiantly. A flush burned in the apples of her cheeks.

"Imryll."

She sneered. "Draz."

"I know that look. You're after trouble."

"And why should it concern you?"

Drazhan studied her dilated pupils and the gentle flare of her nose as she silently dared him to challenge her claim. "Marius," he decided aloud. "You're going to see the man who bought you."

Imryll scoffed, glaring. "Fuck you."

Drazhan physically recoiled. "Hit a nerve, did I?"

"I'm not going to his room to spread my legs for him, believe it or not. He and I have business to discuss." Her eyes darted to the left and right, like she was looking for a way to divert him. "Business that has nothing to do with you."

Drazhan laughed and shook his head. "And they say romance in marriage is a dead notion."

"I'm not *marrying* him," Imryll replied. "And he needs to understand he can't force me into it. He has designs on Torian's throne, and I won't be his pawn. Torian can do with that information as he pleases, but I won't be in the center of it."

Understanding dawned over Drazhan. Quintus had lied to Imryll, and she'd bought the lie. She understood who the man was, but it was too late. It had been too late from the moment she'd stepped onto Easterland soil.

"And you think…" Drazhan cleared his throat and shifted. "You're still so naive, you think your words have any power over him?"

"He finds something appealing about me. I'll use that."

Drazhan laughed. "We both know what he finds appealing about you."

Imryll looked stricken. "That's all I have to offer a man?"

Drazhan braced himself before he could form an apology. "He's dangerous. He's been ten steps ahead of all of you, and whatever you say to him, he'll be expecting and have his response readied."

"Again I ask, what concern is this of yours?" She looked down at her trembling hands and shoved them both behind her. "Move out of my way."

"You cannot sway him."

"Move, or I'll scream."

"Imryll." Drazhan clenched his jaw and squeezed a growl through. A familiar hot tingle surrounded his fingers. "He played you. He's playing you now. You showing up, confronting him, is part of his game."

Imryll took a step back. He saw then the sweat dotting her face, the blood shot through the whites of her eyes. She wrapped her cloak tighter. "You don't think I know that? You don't think…You don't think I'm already aware of how disadvantaged I am?"

"So don't go." He clipped the plea in his voice with a shrug of indifference.

"I have to try."

"Even if he listens, you think he'll keep any promise he makes when he's kept none before?"

"I have to try!" Imryll yelled. She backtracked for her water and drained it in a sip. "I *cannot* stay here. Torian needs a chosen who can give him an heir, and I…Well, it won't be me. If I don't go, there's no deal and the crown falters, and for what? I *have* to get on the ship with him. But whatever awaits me in the Easterlands…It cannot be another prison." She dropped the glass, and it shattered on the stones. She paid no notice. "I won't survive it."

Drazhan's breath hitched. He returned his focus to steadying it. "You go into that room, you give him even more power than he's already taken from you."

"I have no power to give!" Imryll heaved her words, hands thrust to her sides. Her chest rose and fell in harried beats.

"You have more than you realize. Far more."

"I'll ask you one final time, Drazhan. *Why* should I listen to you? You don't even care about me."

Drazhan turned his eyes upward in disgust to keep her words from crashing somewhere dangerous. "You're so dramatic."

Imryll made for the door again, but he stopped her once more.

"Don't go." His voice choked. He tried again, stronger, surer. "Don't go."

Imryll didn't break away. Instead, she turned her eyes up toward him. Her gaze was as cool as ice. "I'm going. And you cannot stop me."

"I could," he said weakly. "If I wanted to."

"But why would you ever want to?" Her eyes narrowed. "You hate me."

Drazhan felt the magic swirl in his hands. *Not now.* "No."

"Ah." She shook her head and laughed. "You love me then?"

A fissure split his chest down the center. "No."

Imryll deflated. She nodded to the side. "I see."

Despite the danger—the very real risk his fingers would turn to claws at any moment—he clamped his hand around her wrist. "Don't do this, Imryll."

Her eyes widened as they both watched the magic attempt to shift him. She tore away and looked up in fear. "You want me to stay so badly? Tell me about your claws."

Drazhan started to shake his head.

"Tell me about the *wulf*."

He paled. "What...What did you just say?"

"Ah...You know exactly what I'm talking about, don't you?"

Drazhan was too stunned to speak. She couldn't know. She couldn't possibly know.

"Don't want to tell me?"

All the moisture left his mouth. He tried to swallow.

Imryll shoved him and moved past. "When you stop pro-tecting your secrets with more care than you ever protected me, perhaps then we'll have something to talk about, Drazhan. Until then...*Leave. Me. Alone.*"

The door slammed.

And something inside of Drazhan shattered.

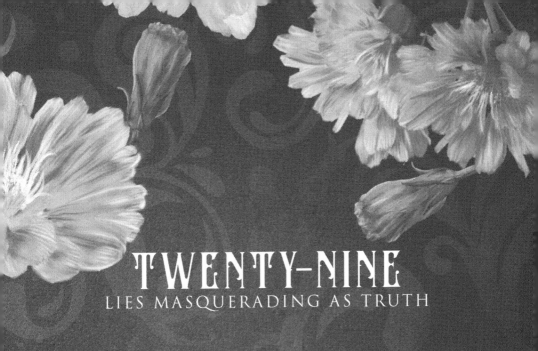

TWENTY-NINE
LIES MASQUERADING AS TRUTH

Despite the late hour, Imryll knew Marius would still be awake, just as all of Duncarrow was after the news of Carrow's death had spread.

He looked up from a broad chair, where he was reading a book he had balanced between one hand and one knee, his other hand swirling a glass of wine in mindless passes.

"Ah," he said. He methodically rearranged himself, securing his glass on the table before adding a strap of leather to his place in the book, which he then set aside as well. He dropped his folded leg to the floor and beckoned her in.

Imryll hoped her cloak covered the raging spectrum of emotions flowing through her veins. She radiated with the power of a thousand unsaid words and the indignity of the wronged. Everyone had been right about Marius Quintus…Even *she* had, in the beginning, when she'd trod with caution, listening to her instincts. Whether he handled her with cruelty or kindness, his decision to employ either would be primarily self-serving.

"How are you feeling?"

"Better," she said. Her next words were almost painful, but necessary if she was to have any chance of negotiating with the capricious man. "Thank you."

"Are condolences appropriate, Imryll?" He poured her a glass of wine, which she refused. "Water?"

She nodded, and he reached instead for the pitcher.

"Or would it be disingenuous?"

"Disingenuous for you to say them or for me to receive them?" Imryll asked carefully. She accepted the water and stepped back, to keep a safe distance between them. She noted her proximity to the door, her need to preserve it.

"We both know how *I* feel," he said with a self-effacing wince. "I never liked the man. His son, on the other hand, is an interesting individual. Wouldn't you say?"

"Whatever I say traps me into an answer you can pick apart as you please."

Marius flinched in amusement. "You certainly are feeling better. There's color in your cheeks again…perhaps too much. Your knight again?"

"It's been an eventful evening. He has nothing to do with it."

"Where is he anyway?" Marius made a show of looking around. "Do you not feel like your shadow is missing?"

"I asked him not to come." Imryll sipped her water, watching him over the top of the glass. "He thinks I was a fool to. But he doesn't know you as I do."

Marius refilled his wine. He held it up to the candlelight, regarding the garnet liquid. "Can we really ever know someone, though? Most men hardly know themselves as well as they think they do."

"I didn't come to barter riddles, Marius." She tightened her hands around the glass, lacing them. "Torian told me about your conversation."

Marius nodded. "I expected he would."

Imryll set her glass down and took a step forward. Her heart raced ahead of her words. "And you didn't think…You didn't think to speak with me first?"

Marius shrugged. "Why would I have?"

Revulsion started in Imryll's shoulders. She rolled them under her cloak, but it was no use. The feeling spread, coating her chest and back and tingling down her arms. "You said—"

"I say a lot of things. I choose my words according to how they suit me in the moment."

"You came into *my* room..." Imryll forced herself to calm. He would claim her flusterment as a victory, and she wasn't ready to lose.

"Imryll, what did you *think* was going to happen?" Marius tapped the side of his head. He took a deep swallow of wine and savored it with a little moan. "Can I tell you how glad I am you're serving Easterland vintage and not some bitter swill from the Northerlands?"

"You should have told me. You should have *explained* things to me instead of deceiving me, thinking I couldn't handle it."

Marius cocked his head. "But you couldn't handle it, Imryll. I can only ask a woman to marry me so many times before I must take her denial as intentional."

Imryll's mouth dropped open in horror. "So you were going to...what...get me there, lock me away, and force me into a marriage I didn't want?"

Marius laughed playfully. "When you say it like that..."

"You *owe* me an answer, Marius!"

He set his glass on the hearth and stepped toward her, making her step back. "I would never harm you. Have I yet?"

"You and I have different understandings of the word if you think you've done no harm to me," Imryll spat. "All so you could... so you could show the kingdom you'd conquered a princess."

"Indeed, we do have different understandings, because I've been nothing but kind to you since the day we met." He crossed his arms. "As for your second charge, more than one thing can be true. I do admire you. I'm fond of you. I enjoy your grit, your wittiness. Your beauty snared me from the moment the sun caught your red curls on the dock at Arboriana. I have no reason to believe you'd be anything but the ideal wife and partner for me, regardless of your pedigree." He rolled his head back and forth. "But...Your pedigree does solve several problems for me."

"My *pedigree*? Am I livestock?" Imryll asked, incredulous.

Marius continued, unmoved. "I've appreciated your pragmatism in the past, and I implore you to apply it here. Just because our marriage involves an enticing level of political expediency does not mean we can't be happy with the arrangement. It doesn't mean you cannot still have more freedom than you have here— and the added joy of living somewhere you are surrounded by more beauty than you know what to do with."

Imryll blinked away the dizziness threatening her. Marius watched as though he had full access to the turmoil running rampant within her. "You aren't...denying you're using me to take the crown."

"Your words, not mine, princess."

"If you want anything from me but willful disobedience, you will speak plainly!"

Marius moved in on her, sending her backward until she was pressed to the wall. He planted his hands on either side of her face, pinning her in. "How's this for plain? Whether you want this or not, you're already mine."

She squinted against the intrusion of his hot breath.

"The queen sold you to me. Yes, like you were livestock. And what's more, with Carrow already turning to rot, your dear Torian did nothing to undo the sale. He spoke hardly a word in your defense when I told him my intentions of sailing with you tomorrow and making you my bride. The *one* man with the power to stop me didn't."

Imryll's mouth trembled. She fought away tears.

"He didn't only fail you, Imryll. He failed himself. His people. His crown. For I saw in his eyes he knew what this meant for his future. He *let me win*. So even if you had a choice in this, the only one that leaves you with a life worth living is one with me. Certainly there's nothing for you here when Duncarrow falls."

Imryll lifted her quavering chin. "I would rather fall with Duncarrow…I would rather *die* than be the pawn of another man's games."

Marius pressed his forehead to hers and rolled it, laughing. "Oh, Imryll. You sweet, delicate girl. I suppose you would see the world thusly, having been reared in the shadow of such foul propaganda. It's the *Rhiagains* who have come to *our* world and demanded what was not theirs. There was never any chance of that lasting after what Carrow did across our lands. Why, your own guard, Wynter, bore the full brunt of the king's wickedness. He watched all of Witchwood Cross burn to the ground, his family with it."

Imryll felt a fresh wave of sickness begin to rise. She shook her head.

"Are those the kind of men you want to align yourself with? Usurpers? Cowards?"

"You'd say *anything* to rationalize your scheming," she said before her tears overflowed.

"As I said. More than one thing can be true, Imryll." He pulled his face away from hers and smirked. "It's a lesson worth learning early, or risk learning it often." While she was pondering his words, he reached into his trunk and withdrew a burnt coil of metal. He threw it at her feet. "You left something in the chalet."

Imryll gaped at the remains of her royal circlet. She shook her head because it was the only action she could will her body to take. The rest of her remained frozen in suspended horror, wrapped in the cruelty of lies masquerading as truth.

"You'll go," he said with a short laugh. He kicked the circlet into the corner. "And when you've calmed down and can speak reasonably, you'll see this isn't the trap you've made it out to be in your clever, overactive imagination."

"I won't," she rasped. She forced herself not to look at the melted silver…the gnarled evidence of her greatest weakness. "I won't do it. You'll have to kill me."

Marius sputtered. "That would be immensely counterintuitive, Imryll." He traced his mouth along the outer edge of her jaw. "Guardians, you're beautiful. You even smell like desire. You'll find I'm a generous lover, even if you're too stubborn to appreciate it." He moved his lips toward hers and said, "But if your own life means so little, allow me to make clear what else is at stake if you don't board that ship with me in the morning." With one hand, he ripped her cloak away and hurled it to the corner as well. Imryll folded her arms over herself. "If you don't come willingly...If you try to do something *foolish*, then the king's life ends. Now. Not later, in a war he can't win. But tonight."

Imryll turned her head to the side and sobbed in shame. She loathed herself more in that moment than in any before. She'd never been so weak, so ineffective and outmatched.

Marius took a step back, giving her a small amount of space. His voice brightened. "In fact, my men are with him now."

Imryll whipped her head back toward him. "What does that mean? With him?"

"They've taken him to the lyceum, under the guise of a secret meeting with me. If I arrive smiling, Torian and I shake hands and wet the vellum and the deal is done. If I send someone else in my stead..."

"No." Imryll shook her head. "No. You wouldn't dare. Not here on Duncarrow."

Marius twisted his mouth into a bored scowl. "Wouldn't I? Your guards have grown fat from inaction. The king's men on Belcarrow are hours away by ship. By then, I could do considerable damage. Irreparable. But I wouldn't need to, because a dead king and a captive princess would do more than any destruction my men could bring down upon this cursed rock."

Imryll inched toward the door. Her breaths were so hard and ragged, she saw spots. "I don't believe you."

Marius pointed a hand at the door. "No? You *could* see for yourself. But I don't recommend going to the lyceum without me. That would be as good as signing his death warrant."

430

Imryll fumbled behind her for the door handle and wrenched it open just enough to squeeze through. She nearly fell into the hall, landing on her hands, but she never stopped moving—half crawling, half running until she was just running.

The halls were alive with grief. The mourning song bellowed down the corridor, set to the macabre tinkle of bells. Everyone she passed gaped at her flying through the halls in a thin gown, tears streaming down her face as she sobbed, open-mouthed, praying to gods she wasn't sure she believed in for it all to have been a bad dream.

She whispered more empty prayers as she approached Torian's apartments. *Please let him be inside. Sleeping. In bed with Ada. I don't care, just please let him be there!*

Imryll nudged the unattended door open with her shoulder and was met with a whoosh of cool air. She immediately took inventory of the room, collecting evidence that confirmed her prayers had been in vain. The fire was nearly dead in the hearth, and the candelabras were unlit.

She rushed to the window and looked out, but she couldn't see the lyceum from this side of the keep. She slapped the window in frustration and decided she had no choice but to go to the lyceum herself, to bring every Rhiagain guard she could find along the way and tell them what the traitor lord had planned. Belcarrow might be hours away, but there was no one on Duncarrow who would benefit from what Marius was planning. Every man, woman, and child would raise arms to protect it from happening.

Imryll started to leave, but her eyes caught the storm brewing outside the window, and she realized she was only wearing her dress now. Her cloak was still on the floor of Marius's apartments. She scanned the room for something suitable for the cold, but all she saw was Torian's robe. It wasn't hooded, but it was warm, and she didn't have time to find something better.

She shrugged it over her shoulders and allowed herself several deep, slow breaths.

They couldn't kill Torian. It simply wasn't…It wasn't possible.

Imryll was reaching for the door when her vision blurred, sending everything in sight into two, three, and one again. She staggered and tripped over the cloak rack, gripped by a sudden attack of wheezing that turned to interrupted gasps.

She hit the floor in the midst of a violent convulsion, coughing, sputtering, and gasping through agonal breaths. A second fit seized her, sending her curling onto her side where she saw in three piles—four, two, one—the surrealism of bloody sprays hitting the stones with her every stilted exhalation.

Her throat locked, allowing no breaths in or out. What remained of her vision turned to nothing as darkness clawed up from within and dragged her down into the abyss.

THIRTY
MY OWN DETRIMENT,
MY OWN DOWNFALL

Five minutes passed.
Ten.
Fifteen.
It was either too soon or too late to go after her. It couldn't
be both.
Sixteen.
Drazhan rocked his chair forward, but instead of landing his
boots on stone, he rolled forward into—
Snow.
Draz.
Cold.
He whipped his head around to gather his bearings, to glean
where the voice had come from, but all he saw was an endless
expanse of white.
Draz.
"Aesylt," he whispered. His breath furled into a white cloud.
The chill in his bones, a thousand icy daggers stabbing through his
thin armor, brought him back to those seven days with the wulf.

He blinked hard. Again. Again. Nothing changed. Snow extended on all sides, as far as his eyes could see, which wasn't far in the blizzard. There was always a blizzard brewing in Witchwood Cross. Springtide was a myth.

Draz. You're in danger.

Drazhan shook his head. He blew hot breaths into his cupped hands and fought a shiver that couldn't be real. He'd fallen asleep while waiting for Imryll. Nothing else explained it.

I know it's been years...too many years...but I can still feel... things. You remember that, don't you? Hraz said I had an overactive imagination, but you knew it was more, even before we opened the path.

It's been years. I'm thousands of miles away.

Ten years. But that's how desperate I was to reach you. You must *come home.*

I'll be home soon. He shouldn't entertain his delusions, but the pleading edge to his little sister's tone hit him like a sack of flour to the chest, even if he were imagining it—and he no longer believed that. *Don't worry about me, Aes. You know I can handle anything they throw at me.*

No. No, if you stay, something terrible is going to happen. I feel it. *Something terrible has already happened, hasn't it?*

I'll tell you everything when I get home.

You're in danger. Your heart is in danger.

Has something happened at home? Is that what you're trying to tell me?

No, nothing has happened. Nothing except the visions are back, and I don't want to lose my brother. I've already lost one.

There's nothing to worry about. I promise you.

You wouldn't tell me if there was.

Aes—

Drazhan was on his knees. He looked up into the fire of the hearth, the lingering cold prompting a chill despite the rush of warmth flowing over him.

"Wynter?"

434

Blackfen's voice pulled him the rest of the way. Drazhan whipped around, scrambling to his feet in dread, wondering what the bowman must be thinking to have walked in on him in such a state.

Drazhan muttered an apology and dusted himself off. "What is it?"

Blackfen hovered in the doorway. "I came to tell you, because it seems everyone else is afraid to. Imryll was seen fleeing Lord Quintus's chambers about five minutes ago. She was very upset."

Drazhan charged forward. "What?" He flexed his hands. "Where was she headed?"

"They said toward the prince's... That is, the king's apartments."

Drazhan rushed forward, clapping Blackfen on the shoulder before pushing past him and launching into a sprint.

Torian's apartments.

His pulse pounded with his steps. His steel jangled at his side, slapping his leg. Eyes of the court followed him as he raced to outrun the horror he'd left for Torian.

Drazhan's boots slid on stone when he rounded the final corner. He saw Torian and Adamina entering the apartments, but before he caught up, the collective screams of the king and his chosen tore through his head like a scythe.

"Ada, go find help! *Now!*" Torian howled. "Evos, go with her, take the guards! All of you, *go!*"

The guards stormed in the opposite direction, tailed by Ada. Drazhan brushed her as they passed. Their eyes met briefly, and he knew.

Torian was on the floor cradling Imryll's motionless body, his mouth open in a scream Drazhan couldn't hear.

He couldn't hear anything at all.

The whole world had gone silent.

Still.

His breaths were no longer compulsory; the world blinked temporarily into darkness, joining the deafening silence.

Torian looked up through his sobbing. He shook Imryll, his mouth spewing soundless curses.

Imryll.

Imryll.

Imryll.

Speak to me.

Say something.

Anything.

Anything.

Imryll.

Everything returned in a whoosh that knocked him forward. Suddenly Torian's screams were *all* he could hear. His nose seared with the stench of something acrid. Moonlight garishly brightened the darkened room.

He dropped to the floor and shoved Torian aside.

"What are you doing?" Torian demanded. He clawed his way back, but Drazhan knocked him away. He shimmied her out of the robe, and she flopped onto the stones like a broken doll. Torian's screaming continued as Drazhan removed his own shirt, covered in the remnants of the cloak.

Drazhan crushed Imryll to his bare chest. He listened for a sign of life and heard the faintest of heartbeats.

He sounded his relief in a feral, guttural sob that stunned the king into silence. It was the howl of a boy who had once faced down a wulf for the right to live. But now he was the wulf, and Imryll was the one who had to fight.

Convulsions seized him. He hadn't been quick enough to keep the poison off his skin, which meant he would have to heal them both at the same time.

If you can hear me, Imryll, help me. Like you did in the chalet. Help me save you.

"Wynter! What are you doing? What are you doing to her? Do you know what this is? What's happened to her?"

What I'm doing is giving up my last chance to dispose of you.

436

But he wasn't giving up anything. As he looked down at Imryll dying in his arms, every other truth of his life disappeared and was replaced by one. There wasn't a choice to be made. Only the illusion of one.

He'd been choosing Imryll of Glaisgain since the moment he'd locked eyes with her in the lyceum.

"Don't touch the robe!" he barked when Torian reached for it.

Drazhan blocked out the king's response. He cradled Imryll, folding his arms around her and twining his legs through her cold ones. Tears ran from his face down onto hers as he released his healing into her, letting it flow back into him like an infinite loop. He pictured his own heart moving toward her chest, restarting the flow of blood in her veins and the breath to her lungs. He watched in his mind's eye as his heart traveled between them until he could not discern where his ended and hers began. His tears landed on her blue lips, on her eyelids that had not opened.

Drazhan exhaled his pain. His fear. His restraint. His cowardice. His *weakness*. He inhaled *her* and replaced the departed pieces of himself with permission for clarity. He said the words in his head to make them real: *If she dies, I will die here with her.*

"Imryll. My Imryll," he whispered. He rocked her to the repeating rhythm of her name, his vigor draining with every urge of momentum. He welcomed it. He would give it all to her. He would give everything to her. Everything. "Come back to me. Come back to me, and I'll make everything right. I'll say all the things I couldn't. I'll give you all of it."

Drazhan's limbs turned to fire as he coiled around her, his mind working against him, sending him horrific images of a world without Imryll. Hope turned to grief, and he sobbed into her hair to expel it, because she needed her dark knight, not the weak man who had let her walk into her own demise because he cared more about revenge than her.

"Wynter." Torian's voice had faded to a whisper. "Please tell me what's happening. Please tell me she's alive."

437

Imryll lurched back with a gasp. She sucked the air so hard, she started shaking. Drazhan shuddered out a sound that was part laugh, part cry. He lowered her to the floor and put both of his hands on her face as he waited for her eyes to open.

"You healed her." Torian's tone shifted. "You healed her, Wynter. *How?*"

Imryll's eyes fluttered open. Her mouth opened and closed several times as she sucked in air. Her head lolled to the side and fell into Drazhan's open palm.

"Draz." She whispered the word as though falling through a dream.

Drazhan bowed his head and shook with tears as he cradled her face in his hand.

"Wynter, you will answer me *now*, or I'll have you sent to the Sky Dungeon the moment reinforcement arrives."

"Yes, I healed her." Drazhan looked at Torian. "And I don't give a fuck what you do with me. Your Grace."

"What's on the robe?"

"Poison."

"*Poison?* How do you know?"

Drazhan met his eyes. Torian's mouth dropped open.

"Call your guards, Torian. Lock me away. Execute me. But if you love her, you'll wait until she's all right."

Torian came to Imryll's side and dropped to a crouch. "You did this to her." Tears ran down his face. "*You.*"

Drazhan nodded through his own tears.

"Who are you, really?"

"Please. Can we do this later?"

"I am your king, and you *will* tell me!"

"When she's safe."

"You insufferable bastard. You put her through so much, and now this?" Torian leaned forward and kissed Imryll's dazed face. "Ryl?"

She blinked up at him.

"I'm going to go find the guards. You have until then to fix this. And then you're leaving this place, Wynter. You're going back to wherever you came from, and you will *never* see Imryll again. Never *speak* to her again. You won't write to her. You won't even *think* about her without the fear of my guard scorching your life to ash. That's about the worst punishment I can think of for you, and it's the price you'll pay for what you've done." Torian glanced at Imryll once more. "It's for *her* I'm letting you live. I could never again look her in the eyes if she knew I'd sentenced the man she loved to death."

Drazhan didn't have the energy for gratitude. But Torian was wrong. The worst punishment wasn't living without her. The worst was not knowing whether his healing would be enough to bring her back from a fate *he'd* caused.

Torian left.

Drazhan was alone with Imryll, but it wouldn't stay that way for long.

Imryll tried to sit. He helped her and she returned to his arms so she could lie upright, unable to hold herself up.

"Am I dead?" she asked.

Drazhan bowed his head with another choked sob. "No. No, you're not dead."

"Why are you crying?"

He cradled her higher and crushed his lips to hers. They curled against the weight of his unabated grief. "I'm so sorry, Imryll. I'm so fucking sorry."

"Why are you sorry?" She weakly lifted a hand and placed it on his face. "Why are you acting like this?"

"I did something terrible. Unforgivable." He spread his lips along her cheeks, her nose, and her forehead, inhaling her and whispering his good-byes before he had to say them. "You're not dead, but if I'd come even a minute later…"

"I don't remember what happened. I was going to go to the lyceum to find Torian…Wait, but he was in here just now, wasn't he?"

439

Drazhan nodded.

"Marius told me…of course. More lies." Imryll turned her head away.

"You asked for my truth before. I couldn't give it to you." Drazhan winced. "I made a *choice* not to give it to you." He didn't have time for rambling. He didn't have time for anything but the most important words.

"Drazhan, I don't understand—"

"I put poison in Torian's robe."

"You *what?*" She wormed out of his arms, tumbling onto the stones. "No, no, no. No. No. You came for the king. Why…No, no, you didn't come for Torian. You would have told me. I would have *known.*" She stopped to catch her breath. "You would have…No, Draz, please, *please* tell me it isn't true."

Desperately he wanted to reach for her, but that was no longer what she wanted. "I came here to avenge my family after Carrow Rhiagain razed my village to the ground to make an example of us. Ten years I trained for this. An eye for an eye. He took my father and brother, and so I came to take father and son." Drazhan's head lowered with the weight of his shame. "And now one is gone and the other safe. All that's left is an inescapable numbness."

Imryll pulled her legs to her chest and scooted farther away. It was the fear in her eyes that broke his heart irreparably. The fear of *him.*

I would never hurt you. Never ever you.

But he had.

And some hurts were beyond repair.

"And…" Imryll's throat bobbed. "Me? You came to…*ruin* me, as part of this vengeance?"

Drazhan couldn't meet her eyes when he nodded.

She sobbed into her hands.

"That was the plan, but, Imryll…" He looked up with a shuddering sigh. "I never expected *you.*"

"I don't know what that..." She stopped speaking and just stared at him.

"When I saw you on the floor, dying, I started to die with you. A part of me did die, and I wouldn't resurrect if I could. It was the part of me that let things get this far."

Imryll bowed her head and cried.

Drazhan closed his eyes to gather what remained of himself and the stolen moment that would be over too soon. "Because I love you, Imryll. I love you so fucking desperately that my heart only beats when it's near yours. I won't even pretend it belongs to me anymore."

Imryll met his eyes with a dazed look. She blinked gently, expelling more tears before dropping onto her hands and knees and crawling to him. She climbed into his lap, and when he wrapped her into his arms, cradling her face against his heart, she didn't fight it. She tangled a hand in his hair and tugged as she rolled her lips against his bare chest and cried.

"Tell me to stay," he whispered. "And I will. I'll spend every last second of my life in the Sky Dungeon if it's what you want."

"How can you say that to me? To me?" Imryll leaned her head back against his arm and looked up at him with reddened, glossy eyes. "You freed me. And now you've broken my heart. You've ground it into dust. You say yours beats for me, but how can that be when you knew killing Torian would be the end of us?"

Drazhan swallowed the worst pain he'd ever felt. "Then tell me to go." He held her closer. "If you want me to go, I will."

"Don't you put this on me." Imryll wiped her eyes on his arm. "Not this time."

They both looked toward the door at the thud of boots in the distance.

"I feel..." Imryll nestled against his chest and released a scream into his flesh. "I feel as though my entire world is crashing around me, and there's nothing to break my fall. Lies everywhere. Deception upon deception, to the point I question even my own truths. You tell me I cannot trust Marius? Well, I never *loved*

441

Marius. But I loved you." She kissed the underside of his chin with a whimper. "I only wanted you to let me in a little. I don't think I was asking for much."

Drazhan inhaled a shaky breath. "Ask me anything."

"It's too late."

"*Anything*, Imryll. The guards will be here any second."

"Your claws." She looked up at him in defiance, expecting another lie.

"You were right. They're a part of me. I earned them when I bested the wulf in the Hunt—"

Imryll's eyes widened. "The Hunt."

He nodded and rushed to finish. "I had seven days to either outlive the wulf or kill him and take his heart. I made it all the way to the seventh day before he cornered me in a cave, and I...I don't remember what happened, but it was like stepping out of my skin and becoming...someone else. And the next thing I knew, his bloody heart was in my hand, and I *was* someone else."

"The boy and the wulf," she whispered.

"What?"

The guards were close. Entering the hall.

Imryll leaped up and wrapped her arms around Drazhan's neck. She pressed her lips to his and kissed him so passionately, he almost forgot there were men coming to take him away from her forever.

"I love you," she said, breaking away just enough to speak. "I love you to my own detriment. My own downfall." She met his eyes for what he realized—with a sinking, crushing feeling—would be for the last time, just as the guards burst through the door. "But if you love me as much as you say you do...If you really love me, Draz...Yes, I do want you to leave. I *need* you to leave. If you want me to believe your heart beats for me? Belongs to me? Then take it away from here and never come back."

"Princess," Evos said, rushing forward. The other guards swarmed in and jerked Drazhan to his feet.

Drazhan didn't fight.

He held his hands out in surrender.

His eyes were on Imryll, watching her watch him. He didn't break the shared gaze until he was forced to when they shoved him into the hall.

He left his heart on the stones of the king's apartments.

If she couldn't bear to keep it, he no longer had any use for it either.

Drazhan stood on the bow of the small ship King Torian had requisitioned for his return to the mainland. He watched the sea, dark and forbidding, crash against the stones of Duncarrow as dawn broke. It carried him away from the place where he'd gone to make himself whole again and instead had left the most important piece of himself behind.

Every inch of him ached to be back there.

Sparring with her.

Kissing her.

Loving her.

Squandering not a single moment.

Imryll.

A gasp curdled from the back of his throat. He staggered back from the ledge. "Captain. Captain!"

The captain jogged from where he'd been huddled with his men. "What is it? Has something happened?"

"We have to turn back." He tapped the railing. "We have to turn this ship around, *right now*, and go back."

The captain turned his head with a pensive frown. "Ahh, son, I'm afraid that won't be possible."

"The tide is fair. There's still time—"

"It won't be possible, Syr Wynter, because the king will not allow a return. If we turn this ship around now, it will be your neck *and* mine."

Drazhan's eyes darted back toward the sea. He was a strong swimmer—or had been in his youth. The Howling Sea was more precarious than the White Sea, and he'd once swum from the coast of Witchwood halfway to Wulfsgate, albeit in shifts, but—

"I can read your mind, and let me assure you…You wouldn't make it." The captain thumped a hand on his shoulder. "A real man accepts his fate for what it is. Doesn't go trying to change it at the expense of others." He lowered his voice, burying it in the roar of the sea. "She'll be halfway to the Easterlands by now anyway. Such is life."

Imryll.

This time, he sent the word to her, reaching across time and sea and space.

Imryll.

Forgive me.

Her silence cut the final thread still tethering them together. Drazhan reached for it, but it was already gone.

BLOOD
OF THE WULF

448

THIRTY-ONE
FANGHELM KEEP

Drazhan finished lacing and strapping his boots. He checked the ties on his vest and trousers. Layering on two separate coats of fur came last, and those, too, he laced, because the wind coming off Icebolt Mountain put the salty gusts whipping across Duncarrow to shame.

He moved down the long hall, past the tapestries narrating the arduous saga of Witchwood Cross, the story of how the early men of the Cross had faced down a pack of wulves and won the right to build their town and settle, after they had been exiled from the Easterlands for witchcraft. The resulting Lycan War led to significant losses on both sides. The details could be found in cave carvings made by the men of the Cross, or in the tapestries in Fanghelm Keep. A grudging agreement between man and wulf, negotiated by a beast whisperer named Darek Summerton, shaped the men and the village for generations.

Darek, the only man who could commune with wulves, became the leader of the exiled witches, changing his family name to Wynter, out of respect for their new home, and building

Fanghelm Keep in honor of man and wulf alike. He claimed the truce made with the wulves required an annual midwinter sacrifice by both sides, where a treasured son of the Cross and a cub from the pack's leader would spend seven days alone together in the wilderness. At the end of the Hunt, if the young man was slain, the wulves earned the right to roam the woods free of hunters' arrows until the following midwinter, leaving the men to rely on salted meats and imported vegetables. If the wulf was slain, the pack agreed to go into hiding for the coldest months and allow the men to hunt and restock their stores.

If both man and wulf survived, the wulves claimed the victory.

Over the years, the wulves won more than they lost. Starvation became a common way for people of the Cross to perish; one in three children didn't reach the age of one. The village spent more than they had in their coffers to trade with Wulfsgate and others to keep even the most meager meals on their tables.

The year Drazhan bested the wulf and emerged from the woods with its heart in his hand came at the end of nearly twenty years of losses. Their population had dwindled so much, there were talks of relocating once more. Stunned, still reeling from a confrontation he couldn't even remember, fifteen-year-old Drazhan returned to the village carrying hope in his hands.

The next few winters should have been a period of great prosperity.

Instead, the heir of Witchwood Cross returned to the aftermath of the campaign the Rhiagains had waged against the Cross. Most of the town had been razed, over half their remaining population slain. The corpses of Ezra and Hraz Wynter hung on crosses on either side of the town gates, their eyes and tongues taken as trophies.

Drazhan had found Aesylt stumbling down the dusty, smoky main road, her face covered in the ashes of their people. She'd collapsed into his arms, and it wasn't until days later she finally told him all she'd seen.

The horrors. The screams. The smells. She'd hidden under her bed, her hands clapped over her ears, waiting to be killed.

And when they were done, they did come for her, but not to kill her. They wanted Aesylt to bear witness to what happened to men who raised arms against the "rightful" crown of the White Kingdom.

Fanghelm was one of the few buildings not brought to rubble. It remained as it always had, a monolith atop the tallest hill in the Cross. The Rhiagains had left it to drive enmity between the Wynters and their people, but the usurpers had underestimated the resolve of a community that was no stranger to persecution. They spent their tears over the coming days and then turned them to the unthinkable task of rebuilding their village, alongside their new young steward.

Aesylt stopped speaking.

And Drazhan started training.

For every word his little sister couldn't say, he pushed harder, training longer, until he knew nothing but the tingle of his claws and the roar of his furious anger—claws he couldn't remember earning any more than he remembered besting the wulf.

He'd promised his people to return with the blood of the Rhiagains staining his hands but had instead returned in shame.

But as he rode the rented horse through the gates for the first time in almost two years, past faces he'd known all his life, what Drazhan saw wasn't disappointment but relief.

We never needed revenge, Steward. We're just happy our wulfling is home safe, with his people, where he belongs.

And then he received the greatest gift of all: the beautiful, chilling sound of his sister's voice, older and deeper but still as lovely as music.

"Brother," she said, wrapped in Hraz's bulky furs as she welcomed Drazhan back to Fanghelm. "We're *so* glad you're home."

Aesylt watched her brother take a hard swig of alc and shove an unruly hunk of bread in his mouth. He was out of his chair and moving again before he'd even begun to chew.

451

Drazhan hadn't stopped moving for weeks. She'd never seen him so restless, not even in the years he'd punished himself for the sacking of Witchwood by throwing himself into a senseless quest for revenge.

"All right! Easy." She shook her head and marched toward him to remove the bread from his mouth. "Sit. Eat."

"Not when there's work to do," he muttered and snatched the bread back with what was almost a smile. "I've been away too long."

"It's the same work we've all been doing for ten years. It will be there in an hour when you're fed and ready to spend your energy," she said, guiding him back to the bench. "Sit. *Please.*"

Drazhan grunted. It seemed to have become his favorite sound. She wanted to roll her eyes every time, but he'd never taken well to being laughed at. Their father had done enough of that when he had been alive, goading Drazhan into being something he was not.

In the end, she supposed, the cruelty had worked. Because the man grudgingly sitting across from her with a permanent scowl was every bit the warrior Ezra Wynter wanted his son to be. The sweet boy who used to make up bedtime stories and carve dolls from pine branches was no more than a distant memory.

Drazhan made a show of tearing the bread into smaller pieces for her, holding each up for her inspection, like a child made to eat his root vegetables.

Aesylt shook her head. "You're an utter mess."

He grunted again.

"You know, making wulf sounds doesn't actually mean you *are* a wulf?"

Drazhan twisted his jaw as he finished chewing.

"Are you ever going to tell me the truth?" Aesylt leaned over the rough wooden table, dipping her chin onto her hands. "Not the version of it you think I can handle."

He washed the bread down with another swallow of ale and pushed the empty mug away. "I failed. There's nothing more to tell."

"Well, I don't believe you," she said with a shrug. "Nor would I consider your sparing a man's life a failure."

He scoffed and swiped crumbs from the table. "You wouldn't understand."

"I can handle it, Draz."

"You're a—"

Her eyes narrowed. "Don't you dare say child. I'm old enough to take a husband."

"The fuck you are!" He reared back. "I won't even entertain the thought for another five years."

Aesylt laughed. "By then I'll be an old maid."

Drazhan snorted. "A *vastly* underrated thing to be, in my estimation."

"You're impossible."

"And you're my responsibility." Drazhan flattened his palms on the table. She felt his boots tapping in nervous rhythm. "Now can we go, Aes?"

Aesylt deliberated. Was it time to ask the question?

If not, would it ever be?

She took a deep breath. "What's her name?"

"What?"

"The one who broke your heart."

A loud screech filled the otherwise-empty Great Hall when he shoved his bench back from the table. "Let's go."

"Tell me." Aesylt reached a hand across the table. "*Please.* You're all I have left in this world, and I'm all you have. How can that mean what it needs to if you won't even talk to me? *Me,* Draz?"

Drazhan shook his head and cast his gaze across the room with a hard sniff. He blinked hard and inhaled through his teeth before slowly blowing the breath out. "Her name was Imryll. And I cannot...Don't ask me, Aes. Respect that I...I cannot. Not now. Not ever."

"The *princess*?"

"Aes."

Aesylt's heart sank toward the stones. Confirming her theory filled her with so much sadness, she didn't know where to put it. It should surprise her he'd fallen for the one woman in the realm who was wholly unobtainable, but it didn't. Happiness was an experience Drazhan would never allow himself.

"Did you…Did you love her?"

"I never stopped." He dragged his hands down his face. "Satisfied? Because we've got work to do in the village."

Aesylt nodded. She wasn't satisfied. She could never be satisfied with the pain she saw etched in her brother's face, forming lines at the edges of his eyes, dips around his mouth.

But she'd confirmed what she'd known in her heart.

Even if for only a little while, her brother *had* been happy.

And it gave her hope he could be happy again.

Drazhan dumped another load of stone into the stonesmith's pile. He paused long enough to watch men hoist it onto wagons to take back into town, and then he turned the cart around, allowing himself a deep breath before returning to the quarry. His shoulders screamed with satisfaction. Pain was progress. And the Cross needed all the progress men could offer.

He'd worked from dawn to dusk every day since he'd returned home, alongside his men, his people. They would tell him to go home, to rest, but they didn't get to go home and rest, so neither would he.

After a decade of rebuilding, the village was almost restored, but another year or more awaited them before they could step back and call their work finished.

A snow squall swept down off the pass, reducing visibility to nearly nothing. It might slow or even stop other men, but resilience was in their blood. They'd been witches and then nomads and then persecuted, but they'd never been defeated.

Fezzan Castel handed Drazhan a wineskin. He shook it when Drazhan didn't accept it right away.

"Thanks," Drazhan muttered and took a light swig, enough not to be rude. He caught Aesylt across the road passing out loaves of bread. Her friend, a boy named Lyandyr, filled mugs with ale from two large casks sitting at the edge of their wagon. Lyandyr snuck looks at Aesylt, mopping his brow or shifting his attention to the storm rolling off Icebolt. Aesylt blushed and pretended not to notice.

Drazhan scowled.

"Ahh, let 'em be, wulfling," Fezzan said with a chuckle. "It's about time anyway, isn't it?"

Drazhan bristled. "If you're suggesting what I think you are…"

"Noooo. Course not." Fezzan shook his head with the twitch of a grin. "But what of our steward? Is it not time for a wife and cubs at Fanghelm?"

"Don't think I'll ever have children, Fez."

"One of you has to."

Drazhan clapped him on the back. "Or perhaps Fanghelm belongs with a Castel or a Garzykk, and not a Wynter."

Fezzan snorted. "Blasphemy."

"We have bigger priorities right now, wouldn't you say?"

"What do we build for, Steward, if not a life to pass on to the next generation? What motivation is there, for any of this, if we don't persist, as we always have?"

Drazhan lifted the arms of the cart back to his shoulders. "Dusk is coming. We go now, we have time for one more quarry run before we have to call it."

Fezzan watched him for several moments before he shook his head and grabbed his own cart. "Sure, wulfling. All right."

THIRTY-TWO

BAD FOR THE HEART

Torian paced behind the throne in the banquet hall. Clarisan had suggested he take the meeting in the king's smaller, private office, a cramped, cloistered space that had always intimidated his father's visitors. But Torian had a different kind of intimidation in mind.

"You're ready for this," Clarisan said. Her eyes followed his movements. "You *are*."

"I don't need reassurance," Torian said. "But thank you."

"Then tell me what you do need. Tell me how I can serve you."

Most of his inner circle never asked him that. Instead, they had for him only assertive demands couched as suggestions. The power moves had been more exhausting than he'd expected—they had been especially displeased at his decision to send his three realm chosens back to their families—but they'd worsened after Torian treated the scheming bastard Marius Quintus like the traitor he was.

After Torian watched Drazhan sail away, secure in knowing *that* problem, at least, was behind them, he'd returned to Imryll and asked her to tell him everything. And she had, right down to Marius threatening to kill his newly crowned king to keep her from refusing his offer.

I don't need you, your men, your land, or your alliance. Your peers will not shame themselves so, when I approach them with even better terms than I offered you. Leave before I throw you in the Sky Dungeon and start an expensive war that you'll lose, for we now have full support from the Westerlands.

Marius had not expected that, but neither had the dukes. When Marius departed with his men—*without* Imryll—Duncarrow slipped into chaos. Drushan and the others acted as though Torian had thrown the kingdom into crisis, and maybe he had. But letting Marius Quintus hold the crown hostage wasn't an option either.

Letting him *threaten* Imryll.

Then, three weeks later, a raven had arrived from the Easterlands.

Requesting permission to send an envoy to Duncarrow to reopen negotiations.

"You're here to keep Oakenwell from puffing his chest too much," Torian said. He rolled his neck with a series of pops. "We both know why he's here and not Quintus himself."

"A shamed dog stays in his corner, where he belongs."

Torian laughed. "That's one way to look at it. Another is he knows I'd throw him in the Sky Dungeon if I ever saw his face again after what he did to me. To Imryll."

Clarisan winced playfully. "Going to be a rough alliance then."

Torian shrugged. "We'll just deal with his lapdog." He grinned. "Or should we say, *your* lapdog?"

Clarisan flushed. She fussed with the collar of her dress. "You make too much of an innocent flirtation."

"Do I?"

"Doesn't matter either way, does it? I'm here. He's there. He probably already has a wife and children—"

"He's a widower, with one son."

Clarisan averted her eyes.

"Father isn't here anymore to hold you back," Torian said. He studied his lovely, intelligent, clever sister, wondering what happiness would look like to her. If she'd even recognize it. "If you want to marry, Isa, I'll see it done for you."

Clarisan chuckled nervously. "Well, I certainly wouldn't want to wed an *Easterlander*. Did you see how many different kinds of plants they serve at their supper tables and call it *food*?"

"Your Grace. Steward Oakenwell has arrived," Duke Rahn said from the doorway. "Shall I send him in?"

"Please. Yes. And Rahn? I'd like you to stay for this meeting."

Rahn frowned. "Drushan is expecting to join you."

"Perhaps it's time reality matches my expectations, not his."

Rahn grinned to the side. "Perhaps it is, Your Grace." He left to collect their visitors.

"I plan to extend an invitation for Oakenwell and his men to dine with us tonight," Torian said while they waited. When Clarisan didn't react, he said, "I'd just as soon watch him sail away as soon as he says his piece, but I thought you might appreciate the opportunity to speak more casually."

Clarisan rolled her eyes. "Tor. It's really much ado about nothing."

"Just the same."

Clarisan turned and motioned for him to take the throne. Seconds later, Steward Oakenwell entered the banquet hall, with Rahn on one side and another well-plumed Easterland man on the other.

Oakenwell approached the platform and lowered into a reverent bow. "Your Grace. Lady Clarisan. Allow me to extend my condolences in person for the loss of your esteemed father, our late king."

Torian nodded.

"And my gratitude for allowing me to port and speak on behalf of Lord Quintus."

Torian waved the man up. "I had half a mind to refuse. Curiosity won out. Know that I am only so curious though, Steward. Also demanding my attention are a thirsty council and a ravenous princess, who is very eager to provide me an heir. Do not take these moments for granted."

Oakenwell nodded. His gaze briefly switched toward Clarisan before he turned back with a light sigh. "I understand, Your Grace. As does Lord Quintus. He can admit when he's been outmaneuvered."

"Admitting this does not make up for the harm done, particularly to Lady Imryll, who remains deeply afflicted by the trauma from that period. What does Lord Quintus offer to assuage the damage?"

"He does have a message of apology for Lady Imryll, if I may."

"You may not." Torian lifted his brows. "You were about to explain the reparations Lord Quintus intends to make."

Clarisan pulled her lips in with a muted grin. Oakenwell noted it with a hard swallow and seemed to force his focus back to the king.

Torian would allow it. For Clarisan.

"He is doubling his offer of men for Belcarrow, Your Grace. And rather than a twenty percent tax for the privilege of playing host to the Resplendent Reliquary of the Guardians, he will pay thirty."

"Forty," Torian stated. "Fifty if your next response is to negotiate."

Oakenwell closed his mouth and nodded. "Forty then."

"Hmm." Torian lifted one leg over the other and leaned back against the plush velvet. "And that, you suppose, makes up for an assertation of treason against a king, and threatening to abscond with a chosen of Duncarrow?"

Oakenwell laughed nervously. "Ah, well, Your Grace, Lord Quintus has always been one for his game. He wasn't *really* threatening your person. He would never do that."

"No? He'd just let Imryll think he would, so she'd comply with his ludicrous demand. I am not my father, Steward. And I am certainly not my mother. Lady Imryll almost *died* that night." He put the memory out of his head before it took over his waking thoughts, as it had his nightmares. "And that would not have happened if your lord had not put such terrible thoughts in her head."

"Lord Quintus is *deeply* regretful of what happened after she left his apartments, but he would want me to, respectfully, remind Your Grace that it was not he who put the poison in your robe."

"You split the wrong hairs, sir!" Clarisan declared. She took a step forward and landed on Torian's right. "Our king is telling you someone very dear to him was wronged and hurt, and your response is to deflect accountability? I believe he asked for *reparations*, Steward, not excuses."

Oakenwell stared at Clarisan, slack-jawed and wearing a look so wounded, Torian nearly called him out on it. "Lady Clarisan—"

"Your business is with the king. Not me."

Oakenwell reluctantly returned his flustered gaze back to Torian. "Forgive me, Your Grace. Lord Quintus understands his games are neither welcome nor acceptable, and will never again seek to play them in your court."

Torian tapped his father's ring on the arm of the throne. "That's a start."

"Is there an offer that would be pleasing to Your Grace?"

"Pleasing? You better hope so, with the Westerlands ready to rally at my command." Torian laughed. When he left Oakenwell, he'd go straight to Imryll's chambers, where he already knew what he'd find: Imryll in bed. Refusing to eat. Hardly speaking. Tasmin would be with her—or Teleria or perhaps even her brother, Octavyen, whose work in the Westerlands had probably saved the crown.

What would *please* Torian was to go back in time and never have dealt with Marius Quintus at all.

What would *please* Torian would be to have his Imryll back. Not as his chosen—it was no secret she carried a child who wasn't his—but as the one person he could laugh with, play with, and confide in. Whom he could talk to about Adamina's unnatural

461

sexual appetite or how the dukes wore perpetually constipated looks, whether he took their guidance or dismissed it.

What would *please* Torian was for Drazhan Wynter to die a natural death, so Torian could eliminate the niggling fear the man would renege on his promise and return to Duncarrow, forcing Torian to kill him.

"I will consider Lord Quintus's offer."

Oakenwell bowed with a relieved exhale. "Thank you, Your Grace."

"You are welcome to stay and sup with us." Torian winced in his sister's direction. "That is, if you have not irreparably offended Lady Clarisan."

Oakenwell glanced at Clarisan with a hopeful look.

"Not…not irreparably, no," Clarisan muttered.

"Good. That is all." Torian stood and left.

"Today. Today will be the day you leave this room and come with me to supper," Tasmin said, in the placid tone of a physician handling a patient they expected to fall apart with the lightest touch.

Imryll supposed that wasn't untrue.

"I can eat just as well in my chambers," Imryll said. She was curled on the settee, which she'd pulled near the fire. "If I can even keep anything down. Mortain is overdue for his weekly visit, and I can hardly stand to even think of the smell of food."

"Then…Then come and simply sit with me. At my side. You can sip on water, if it's all you can handle."

"And give everyone yet another reason to talk about me?"

Tasmin sighed, unable to hide her exasperation. "Imryll. I love you. Dearly. But by staying in this room, you're *giving* them something to talk about. Don't you understand?"

"Understand?" Imryll pulled her knees as high as she could, but her belly had become sensitive enough to restrict the attempt. "I understand everyone in Duncarrow knows I had inappropriate relations with my guard, who then abandoned his post and me."

462

But that was the amended truth. It was what she and Torian had agreed on as the accepted story, after he'd told her he'd let Drazhan leave unharmed on the condition he never again attempt to contact her in any way.

"Well, he was a *very* attractive guard…"

Imryll couldn't help but laugh. "I'm sure it's enough to soften my failure as First Chosen."

"You never wanted Torian. Now there's no pressure for it," Tasmin said reasonably.

"I can't weather the arrogant grins Adamina gives me anytime she visits, like she's won something even though I never wanted it."

"She'll be queen, which I suppose is what she wanted all along, but would she have chosen Torian if he weren't a king? Do you really think she'll be happy?"

"We'll never know." Imryll's thoughts started to drift back to that night, but she'd gotten exceptionally good at killing them before they took on life. And oh, how they tried. Day, night. In her dreams and nightmares alike. She replayed Drazhan's words over and over and over and over until they meant nothing…until her broken heart, instead of mending, turned to stone.

But to keep out the pain, she could invite no joy either.

"Fine. We'll eat here," Tasmin said reasonably.

"No. You go." Imryll clutched her shawl tighter and smiled feebly. "You've spent too many hours in here with a disgraced woman. You'll never find a husband if they think I've rubbed off on you."

Tasmin scowled in clear disgust. "A husband? You're not serious?"

"Duke Rahn is unmarried."

"You realize it's because he *wants* to be, right?"

"And a catch," Imryll said, ignoring her. "If I wasn't already a complete disgrace to the Glaisgain name—"

"Pardon me, Lady Farrestell. You need to leave."

Imryll started and nearly fell off the settee at Mortain's voice. She hadn't heard him come in. From the startled look on Tasmin's face, nor had she.

Tasmin turned toward Imryll, not Mortain. "Do you want me to stay?"

"Lady Far—"

"I asked Imryll."

Imryll shook her head with a wave of her hand. "I've been waiting for him to come ease me. Maybe it will put me in better spirits, and I'll come down after."

"Mm. Sure it will." Tasmin narrowed her eyes at Mortain, but she moved toward the door. "I'll return after supper."

"That's not necessary, Tas."

"Just the same."

When she was gone, Mortain made a disgusted clucking sound. "Duchess Teleria has her hands full with that one."

"I don't think the duchess quite sees it that way," Imryll muttered. She made room on the settee, but Mortain didn't join her. He instead knelt before her and took her hands in his, tracing the oddly soothing concentric path once again, easing her suffering more and more with each pass.

When he was done, he didn't leave. He settled in against the hearth and watched her with a steady, inquisitory gaze she couldn't interpret.

"You have been neglectful, Imryll."

Imryll snorted and rolled her eyes. She'd never have dared to do either in his presence before the past few weeks, but she'd grown almost comfortable around him. Sometimes she found a crack in his demeanor and split it wide enough to see a hint of humor. A hint of warmth.

"You're amused by your failure?"

"Only wondering where I should slot this one in against all the others."

"Self-pity is unappealing. It's beneath you."

464

Imryll batted her lashes at him with an exhausted smirk. "If I agree with you, are we done?"

"No," he said, drawing a breath that said he was just getting started. "I gave you plenty of time, and there's no reason…" Mortain made an upside-down V with his hands and tapped them against his sharp chin. "Even allowing for the trauma you've experienced, and the changes to your emotional state with a child growing within you, you have been *especially* obstinate."

"Obstinate?" Imryll's mouth dropped open with a short laugh. "Is that your clinical diagnosis, physician?"

"And the tongue on you." He looked at her as though she'd sprouted a few more heads. "I'm going to ask you about your visions, though I already know what you're going to say."

"Well then, let's not waste precious breath on the matter." Imryll leaned forward and snagged a poker. She prodded the logs to urge new life into the flames.

"You've been writing again."

She felt the blood drain from her face, but the rush of fear didn't follow. Those who had punished her for writing no longer had the power.

"Your guard left the vellum for you. So you would pick up where you left off."

"And?" Imryll wiggled her fingers and then pulled them in for a hard clench. She'd suspected it was Drazhan who had stuck the thick roll of vellum and ink under her bed, but hearing it confirmed added to her painful confusion.

"Has the king ever done such a thing for you? Taken heed of your passions and fed them?"

"You know he hasn't."

"So why would a man you've forsaken spend his final hours on Duncarrow searching for *paper* to slip under your bed?"

Imryll lowered her voice with her eyes. Her chest fluttered when she remembered Drazhan's genuine interest in her writing. He'd wanted to know why she'd stopped, and she hadn't been able to give him an answer that satisfied either of them.

"I don't want to talk about Syr Wynter," she said.

"Does he know you were transcribing visions?" Mortain asked.

Imryll shook her head. "I told him they were stories."

"Stories?" He seemed surprised. "Though, they are stories, aren't they?" He spread his hands down his dark cloak with a sharp inhale. "You wanted to know why you're having the visions. Where the magic comes from. You asked me this before."

Imryll shrugged. "I did. Before."

"But not now?"

She looked up. "Does it matter?"

Darkness passed over Mortain's beady eyes. "There is *nothing* in your life that matters more."

"Have to disagree with you there, Mort." Imryll enunciated the T more than usual as she wrapped a hand around her belly. Soon, she wouldn't be able to chalk up its rounding to an unflattering dress.

He nodded at the swell under her dress. "You think your child has nothing to do with this?"

"I try not to do much thinking these days." She sneered and tapped her chest with her palm. "Bad for the heart."

Mortain bowed his head in thought and held the pose for several moments before looking up. "I'm disappointed you couldn't hear the oracle's pronouncement for yourself, Imryll. It would mean so much more to you if you had. Without those words, you wouldn't even be alive."

Imryll stilled.

"I see that got your attention. Did you know we were not always from Ilynglass?"

Imryll tried to shake her head but could only twitch. The dread that followed came without warning.

"We ended *up* in Ilynglass when the world was sundered into pieces. My fellow Meduwyn and I have spent several millennia searching for a way back to the light, to our home and our rightful font of power. The oracle told me the answer was here, in what men insipidly call the White Kingdom."

"What do you mean, sundered?" She tensed her shoulders to fight off a chill that had nothing to do with the cold.

"Another story, Imryll. For another time. But 'Beyond' is only the way men explain the concept of different worlds. But they were one world once. And they could be again."

Imryll absorbed his words in breathless wonder. No one had ever spoken so brazenly about their past around her. His words bordered on treason. But who would ever punish a creature like Mortain?

"Not all of the Meduwyn had faith in the oracle's pronouncement. Some had grown fat and lazy, comfortable in their prosaic lives. They'd forgotten the Light. If the oracle had not given me a private scrying…We might have stayed. But she told me something else, and it was for *that* I convinced the others our only chance of survival was to leave everything behind and sail for the White Kingdom."

Imryll didn't know whether her awe came in the form of a comment or a question. Indecision stayed her words.

"Do you know who the Ravenwoods are?"

She swiftly nodded, happy to have an answer finally. "Priestesses and priests who live in the mountains of the far north. A matriarchal society of raven shifters."

Mortain shook his head. "You sound like you're reciting one of Duke Rahn's instructions."

Imryll flushed at his correct assumption.

"Like us, the Ravenwoods fled Ilynglass when danger found them."

"What kind of danger?" Imryll didn't want to be so tranced by his words—to be snared by them in an equal measure of thrill and fear.

Mortain grinned. "*Me.*"

"You?"

He laughed, the sound short and dark. "The Ravenwoods and I have a very old score to settle."

Imryll shivered at the grotesque way his mouth moved, like his face was reforming itself to mimic joy.

"The oracle's path demanded patience, but a hundred years, measured against thousands, is just the middle of an exhale for someone like me. In roughly three hundred years, I will have my vengeance. I've seen it."

"And what do the other Meduwyn have to say about this? About leaving one world behind for another so you could follow some ancient grudge?"

Mortain's smile sent ice into her veins. He folded his hands and didn't answer.

"All right," Imryll said, breathing slowly through careful words. "Why are you telling me this?"

"Have you ever noticed the way your mother shrinks in my presence?"

Imryll quirked her mouth. "Everyone does. They're all afraid of you, even if they won't admit it."

"She's not afraid of me, Imryll," Mortain said. "She's ashamed."

"Of?"

Mortain looked at the dark side of the room. "The oracle showed me a daughter. She showed me how this daughter would come along, and who this daughter would meet. How she would stand with the boy who had taken the heart of a wulf and carried it home to his people."

Imryll's hands froze, unable to bend, to move. Her tongue shifted to the roof of her mouth.

"*You* are my daughter, Imryll. Spare me your objections, your horror, your denial. You want to know where your magic comes from? From the ancient power of the Meduwyn, of which there is *no* equal."

Imryll was weightless. She gripped the bench, waiting to be blown away, carried across a wind and into the sea. Her empty gaze pointed not at Mortain but beyond, and in the distance, she saw the long trail leading up the mountain. She saw the wulf coiled to strike. But this time, *she* had conjured the images. She'd sought them from the broken place in her mind, where the fortress no longer had the stones to support her bid for survival.

The mountain and the wulf disappeared. In their place were the realisms that had shaped her life, birthing the desire to leave Duncarrow for a better one. Drushan's biting words and cruel smiles. His quickness to sell her to the highest bidder. But wasn't Melantha's craven obedience almost worse? Time and time again, she'd chosen still waters over her daughter's safety.

Imryll tried to swallow, but it caught in her dry throat and turned to a sputtering cough.

Mortain continued as though oblivious to the conflict splitting her world down the middle. "And your knight? The boy who took the heart from the wulf? The oracle showed me this, but I needed to see it with my own eyes. When the boy was ready for his test, Carrow was already preparing his men to make an example of Witchwood Cross. I watched Drazhan Wynter earn the name his people would forever know him by, and while he slept, tortured by the horrors he'd returned to, I imbued into him my magic and turned the wulfling into a wulf, so one day he would be ready for you. *Worthy* of you."

"You." She pushed the word out through strained breaths. Her voice cracked. "*You* killed all those people? Drazhan's family?"

"Men were going to die either way. Carrow was hungry to strike back at the Uprising." Mortain exhaled with a contented huff. "I only showed him the best option."

Imryll couldn't fight the contortion of her expression, the pain rolling up from her chest and screaming through her clenched jaw. "You're lying. I don't know why you would…why you would say such things. Why you…" She brought her hands to her mouth and moaned into them in horror.

Mortain charged forward and leaned over her until he was inches from her face.

She sobbed and angled back.

"We are *not* going to play the foolish word games of mortals! I am giving you your truth. I will not dignify ridiculous questions with answers, and I will not abide you retreating into yourself, because you are *better than that, Imryll*! You are half-Meduwyn, my progeny, my *future* as told by the oracle. And I have secured yours by making that boy worthy, by showing him a path to the vengeance he so craved, so he could instead find what he *needed*. And if you were not so cursedly stubborn, you would have seen all of this by now. You would be in Witchwood Cross, where you belong, where your descendants will keep the Ravenwoods subdued until the time comes for me to do it."

"No," she whispered. "This has to be some kind of nightmare."

"Deny who you are one more time and I will place my hands on either side of your head and *force* you to confront these visions, which I promise you will be far less pleasant!"

Imryll shrank away. She wanted to defy him, to stand and face him down and renounce every last one of his lies. Renounce *him*.

But she couldn't.

Not because she was afraid of him. Somewhere between his seething words and his spittle spraying her face, she realized she wasn't afraid of him, not anymore.

Imryll couldn't renounce his lies because they *felt* like truths, which scared her more than he ever had.

"Ahh." He withdrew and towered above her. "So we're done with insipid denials."

Imryll only hesitated momentarily before she nodded. She no longer felt in control of any words she might speak.

"Drazhan Wynter was always meant to come here. To win you. To conquer you."

"You're saying he had no free will? No choice?"

"*Choice* is all he had, Imryll. Everything he's ever done was a *choice*."

Her upper lip curled upward in a sneer. "Did your oracle see him *choosing* to put the poison in Torian's robe?"

"You harbor unresolved feelings about what Wynter did."

470

"Unresolved..." Imryll scissored her jaw, laughing. "He tried to *kill* Torian! He would have succeeded, if I hadn't accidentally come across the poison myself."

"Your wulfling lost his father and brother to Torian's father. Half his village."

"Because of you!"

"Does that weaken his crime in your eyes, or make it worse?"

"I don't..." Imryll swallowed. "No matter what you saw, there is no future of mine that involves Drazhan Wynter." Saying the words aloud brought a wave of fresh pain washing over her.

Mortain sounded a short sigh. "There is no future for you at all without him."

Imryll couldn't look at him. Everything that had once unsettled her about him gutted her. His mouth was her mouth. They had the same eye shape, even if his were lifeless and cold. She'd never seen herself in Drushan, but she'd never wanted to.

It wasn't the time to make sense of it. She might never. Deciding something was true wasn't the same as accepting it as her truth, and that was a choice only she could make, no matter what he said. "You don't realize this, but you've freed me. Now I know it was never love."

"The oracle saw you take him to your bed, Imryll. Not give him your heart."

"But what sense does that make? Why would anyone willingly follow someone they didn't love?" She shrugged. "I wouldn't."

Mortain turned his hands out. "Loving him wasn't necessary. But if it makes it easier for you to stand at his side, so be it."

Her head shook wildly. "He's in Witchwood Cross. I'm here. That won't change."

"I have a ship prepared to take you up the coast, all the way to Wulfsgate, where you'll finish the journey by carriage."

Imryll burst out laughing. "I *never* want to see him again. Ever. For any reason."

"Be that as it may—"

"*I won't be getting on any ship!* I don't *care* what the oracle said. I don't care if you're my father. I don't care about the Ravenwoods, about any of it. Everything you've said to me tonight only reinforces my desire to never follow *any* path you lay for me, because then I really will have become a prisoner."

"You will leave," he said calmly. A crack formed in his careful facade. "This is not up for debate."

"Do you plan to truss me and throw me in stowage?"

"No," Mortain said. He went to the drink table and poured her a glass of water. He handed it to her and waited for her to take a sip. "I would never do anything to harm you or your child. That child is our future. My grandson."

"Grandson?" Imryll's fire cooled. "My child is a boy?"

"Yes. And that boy will be raised with his father in Witchwood Cross." He nodded at the mug. "Drink. You'll want your wits for this next part."

"What—"

"*Drink.* And no more wine, Imryll. Men refuse to see reason on the matter, but it can harm the child." He inhaled and smiled at her compliance. "There. Now that you're hydrated, let me explain something to you. If you are not on the ship tomorrow, something terrible will happen."

Imryll's fear switched back to disdain. "Something terrible will happen? Is that supposed to scare me, your vague threat?"

"If you had any sense, yes."

"And you're not going to tell me what this terrible thing is?"

"I could, but I don't think I will," Mortain said slowly. "Your energy should be spent preparing for your trip north."

"Why do you care so much about the Ravenwoods? What are they to you?"

"It doesn't matter," he said with a tight, thin smile. "Because my reckoning with them will not happen in your lifetime or your child's or theirs. What's been put in motion on Duncarrow will last hundreds of years before it's spent of use."

"Then why—"

472

"I don't need you to do anything, Imryll," he said wearily. "Except go."

Imryll pitched forward, but Mortain held out his hand. Magic held her in place, kept her from pushing against the invisible cage he'd trapped her in.

"You have until tomorrow night to shed these useless mortal emotions and do what you were born to do. If you don't, the consequence will haunt you for the rest of your life. Unlike Lord Quintus, I don't bluff."

Mortain marched to the door. When he reached it, he flicked his wrist, and she stumbled forward. "I take no joy from threatening my own daughter. But if I need to kill every man, woman, and child on Duncarrow to ensure she embraces her destiny, then it will be but a minor inconvenience for me to see it done."

Mortain shut the door. Bolted it from the other side.

Imryll reached for it from across the room before she crumpled to her knees in numb disbelief.

THIRTY-THREE
SPINNER OF LIES

*N*o matter how fast he ran, he could never catch up to her.
       She raced down a hall that never ended, her robe flapping
in arduously slow motion and her hair catching wind and bouncing
with every desperate stride. Even so far ahead of him, Drazhan could
feel her torment, mounting with every burst of forward momentum
and turning into something so powerful, he knew if he couldn't reach
her, it would kill her.

   He called to her.
   Over and over.
   Screamed her name.
   Over and over.
   But his voice had no sound. Her bare legs pumped faster than his.
Her red curls framed his view of her in a blaze of fire.
   Imryll.
   This time, he sent it into her head.
   Imryll!
   IMRYLL!

Drazhan awoke soaked in his sweat. He grappled for breath as he blindly reached for his waterskin on the bedside table.

But it wasn't there. Aesylt had it in her hands, and she offered it to him as she lowered herself to the edge of the bed.

Drazhan swallowed the entire contents in one continuous, brutal gulp. He shook the remnant drops over his head with a blubbering groan.

Aesylt took the skin from him, capped it, and placed it on the table. "Another nightmare?"

He nodded and slid farther up the bed, bracing for the internal tethers that would secure him to his waking reality.

His sister looked down at her hands. "Maybe you shouldn't have come back."

Drazhan blinked himself awake. "What? Why would you say that?"

"Draz, you're not *well!* Don't tell me I'm imagining this—or overreacting. I *know* you."

"Aes, I had to come home. For her, but also for you."

"Because I sent for you," she said, sighing. "But I didn't know leaving would be worse for you than staying, or I never would have…taken our path again…" Aesylt recoiled when he reached for her, moving farther down the bed, out of his grasp. "Don't ply me with hollow platitudes. I missed you terribly, but I'm not the little girl who stumbled out from under her bed to see her world burned. Not anymore."

"Aes…" Drazhan sighed. He dragged his hands down his face with a pained moan. "I'm supposed to be protecting you, and I'm failing miserably, aren't I?"

"Yes," she said with a flippant tilt of her chin. "You are. Keeping me in the dark isn't protecting me. It breaks my heart to see your own so shattered." She shook her head at her lap. "But I didn't come here to chastise you." When she looked up, the fear in her eyes chilled him. "We have a visitor. From Duncarrow."

Drazhan lurched forward. "*What?* Who?"

476

Aesylt shrugged and shook her head. "He won't tell me his name, but he assures me he's not here to harm you or to punish you for what happened. He says...Well, he says he wants to talk."

Drazhan inhaled hard. "How many men?"

"That's the thing, Draz." Aesylt twisted her mouth into a frown. "He's come alone."

Drazhan peeled the blanket away and started picking his clothes up off the floor. "How can that be?"

"I don't even see a horse or a carriage, a cart...anything. Truthfully, I don't have any idea how he got here at all."

"Did you actually see him arrive?"

"No. Ilsa woke me."

"Did *she* see him arrive?"

"The knocking is what woke her."

Drazhan buttoned his shirt in a rush. "What does he look like?"

Aesylt held out her hands. "I don't know, dark hair? A bit pale. He has the oddest eyes..."

He paused as he reached for his sword belt. "How old?"

"That's just it; I can't place it. He could be thirty or seventy, and I'd believe either were true."

Mortain.

Drazhan fastened his sword belt and turned with a hard look. "Go to your room. Lock the door. Do not come out until I tell you it's safe."

"But, Draz—"

"Do as I say, Aes!"

She backed away, horror pooling in her eyes.

Good. Fear was the only thing that would make his stubborn sister listen.

He could soothe it later, after he'd dealt with the slippery sorcerer.

Drazhan left Mortain waiting half a tick of the moon. He did it to give himself time to balance his thoughts, but also to send a message to the sorcerer. Duncarrow might cow before the creature like supplicants, but in Witchwood Cross, they had no love for Meduwyn.

The creature was sitting in the late Ezra Wynter's study—in the man's very chair, lit by a single candelabra on a tall shelf. He didn't stand to offer the steward's chair to Drazhan, instead gesturing at where the visitors would sit.

Drazhan chose to stand. "You have one minute to tell me why you're here."

Mortain spread his hands with an affronted look. "One minute? That won't do at all."

It happened so fast, and it wasn't even intentional. Drazhan's claws descended in a rush of rage and magic, thrust out at his sides in a fighting stance.

Mortain laughed. "You can't hurt me with those, wulfling. I'm the one who gave them to you."

Drazhan flexed his claws. They tore at his flesh, sending spines of pain into arms that didn't share the feral swell. "A skilled liar is still a liar."

"You don't remember?" Mortain reclined in the chair with a thoughtful pause. "Well, of course you don't. You'd just returned home after seven grueling days in the ice and snow, covered in the blood of a wulf no one thought you could kill, and found your entire world had changed. Even I might have needed a moment to collect myself."

Drazhan grimaced. He peeled his lips back, the magic still building his claws to full form.

"I know, Drazhan, that *you* know those claws didn't come from claiming the wulf's heart. How many men had succeeded in the hunt before you?"

"Twelve." Drazhan forced the word through the rough clench in his jaw.

"Twelve. And how many of them turned into wulflings?"

"That's not my name, sorcerer."

"Is that not what your own people call you? The wulfling who emerged from the forest, carrying hope in his hands?"

Drazhan's chest heaved, but his claws had already begun to retract. "Say what you mean, spinner of lies, and then leave."

"You were a strong boy. They underestimated you," Mortain said. He ran a finger along the desk, pulling back a thick layer of dust. "Especially your father. No one but you can take credit for what happened that night in the forest. Wasn't magic. Wasn't luck. Your claws? Those came after."

"You weren't even there, sorcerer," Drazhan spat. His hands became hands again, and he wrapped one around his sword hilt. "Why are you here now?"

"A sword won't do it either. You cannot kill me with anything, wulfling, because I've imbued you with some of my magic, which makes me impenetrable to you. And, fortunately for you, the reverse is true."

Drazhan snorted and gripped the hilt tighter, despite Mortain's claim. "What foul nonsense is this?"

"That night, while you slept, dreaming of what a lesser man had done to your people, I gave you a piece of me. I wrapped it in your hands and bid the magic to transform you into the truth that lived in your heart. And this magic carried you through the years, through your vengeance, through your training...through your acquisition of Imryll and everything after."

Drazhan laughed. "I've always had magic. I was born with it."

Mortain's pleasant mien crumbled into the first twinge of anger. "*Weak* magic. The magic of men, of mortal, infallible creatures. Even your Medvedev blood is too diluted to matter. Tell me, wulfling, when did your healing become so powerful?"

"I've always been able to heal." Drazhan's mouth drew into a tight scowl.

"That isn't what I asked you," Mortain said. "Stalling is a tactic of men. You are more than that."

Drazhan flexed his hand, twitching his fingers before resettling them around the hilt of Stormbringer. He breathed in, then out, forcing both through the tension that had become a part of him since leaving Duncarrow. He didn't dare release it. It was the only thing holding him together.

"I do not go around offering my magic to just anyone," Mortain said, boring holes in Drazhan with his dark, soulless eyes. "When I came to you that night, I did so knowing you were the only man deserving of my daughter."

"What daughter? Can you even have those, with what you…" Drazhan waved a hand in disgust. "With what you are?"

"I very much *can*, though I have but one. Imryll."

Drazhan's hand slipped off his sword. "Leave."

"And we were doing so well," Mortain said with a vacant laugh. "I could spend all night and into the following day telling you how it all came to be, because I have nothing *but* time and patience, wulfling. *You*, on the other hand, are short on both, and so we'll come to the point." He pushed back from the dusty desk, untouched since Ezra's death until today, and stood. "Imryll is carrying your child."

Drazhan swayed sideways a step. The flame tips of the candles winked from his vision. Everything around him blurred into an oppressive cluster of dense air and closing space. "You're lying," he choked out.

"She was carrying your child when you poisoned her."

"No…" Drazhan sputtered through a violent wave of nausea. "No."

"And now she's forsaken, a discarded chosen ruined by the man who was sent to protect her. A woman of no house, no name. Her only visitors are the unfortunate Farrestell women and her tenderhearted brother. She hasn't left her apartments in weeks, and if I didn't visit her, she'd be too sick to eat or drink."

"No—"

"Ah, yes, I see you're surprised to learn she's not with Lord Quintus. Long story. Tedious and unimportant. If the king were not so fond of her, she'd be wasting away in the Sky Dungeon, her eventual child sent into the care of strangers."

"I...don't...believe...you."

"What you mean to say is you don't *want* to believe me, because accepting this truth means you abandoned her to a life of stifling exile when you fled Duncarrow under the cover of darkness."

"She *asked* me to go," Drazhan replied. "She *said*..." *If you really do love me, you'll go.* "Unlike you, who is still...still *standing* here, with your smirking and your smug revelations, I respect someone when they ask me to leave."

Mortain pulled his mouth into a surprised scoff. "Oh? Did you respect Imryll when you lied to her and used her to get close to the prince?"

Drazhan started forward, returning his hand to his sword. A thousand words and twice as many sensations whispered in his ear, but if he addressed even one, he would explode into a thousand tiny, useless pieces. "I should send your head to the king."

Mortain feigned a yawn. "We've been over this. You cannot kill me. Nor I you. Nor either of us Imryll, and so on and so on, ad infinitum. Can we move on already?"

"I can prove you're lying, because my poison almost killed her."

"*Almost.* You were nowhere near her when she slipped the robe on. She was healing herself, wulfling, even before you found her."

"Even if this isn't a lie—"

"Lies are beneath me. When I choose to spend my words, I spend them with care. I've given you more than most get in our entire acquaintance. None of them were owed to you, but you're too mired in your emotions to understand the *gift* I bring in telling you what Imryll will not."

"She made her desire clear when she told me to leave." Drazhan's mouth filled with cotton, which also stuffed his throat. He tried to swallow it down, but it only made it worse. *A child. A child. A child.*

No.

Not here.

Not in front of him.

"My daughter has lived her entire life lacking clarity," Mortain said with a weary sigh. "She's never belonged to Duncarrow, and she knows this. She's spent her life searching for purpose, only to turn her nose up when it finally presented itself. She knows this now, but…Ah, what will she do with it? Sadly, I know the answer. I've seen her stubborn refusal to embrace her purpose, and so I have no choice but to take something very dear from her."

Drazhan's fury returned, swirling not only through his hands but up his arms, circling his chest. "You even *think* of touching her, sorcerer—"

"She's my *daughter*, Wynter. Even if I could hurt her, I wouldn't. She carries the future inside of her, and it must be protected at all costs." Mortain sifted through the old stack of vellums on the desk. "No, this will toughen her. Steel her. For the sake of your son, who *must* survive but who will not, and nor will Imryll, if she stays on Duncarrow."

Son. Drazhan squinted to clear the intrusion of unwelcome revelations. "Why would you…Why wouldn't she survive?"

Mortain locked his eyes onto Drazhan's. "Imryll has two paths, and she can take either, though she must only take one: the one where she finds her way back to you. Through your son, an incredible ancestry will live on." Mortain sighed with a rolling stretch of his shoulders. "And the other…The other will come to pass if she remains on Duncarrow, where she will be murdered by the man who believes himself to be her father. Drushan, rent by the shame he believes she's stained their name with, will take his own dagger to her heart."

Drazhan reached for a nearby bureau and rolled his hand along the chiseled edge, inviting the sharp pain, the trickle of blood beading from the cut in his palm a welcome alternative to the devastation brewing within him.

How many times had he replayed his final words to Imryll?

Her words back?

The annihilation in her eyes from the destruction he'd wrought on her life.

I love you to my own detriment. My own downfall.

"You said…" Drazhan bore down on the pain to finish his words. He had to know. Lies or not, he needed to know all of it. "You said you were going to take something from her?"

Mortain tapped the air. "What does she care about most, wulfling, other than you?"

Drazhan recoiled with the horror of his comprehension. "No."

Mortain's head tilted. "I thought you *wanted* him dead?"

"No, I…not anymore." Drazhan said the next words for himself, freeing them for the first time. "There's no peace to be found in harming the innocent. It would make me no different than his father."

Mortain processed this. He made a little chuffed sound. "Well, cheer up. *You* were never meant to kill him. His legacy will live on through the son Adamina of Privaine doesn't yet know she carries, and the Rhiagains will reign unchallenged for the next three centuries. Nothing you did or could do was ever going to change it."

Drazhan shook his head. "Don't do it, sorcerer."

Mortain dusted his hands out to the side in a soft sweep. "Ahh, but it's already done. The same knife Drushan would have wielded against Imryll, his wife now wields against the king. She doesn't *quite* understand her motivations…what drives her to take each grueling step toward a future she doesn't remember planning. She doesn't know she'll spend the rest of her miserable days rotting in the Sky Dungeon, wondering why or how she could have ever turned against the one man capable of securing her family's power." Mortain shrugged. "And I'll certainly never satisfy that weak, simpering woman with an answer."

"Mortain…" Drazhan sputtered through several attempts to speak. "Call it off. Don't do this. You will destroy her. She won't come back from this."

"You've already done that well enough, wulfling." He glanced out the window into the darkness and snow. "If I don't leave now, I'll miss the best part."

"Call it off!"

"No." Mortain marched around the desk and brushed past Drazhan with a hard nudge. Drazhan turned and followed him, hardly able to match his pace as the sorcerer all but flew down the hall, gaining speed with every nimble, soundless step.

"Mortain! Call it *off*!"

Mortain burst into the night and leaped down the stairs before turning with a light spin and a bow. "If you'll excuse me, I have a daughter to comfort."

Drazhan raced down the steps after him when an explosion of red-and-gold light sent him skittering back in the dirt.

He gaped, in breathless awe, as Mortain shifted into a phoenix and twirled into the sky before flying away.

THIRTY-FOUR

PHOENIX

Two days had passed since Mortain had locked Imryll inside of her apartments.

On the first day, Tasmin had banged on the wood for so long, Imryll was surprised she hadn't cracked her way through.

By the second, Tasmin had Octavyen and Rahn engaged in helping, but they couldn't get it open either.

We need to involve the king. We need to break the door down, Rahn had said, but Imryll made them all swear not to make a scene. Mortain wanted her to learn a lesson, and circumventing it would get others hurt. People she cared about.

And they'd never be able to open the door, no matter how many men they assembled.

Because it wasn't a key locking her in.

It wasn't a slab of wood keeping her from leaving.

It was Mortain's foul magic.

Imryll waited for the crash, the moment when Mortain's mad revelations would weaken her and send her into a downward spiral, but it never came. Terrible truths were still truths, and while

485

she wished she could deny the foul words and dismiss them as more deception, more lies, she knew in her heart it would be the same as denying herself.

Mortain had been there for every important moment of her life. Why had she not pushed harder to understand why he didn't afford the same treatment to others? Why not Adamina or Tasmin or the other young women…or even *men* of the court? Why had Drushan never questioned the sorcerer's interest in his only daughter?

Perhaps he'd always known about Melantha and Mortain, and why the youngest Glaisgain child was similar to her brother but not the same.

Imryll could feel her son in a way she could not before Mortain had given him identity. *Aleksy,* she heard in her mind, in the hollow recesses of a heart that still beat unevenly. She couldn't say where the name had come from, only that it was the right name, the *only* one.

Aleksy the wulfling.

Part witch, part sorcerer, part wulf, part sceptre.

Aleksy would be his father's son in so many ways, it left Imryll hollowed. It was no longer a matter of whether she missed Drazhan or not, but whether she felt safe admitting how fragmented she was without him. Mortain's story had softened her loathing, but could she ever forgive Drazhan for what he'd done, no matter how damaged he'd been when he had come to Duncarrow with vengeance flowing through his blood? How could she forgive the way he'd loved her with one hand and plotted to hurt her with the other?

Imryll didn't have the answer.

She only knew how hard it was to breathe without him near.

Drazhan had said his heart belonged to her. But if that were true, why did it feel as though there was a hole in her chest where one should be?

Aleksy will close the wound, she thought, but that was unfair to her son, who would change her life—maybe even save it—but would not be responsible for her happiness. If she'd learned any lesson from the tempest of the past months, it was that expecting others to facilitate her peace assured the opposite would happen.

"Draz." She whispered his name through tears she no longer tried to hold back. They weren't a weakness at all, she'd realized, just another way to use strength. No one was impenetrable. If they were, it meant they had nothing to fight for. To live for.

But if she fought for Drazhan…if she *lived* for Drazhan, was it not equivocal to living for Mortain? Wasn't that exactly what he'd wanted with his interventions and machinations? How could she live with being a part of that?

Hours had passed.

Days.

She'd paced the room a hundred times.

A thousand.

Snow filtering in soft waves outside her window turned to rain that hammered the earth and sea. Wind whipped so hard, it seemed the great tower of Duncarrow would bow and snap.

She had only one more apple and the meager remainder of her water jug left.

As she lifted the last piece of fruit, regarding it with numb finality, her door finally clicked and swung open.

Torian waited for Adamina to leave before he dressed. If she knew where he was going, she'd be furious, though there was no reason for her to be. He was actually a little proud at how well he'd risen to her overly ardent nature, going well beyond what was reasonably expected of their shared duty. No doubt she'd be with child soon, which should ease her intensity some. But even that would not be enough for her if she knew Torian was going to see Imryll.

He hadn't seen her in almost a fortnight. She hadn't left her room, though that wasn't anything new, and he'd meant to go to her sooner. He really had. But there was always something pulling him back, demanding his attention. The dukes were always whispering some new idea in his ear. His mother, unwilling to accept her power had been neutered, still tried to manipulate him. He'd decided to send her to the mainland, to live out her twilight years as a matron of the reliquary, but he hadn't figured out how to tell her.

The call to sleep was stronger than his desire to see Imryll, but he couldn't shake the sense the gods were deliberately delivering obstacles to keep him from her.

Evos stirred outside the room. Torian waved a hand to indicate he should return to his chair.

"You can stand down, Evos. I'm only going to see Imryll."

"Are you certain, Your Grace? There's no need for relief on my account. I live to serve you."

"I am." Torian smiled tightly. He liked the man, but even looking at him stirred memories of Janus. Torian hadn't known how much the guard had meant to him until he was gone, and competent as Evos was, there was still a hole in Torian's life that couldn't so easily be filled. "And tell the others they don't need to follow me either. It's late. I won't be long."

Evos bowed with a slightly flustered look. But the only threat to Duncarrow had been sent away weeks ago and wouldn't be returning. Only a few knew the true reason, and though Evos was one of them, he hadn't taken Wynter's exile as an excuse to relax. His vigilance had only increased.

Despite his clear reservations, Evos darted ahead to deliver orders to the guards, who all wore the same wary look as their superior. Torian ignored them and exited into the main hall and then down the next one leading to Imryll's.

Godivah had been on him to move Imryll into a smaller suite of rooms—when she wasn't advising him to exile her from Duncarrow altogether—and give the First Chosen's to Adamina. But it had never been Torian's choice to set Imryll aside. He would have made her child his own without question, no matter the cost to the Rhiagain supremacy. It was Imryll who didn't want that, and he'd discarded her wishes too many times in the past to do it again.

He rounded another corner and came to a halt with a startled gasp. In the center stood a disheveled woman in a flowy white gown. He strained in the dim light and was stunned to see it was Duchess Melantha.

Torian furrowed his brows in concern as he approached. "Duchess? Is everything all right?"

"There you are, Your Grace." Melantha stumbled forward, barefoot, with a grim smile. She sounded distant, still caught by slumber. "I've been looking for you."

"I've been in my apartments for hours." He started forward tentatively. "What is it? Is it Imryll?"

"Imryll?" The duchess looked confused. "Oh. No. No, it's not Imryll."

Torian's heart fluttered with each anxious step. Something was wrong with the duchess. Very wrong. "And you? Are you all right?"

"Me?" Melantha hobbled forward a few more steps. Her unnerved face revealed itself in a band of moonlight falling across the stones. "Of course I'm fine, Your Grace. Why would you ask?"

"It's just…You seem…" Torian held out both of his hands, as though apprehending a dangerous madman. When he realized it, he chuckled to himself and shook it off.

When he drew near, the duchess stumbled forward, and Torian lurched just in time to catch her before she hit the stones.

A sharp, piercing jolt seized him. The pain shot to his head so fast, he dropped her before he pitched sideways, to the stone wall.

Torian gulped the dense air before looking down. He swooned at the sight of a thick bloom of crimson spreading outward from the hilt of a dagger protruding from his belly.

Melantha peered up from the stones, her lips peeled back in a sneer. She started cackling. The harsh, unforgiving sound deepened his pain, further darkening the hall, and it was all he heard, bouncing off the stones and drumming through his ears, as he slid down the wall.

He wheezed, his shaking hands trying to land on either side of the hilt, but blood spurted around the steel with every labored breath.

"Melantha," he said weakly. He met her eyes through heavy blinks, but he didn't recognize her at all. The Melantha he'd known all his life was gone. He didn't know who he was looking at.

A shrill scream at the far end of the hall had him rolling his head to the right. Imryll came flying toward them, her eyes widening in horror at a scene Torian still didn't understand himself.

And you never will, you fool. Because you're dying. You're going to die without ever knowing why.

Imryll dropped to her knees in an ungraceful dive. "*Tor.*" Her hands trembled as his had, as she surveyed the damage. When she looked up, her eyes held confirmation of what he already knew. "We need to stop the bleeding." She glanced back at her mother and then at Torian again, shaking her head in astonishment. She growled as she tore at the sleeve of her dress, unable to rip the fabric. "I'll go find Evos."

Torian reached out to stop her. He could hardly see her face anymore. In the seconds he'd watched her assess his fate, he'd left more and more of the world behind, until there was just her. The dark spots in his vision blurred her face, but she was there. Imryll. His Imryll. His first and only love. Even if fate had allowed him a longer life, nothing could ever come close to the youthful purity of first love, before experience had left him stoic and embittered.

"Stay," he pleaded.

"SOMEONE HELP US!" she screamed. Her gaze whipped from his mortal wound to his face, then back again. She'd clamped her hands around the dagger, but blood spurted through her fingers and around the edges of her hands, pumped by the receding thrum of a heart racing through its final beats. "It's…It's all right, Tor. It's all right. It's going to be fine."

"I thought we promised no lies," Torian said, dipping into the receding well of his remaining vigor to offer her one final smile.

"HELP US!" she howled again and then moaned as she said, "I'll go get someone. I'll—"

"No." Torian groaned and laid a bloody hand against her cheek. "I don't want to die alone, Ryl."

Imryll's face squinted into a hard sob. She grimaced and forced it back, shaking her head. "Don't talk like that. Stay right here. I'll—"

Torian grabbed her other hand with his free one. "Ryl. It's done. It's over. Sit with me."

"I *can't*," she sobbed. Tears cut through the blood staining her cheeks. "This isn't happening. This isn't real."

"It is." Torian coughed. When he saw what was in it, he understood he was even closer to the end than he'd realized. The defeated terror in her wide eyes said she knew it too. "I love you. I have always loved you. You need to leave Duncarrow because the others won't…They won't be as kind to you and your child."

"Stop speaking like this!" Tears streamed down her face in streaks, but she'd given up trying to get away. "Is there *anyone* who can hear me? HELP us!"

"Shh. Listen to me."

"*Please!*" she sobbed, and it wasn't clear whether she meant the word for him or some higher power.

"You…have…to go," Torian said. It was all he had left, and it wasn't nearly enough. It wasn't…

Imryll brought his hands to her mouth in a quaking, sobbing kiss. "You are so, so dear to me, Tor. Irreplaceable. You were the first person who ever *saw* me." She broke away with a sharp cry. "And I see you now, and I love you. I love you, Torian Rhiagain. My truest friend in all the world."

Torian closed his eyes as her words washed over him. He repeated them in his mind through his final, ragged breaths.

"TOR!"

He smiled one last time. For her. For himself.

And then Imryll, and the world, faded to black.

Drazhan awoke in the barn to a large, tight vise closed around his heart. Loose, scratchy hay greeted him, followed by the distinct scent of cattle excrement.

It was dark. Night still.

He tried to make sense of a situation that offered none. He didn't remember how he'd gotten there or why he'd come at all. The last thing he remembered was...

Mortain.

Imryll.

The vise tightened. He saw her again, flying through the halls of Duncarrow, covered in blood and angst. He listened for her screams, but they never came. They either had no sound, or she'd given them up for something more useful.

Drazhan used a nearby bale to climb to his feet. Unsteady, he ambled toward the barn doors, his vision splitting in two, dividing himself across two realities.

Imryll.

Drazhan lunged for the door but missed and landed first on his knees and then his face.

Imryll.

"I'm coming, Imryll. I'm coming." He panted before passing out once more.

Imryll fell back on her hands, slipping in the blood. The ringing in her ears started low and distant, building to a sharp crescendo that eclipsed the remainder of her senses.

In a deadened stupor, she glanced back at her mother, lying on her side with her arm stretched above her head as though sleeping.

The ringing intensified. Her eyelids grew heavier with each blink. She slapped her bloodied hands around on the stone for purchase, finding none. She swung to her side and pushed up from her knees and nearly fell over Torian's corpse—

No, no, no, he's not dead. He cannot *be dead. He*—

She stumbled to her feet. She held her bloody, shaking hands out before her, turning them in the dim light. They no longer looked like her own. Her tongue felt foreign as it rolled inside her bloodied mouth. The lungs trying to claw itself from her chest did so because they were done with her vessel and were ready for another.

Imryll swayed, kicking her mother's arm in her effort to steady herself. She slipped again and slid forward into a messy jog, but as her legs lifted and fell and pushed, she sank into a rhythm—the only rhythm, a *perfect* rhythm—that silenced the ringing. She left a part of herself in the hall, but she didn't need it anymore. The thought lifted her, carrying her forward, around corner after corner, until she reached the main hall.

If you are not on the ship tomorrow, something terrible will happen. The consequence will haunt you for the rest of your life.

She was on fire from the inside out, her flesh radiating with heat and light and an urgency greater than any she'd known before. Only a handful of people were awake and moving about the keep at the late hour, but she didn't stop to tally them. One face threatened to give her pause: Mortain, leering at her in inquisitive anticipation. *I will die before I ever follow any path you set for me,* she thought as she left him and his cursed truths behind.

She ran faster, her curls flying behind her like a waving flag. Her nightgown was a bloody mess as she left crimson footprints where her bare feet struck the stones, skipping stairs on her desperate spiral toward the ground level.

Imryll didn't stop when she hit the rain-sodden rocks of the courtyard. Without all the twists and turns of the keep slowing her, she picked up speed, riding the tailwind as she raced toward the collage of rocks that separated her from the sea.

She didn't think of Torian slumped in the hall, nor her mother, covered in the stench of her inexplicable act. She released the past few months into the rainy night, laughing as the Choosing, Godivah, Carrow, Marius, Ada…all of it remained behind, unable to follow her to a future she couldn't yet comprehend.

Only Drazhan and Aleksy were with her as her feet lifted off the stones, curling into talons. She drew a final, gasping breath before her legs bent and drew inward, her flaming arms becoming brilliant red-and-orange feathers at the same moment her mouth elongated into a perfectly curved beak.

Imryll of Glaisgain had one final thought as she shifted into a phoenix and left Duncarrow behind.

Here I am.

THIRTY-FIVE
FOUR MONTHS, SEVEN DAYS,
AND SIXTEEN HOURS

S *he turned into a brightly plumed bird and flew away.*
    That was it.

The only information anyone had about the whereabouts of Imryll of Glaisgain following the murder of King Torian.

She'd been gone almost a fortnight by the time Drazhan docked at Duncarrow with a handful of trusted men. Word of Torian's demise had reached the Cross by raven the day they were readying to depart. Though he'd once wished for nothing more than the destruction of Carrow and his son, Drazhan had spared a moment of silence for the kind young man whom Imryll had loved so dearly. He beseeched the Guardian of the Unpromised Future for Torian's swift passage.

Duncarrow had been a chaotic mess when they reached the port. All eyes were on the grieving Adamina, within whom their last hope either flourished or perished. A hasty regent council had been assembled, consisting of the usual figures and Clarisan Rhiagain, who was the only living person left on Duncarrow with the right bloodline. But crown matters were far from

495

Drazhan's thoughts when his bootsteps rang across the familiar halls.

Clarisan had been the first to tell him Imryll was gone. She turned her nose at the rumor Imryll had shifted into a bird and disappeared into the twilight sky, but then, she hadn't seen Mortain do that very thing only a fortnight past.

It was to Mortain he'd gone next, but one look into the creature's fraught eyes told Drazhan the sorcerer didn't know anything either.

You can't sense your own daughter?

Not if she doesn't want me to.

Not if she doesn't want me to was enough to rekindle Drazhan's hope that she *was* still out there...that she hadn't joined her ancestors at the bottom of the White Sea.

Drazhan departed the same day, but he'd left with more men than he'd arrived with. Blackfen resigned from the Queens' Guard, and Owen, who had become Adamina's second guard, did the same. They turned their posts over to Garrick and Waters, who had both been reduced to members of the Rhiagain Guard when Torian had sent the realm chosens home.

I promised the princess the day of the tournament that I'd protect her no matter who won. So I'll take the Westerlands, Wynter. No one knows those lands better than a Blackfen.

Aye, and your secret, Stormclaw. The magic in your hands? Dies with us. So I'll take the Southerlands. Need salt and sand leading that charge. None better than a Strong for the job.

Overcome with emotion, Drazhan accepted their offers, realizing that although he'd lost so much, he'd also gained in the unexpected brotherhood he'd found with his fellow knights.

Others, like Octavyen, insisted on coming along as well. Drazhan wouldn't stop any man who wanted to help.

Drazhan had gone first to the Easterlands, to the last man he ever wanted to see again: Marius Quintus. But Quintus had already sent men to scour the Easterlands when word had arrived that Imryll had vanished. *You're welcome to conduct your own search, but she's not here, Wynter. I even had the men check your little love chalet, but it seems someone finally had the sense to tear the relic down.*

He didn't trust Quintus a whit, so he'd conducted his own search, covering every corner of the Easterlands. But Quintus wasn't wrong. The chalet wasn't there, and neither was Imryll.

That left the other three Reaches.

Though he had help on all sides, Drazhan refused to leave the most important mission of his life to chance.

He traveled from village to village, all over the Southerlands, Westerlands, and even returning home temporarily to the Northerlands. He slept every third night, one or two hours at a time, eating on the ride. With something constructive to focus on, his ability to meditate returned, and if he wasn't knocking on doors or scouring markets, he was using the skill to pour over all he'd learned, to find *something* to hang his hope on.

Four months, seven days, and sixteen hours from when he'd started his mission, hope brought Drazhan Wynter back to Whitechurch once more, exhausted, spent, and desperate.

You can't sense your own daughter?

Not if she doesn't want me to.

I even had the men check your little love chalet, but it seems someone finally had the sense to tear the relic down.

It's no longer there.

Drazhan allowed himself his first and only full night's rest on what he prayed would be his last evening on the road.

If he was right, then the one part of his quest remaining was also the one he most feared.

The man who had never known the right words would have to find them.

Drazhan turned off the main path and entered the forest, headed toward the chalet. But as before, it was gone. The night he'd taken Imryll there, it had been visible from the path, but there was nothing, not even the remnants of a foundation or forgotten stones and timber left behind.

It was like it had never existed at all.

He dismounted and navigated the rest of the way from memory. The past rushed up, and he again felt Imryll draped limply in his arms, against his chest, as he ran her the rest of the way to the chalet. He would remember the run forever.

A nauseating wave stole over him. He backed up a few steps and felt immediately better. With a determined frown, he started forward again but was met with the same odd sensation, like he was trying to enter a place that didn't want him.

Drazhan suddenly felt like a great fool. What his mind had been hypothesizing the past few days was impossible. It defied everything he knew about his world, about magic.

But Imryll's magic wasn't from *his* world. It had come from somewhere far more ancient and forbidden.

You can't sense your own daughter?

Not if she doesn't want me to.

He rolled his shoulders back and closed his eyes, slipping into a meditation. He could afford no external intrusions. Doubt had no place. Fear even less.

Drazhan turned his face toward the sky with a weighty exhale. He said a silent prayer to the Guardians and lowered his gaze back to where the chalet used to be.

Where he believed it *still* was.

Hiding.

Imryll.

He waited for signs. He didn't know what to look for, but meditation had sharpened his mind and opened it to all possibilities.

I know you're there. I think I even know how you did it.

Lightning tore across the sky. Thunder boomed seconds later.

But the chalet didn't appear.

It's me, Imryll.

Nothing.

Everything that gives my life meaning is inside that chalet. I know I have no right to ask anything of you, but...

A soft drizzle rained from the sky. Another roll of thunder, closer.

If you're in there because of me...because you're afraid of me, I can't fault you. And I'll...I'll accept it. I will, if it's truly what you want. If that's the right thing for you, I'll leave here and never return. But I can't go until I know you're all right. Until I know our son is all right. Give me that and I'll go.

It was a lie, the worst he'd ever told. There were some things a man could never move on from.

But if she asked him to go, he would.

He'd know then her decision was final.

Im—

Drazhan fell back at the intrusion of a thick push of air. His hands came up in protection as the world...fluttered. The air rippled into waves, and between the ripples he could see...

The chalet.

He lowered his hands.

The small cabin continued to dance in and out of focus, both there and not, until the air settled.

Drazhan heard a horse snuffling and glanced to the right to see Enzi, free-grazing in forestland that hadn't been there at all moments before. Beside her was a wool blanket, hanging from yarn strung between trees, as though drying from a recent wash.

His eyes were drawn back to a deep creaking groan when the door swung open.

Drazhan left his hesitation behind, straightened, and entered.

Fire crackled, filling the small structure with an inviting warmth. A deep, nutty scent permeated the air, coming from a rusted pot hanging from the interior hook of the hearth.

"How did you know?" Imryll raised her hand. The door slammed closed behind him, touched only by her magic. She lowered it back to her side.

Drazhan choked on his breath at the sight of her. She was still the same—the same woman he'd reluctantly, grudgingly fallen in love with—but she was so changed, he could hardly wrap his mind around the differences.

Her red hair was coiled in a knot atop her head. She'd fashioned a crude dress out of the discarded cloak from that long ago night, and pieces of a blanket. Her skin was ruddier, as though she spent most of her time in the sun, and a soft but tired expression painted her golden, freckled face. His gaze meandered down to her hand resting on the swell of a belly, which was unmistakably with child.

"Draz?"

Drazhan looked up with a start. He tried to meet her eyes, but there was an earnest depth in her amber irises that gutted him. He could drown there, he thought…and would, if she invited him to.

"Mortain…" he sputtered.

Imryll's eyes flicked briefly upward. Her hand mindlessly stroked her belly through the thin dress. "So you know."

"That he's your father." Drazhan nodded. "He told me."

Her eyes narrowed in distrust that left his heart fluttering in fear. "When?"

"He came to Witchwood Cross."

Imryll laughed and rolled her eyes. She reached sideways for a mug and took a deep sip before handing it to him. "All I have is water and…more water. Turns out the cistern is pretty useful."

Drazhan shook his head. He watched her smooth, confident movements in confusion that only deepened his love. No desire he'd ever had was stronger than seeing her exist in the safety of a world she'd created for herself, while he was unable to take her into his arms and crush her to his chest.

She set the mug down. "So, he told you about me. That doesn't explain how you knew to find me *here*."

"Instinct," he said, cringing before the words even landed, hoping they were not the wrong ones. "I came four months ago—"

"Four months ago?" She reared back in surprise. "Has it been that long since I left?"

Left. She hadn't said *flown away,* but it didn't mean she hadn't. The distance she kept meant there was distrust there still. "Four months and some days. Yes."

"I stopped counting after a fortnight," she replied. "Seemed rather pointless. As long as I knew when to expect the sun and the moon, I had no use for the specifics."

Drazhan gestured around. "You've been here all this time?"

"Most of it," she said. She shifted her second hand atop the other and then they split opposite ways, encircling her belly from both sides. "I didn't know how to get here, so I had to find my way."

"And the ward you created, over the chalet..."

"Unintentional," she said with a soft laugh that made him weak. "I was so worried about Aleksy—"

"Aleksy?"

She smiled down at her belly. "Our *son,* Drazhan. That's going to be his name."

Drazhan gripped Stormbringer's hilt, because if he didn't hold on to something, he was going to fall. "That was my grandfather's name."

She looked up in surprise. "It came to me one day, and I knew it was right." She braced herself on the back of a chair. "I was afraid of what would happen to him if I was found, and I envisioned a place where he could be safe from harm. I didn't know what would come of it, but then I watched several bands of men ride right by the chalet, oblivious to its existence. That's when I knew what I'd done."

"That's not realm magic."

Imryll tilted her head. "Is that a question?"

"I don't know." He aimed a laugh at his feet. "All these months, I thought of what I might say to you when I saw you, and..."

"And what?"

He winced and looked up again. "None of it feels right anymore. It doesn't feel...enough."

Imryll nodded thoughtfully. She glanced around and gestured at the table. "Want to sit?"

He pushed away the memory of taking her for the first time on the very same table. "All right."

When they were both seated, Imryll asked, "What else did Mortain tell you?"

Drazhan opened his hands. "He's the one who gave me my claws, he says."

"I suppose that would make more sense than you just having them." Imryll was looking at his hands. "I don't think he's lying. But something tells me he left out the role he played in what happened to your family and people."

Drazhan exhaled in slow comprehension. Of course Mortain had been behind Carrow's choice of Witchwood Cross. Carrow Rhiagain never made a decision Mortain hadn't made for him.

Imryll smiled tightly. "I'm sorry, Drazhan. Truly."

He shrugged. "That should have reopened a wound for me, but all I feel is...relief? Better to know than not, I suppose."

"He's a monster who has guided both our lives for far too long." Imryll's face flushed with a quick rush of anger. "If he could find me here, he would have."

"He told me he'd never be able to if you didn't want him to."

"All this trouble he went to, and when it really matters, he can't even break through a ward created by his own magic." She angled her face away in bemused disgust.

Drazhan held his words until he was sure she was done speaking. "Imryll, I...I am so sorry about Torian."

Her mouth twitched. She passed a thumb along the corners of both eyes. "I thought you'd be happy to hear the news. You wanted him dead."

"No," Drazhan said. "Not anymore. If I could have saved him, I would have."

"Hmm." Her expression was impassive. He couldn't tell if she believed him.

"And Aleksy, he's..."

"Well," Imryll answered with a glance downward. "He's certainly putting my limited foraging skills to the test though. I've never been more ravenous in my *life.*"

Something in the light, casual delivery, the way she spoke of their *son,* of the start of her life as a mother, snapped the tight control he'd brought into the chalet. He tried to laugh, but it erupted into a sob. He buried his face in his hands in shame.

"I forgive you," she said, so softly he looked up to hear her better. Her smile was sad. "I feel like I understand you better now. And if I had the power, Drazhan, I would take down the creature who hurt you so deeply...who took Torian from me...but for all the magic Mortain has given me, he still has so much more than I ever will. It's why I'm here and not out there, fighting back."

"I'm the one who was supposed to protect you." Drazhan's voice splintered with his heart.

"Ah, but you did. More than you know."

"I love you, Imryll," he blurted, unable to hold it in any longer. "I need you to hear it again, here, now, so you know it wasn't said because emotions were running high. I *love* you, Imryll. Then. Now. For whatever is left of my wretched, cursed life. And if I had any doubt of my own words, the months between us made this feeling so powerful, it's replaced everything else."

Imryll bowed her head. She rolled her bottom lip into her mouth and held it there.

"I didn't say that to make you feel—"

She wiped her eyes and looked up. "I love you, Drazhan. I absolutely, unequivocally, to the end of my days love you, and nothing you've done has erased this love, even when I wished it would. I wanted to banish you from my heart, but...How can I? When you saved me? Freed me?" She took a deep breath in. "When you gave me a son."

503

Drazhan spread his hands over the splintered table. "Do you know why I'm here?"

"Yes. Or no. I don't know, honestly. When you were outside, you said you were worried—"

"Imryll, you have something vital of mine." He laid both palms, one atop the other, over his heart. "Something I can't live without."

Imryll swallowed. She blinked through hooded eyes. "But what…What do you make of Mortain's role in everything?"

"His role?"

"He created me. He made you. He *wanted* us to be together."

"And you think he used magic to see it done?"

Imryll's eyes filled with tears, but they didn't spill. "I don't know, Draz."

Drazhan pushed back from the table and dropped to his knees before her. He gathered her warm hands in his and pulled them both to his chest. "No magic can tell my heart how to beat. Who to love."

Imryll squeezed her eyes closed with a pained sigh. He felt the same thing break in her that had broken in him, something he knew only she could heal. But could he heal her?

She bent her fingers back to collect his and wound them into a knot. "I haven't known fear in months. I never want to know it again."

Drazhan shook his head with a gentle laugh. "Imryll, I can't promise you a life without fear. No one can. But what life is there to be found here, shielded from the world? From life? From joy?"

Her wide eyes broke his heart. "And if he finds us?"

Drazhan lifted off his knees and pressed his mouth to her forehead. Held it there. "He will. He will find us, but he can't hurt us. He'll have to live with knowing that though he orchestrated our meeting, he has no control over where our story goes from here. None."

Imryll folded her head against his chest, and when he slid his arms around her from behind, to gather her, she relaxed into the gesture, wrapping herself against him.

"Tell me what you need, Imryll. Whatever it is, I'll do it."

"I haven't talked to anyone except Aleksy in months, and I'm already tired of it," she whispered against his shirt. Her lips rolled against the fabric. "You don't need me to tell you what I need, Draz. You already know."

Imryll climbed into his lap and undid each of his shirt buttons one by one, teasingly slow, enjoying the strain in his jaw. His hips thrust against her gown, but she wasn't ready to give him what he wanted. She hadn't realized how much she'd missed it—*him*—because she hadn't wanted to. She'd sealed every last bit of him away in a box and locked it. Until he'd stood outside the chalet and called to her, she'd thought the key was lost forever.

Imryll had felt him approach before he sent a single word. *Stay strong*, she'd told herself, only to realize she no longer knew what that meant.

Everything that gives my life meaning is inside.

How those words had wounded her. They'd dragged her back down to the depths she'd run from and forced her to confront why she'd run at all. She'd died and then been reborn—and all before he'd said, *Give me that and I'll go.*

Unexpected fear tore through her at the thought of Drazhan leaving. Softening the ward for him hadn't happened consciously, but neither had the creation of it.

She peeled his shirt down off his shoulders, and when she did, her hand brushed the raised flesh of his scars. He flinched, but she spread both hands deeper across his back, feeling the path of his history and showing him her intention to know him, scars and all. Daring him to challenge her, as he once had.

"My wulfling," she whispered, and his tension disappeared. "You worked so hard for these. How hard will you work to save yourself from me?"

"Imryll," her dark knight growled, winding his fist through her knot of hair. Desire burned in his eyes, tinged with muted violence. "I'm going to explode."

"Not yet," Imryll commanded. She rocked over him, asserting her dominance. He needed to know some things would be different. There was no returning to the timid girl he'd subdued with his feral grunts and illicit words. She still wanted those things— maybe more so—but more than anything, she wanted Drazhan Wynter to *see* her.

See what she'd become.

Decide whether he could love what was before him.

"Look at me," she whispered as she released his shirt the rest of the way. "Drazhan."

His throat bobbed, and she felt him brace. He blinked hard and met her eyes, and she waited, to be sure he wouldn't look away.

Imryll urged the fire into her eyes that had become innately hers. She felt the flicker as it passed across her irises, changing their color and depth. Letting him see her shift form was too much, but if he could gaze into her flame and not shrink away...

Drazhan dragged his thumbs along the soft flesh on the outer edges of her eyes. "I already know, Imryll. I already know." He crushed his forehead to hers but didn't break her gaze. "You can't scare me, my love. We both have the capacity for darkness, but we know who we are. We *know* who we are. We showed each other the void, and we can *choose* to stay in the light. Together."

Imryll killed the flames and kissed him, her tongue prying his mouth open wider. His groan vibrated her tongue as she dug it toward his. She fumbled with his belt and pants with one hand, but she couldn't release him fast enough.

Drazhan helped her, and together they freed him. Together, they lifted her tattered dress and guided him into place. She had to angle herself back to do it, the roundness of her belly too much for their old way. He broke their gaze only long enough to watch himself push in.

Imryll's head fell back as she took him in. He was still the perfect fit, the *only* fit, and with each and every roll of her hips, the months, days, and hours melted away.

"I see you," he said between demanding kisses. "I know you. I love you."

Imryll let him take over the motions. She wrapped her arms down his back and traced the scars she knew he'd earned in the greatest fight of his life. She listened for his throbbing pulse and rode the rhythm of it, setting her long-buried vulnerabilities in his hands, knowing they were safe there.

Drazhan pulled her face back and looked deep into her eyes as he crested and crashed. He slipped his fingers between her legs to finish her, but she shook her head.

"Hold me instead?" she said, sliding off of him and turning sideways in his lap. "Both of us."

Drazhan gathered her in his arms and set his chin atop her head. She felt his chest shudder. "I'll hold you, Imryll. Because the only thing I want more than to watch you come is to wrap my arms around you and never let go." He tilted her head back and looked into her eyes. "But this time, we're not running away from each other. Do you understand?"

Imryll nodded through her exhaustion of the long days and nights she'd spent alone with her thoughts, getting to know herself for the first time. "I don't want to run anymore. I just want to be safe. For our son to be safe."

"Aleksy will be. *You* will be," Drazhan insisted, holding her tighter. "Mortain has no power over either of us. The same magic he used, to guide the future he wanted, keeps him from using it to hurt us. Let him come. Let him beg, whine, plead, threaten. He can't touch us, Imryll. Especially not when we're together."

"You're going to ask me to leave this place, aren't you?"

He nodded and kissed her again, more firmly this time. "You did so well keeping our son safe here. I'm in awe, Imryll. I'm so proud of you. What you've done here is phenomenal. But when he arrives, he needs room to play, to grow. To thrive. And his

507

mother…" Drazhan's voice choked with emotion. "She deserves those things too."

"And when you tire of me?" Imryll asked. The question no longer came from a place of insecurity but practicality. "What then?"

"There's no future where I would ever look at *any* woman the way I look at my wife."

"Your wife?" Imryll laughed at what would have, once, been an utterly absurd notion. Imryll of Glaisgain marrying the dark knight who'd come to ruin her? "Was that a proposal?"

"I'm not asking." His eyes darkened. Desire stirred between her legs.

"Awfully bold," she muttered, dodging his hard look.

Drazhan ripped her breath away with a ferocious kiss. "You wouldn't have me any other way."

EPILOGUE

Imryll stood upon the teetering stack of crates with blind trust. She only needed a few more moments to lift the shingle onto the hooks, and that was all she was going to get, because if Drazhan saw her doing something so dangerous, he'd lose his mind.

Aesylt kept darting her gaze around from below, only to turn it back on Imryll with fretful head shakes. She tried to steady the crates, but they both knew there'd be nothing she could do if it all went toppling.

Imryll grimaced and reached for the last hook, bracing one hand on the freshly built roof, the other so far beyond the crates, she was stretched from toe to finger.

"Imryll." Aesylt moaned, barely above a whisper. She shifted in the cold. "Draz will do it when the men bring the ladders back."

"I know he would, Aes, but…" Imryll closed her eyes and let her hand guide her, feeling around the metal post until she reached the end—the hook. "This was my passion, and I won't have anyone say I didn't pull my weight."

Enzi, tethered nearby, made a soft snuffling sound Imryll interpreted as approval.

"How could anyone say that when you've been out here, day and night, building right alongside the men?" Within Aesylt's castigation, Imryll heard pride.

"How is that different from you out here, day and night, feeding them?"

"It just is." Aesylt sighed. "Don't you have any magic you can use for this?"

"I'm still learning what I can do. Besides…It's more gratifying to do it the hard way." Imryll stuck her tongue out, balanced the edge of the sign, and…*clink*. Hooked.

Aesylt released a breathy groan of relief. "All right. Now get *down*. Please?"

"Now? I thought I'd host a tea party on the roof." Imryll teased, but she carefully climbed down. When she reached the bottom, landing in a dense pile of packed snow, she released her own careful sigh and glanced up to see her handiwork.

Books of All Things, the sign said. She'd carved it by hand, a new skill she'd added as she sought to make herself a contributing resident of Witchwood Cross. Some of the men in town had frowned at her idea of a village library and school, because paper was nearly as valuable as gold. But what lay within the pages of books was worth far more than that.

Drazhan had given much of his wealth back to the Cross to fund the rebuilding efforts, and yet he still had more money than any man needed. When she'd first broached the idea with him, her vision had been so much smaller—perhaps a library within Fanghelm, or a group who came together once a fortnight to listen to a reading and learn their letters.

But then he'd walked her down to a spot at the end of the main road and showed her the remnants of the needlework shop his late mother had used to run.

Epilogue

Make it your own. You want to build a library, to educate the world? There's no reason not to.

Imryll's thoughts had been riddled with doubts in the early days of the build. Books were frivolous, not essentials. They had bigger priorities, more useful ones. In her weaker moments, she recalled Drazhan's first assessment of her idea, back on *The Sweet Yvaine*, when he'd dismissed her dream as idealistic—even though she knew he'd said it out of anger and regretted every word.

But the Witchwood rebuild was nearly complete. And with every passing day she spent clearing out old timber and replacing it with new, more and more citizens stopped by to learn about what she was doing. Women, mainly, who had never been taught their letters and wanted better for their daughters. But men too.

Aesylt came every day to help. Drazhan divided his time between the library and the finishing touches on the rest of the village's reconstruction.

Aesylt looped her arm through Imryll's as if expecting Imryll to clamber back up the crates. "Now that it's done, what's our first order of business?"

Imryll leaned in and set her head against Aesylt's. She'd always wanted a sister, and the one she'd gained exceeded even her greatest dreams of one. Aesylt was warm and loving, an incredible support for her family, but she also had a spark of her own that burned so bright, Imryll wondered who would be worthy of kindling it. Drazhan was unlikely to let any man consider courting his sister. He'd already driven away a dozen.

"Well, we'll have to find a teacher," Imryll said. She twisted her mouth. "One who knows the old languages and the new."

"But the old languages are forbidden."

Imryll grinned at her sister. "And who would ever come this far north to enforce it, hmm?" Her smile nearly faded when she remembered that Mortain had visited twice…and he'd only keep coming back. He couldn't hurt her or Drazhan, but it didn't mean he'd given up on his vengeance with the Ravenwoods. It was a

511

battle they'd never stop fighting. "The old languages are a part of your people. We can't let them die."

"*Our* people," Aesylt stated, smiling back. "You're one of us now, princess. Better get used to that if you're going to make us read books and learn things." She feigned a disgusted look.

Imryll gave her a playful shove, but Aesylt's kind words settled around her like a warm blanket. She'd been in Witchwood Cross little more than six months, but it felt more like home to her than Duncarrow ever had. She looked forward to their long nights gathered around the village bonfires, meeting the people who made up her husband's small but comfortable world. They all loved their wulfling, and they seemed to love his she-wolf as well. *The one who finally tamed him*, they said, and Imryll wondered what he'd been like before tragedy had hardened him.

Drazhan came around the corner towing a cart behind him. His sleeves were rolled back, revealing muscled arms streaked with the same dark dirt he had on his face. Strapped to his chest in a sling Aesylt had made him was a soundly sleeping Aleksy.

"If he wasn't already married to you, women would be lining up, him looking like that," Aesylt muttered with a laugh. She grew serious. "He reminds me a little of the boy he was, before…"

Imryll squeezed her. "We all have our wounds, Aes. Some close slower than others. We'll all get there. I promise."

"I've never seen him need anything the way he needs you and Aleksy. He really loves you, Imryll. You've been the only thing big enough to overshadow his pain."

"It wasn't me," Imryll said as she watched her husband lower the cart and stretch, then tilt his waterskin back for a sip. He used the remnants to clean his face before he dropped a kiss on Aleksy's sleeping forehead. "He had to learn for himself there was no vengeance that would do anything other than destroy him. There's no peace in revenge. Just more pain without end."

Drazhan approached and greeted her with a kiss so indecent, it had Aesylt gagging.

"You think Aleksy dropped out of the sky, do you?" he growled at his sister, grinning. He kissed Imryll again and carefully unwound their son and passed him over. "He's been sleeping all day. Starting to wake up now."

"Should be a long night then," she said, chuckling.

"I'll take him tonight," Aesylt said. "I don't mind."

Imryll kissed her son and shifted him to a better position against her shoulder. "You don't have to look after him so much, Aes. You already do so much."

"It's not a chore for me," Aesylt insisted. She tucked her pale golden hair back off her face and gathered it into a rope, bringing it around her shoulder. "I love Aleksy and the light he brings to Fanghelm—that you both do these days." She grinned. "Besides, no one, infant or adult, should have to listen to the way the two of you carry on after dark."

Drazhan and Imryll exchanged glances. "You're too young to know about any of that," he groused.

"I'm a year younger than your wife, *wulf.*"

"Yeah? Changes nothing for me, *cub.*" He rolled his eyes at Imryll. "She acts as though the men who have made their claims are even worthy of dining at our table."

"Lord Dereham himself offered a son!" Aesylt exclaimed. "How much more worthy can a man be?"

"Worthier," Drazhan said. He sniffed the air. "Storm is shifting. We'll need to be indoors before it does."

"Another squall?" Imryll glanced up toward the fog-covered Icebolt. At the top, the Ravenwoods lived in shrouded seclusion. She'd not seen one, though she'd thought perhaps she had once—a dark bird, bigger than all the others, passing over. The temptation to shift into her avian form and fly up to meet them had been stronger than she'd like to admit, but she wasn't ready to address that side of herself.

Drazhan and Aesylt knew the Ravenwoods personally though. They even had a relationship with some.

Imryll didn't have to meet the Ravenwoods to know she'd never let Mortain harm a single one.

"Wintertide never leaves quietly."

Imryll started to say how eager she was for springtide but then remembered that the far north only had one season: cold.

"I'll take Aleksy while you two finish up here," Aesylt said, not waiting for permission. She gently peeled her nephew away from Imryll and swaddled him in her apron before she started up the hill to Fanghelm.

Drazhan tilted his head and inhaled the icy air. He smiled into the exhale, but his eyes widened when he saw the sign. "Books of All Things," he read. "You did beautiful work with it. But you know what I'm going to ask?"

Imryll bit her lip to suppress a laugh. "It was *fine*. I was never in any danger."

His lips curled back when he eyed the scattered stacks of crates. "Please tell me…"

She craned up to kiss him. "Better you don't know."

"Mm." His groans melted in her mouth. "We'll have to fuck inside before you open. Every corner."

"Oh? Will we?"

"Tradition." He slid his hands under her ass and lifted her higher, kissing her deeper.

"So if I…" she asked through breaths, "were to ask around, everyone would tell me they do the same when opening a new business?"

Drazhan lifted her and guided her to the wall. "Best not to ask." He was hitching her dress up over her ankles when he froze and carefully lowered her back to her feet.

"What is it?"

Drazhan stepped out onto the road. She watched him squint, then move his hand to his sword. She jumped out to see what had startled him, but her apprehension quickly turned to joy.

"Tas!" Imryll cried. She flew across the road and enveloped her friend in a strangling embrace that had Tasmin begging for mercy. "What are you doing here? How did you…"

"Know you were here?" Tasmin thumbed behind her, at where her mother, Duchess Teleria, walked beside…

Duke Rahn.

"I'll let the duke explain," Tasmin said. She leaned past Imryll to get a view of Drazhan.

Imryll felt Drazhan go entirely still several paces behind her. She knew what he was thinking: Duncarrow had sent friendly faces to accost Imryll. But Drazhan didn't know Rahn Tindahl. He was a scholar of words and letters whose passions were wasted on Duncarrow. He valued knowledge over obedience, education over blind fealty.

Imryll held a hand to her side to stay her dark knight. She turned toward Rahn, who was on his knees in obeisance.

"I'm not a princess anymore, my lord…if I ever was. Stand up." When he returned to his feet, she asked, "Where are your men?"

"Men?" Rahn tilted his head.

"Guards…advisers."

Rahn tossed a grin back at his fellow travelers. "Duchess Teleria makes a fine adviser. As for guards, there's a dearth of those on Duncarrow, and I saw no need to contribute to that."

"What do you mean?"

Rahn passed a wave and a nod to Drazhan behind her. It did nothing to relax her husband. "If you'd oblige us with some ales and warmth, we'll be happy to tell you everything."

Drazhan reluctantly watched Imryll join the unexpected visitors at the table, but he had no intention of coming any closer to the hearth. He observed in terse silence as food and drinks were brought out…as they all dug in, ahead of words.

If they wanted to hurt me, Draz, they'd have sent someone far less honorable than Rahn Tindahl and the Farrestell women.

Enjoy their company. Catch up.

And you? Won't you join us?

I won't relax until there's reason to.

515

"Duncarrow is in chaos," Rahn said, after he'd eaten his plate clean. He sat back with a weighty exhale, sharing a quick glance with Teleria before he continued. "The power shift with King Torian's death has left a void. Godivah, without her husband or son to buoy her, has been relegated to an aging dowager, but I'm afraid it's only made it easier for ambitious men to climb. The other dukes swarm poor Queen Adamina, though she listens to none of them. Only to Lady Clarisan does she confide."

"Rightly so," Tasmin said with a snort.

Rahn nodded. "Perhaps. But neither will Duncarrow follow the rule of two women. The next fifteen years or so will be hard times as they watch and wait for young Prince Farian to come of age."

"Oh, and remember the whole 'dozen marriages by wintertide'?" Tasmin quipped. "No one's saying *that* anymore. Half the women want to find a mainland groom, and the men are too big of fools to know how to stop them."

"Carrow was wrong for wanting us to be so isolated. How can the Rhiagains manage a realm they have no stake in?" Imryll turned back toward Rahn. "You said there was a lack of guards?"

"Many left when they saw he and his friends do it." Rahn nodded at Drazhan. "I guess they didn't know they could."

"To be fair, they *couldn't*. Not when Carrow was still alive," Teleria said.

"Well, they can now," Rahn said with another hard swallow of ale.

"Duke Rahn, I know—"

"Just Rahn, Imryll. Please."

Drazhan rankled at the soft way Rahn talked to his wife.

Imryll smiled. "Rahn. I know you didn't come all the way to Witchwood Cross to tell us about the prince's birth, which is now old news. And if you didn't come to civilly accost me on behalf of the queen or her council, then why *are* you here?"

Rahn picked at a slab of bread. "Imryll...if I may..."

She nodded.

Drazhan readied himself for the possibility of anything.

"As far as I know, Torian Rhiagain was not possessed of even an ounce of magic. But…" Rahn sighed sadly. "He had a feeling about his future, a strong sense about things that, unfortunately, proved true."

Imryll's jaw went slack. "Torian knew he was going to die?"

Tasmin reached a hand toward her.

"That might be too powerful of an implication. Perhaps he was simply responding to the surrounding instability, with his father so ill and the other dukes swarming in like vultures." Rahn shook away the bread and folded his hands together over the table. "Even as a boy, he seemed to trust me. Maybe because we weren't so far apart in age as he was from the adults in his life, but whatever his reason, he confided in me over the years, from time to time. I remember when he told me how much he loved you." He made a soft sound.

Imryll bowed her head with a sorrowful inhale. Drazhan fought the urge to go to her. It wasn't what she wanted.

"Right before his father died," Rahn said, "he came to me and said he'd like to make arrangements for some things, in the event of his untimely passing, and that he would like *me* to be the only one who knew of them."

"I didn't realize he talked to you so much," Imryll said.

"Not as much when he aged out of my classes." Rahn smiled. "I told him, of course, I would do anything he needed. And he then asked me to look after you."

Drazhan couldn't hold back anymore. "While thoughtful of our late king, Imryll has everything she needs already."

Imryll screwed her mouth at him before turning a more earnest look on the duke. "Go on."

"He asked me to make sure none of the others ever tried to exile you or harm you in any way." Rahn nodded to himself. "But what he really wanted me to know was that if you were ever to leave, to abscond in the dead of night when no one was there to stop you, that I should come here to Witchwood Cross because it's where your heart would be. And now I see, with my own eyes, that you are well."

Imryll released Tasmin's hand and crossed her arms over her chest, looking up. "I see."

"Are you all right?" Tasmin asked.

Imryll nodded.

Drazhan stepped forward and dropped his palms onto the table. "You have fulfilled your promise, Duke Rahn. Your conscience should be well satisfied, and a return trip to Duncarrow imminent."

Tasmin shot a look at her mother and then buried a smirk in her lap.

He knew what they thought. What they all thought. That he loved to hear himself roar and growl. He didn't care. Those roars and growls kept danger from his doorstep, and his family safe. They allowed him to sleep at night.

"I appreciate you telling me," Imryll said. She sounded far away. "And for being such a good friend to Torian. I loved him very much." She glanced at her friend. "Though I am so, so grateful to see you, Tas, Duchess…I don't understand why you all took such personal risk to come see me."

"I'll answer that," Teleria said. "It seems the Farrestells have officially outstayed our welcome on Duncarrow, and it's no longer tenable for us to remain there. Tasmin and I decided to accept an offer from Lord Quintus to come to his court, and we agreed… but Tasmin wanted first to see you, so we came along with Rahn."

"The Quintus court?" Imryll balked. "Absolutely not."

"It's decided—"

"All respect, Duchess, but it is *not*." Imryll leaped out of her chair, toppling it. "That man…no. I won't hear of it. It is not your only option."

"He's a capricious man but a compassionate ruler who takes care of his people. It's all anyone can ever ask for."

Imryll shook her head as she gathered her breath. "No. There has to be—"

"Here." Drazhan said it without thinking, but it was the right thing to say. He knew it the moment his wife's eyes lit up in stunned gratitude. "You'll stay here, in the Cross. At Fanghelm if you like, or there's some unclaimed properties around the foothills in need of new tenants."

Teleria and Tasmin looked at each other in confusion. "We didn't come here to sway you into an invitation," Tasmin said. "I only wanted to see you."

"Stay," Imryll insisted. "Unless you have your heart set on the Easterlands, *stay*. If you really want to go, I won't stop you from pursuing happiness there. But if there's any doubt in you about whether that's the right place to land, stay here, with us. You would be doing me a great favor." She clapped her hands over her heart. "Aside from Torian and my brother, you're the only family I really had on Duncarrow."

Tasmin laughed. "Well, *I* didn't have my heart set on living in the trees, but I'm not sure the cold is much better."

"I'll take the cold any day," Drazhan said. "Anything that makes my wife smile…" He smiled at the thought. "You're welcome here. Both of you."

Imryll sighed in clear happiness. But it faded some when she looked at Rahn. "And you? What will you do?"

"I thought I might offer my aid to the Reliquary when they finally break ground. I'd like to help shape their scholar's program. Time will tell if they'll even be open to my ideas, but I can try."

"You're a scholar?"

They all turned toward Aesylt, standing in the doorway.

"Yes. I am," he said, breaking into a broad smile.

Her smile was just as big. "Well, Imryll was just telling me today how we are in need of one."

Rahn looked at Imryll. "Is that true?"

"It's nothing much right now. A building. Some books." Imryll met Drazhan's eyes. "But I have high hopes for it."

Drazhan hadn't missed the untoward glances shared between Rahn and his sister, but he could manage that. What he couldn't

519

do was be the cause of Imryll's disappointment. Never again. "Why don't you stay on then? When you're not helping my wife, we could use another teacher in the village."

Rahn frowned. "I would never wish to impose."

"This is precisely the kind of imposition we welcome!" Aesylt exclaimed. When Drazhan chastised her with a look, she smiled once more and disappeared.

"Your sister is brimming with life," Rahn said, his eyes still fixed on the place where she'd stood.

"And more than a little young for you," Drazhan retorted. "But she's training to be a teacher herself, and if you could take her under your wing…" He clenched and reminded himself it was the right thing to do. "You'd be doing me a favor."

"Are you certain?"

One look at Imryll's hopeful face was all Drazhan needed to answer. "Welcome to Witchwood Cross."

Aesylt found Duke Rahn sitting alone in the dining hall, nursing a broad mug between his hands. He aimed a determined look into the fire with tired, glossy eyes.

She secured her hold on Aleksy and entered quietly, not wanting to draw the duke too far from his thoughts.

"Lady Aesylt," he said. His serious expression dissolved with the addition of a soft smile. "Ah, and our little one. May I?"

Aesylt warily approached. Other than her brother, she'd not seen many men hold an infant they had not been forced to take.

But Rahn held out his arms, creating a perfect cradle that made her heart skip. He grinned down at Aleksy, who was finally starting to calm down for the evening. "I can't decide who he looks more like. What do you think?" He met her eyes with the question.

"Ah…I don't…Imryll, I suppose. Though he'll have his father's scowl."

Rahn shook his head with laughter. "I didn't really know your brother on Duncarrow, but I remember *that*."

"What's it like?" Aesylt asked. She chided herself for the question, which she knew would anger Drazhan. Duncarrow was a forbidden subject, one sure to put him in the foulest of moods.

"Duncarrow?" Rahn rocked Aleksy with a considering look. "Isolating. Rocky." He chuckled. "Different. To most who live there, those are not negatives. Isolation is safety. Rocks are protection. Different sets them apart, makes them special. Am I rambling?"

Aesylt quickly shook her head. She slipped into a chair at the end of the table, fearful of sitting too close. "No, not at all."

Their attentions were drawn toward sounds echoing from the hall.

Aesylt rolled her eyes before she could remind herself it wasn't ladylike.

Rahn chuckled, regarding Aleksy with a dreamy look. "They enjoy each other. Nothing wrong with that."

"Every night?" Aesylt scoffed. "It's indecent."

"Is that why you have Aleksy?"

She quickly shook her head. "They've never once asked me to. Imryll is a wonderful mother, and Drazhan…He's become someone I almost don't recognize but want to, you know? I want them to…" She scrunched her nose with a groan. "*Enjoy* each other, if I can see him this happy all the time. But the truth is, my lord, I like looking after my nephew. Gives me a sense of purpose, one I haven't had inside these walls in many years."

"Not everyone sees a need in purpose," Rahn said. "They're content to play whatever role fate set for them."

"Not you," she said, then drew her lips in when she realized it sounded like an accusation.

"Not me," he agreed. He rose and brought Aleksy back to her, settling the infant neatly into her arms. He was close enough she felt his soft, even breaths.

She looked up and met his eyes.

"I don't know if my purpose is here. But in the attempt to discover the answer, I would love to take you under my wing, as my disciple." He stepped back before her heart exploded. "Perhaps together, we may better understand our respective purposes." He nodded. "Good night, Aesylt."

Her voice cracked. "Duke Rahn."

He looked back from the entrance toward the hall with a shy smile. "Just Rahn."

Aesylt held her exhale until he was gone and her heart could safely sink to the stones unnoticed.

Imryll clawed her way down her husband's back the way he liked, wriggling under his unyielding thrusts. His palms cupped either side of her face, keeping her from turning away, from closing her eyes to channel the unrelenting pleasure that was so intoxicating, she could hardly breathe. As though only through escaping it could she truly experience it.

It was like this every time. A violent wash of pleasure and pain that left her needing more than she could handle.

But he tested it. Every time.

He pushed her limits a little further, and further still, until she no longer knew anything but the pleasure.

Drazhan panted, his mouth slack as he dutifully kept his eyes fixed on hers. The urge again to close hers, to brace for everything he gave, almost overcame her, but it was the raw, perfect desire in his eyes, the cords in his neck, and the taut pull of his jaw that she could see, for as much as he gave, he still held some back.

She was already so sore. No, she was *always* sore, because each day was a greater test of their boundaries. So far, they hadn't found an edge they weren't both utterly enthusiastic about eradicating.

Imryll's tender clit throbbed with every forward thrust. He'd pushed that to the limit too, rolling her over his face until she'd come so many times, she'd stopped bothering to count. But her body betrayed her, asking for even more as his thick base skimmed her in taunting strokes.

Drazhan's mouth parted wider, his eyes rolling back. She felt him tighten under her hands, his muscles flexing and rippling as he reached his climax. A savage grunt rumbled from the back of his throat as he crashed over the edge, jerking wildly as he spilled over an hour's worth of pent desire into her.

She waited for him to finish, enjoying every clench and twitch of his face as he tried to maintain some composure. But when he finished, he didn't roll away. He tightened his hands on the sides of her face with a deeply serious look that almost brought old fears rearing back.

"I don't say it enough," he said, breathless. He blinked sweat from his eyes. "Not nearly enough."

"What?" Imryll reached up to wipe his face.

"How much I love you." Drazhan bowed down to kiss her. It wasn't the kind that had Aesylt snickering; it was gentler, belonging to private moments when they existed in the space in between the worlds together. "Since Aleksy was born, and we've both been so busy, all we get are these sweaty interludes, and oh…Guardians, how I look forward to them." He laughed, and she laughed with him. "But I do, Imryll. I love you in a way that no magic, no war, no words could change. There are times, when I look at you…" He finally broke their gaze, long enough to take a deep breath and gather himself. "And I can't believe you're real. I convince myself that the second time I came to the chalet was a dream. That there was no ward. No you. And we just…"

Imryll gripped his head and pulled herself up to kiss him. "But there *was* a ward. And I *was* there. If you had come a year later, ten, it would've been the same. And now I'm here. With *you*." She pressed her nose to his. "Home."

He lifted himself and lay down beside her. "I hadn't let my thoughts travel that road in some time, not until your friends showed up tonight."

Imryll rolled to her side to face him. "Do you regret asking them to stay?"

"No," he said quickly. He turned his head on the pillow toward her. "No, I don't. You came here knowing no one except me. You've fallen into our ways so smoothly, but it's easy for me to forget you left all your people behind to come here, with me."

"I have no complaints," she whispered. "None, Draz. I have all I need."

"And tonight I had the opportunity to give you more." He found her hand under the blanket and twined their fingers together in a tight knot. A devious grin spread across his face. "Which I very much enjoy, especially when you've been such a good girl..."

Imryll swallowed hard. "Have I, though?" She steadied for what would come next.

Drazhan swung her atop him with one strong arm. "We still haven't dealt with your insubordination earlier with the crates. Will you promise to behave from now on?"

Imryll leaned in and let the magic words come to life in her mouth before she spoke them.

"Make me."

The Book of All Things continues with a new story in
The Poison and the Paladin.